n-Space

Stories, Poems, and Music of the Future

Chris Martin

iUniverse, Inc.
New York Bloomington

n-Space
Stories, Poems, and Music of the Future

iUniverse books may be ordered through booksellers or by contacting:

iUniverse
1663 Liberty Drive
Bloomington, IN 47403
www.iuniverse.com
1-800-Authors (1-800-288-4677)

ISBN: 978-1-4502-6091-6 (pbk)
ISBN: 978-1-4502-6090-9 (ebk)
ISBN: 978-1-4502-6089-3 (hbk)

Library of Congress Catalog Number: 2011906528

Printed in the United States of America

iUniverse rev. date: 4/2/2011

Acknowledgments

David Bernardi, my editor, provided well-deserved criticism and many excellent suggestions.

Sharon, my wife, listened patiently to repeated readings of the manuscript and shared her insight and commentary from a mother's perspective. She is, in a very real sense, Jana's mom.

Semhar Kibrom Michael took time from her graduate studies in mathematics at the University of North Dakota to review my calculations.

Kaci Lemler, undergraduate student in mathematics and mechanical engineering at the University of North Dakota, assisted in proofreading and content analysis.

Victoria, Suzanne, and Emily, my daughters, provided consistent encouragement. I am grateful that in many ways, I can truly say that they are all Jana, and Jana is all of them.

Contents

Introduction

This book expands the genre of didactic fiction; it contains stories that teach.

The futuristic adventures of the heroine, Jana Maines, take place in a variety of environments in space and on diverse terraformed planets served by the Space Trading Coalition. The settings are classic science fiction, yet they contain many elements of everyday life, because the basic nature of people remains constant. What concerns people today are the same things that will concern our descendants a thousand years in the future, or what concerned our ancestors a thousand years in the past: finding food, shelter, companionship—and seeking a purpose for life beyond mere survival. Technology might change the way we address these concerns, but it cannot change our desire for them and our need to meet them.

Jana is an ordinary person who confronts unusual and challenging situations with courage and determination. Like all of us, she is not perfect, and though deeply motivated by her convictions, she struggles with uncertainty and doubt.

Almost every idea or concept presented in this book is based upon historically recognized scientific or philosophic principles. These principles are imaginatively applied, and such speculations may prove to be unattainable. But they are not complete flights of fancy—they are rooted in fact.

In order to broaden the literary experience, multiple story formats are utilized: prose, poetry, and written music. The stories are generally in chronological order; the exception is the final poem, "The Wind." Although Jana is never named in this story poem, it describes her as a child as she spends an afternoon with her father.

Footnotes highlight topics of interest that are briefly explained in a technical section. A small glossary defines words shown in **bold** print.

Academic topics include secondary level algebra, geometry, chemistry, and physics. The steps of the calculations are shown as a review for readers familiar with mathematics and as an introduction for those with less experience.

Beyond entertainment, this book encourages the reader to reflect upon the amazing beauty and precision of creation, to wonder at the miracle of existence, and to appreciate the complex mixture of pain and pleasure in every human relationship.

The Derelict

To desire the truth and reject the lie—our highest calling before we die.

Truth whispers in a quiet voice as Hell's citizens arrive by their own choice.

—*Meditations on the Canon,* Book V:XXX:IXX

Chapter 1

The space transport, *Phoenix,* fell through a crack in the sky on schedule as it completed one of the many *n*-space jumps on its run from Freeman's World. On this portion of the route, the great ship carried almost a million metric tons[1] of pure copper for the fledgling electrical industry on the metal-poor planet of Katania. Between jumps, the ship's crew of two, Captain Rif Larkin and First Officer Jana Maines, settled into a standard inter-jump routine. The captain went **aft** to the habitation section of the ship to take an exercise break, while Jana remained forward in the flight station and stood the first watch. She immediately began one of her primary tasks: measuring the angular separation of several pulsars to fix their present 3-space position in order to make the calculations for the next jump.

A warning chirp from the forward-looking long-range radar interrupted Jana's navigational work. It had detected an object—a highly unusual occurrence in deep space. Even so, the situation held an element of potential danger that she had to evaluate. Her brows narrowed in concentration as she tapped instructions onto the screen to change the radar's wide-angle search raster scan[2] to a focused pattern centered on the tiny, distant blip. Once the object was centered, the track-plotting computer began its analysis.

A few scans provided enough data to confirm it was not on a collision course, but the Doppler shift[3] of the radar reflections indicated that the object was nevertheless approaching. The strength of the radar echo indicated it was largely metallic, but the returns varied.

The object had to have an irregular shape and was probably tumbling. As the distance shrank to a thousand kilometers, Jana realized that it could be a ship—an *old* ship. No modern vessel would be out here in deep space, radio-silent, and in an uncontrolled spin.

Once more, her fine brows knitted in thought and she absently brushed a wisp of short, blonde hair back from her forehead as she studied the data screens. She pursed her lips, took a deep breath, and tapped a small communication panel with a short, pink nail. Seconds later, the face of Captain Larkin appeared. His sandy hair, touched slightly with gray at the temples, stuck to his damp forehead.

"Yes, Lieutenant?" he asked, breathing heavily from his running exertions in the ship's axial ring.

"Sorry to interrupt your exercise, sir, but I've detected an object." Her eyes flicked from the comm panel to the data screen and back. "It seems to be an **anomaly**—not natural."

They had both heard stories of ghost ships—the ***Flying Dutchmen*** of space. Investigation of most reports proved them exaggerated travelers' tales of some inert piece of space junk forgotten in planetary orbit after the anarchy of the last intersystem war. However, no one had found anything in deep space before, hundreds of **light-years** from any known, developed star system.

"Not natural, huh?" The captain seemed more concerned than excited. He rolled his mouth and frowned in thought. "You've recorded everything?"

"Yes, sir," Jana replied as she quickly verified that her findings were noted in the ship's log.

"I'll be right up," he said shortly and his image on the comm screen winked out.

Jana sat back with a quiet creak from her seat, once more brushed back the stubborn wisp of hair, and returned her attention to the data screens while she waited for the captain. Her petite fingers danced across the control panel time and again as she as she attempted to obtain and analyze the raw data.

The *Phoenix* was a cargo ship—what space crews called a "box hauler." Its onboard computer and sensing equipment met the requirements for deep-space navigation. They were not designed for research and analysis, so it took a great deal of effort to coax more than basic information from the gear. To Jana, the task was more than a personal challenge. Crewmembers who demonstrated creativity and initiative might earn a coveted slot on one of the far more exciting and lucrative exploration or research vessels. Even if that didn't happen, there remained the possibility of the considerable prize money that she might earn from her discovery.

Ships once more plied the space lanes after a two-century hiatus—working ships, simple in design and Spartan in amenities—but sturdy and reliable. The *Phoenix* was just such a vessel—four hundred meters long, fifty in diameter, and aerodynamically designed with triple-redundant fusion reactors on the tips of its three great fins. The ship could, with the assistance of appropriate ground support equipment, lift its cargo from the surface of one planet, travel through interstellar space, and deliver the cargo to the surface of another.

More than seven hundred years earlier, at the close of the First Age of Space, multidimensional space travel was discovered. This mode of travel utilized a device known as the *n*-drive, enabling movement in higher, or *n*-dimensions.[4] Several centuries of exploration, known as the Second Age, followed, and humanity rapidly spread throughout the universe. More centuries passed before economic decline and intersystem war destroyed most of Second-Age civilization and left colonized worlds war-ravaged and isolated. Additional centuries went by, and a powerful cartel of merchants, traders, and investors slowly emerged from the worlds less devastated by the war. This group formed the Space Trading Coalition, the STC, which used its profits and interstellar capacity to expand its markets. To this end, the alliance organized trade, funded scientific exploration, and frequently served as an intersystem de facto government.

The great conflict had destroyed much more than just the technical knowledge of the Second Age. Historical records were also lost, including the locations of many of the planets that had been **terraformed** and settled. The object Jana had found might be a ship from one of these forgotten worlds. The possibility tantalized her. Cosmo-archaeologists were eager to rediscover scientific artifacts or records that such a ship might contain. Because the STC usually awarded prize money for anything of historical value, Jana's discovery would not only reflect well on her performance report, but it could considerably enhance her personal finances as well.

Thumps from the crawl tube and a whiff of sweat announced the captain's arrival. He slid wordlessly into the left seat and then studied the computer holo-screens while he reviewed Jana's summary. His apparent lack of activity belied the complexity of the job; Jana knew his mind was working rapidly. She admired his skills, and though they had been together for only several days, she had found him to be pleasant and competent. She fervently hoped he would be satisfied with her level of performance. His endorsement on her training syllabus was critical if she ever hoped to have a command of her own. She bit her lip as she studied his face, puzzled by his deep frown and self-absorbed silence.

After several moments, Larkin grunted. "Good work, Lieutenant. Very thorough."

"Thank you, sir," Jana replied, breaking into a relieved grin. "Shall I plot an intercept course?"

"*Negative*!" His response came with unexpected force.

"Sir?"

"Well, you snagged us a real derelict for sure—probably one of those tubs left over from the war." He frowned at the screen. "Odd, though, that it's out this far."

"That makes it of especially great interest to the historical teams, don't you think?" she asked hopefully.

He regarded her briefly, deepened his frown, and returned his gaze to the image on the monitor screen. "Yes. And we'll leave it for them." He rubbed his thumb on his chin before he continued. "There was a crew that found a wreck in orbit over Edgeworld. It was mined. It vaporized when they were about a hundred clicks out. The crew survived because they were in planetary orbit and could drop a lifeboat. We can't afford to repeat their mistake out here, and I'm not inclined to risk my ship, in any case."

Jana stared at the monitor. The three-dimensional image, grainy from magnification and light-enhancement, showed the distant, ancient ship slowly rolling in the holo-screen. Its three egg-shaped modules, connected by a network of exposed ribbing, seemed quaint and benign.

"If it is a bomb," Jana wondered aloud, "why would they send it out here where no one would be likely to find it?"

"People do strange things in war," Larkin shrugged. "And it might not be intentional. It could have been cut adrift, or it could have wandered off target and been lost."

"I still think we should investigate," Jana insisted. "We don't know what this ship contained. It seems to me it would be worth a look and marking it for a prize claim."

"I have no desire to risk losing my bonus percentage for this run by coming in late to Katania, and I see little profit in risking my ship to idle curiosity. We can drop a radio marker buoy. It'll eventually be recovered."

"But that means no one might examine the ship for a long time. There might be valuable records or artifacts—"

"*Might* be," Larkin cut in. "More than likely *won't* be. We're looking at space junk—a derelict. There's nothing of value over there that can't wait. Whatever it contains has been out here for several centuries. A few more years of waiting for a real research team or prize crew won't make any difference."

"Yes, sir." Jana sighed with disappointment and gave a longing look at the derelict.

Larkin studied the radar display. "Prepare to launch the marker buoy. We still have almost eight hundred clicks of separation. If that tub is mined, I want the buoy to set it off while we're still far enough away to outrun the blast shell."[5]

Jana nodded, and her fingers danced over the control panel as she programmed the marker. "Buoy prepared for launch," she announced when it was ready.

"Get it out there, Lieutenant."

She tapped the instruction onto the screen. "Marker away. It will be within a hundred clicks in less than fifteen minutes."

"Position us so we can immediately go to full acceleration away from that ship. If it goes up, we'll stay ahead of the blast until charge-up is complete and make the jump before it reaches us."

"Aye, sir," Jana acknowledged. External thrusters winked, and their bodies tugged against their restraint harnesses as the *Phoenix* turned so its stern faced the derelict, readying it for maximum acceleration away from the other ship if necessary. The image on the monitor flickered as the view changed from one external camera to another and then steadied as the ship stopped on its new heading.

"Main engines ready," Jana announced. In the quiet moment that followed, she inadvertently sighed.

The man studied the woman's face. "Why are you so interested in this derelict, anyway?"

She looked thoughtful. "The probability of finding it was so small—I just have this feeling that the discovery of this ship was no accident."

"Murphy's Law," Larkin snorted, "*Whatever can go wrong, will go wrong.* And you have a feeling? What's that supposed to mean? When you get your own ship—*if* you get your own ship—you'd best chart a course clear of intuition, calls to destiny, and other such nonsense. You go by the facts and by the book. And right now, the facts say that ship is a dead hulk. The book says it has zero priority. If it doesn't blow, the log will verify we dropped the radio buoy and we'll leave it at that. You'd best keep in mind that you never risk the ship or the schedule without a very good reason, Lieutenant."

Jana fought back any further protest. She bit her lip and watched the blip of the buoy rapidly close in on the other ship. "One hundred clicks," she reported. "Buoy is slowing to match velocities."

"Stand by the engines ..." Larkin growled in a tight, low voice.

A trill from the electromagnetic field sensor, or EMF detector, broke the tense silence and another indicator flashed on the screen. Jana started and inhaled sharply, and the captain exhaled in surprise. A signal was coming from the other ship. The derelict *wasn't* dead!

Chapter 2

Jana acknowledged the alarm to silence it while the EMF detector continued to register the signal's weak but steady presence.

"What do you think, Captain?" Jana asked with an edge of growing excitement in her voice. "Is it a hail—perhaps a distress call?"

Larkin cleared his throat but did not immediately respond. "No," he finally said. "There can't be anybody left alive on that ship after all this time. It must be the **spurious** noise of some failing gear." He stared at the screen thoughtfully and rubbed his chin before he continued. "But I'll give whoever tossed that crate into deep space a lot of credit for building *any* system that can last as long as that thing has."

"But the ship didn't go up—and we're getting a signal from it. Doesn't that change the scenario?" Jana pressed.

"Not in my judgment," Larkin sniffed. "We're still nearly a thousand clicks out, and we'd have to spill reaction mass to match course. That tub has considerable roll—on several axes—so we can't dock. The only way to get aboard would be using a maneuvering pack. Then you'd have the problem of making contact without getting hit, and just holding on would be another dangerous chore. And then how would you get in? We'd have to find an airlock—if there is one—and hope that it was still operating. If entrance was gained, then what? We have no layout. We don't know what disease or radiation leak may have killed the crew. It might very well be booby-trapped."

He sat back and folded his arms. The look on his face remained determined as he studied the data screens in hard silence. After a moment, he snorted, rubbed his chin, and grimaced. "I might reconsider if we knew for certain that the signal is a distress call, but even then we're not really able to offer much assistance." He paused again in thought before he continued. "See what you can make of that signal. We've got to wait for charge-up anyway so you might as well practice your analysis skills. In the meantime, I'm going to get cleaned up."

"Aye-aye!" Jana acknowledged enthusiastically, and she immediately set to work.

Despite his expressed intention to leave, Larkin settled back, once more folded his arms, and silently observed the junior officer for a few minutes.

"What brings you out here, Maines?" he suddenly asked.

Jana glanced up, then turned back to her display, bit her lip, and considered how to answer. "I'm in training to be a star pilot. And I hope, one day, perhaps to be a captain." *He must be testing my ability to work with a distraction*, she thought, so she continued to try to analyze the signal.

"Yes, but I'd like to know *why*?" the man probed.

"Sir, that information is already in my psychological profile."

"I've looked at it," he admitted, "but records like that are academic. When it comes to formulating a professional evaluation, I often find it useful to collect my own data."

"Oh."

"So why did you choose the space service?"

"It seemed the best choice given the circumstances."

His heavy brows rose. "And what were those circumstances?"

She paused and looked up. "How much detail do you want?"

Larkin shrugged. "I'll let you know when I've heard enough."

Jana sat back, unable to concentrate. The captain seemed to be doing more than simply providing a distraction. *Maybe he's seeing if I can prioritize.* She took a deep breath before she spoke. "I grew up on Ceres, a frontier agricultural planet. Life seemed simple there. The only advanced technology we had was the equipment for producing grain."

"Sounds typical for a frontier world—harsh living conditions and little chance for advancement. What tech level was it?"

"We were mostly at level three on the Irwin-Flyger Scale[6]—late post-industrial. There was also a smattering of some level four that supported the fusion generating station and the spaceport."

"I can't fault you for wanting to get off a backwater dirtball like that. But I suspect there's a part to this story that doesn't involve your home world's low level of industrial development."

She nodded. "My father is a farmer—a good farmer. He and my mother arrived a few years before I was born, but by the time I left they had developed over five **kilohectares**. The farm is his legacy. He means to give it to my brother."

"But not to you?"

"There was no need. In our culture, a man provides for his wife and family. I would have a stake in my husband's property."

The captain tapped a data screen and examined her record. "But I see you were never married."

"No." Her voice was flat.

"Hard for me to believe that you had no prospects."

"I did."

"And?"

She faced him. "He was unfaithful and vindictive. I *had* to refuse him."

"There were no others?"

"Did I mention that he was vindictive?"

Larkin nodded.

Jana turned away and studied the image of the derelict on the monitor. "He was very angry when I broke my pledge. He swore retribution on my entire family for the humiliation he said that I brought to him. His father has a huge and profitable operation, so he has the means to do it. Given time, he will force my father and brother off their farm."

"It might not be that bad. Anger cools."

She shook her head. "My father used to say, 'Passion cools, but anger goes to seed.'"

"So the prize money for this derelict is what is important to you."

"Only in that it could help my father and brother. They've been able to survive financially so far, but if a bad year comes—and eventually, it will—they'll need a buffer. A salvage reward could provide that."

Larkin shifted in his seat. "I can sympathize, but I can't be sympathetic. With the information we have on this derelict, I simply can't justify risking you, my ship, or the schedule."

Jana bit her lip, blinked rapidly, and stared at the screen. "I understand, sir."

A brief silence followed. Then Larkin cleared his throat. "In case you're wondering, I'm not happy with the decision I have to make—but I have my orders too."

"I said I understood, sir!" Jana repeated more strongly than she'd intended. She immediately regretted her tone. Having a petulant attitude toward a superior officer was never a good idea, but it could be especially damaging now since it was obvious the captain was evaluating her. But the words were out and she couldn't take them back. She blinked rapidly and struggled to appear composed.

Larkin's seat creaked and he rose. "I am sorry, Jana," he said, and then his footsteps faded aft.

Jana forced her mind back on the analysis, finding a calming effect in the distraction of the technical challenges. She continued studying the displays, and when she finally took note of the **chronometer**, she was surprised that she had been at work for over an hour. By now, the *Phoenix*'s main capacitors were nearly charged. Energizing the *n*-drive would catapult them out of ordinary 3-space, when they would, as some pilots said, "*fall through a crack in the sky*"—the slang expression for translineating through *n*-space from one locus in 3-space to another, dozens or even hundreds of light-years distant.

The signal from the derelict continued its plaintive beeping. It was an old-style radio signal, a low-frequency electromagnetic wave.[7] Even though this type of energy rapidly dissipated and was limited to the speed of light, it was simple to generate and to detect. That fact alone made it seem likely to be a distress call. Logically, a call for help should be obvious and easily understood. Jana made a **wry** face as she realized that "easily understood" was a relative term.

She listened again to the beeps. The series began with three short pulses, then three longer pulses, and ended with three short pulses: *dit-dit-dit, dah-dah-dah, dit-dit-dit*. After a pause, the sequence repeated.

The computer attempted to analyze the pattern in terms of binary[8] or other base numerical data, but the library of obsolete radio communication protocols[9] and the amount of data from the signal itself were both very limited. The computer did not find a match. She was disappointed, but not surprised.

"Down to three hundred clicks," Larkin observed quietly when he returned and scanned the screens. "Anything new?"

Jana shook her head.

He brought up a display of the signal. "There doesn't seem to be much information in these packets," he observed.

"No, sir," she agreed. "I haven't found anything coded into them. There certainly appears to be no amplitude modulation."[10] She gestured to the time domain display. "You can see the signal goes to maximum and stays almost perfectly level until it cycles off." She tapped the screen. "The spectrum analyzer[11] shows a single frequency. That rules out any frequency modulation. I tried analyzing the shape of the packets, but the only difference is their lengths—either 300 or 600 **milliseconds**." She made small fists on the console in frustration. "The transmission *must* mean something! A research ship might be able to decode it, but we don't have analysis computers and our databases are just too limited."

The captain stroked his chin. "Long ago they used various binary codes for message communication, but if that's what this is, the data transfer rate would be pitiful. I can't imagine any computers operating that slow."

"Unless," Jana thought aloud, "it's *not* computer code!"

"*Manual* encoding and decoding?" Larkin sounded skeptical. "It seems unlikely they would have used anything so inefficient."

"They probably wouldn't under normal circumstances," Jana agreed. "But if the primary communication systems failed, their backup could be very crude—or they might have assembled a makeshift transmitter."

Larkin grunted and shook his head. "I commend you for your imagination, but I think life support would fail long before comm systems."

"But there could be some peculiar set of conditions—"

"Peculiar is right," Larkin said, cutting her off in irritation. "Suppose there is someone alive over there. They'd have to be over three hundred years old! How plausible does that seem to you, Lieutenant?"

"Not very plausible, sir," Jana acknowledged and bit her lip. She stared at the image of the vessel on the screen as it continued its slow approach.

The man regarded her, and his face softened. "Look, I'm just suggesting you rein your imagination in a bit. You've done **yeoman's work** trying to evaluate this data, but don't let your personal concerns cloud your judgment. You need to demonstrate that you can prioritize and keep focused on what's important."

"If that signal is a distress call, then it *is* important, isn't it?"

"We don't know that it's a distress call."

"You are right, sir. We don't *know*. But it *could* be. I am trying to find out."

Larkin let out a long and breathy sigh. "Are you familiar with the expression, '*don't hunt for dragons*?'"

She shook her head.

"It means that you are on a futile and dangerous quest. The search is futile because dragons are imaginary creatures. But even if you somehow did find one, it would mean big trouble—they were supposed to be ferocious monsters. In other words, you don't really want to find what you are looking for."

"Are you ordering me to stop searching?"

The captain looked away. "No. I can't. There's already too much in the log." His voice took on a harder edge. "But command decisions have to be balanced between the strict reading of an order and its practical application. You're out of balance when you can't focus enough or when you are *too* focused."

Jana's eyes moved uncertainly from Larkin's face to the screens and then back to him, unsure if his words were meant as counsel or reprimand. A flush crept up her face, but she managed to maintain her composure. "I shall endeavor to ... to keep my priorities in proper order, sir."

Larkin nodded assent. "Of course, Lieutenant." He sighed and turned back to the screens. "But that's all for future reference. Right now, we've got to deal with this stinking derelict."

"I'll check the computer library for any entries of noncomputer distress codes," Jana offered thoughtfully. She tapped the screen to initiate the search of the ship's library.

The captain grunted but otherwise watched quietly as the computer compared the signal to the limited library of manual distress codes and emergency signals used on the multiple planets served by the STC.

"Ah!" Jana announced in surprise when the computer actually found a probable match. "It appears to be an ancient distress signal from the First Age of Old Terra. The signal, consisting of three short pulses, three longer pulses, and three short pulses, was derived from an archaic digital alphabet known as the International Morse Code. Old Terra was divided politically into nation-states at that time. The system was retained for emergency purposes on some worlds even into the Second Age."

The captain nodded, and she continued.

"This method was initially developed in the early days of electromagnetic communication. The only way to get information onto the carrier signal in those days was to turn the transmitter on and off. The method was known as *continuous wave modulation*. By common agreement, the nation-states adopted various combinations of long and short pulses that represented letters, numbers, and other symbols. They included abbreviations for common messages or phrases. The series of three short, three long, and three short pulses was the emergency code."[12]

"So it *is* a distress call," Captain Larkin said softly, knowing that their orders required them to make every effort to lend assistance to a ship that called for help. He growled in frustration. "This is a surprise—and I don't like surprises. They're dangerous."

"Standing by to transmit a response," Jana announced.

"Proceed," the captain ordered. "But I don't expect anything to happen. All we're hearing is more than likely just a recorded message."

Jana programmed a response using the archaic digital code and initiated the transmit sequence. A moment passed, and then the other ship stopped transmitting. Jana glanced at the captain. The lines on his face deepened as he stared at the displays.

Then a new sequence of beeps suddenly began: one short, one long, one short: *Dit, dah, dit.* Jana consulted the database to decipher it. "The ship is acknowledging!"

Larkin leaned back in his chair and closed his eyes.

"What do we do, sir?" Jana asked.

Larkin's jaw worked silently before he spoke. "Lay in an intercept course." His tone was reluctant. "And calculate the reaction mass we'll have to spill to match velocity with that stinking tub."

"Aye, sir," Jana responded, an edge of excitement back in her voice.

"This is not a stroll in the park, Lieutenant!" Larkin's tone was severe.

"No, sir," she agreed soberly. Her shoulders sagged slightly as she stared at her hands.

He regarded her, then shifted his attention back to the monitor screen and made a face. "They say bad luck comes in threes. We've had the rotten luck to find this crate. Now we're forced to investigate it. I'm not looking forward to the third stroke."

"I don't believe in luck, sir."

"You're still young," he insisted. "I've seen too many things happen—good and bad—for no apparent reason. If luck doesn't explain it, I don't know what else does."

"We may not understand the reason, but that doesn't mean there isn't one. One person's seemingly bad luck might be the answer to someone else's prayer."

He sniffed and stared bitterly at the screen. "If the Divine takes the time to answer prayers, then he has a strange way of doing it."

"I agree, sir."

The man jerked his head up, the lines on his face deepened to a questioning frown.

"Our human perspective is limited," Jana explained. "We shouldn't expect the purposes of an infinite mind to be completely understandable to us."

The man looked back at the screen. "Are you telling me that you think God answers your prayers, Lieutenant?"

"I'm saying that, in my experience, prayers are often answered in times and in ways we don't expect. Our petitions to God are requests, after all, not orders."

"What about your father and brother? It doesn't seem like you've gotten an answer there." His harness clicked as he unfastened it.

"I was thinking I just had."

Larkin's mutter was low and indistinct.

"Sir?"

"I said I need a short break."

"Aye," she said.

He rose to leave and then stopped and looked over his shoulder. "You found us a dragon, Lieutenant. For whatever it's worth, say a prayer for the both of us."

She looked up and nodded. He turned and headed aft.

In the captain's absence, Jana computed the angle and duration of the engine burn needed to bring them alongside the ship. When ready, she announced to him that she was about to make the velocity adjustments. He reported that he was braced for the burn and she fired the engines.

A short time later the ships were as close together as was prudent, and Jana completed another brief burn to match speeds. The derelict hung steady about two kilometers off, and its image filled the screen.

She had been able to determine that the ship was two hundred meters long and fifty wide, and **pitched**—turning end over end—at a rate of one revolution every 110 seconds. It also **rolled** on its long axis at a rate of one revolution every 103 seconds. Its **yaw**, or the rotation time from side to side, was a leisurely 400 seconds.

The **ambient** light in this region of deep space was dim by human standards, but light amplification on the visual scanner revealed only what appeared to be a small amount of superficial damage near the derelict's stern. She could not be certain of the extent of the damage because the exposed ribbing obstructed her view of the pressure hull.

"How's our dragon? Any new data?" Larkin asked by way of greeting as he returned.

"Yes. There is some damage near the aft thrust tubes," she reported. "Something must have hit the ship. It doesn't appear that it was enough to take it completely out of commission, though it does explain why it's tumbling. But I found something of even greater interest." Jana pointed to several bright patches on the holo-screen image. "The infrared scan indicates a number of hot spots. I think those might be waste heat from equipment in operation."

Larkin exhaled unhappily. "What else?"

"As you can see from the monitor, the ship was constructed in three main modules. Despite the slight damage, the aft module is emitting a small amount of ionizing radiation.[13] A small reactor could still be in operation."

"A fission[14] reactor would have run out of fuel a long time ago," he countered.

"It's unlikely they used fission," Jana explained. "The thrusters show almost no residual radiation. There is also the problem of deteriorating fissile material. I can't imagine *anyone* using fission for deep-space travel. They must have used fusion[15] just as we do. It's the only logical possibility—and the radiation levels are just what we would expect from a fusion unit."

The man studied her as if puzzled. "Why don't you give it up, Maines?"

"I'm just thinking how I'd feel if I were over there calling for help. I wouldn't want a potential rescue ship to give up too easily while they were looking for me."

"There's nobody over there, Lieutenant—there can't be. But, just as a theoretical exercise, do you have any indication where they might be, if they were?"

"The radio signal emanated from an antenna assembly somewhere amidships. We were too far out for me to get an exact fix on the source before it stopped transmitting. I think the most likely location for the crew is the forward module. There are a few warm spots up there, as well. *Something* seems to be operating."

Larkin studied the data screen and the visual monitor. The derelict's aft thruster section swung slowly across the screen. He wondered how long it had been since the other ship's ancient reactor had belched mass from those tubes, and from where they had made the *n*-space jump to arrive here in this lonely corner of the universe. He wiped his hand over his lined face, shook his head, and regarded his junior officer with a questioning half-smile. "Do you enjoy being my conscience, Lieutenant?"

"It's a dirty, thankless job," she rejoined, taking his weak humor as a welcome invitation to be conversational. "But someone has to do it."

The senior officer gave her a studied look. "Speaking of dirty jobs, have you seriously considered how hard it's going to be to board that wreck?"

"I have, sir," Jana answered quickly.

"You have? Do you know what it's like to hang in deep space, knowing that a failure of any component of your maneuvering pack, your suit, or the slightest mistake on you own part can leave you stranded while your pressure bleeds down to a vacuum? And while you're over there, for half of the time you will be out of contact because of the ship's radio shadow.[16] You've thought that all out?" His voice was low; his gaze was steady, probing.

"I think so, sir."

"You *think* so?"

The rise in Larkin's tone subtly accused her of thoughtlessness. Heat rose again in her face. She looked down, bit her lip, and then looked up. "Even if I haven't, I feel morally obligated to make every reasonable effort to help someone in distress—whether that person is someone on that ship or … someone in my own family."

The captain's face softened slightly. "I know you want to help your family. But think about this: if something happens to you and you don't make it back, they won't have *anything*."

"I believe finding this ship is providential—that I've been given an opportunity. As a follower of the Way, I think it would be an act of ingratitude to ignore it."

The captain shook his head. "You're quite the philosopher, Jana. Is a dead and ancient philosophy going to be enough to sustain you when you're out there alone?" He waved his hand toward the screen.

"I don't believe I will be alone. And a dead philosophy doesn't sustain me. It is a living faith."

"Faith," growled the man, "makes poor reaction mass." He exhaled in exasperation and then continued. "I'm losing time out here, and I might very likely lose my first officer. I've got no objections to your personal beliefs, Lieutenant, but I have to draw the line when I think those beliefs are preventing you from carrying out your duties."

She wanted to shout, *My family is counting on me—I just can't let this blessing of Providence slip away!* But she knew such an outburst would be unwise. "With all due respect, sir," she responded, taking a quick breath, "it is precisely my faith that motivates me to fulfill those duties." Somehow, she found the strength to look up and meet his hard gaze.

Larkin threw up his hands. "Enough of this! A philosophical discussion has no bearing on our problem. We've got to deal with the situation here realistically. I need to be sure you understand the difficulties involved with what you propose to do."

"I understand the seriousness of the difficulties, sir. But we have been given—" she caught herself and began, again. "We have before us an extraordinary opportunity to investigate an artifact of great historical interest. I think the most realistic course of action *is* to investigate a relic that remains functioning beyond all expectations—and that is broadcasting a distress call."

"*Relic* is an appropriate description. Distress call or not, you'll be poking around in a graveyard," Larkin muttered. "You might find something of interest, but don't expect it to be pleasant." He paused and continued. "But let's consider the impossible one more time. What would you do if you found someone alive over there?"

"If they could stay with their ship, I'd leave them aboard and we would send a rescue team as soon as possible. If not, I would transfer them back here using the inflatable life pods."

"What about quarantine? They developed some nasty bugs during the war. What if your survivors are contaminated?"

"I think that's unlikely," Jana replied. "Weaponized diseases are designed to kill quickly. The fact that someone over there might be alive after three centuries argues against such contamination. If necessary, we can use the suit-up chamber for a quarantine area to keep them isolated."

"Very well," Larkin acquiesced in resignation. "But I can only allow one hour for you to play archaeologist. That's the most time we can make that up if we complete the rest of our jumps with no further delays." He paused to give her a meaningful glance before he continued. "Let's get through the watch checklist. Then you get down to the airlock[17] and suit up. Let me know when you're ready. I'll stop the ship's rotation and be down for the safety inspection."

"Aye, sir," Jana said.

They went through the checklist as quickly as possible. When the captain took the watch, Jana unfastened her harness and rose to go.

"One more thing, Lieutenant."

The woman stopped and turned. "Yes?"

"If there is a malfunction—if something goes wrong and you get stuck somewhere—there's no rescue party."

"I know, sir."

"And Lieutenant."

"Sir?"

He looked away and then back to her face. "Don't get stuck."

Chapter 3

Jana left the flight station and moved aft through the habitation section, pausing to use the **head** in her stateroom while the apparent gravity was still present to make the task easier. Before she left her quarters, she paused and softly touched the strings of her guitar that was strapped to the **bulkhead** in its battered case. They resonated quietly in response to her contact. She called the instrument Sebastian. It was one of the few personal luxuries permitted her as a crewmember. Music often comforted her. As her fingers made familiar contact with the instrument, her mind flooded with memories—from the warmth of singing with her family at home to the lonely nights at the academy. But, she realized, there was no time for music now. She gave the strings another gentle stroke with the sudden realization that it could be for the last time. In the flight station, the captain's warnings of danger had seemed theoretical. Here in the solitude of her cabin, staring at her guitar, they became real.

Stop daydreaming and get moving! She took a breath, turned, and quickly stepped out of her room.

Aft of the habitation section was an airlock that kept the *Phoenix* compartmentalized from the cargo section. She passed through its pair of hatches, and owing to the pseudo-gravity effect created by the ship's rotation, she used the short **ladder** beyond almost as if the ship rested on a planet's surface. The artificial weight provided by the ship's spin was critical to preventing the loss of bone and muscle that would otherwise occur in crews that spent extended periods of time in zero gravity. Though it was quirky and lacked the relative uniformity of a real gravitational field, these spin effects were preferable to the adverse consequences to the crew's health without it.[18]

Another airlock in the cargo area opened to the suit-up room. The light blue shapes of two space suits hung on their wall racks. Jana removed her boots and padded across the chamber to the smaller suit. She de-energized her light-duty ship suit, and the fabric sagged as it relaxed. She easily slid out of it and hung it on its rack.

It felt strange to be wearing only her thin fabric body stocking while the ship was cruising in deep space. Explosive decompression of the ship was possible at any moment, and she felt vulnerable and exposed. With relief, she slid into the light blue, multilayered piezo-plastic fabric suit built for working in deep space. It contained additional radiation shielding, so it was heavier than her ship's suit, though still quite thin. In addition to the extra shielding and insulation, like the lighter ship's suit, it contained a piezo-fabric[19] layer that responded to an electrical charge by changing shape. Jana energized it, and the suit conformed snugly to her body. It felt good to be held by *something*.

She pulled on and latched the boots to the lock rings on the ankles of her suit, then fastened herself into the compact life-support pack that contained her oxygen generator and extended power supplies. The seeds of doubt that Larkin's words had planted in her mind were beginning to sprout. Against her will, she thought of all the things she might lose if something went wrong. Images of Sebastian flashed through her thoughts, followed by the faces of her family. And then *his* face, and *his* voice—threatening and malevolent—intruded into her mind and roughly pushed aside the earlier, pleasant recollections. Her eyes narrowed in grim determination and she continued her preparations with renewed energy.

Jana next positioned herself into the maneuvering pack and with bare, trembling fingers made the connections from her suit to the pack's additional air and energy supply. The maneuvering unit was a highly sophisticated motion-control device. When linked via radio to the *Phoenix*'s computers, it transformed her space suit into a tiny, one-person space ship.

She tapped the comm screen on the bulkhead. "I'm ready, Captain," she reported to the tiny image.

"Brace for zero g," he replied shortly and the screen winked out.

Jana took a solid grip on the handholds. The chamber suddenly seemed to slide sideways as Larkin stopped the rotation of the ship. Momentum caused everything inside the *Phoenix* to continue moving in the direction of the rotation[20]—including the fluids in the semi-circular canals of Jana's inner ear that provided her sense of balance. She held on to the handholds and waited for the room to settle down. The familiar, brief wave of nausea passed as the ship came to a full stop and she floated in zero gravity. She maneuvered across the chamber toward the storage compartment and fumbled for her helmet. She pulled it from the bin, then let it float beside her as she put on her gloves and latched them to the suit's wrist rings.

Moments later, Captain Larkin pulled himself through the hatch and floated toward her. He scanned her suit and pack thoroughly, tugged at each fitting, and checked each latch. Finally, he nodded and grunted while raising a slightly grizzled eyebrow at her store of supplies.

"The climbing gear I understand. But a medical kit, Lieutenant? If you get hurt over there, you'll need a lot more than that."

"I wasn't planning on needing it for myself, sir."

He shook his head and studied her face. "You don't *have* to do this, Lieutenant."

"I think I do."

He snorted. "You're on a fool's errand."

"Haven't you ever felt like you *ought* to do something, sir?"

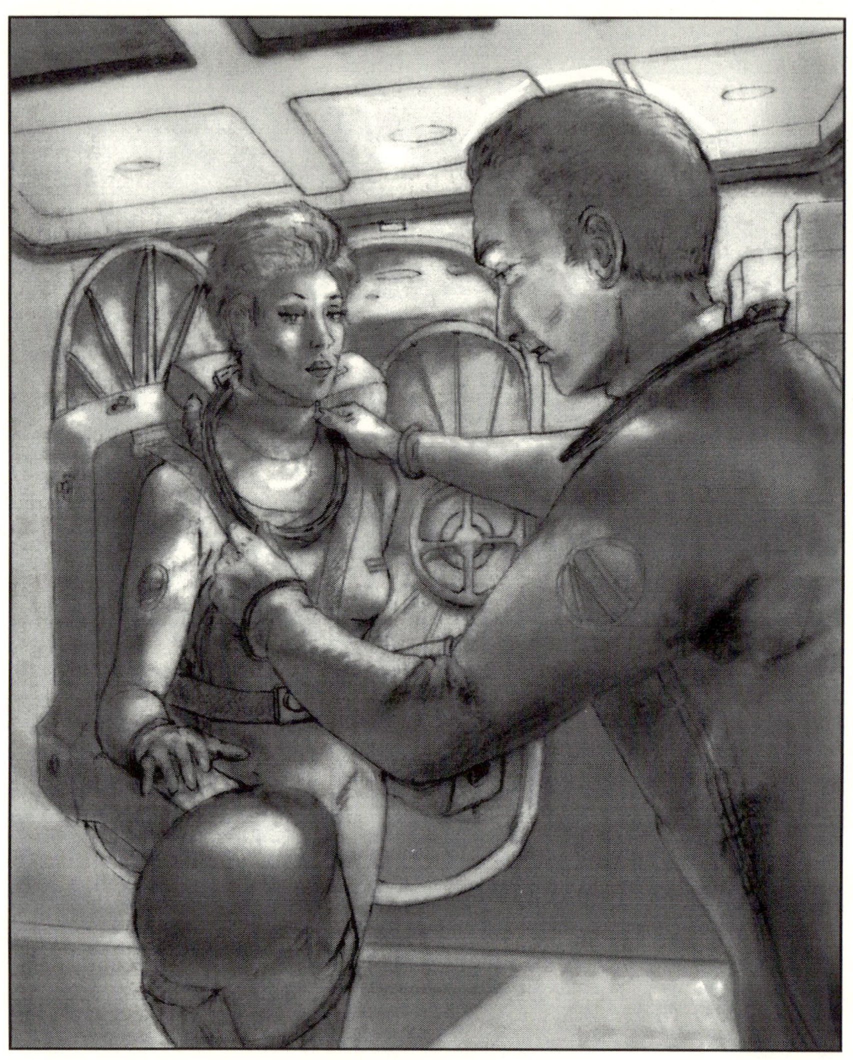

Larkin nodded. "Yes, and it usually involves keeping my behind covered. What you are doing is just the opposite."

Jana looked down, then back up at him. "We have received a call for help. Whatever you think of me, I feel I must try."

The captain took a deep breath and exhaled. "I rarely hope I make the wrong call, Lieutenant, but I'm hoping so now."

"Thank you, sir."

He shook his head and gestured toward the helmet that floated beside her. She placed it over her head and gave it a sharp twist to secure it to the collar ring. Larkin grabbed it and gave it several strong shakes that jerked her head from side to side, and slapped it to indicate he was satisfied that she was ready to enter the airlock.

He reached out, grasped her gloved hand, and gave it a squeeze before letting go and moving back. She nodded, turned, and pulled herself into the lock. The inner hatch clanged into place and she spun the locking wheel that moved the metal pegs, called *hatch dogs*, into an extended, locked position that sealed the door closed. When she tapped the lighting controls, the chamber illumination went red to help her eyes adjust to the low outside light level.

She gave another tap on the pressure control, and the hissing sound of the air being evacuated disappeared as pressure in the airlock dropped to near zero torr.[21] Jana checked her internal suit pressure; the readings projected onto her faceplate. She verified the status of all her suit's components using the built-in suit computer that changed the display at each voice command.

"Say status, Jana," Larkin's voice came over her radio communicator.

"Nominal, Captain," Jana replied. Everything was working properly. "Ready to open outer hatch."

"Roger. Open outer hatch and test maneuvering pack."

"Aye-aye." A short response. Perhaps not long enough for the captain to detect the quiver in her voice.

She reached across the meter of space to the outer hatch, braced herself, grasped a handhold with one hand, and spun the center wheel with the other. When the hatch dogs cleared, the door swung easily into the chamber, and she locked it in place. The open hatchway yawned like a dark pit.

The entire universe is just outside that opening … I wonder what Mom and Dad are doing now? Wait—I've got to focus! A riot of thoughts fought for her attention, but discipline prevailed and Jana forced her mind back to her duties.

The maneuvering pack contained bottles of highly compressed gas that fed ionizing chambers in a number of small nozzles distributed on the pack. Computer control of each nozzle allowed the operator to direct the motion of the pack by voice or eye command. An internal navigation unit helped overcome the pilot's limitations in judging speed and position. The ship also emitted navigational signals from several locations on its hull, enabling her navigation system to fix her relative position with great accuracy.

"Maneuver. Forward. Ten centimeters," she instructed. A tiny burst of ionized gas from the pack's nozzles gently nudged her forward, and then another burst brought her to a complete stop. She completed several other tests and announced she was ready to depart.

"I've plotted an intercept course to the other ship," Larkin's voice came to her ears. "The data link is on channel one."

"Roger. I'm stepping out." Jana's voice sounded so strained that she decided to give up trying to hide it. Her rapid breathing whistled loudly in her helmet.

The dim light of the starry cosmos spread out before her as she carefully pushed past the outer airlock door. The sides of the *Phoenix* curved away—the miniature planet she was about to leave. The glow of the galactic band streamed around her in a smoky horizon. Stars in a multitude of colors and brilliance were scattered throughout the celestial sphere, forming unnamed constellations. The derelict turned slowly in the distance, barely visible in the dim light of a billion distant suns.

"Maneuver. Data link. Channel one," her strained voice intoned. The suit's computer dutifully accepted the command and she accelerated forward across the great, dark gulf.

Chapter 4

The maneuvering pack accelerated forward briefly as it guided her along the calculated pathway to the derelict ship. It would take less than ten minutes at a speed of five meters per second to cross the nearly two-kilometer distance.[22] Her approach would soon take her close enough to be in danger of being struck by the spinning hulk.

Larkin's good. Larkin's real good, she told herself, though she found she was obsessively scanning the suit's readouts. *Everything checks out. All systems working. Relax. Prioritize. Legs, stop shaking!*

"Your flight profile is nominal," Captain Larkin's voice briefly broke into her thoughts, and then there was silence. In situations such as this, the crewmember acting as flight controller would often maintain a light patter to keep the person outside occupied, requesting a status report or personal observation—anything to fill the quiet emptiness that tended to unnerve a human being so far out of its natural elements. But Rif Larkin was, by nature, a man of few words. The fact that he didn't want Jana out there did nothing to increase his loquacity. Jana found the quiet increasingly disconcerting.

Say something, Captain! The plea was mental; the only relief was her own unsteady humming of a tune.

"I'm sending you a destination display," he finally announced as a schematic of red lines outlining the derelict ship projected on her visor. "The green square on the forward egg marks the point that you analyzed as an airlock. You need to get to that location."

"Roger. I see it," she confirmed gratefully past the tightness in her throat.

"The center of gravity is the yellow circle divided into quadrants alternating solid and open roughly amidships," Larkin continued. "Since the ship rotates around the center of gravity, motion is minimized there. It is the safest place to make contact."

"Got it," she said as she eyed the glowing diagrams.

"Ten seconds from maneuver, Jana," Larkin announced.

Oh, my goodness! She took a deep breath. In space, terms such as "up" and "down" were almost meaningless, but from her present perspective, the stern of the ship seemed to tower above her, slowly swinging down like a giant club. She felt the tug of her maneuvering pack push her aside. The stern swung past—scant meters away in the complete silence of the hard vacuum of deep space. She found herself tensing as the pack jerked again, and she seemed to be approaching the wreck at dizzying speed. Her breath came in gasps, intermittently fogging her faceplate.

"Contact in five seconds," Larkin's calm voice intoned. "Get ready for the bump. Matching tangential rotation. Flight path nominal."

"Roger," she heard her voice croak as she swooped toward the gray, alien surface. A narrow girder rose toward her. She reached out, and her gloved hand closed around it in a small but fierce grip. Her body jerked sideways as it matched the rotation of the ship. Despite having an apparent weight of a mere 1 percent[23] of normal, the suddenness of the force from contact with the metal almost ripped her fingers from their hold. She grabbed the metal with her other hand to keep from being flung back into space, pulled herself closer with her right arm, and then used her left hand to attach a line and snap hook to hold her securely. The centrifugal acceleration from the ship's turning swung her feet outward, and she felt as if she were hanging on to the side of a metal leviathan that was trying to throw her off. The line held securely and she took several deep breaths while she attached a second short line. She planned to alternately connect and disconnect these safety lines as she moved forward. That way, even if she lost her hold, at least one line would keep her fastened to the ship at all times.

"I made it!" she announced, her voice steadier now in her triumph and relief. But there was no response. She emitted a small, guttural sound, frustrated at her captain's taciturnity. But her irritation lasted only until she remembered that the ship's rotation had taken her out of sight of the *Phoenix* and blocked the radio comm signals. Each minute of communication was followed by a minute of silence.

I should have remembered that! She chided herself and breathed deeply. *Let it go. Pay attention!* She scanned the network of gray metal ribbing to get her bearings. She knew she had to keep busy. Focusing on the next step would help to keep her thoughts from spinning out of control.

"Display route," she ordered. The suit's computer popped up the red schematic. A blue line traced from the yellow circle to the green box. She would have to hang free, fighting the increasing centrifugal acceleration as she moved forward about sixty meters.

Jana pulled her body against the girder to slack the lines, unhooked one of them, and moved it forward. Then she disconnected the second safety line and moved it forward. She continued this process to make forward progress.

"Nice work, Jana!" Larkin's voice sounded in her ear. Jana exhaled with relief at hearing him again. The small compliment meant more than she had anticipated, and she resolved never again to take small deeds of kindness for granted. "I have you on the monitor," Larkin informed her. "You have ten meters to go. Acceleration at the airlock will be about point zero two g at twenty-five degrees forward."

"I feel it increasing," she replied between breaths. "My feet are swinging forward."

"Hang on. You are doing fine ..." The voice faded in a quiet burst of static as the signal cut off once more. The second small compliment again buoyed her spirits despite the renewed isolation of the radio shadow as the derelict blocked Larkin's signal.

Energized, Jana continued pulling herself forward. Though the apparent force was not great, her arms were beginning to feel the continuous strain from holding them what felt like "above" her. When she made it to the airlock, she planned to stop, cable up to the girder, and let the blood flow back into her arms.

"Two meters, Jana," Larkin announced. "You've made excellent progress."

"I guess those hours of exercise are paying off," she replied in attempted humor.

"They better," the captain responded. "You were on company time."

"Aye," she responded, unable to think of a clever comeback as she concentrated on keeping her grip. A bead of sweat was slowly moving down the left side of her nose. She exhaled forcefully with the effort to cover the last meter, and several small drops of moisture spattered the inside of her faceplate. The suit's dehumidifier would soon dry them, leaving little white circles of salt.

"I'm at the airlock," she announced to the silence of the radio shadow. She cabled herself to a recessed handhold near the airlock and let her body go limp to permit the blood to flow back to her fingers. The stars swirled beneath her feet.

It's a long way down! Jana shook her head as if to cast off the growing sense of morbidity. *Stay focused!* She turned to study the airlock to keep her mind active.

A faded black and yellow stripe, pitted from centuries of micrometeoroid bombardment, marked the perimeter of the hatch. Otherwise, the flat, gray metal appeared to be a basic, manual lock with evenly spaced recessed handholds around it. She reached out, grasped a handhold with her left hand, and spun the center wheel until it hit the stops. She readjusted her grip and pushed up against the hatch. It gave, revealing cold darkness within. She felt the shock through her arm when she released the hatch and it slammed closed.

"Jana, can you gain access to the ship?" Larkin's voice suddenly crackled.

"I think so," she replied. "I'm at the hatch and can open it but the ship's motion forces it closed as soon as I let it go."

"Can you prop it open?"

"With what?" Jana shot back, irritation rising in her voice, frustrated at her inability to gain access.

"If you push it far enough there may be a catch or it may swing far enough to hold itself open."

"I'm trying," she said, her voice on the edge of cracking.

She braced herself a second time, took a deep breath, and pushed against the hatch. The task was difficult. She had to use one arm to brace herself and the other to push against a hatch that was not designed to operate under the influence of the current centrifugal forces. But with great effort, Jana forced it open, stretching her right arm as far as she could and pulling herself hard against the ship's side with her left. Her breath fogged the faceplate at each rapid exhalation as she arched her fingers, trying to push the stubborn door inward as far as possible.

But it was no good. Her arm was too short to push it far enough.

I can't believe I made it this far to be stopped by an open door I can't keep open! The irony was bitter and she made a kicking motion in frustration. The kick suddenly reminded her that she had another set of limbs. *My feet!* She unhooked one of the safety lines and reached across the hatch to attach it to a handhold on the far side. Then she repositioned herself so both feet could push against the outer door. Once more, it gave, and now she could use the full length of her legs to push it up.

The pressure of the hatch through her booted feet suddenly disappeared and she felt it thump against the inside bulkhead of the airlock through her safety cables. The opening gaped, the interior cloaked in inky blackness as dark and silent as a crypt.

"Lights on," she ordered. Twin spots of light appeared from the small lamps on her helmet. "I'm going in," she announced.

"Be careful, Jana," Larkin responded. "Stay calm. Take it easy, and—be very, very careful. We'll lose radio contact completely as soon as you go inside."

"Aye," Jana acknowledged, pulling herself inside the ancient ship's airlock using the handholds and the lip of the opening. She examined the chamber, and her lamps revealed a square control panel above her head with instructions lettered in an archaic form of Basic, the root language from the Second Age.

She studied it a moment and then pressed a switch marked with a circle and spreading rays. Several glow strips in the bulkheads weakly illuminated the chamber and the small control panel's indicators dimly glowed to life.

She pulled the outer door closed and spun the wheel. When the hatch dogs were tight, one of the indicators went green. She nodded in satisfaction and scanned the panel before she pressed a stud marked with an upward-pointing triangle—a control symbol commonly used to indicate an increase. Nothing happened at first, but as the chamber filled with air, she soon felt the return of external pressure on her suit and could hear the faint whistle of gas filling the lock. Another indicator went green and the whistling stopped. She now could clearly hear the rustle and squeak of her suit when she moved. She reached up to spin the wheel on the inner hatch and, once unlocked, pushed it up until it rested on the inner wall. This task was easier than the outer hatch because inside the airlock she could brace her feet and use both of her arms at once.

The open hatch revealed a dimly lit crawl tube. She unfastened her maneuvering pack and gently let it slide "downhill" to the forward bulkhead, but kept her own air supply. It would be foolish to trust this ancient atmosphere. It could be contaminated, and she had neither the time nor the equipment to test its purity.

The spin of the ship created a pseudo-centrifugal-gravity that pulled outward and forward, making the chamber feel canted at a bizarre angle. Jana grasped the handholds and pulled herself what felt like up, into the crawl tube. As she gazed down the length of the tube, the realization struck her that she was inside a ship built nearly three centuries before she was born—and operating without maintenance for most of that time. She paused a moment to marvel at the durability of this old craft's systems, but she noted the failed lighting panels and sensed a growing awareness of the possibility of other imminent failures.

The tube was tan in color, with blue-white lighting panels spaced at regular intervals down its length, though some were dark, which created irregular blotches of shadow down the visible length of the crawlway. The tube branched forward and aft. Forward felt downhill; aft felt uphill. Jana knew that generally, engine rooms on ships were aft and support systems were amidships. Since the crew and control systems were generally forward, she moved in that direction, all the while searching the passageway walls for written clues as to the ship's origin. The only writing she was able to identify was station numbers—a common practice used to mark locations in ships. Jana took a moment to study the numbers, written in an archaic style while her mind pondered the ship's crew. *Who was the last person to use the airlock? What was happening on this ship when that person passed through this crawlway?*

She glanced at the status screen in the lower left corner of her helmet's faceplate and noted the remaining time. Larkin had grudgingly allowed her only one hour to explore so she needed to work quickly but she knew she had to work carefully. Her eyes constantly scanned ahead, trying to detect any hidden dangers—a piece of jagged metal that could damage her suit or any sign of chemical or radiation leakage.

The passageway branched again with a short fork to the right that ended in a closed hatch. Above it a small, green light was inscribed with two short, parallel lines. Jana took that crawlway branch, approached the hatch, and spun the wheel. When the dogs cleared, she pushed the hatch open and peered into a room poorly revealed by a dim lighting panel.

It seems to have been a communications center—but unused in a long time. Two short consoles on either side of the small chamber held several dark screens. A low rack of equipment topped the consoles over otherwise dark panels. At the far end of the chamber, two chairs covered in deep red fabric and mounted on rails that ran the length of the console faced the hatch like silent sentinels.

The aging lighting panel cast a dim glow over the somber scene. A chill crept up Jana's back as she looked at the empty chairs. The angled force from the spin of the ship made the scene eerily twisted, like the nonsensical whimsy of a dreamscape.

She quickly backed away and slammed the hatch closed to block out the melancholy sight. She turned and continued down the passageway.

The next two branches led to rooms that were larger, but crammed with mazes of cable trays and equipment bays. Jana despaired that she might spend precious time simply scouting empty equipment rooms and the echo of the captain's opinion that she was on a fool's errand sounded ever more loudly in her mind. The quiet voice that had seemed to lead her to this place was increasingly difficult to hear above the rapidly rising chorus of her doubts and fears. She noted her remaining time, took a deep breath, and opened the hatch to the next room.

It was the largest so far—about ten meters long and four meters wide. Three double tiers of tanks lined the walls.

Cryonic *hibernation chambers!*

The Second-Age civilization had used this hazardous preservation method, which had employed metabolism-lowering drugs and low temperatures to minimize the crew's need for air, water, and food. Although the artificial hibernation slowed the aging process, it could not stop it. And while the technique greatly extended the time available for deep-space exploration, it carried increased risk to the crew. If a malfunction occurred while they were asleep, there would be no one available to tend to it.

I found the crew! She suddenly realized that if they were alive they would probably be in an advanced state of aging, and she involuntarily shuddered.

Sketchy records that survived from the Second Age indicated a skeleton crew sometimes remained alert on such vessels in order to monitor the ship and respond to emergencies. If something happened to the alert team, the hibernating crew might never be revived. A grim thought occurred to Jana that if something had indeed happened to this ship's alert crew, the term *skeleton crew* might literally be true. Her heart thudded in her ears as the full meaning of the captain's cryptic warning that she might find something unpleasant became a grisly possibility in her mind, and she caught herself staring at the white cryonic units.

Her pulse raced as she entered the room and carefully picked her way across the slanted **deck** to the first of the dozen snow-white containers. She knelt to study the instrument cluster on the first tank, and her heart fell. All the indicators were dark. She quickly scanned the other panels in the dim light. Every one was dark. She exhaled slowly. *They are all dead!*

Jana took a moment to wonder about these ancient builders. She imagined the launch of this ship with great ceremony and pomp. She noted the irony of how the crew had boarded her, full of pride and high hopes, only to silently die alone, one by one, in the quiet, cold depths of space. She was too late—perhaps centuries too late.

The heating elements in her suit could not ward off another cold shudder. Outside, the tanks remained clean and pristine, but she now knew that within each was hideous corruption. She was alone with the dead. The reality of the situation was another severe blow to her earlier optimism and conviction that someone had survived. She found it increasingly difficult to believe she was accomplishing anything worthwhile and a sense of fear began to gnaw more vigorously at the base of her brain—primitive, childlike fear of the dark and of dead things. Against her will, she remembered Larkin's reminder that there could be no rescue for her. *You've got to get out!* A voice inside her head began to scream. *Get out! Get out! Get out!*

No! The dead can't harm me—but I can certainly harm myself if I panic. She shook her head, took several deep breaths, and tried to force her racing heart to slow down. She had been so confident that something important was on this ship. Her eyes anxiously searched the room for some transportable object of potential value, but the chamber seemed devoid of any such significant artifacts. Her mind became a battlefield, as hope fought against despair. Despite her determination, her conviction wavered. *Was the signal simply an automatic recording? Have I been fooling myself? Is there anything here but the dead?* She had been expectant for some sign or sense of guidance, but there was no epiphany, no assurance, and she suddenly seemed utterly alone.

Help me!

Was it her prayer, or someone else's? She found the question strangely encouraging, and for the moment, it held despair at bay.

She left the chamber of death and faced another hatch at the next turn, its entrance partially shrouded and indistinct in the shadows. To move toward it meant to move into darkness. Her mouth was dry, her palms damp and cold inside her gloved hands as she advanced anyway and spun the door open, dreading what she would find as she passed through the hatchway.

The monotonous, dim blue-white light revealed only three cryonic tanks. The two far tanks were sealed, and their indicators were dark. But the third tank was open—split down its full length! A body, dressed in a simple green coverall and white socks, lay curled outside the chamber, looking as if it had slid out. Jana sucked in her breath. Even at this distance, she could tell the shrunken frame had undergone severe muscle atrophy.

The poor thing! I hope he didn't suffer.

A small console at the far end of the chamber now caught Jana's eye. It displayed several lights. *Is that the communication panel that generated the distress call? If so, who had operated it?*

She cautiously picked her way across the canted deck toward the hibernation tanks, which were braced in their positions. As she neared the open vessel, she studied the body. Despite being out of the protection of the chamber, it was well preserved. Jana stared hard at the figure, now just a meter away as it lay on the open top of the tank. *How long has the body lain there?*

It's not a man—it's an old woman! The realization came with a start. The figure's thin, white hair was matted against her skull, and her skin was wrinkled, pale, and traced with a network of dark veins easily visible even in this dim light. Jana froze when the eyeballs rolled under closed lids. This was no corpse, a but living human being!

A flood of compassion swept over her, pushing aside her self-absorbed, morbid dread as a fresh breeze blows away a puff of smoke. The wave of empathy moved her to help this traveler, this long-forgotten spark of life; her thoughts were no longer simply on herself.

Her prayer for guidance was wordless but sincere as she knelt beside the figure and pulled the small medical kit from her belt. She slipped a cuff over the thin arm, pressed a button, and watched the analysis appear on the tiny screen. The old woman's breathing was shallow and slow. Her heart rate was less than forty beats per minute, with blood pressure and body temperature both dangerously low. *She's barely alive!*

The microcomputer readings on the medical cuff indicated that the woman had emerged from the hibernation tank within the last several hours. Jana calculated that as being about the time the *Phoenix* had dropped out of *n*-space near the derelict and started scanning it with its radar.

The computerized kit prescribed a dose of **epinephrine**, two liters of **saline intravenous** solution, and a warm blanket, but all that Jana could provide was one epinephrine applicator. She touched it to the woman's arm.

Jana stroked the woman's lined face with her gloved hand. The glove made it seem impersonal but she knew she dared not expose herself to whatever **pathogens** or toxins might be in the atmosphere of the derelict; there was no way to know exactly what had killed the rest of the crew.

"Can you hear me? Can I help you?" Her voice sounded mechanical though the small speaker built into the outside surface of the helmet. She listened for a reply, but the external microphone only detected the rustlings, scrapes, and thumps of her own movements.

Finally, the old woman stirred. Her eyeballs rolled, and her lids drifted open. Rheumy, gray eyes stared sightlessly for a moment before coming into focus and settling on Jana. She blinked and stared. A tear trickled from her eye and rolled slowly into her ear.

Jana smiled and tried to be reassuring. "Can you speak?" she asked, slowly, hoping to make herself more easily understood.

"You be cohort?" the ancient voice croaked. Jana recognized the archaic language of Basic through the thick accent.

"I am Jana Maines, an officer of the Space Trading Coalition vessel *Phoenix*. I am here to help you."

With obvious confusion and effort, the woman reached a withered and veined hand to touch the faceplate of the young woman's helmet. Jana brushed a gloved hand against the parchment-like face. A faint grimace revealed gray teeth and receding gums.

"We be arrived," she whispered. "Our science … be … triumphed. We did find our New World. Here, we to be building … paradise."

Jana shifted her gaze to the medical cuff and caught her breath. The woman's vital signs had not completely stabilized. The medical cuff's prognosis was still death within twenty minutes if she did not receive advanced emergency care.

"Our crew … the best crew," the old woman continued. "We be not failing … the Home World."

Jana's focus moved from the cuff to the woman's face and then once more to the cuff as she pondered what she should say. She could say nothing, and let this woman die believing she had fulfilled her mission, or she could confront her with the painful truth that they had not succeeded. Few would begrudge her silence. Larkin would probably consider saying anything as another dragon hunt.

Jana remained silent and tried to smile as she touched the woman's face. She took the old, bony fingers in her gloved hand and patted them gently. Her mind spun as she searched for a way to comfort the last, dying crewmember of this ghost ship, but the right words eluded her. The truth was hard—yet anything less seemed hollow. She breathed another prayer for guidance, for some light in the dim bowels of this ancient, dying spaceship. In quiet reflection, her mind moved back across time and space to the fields of Ceres, the agricultural world upon which she had grown up. Long dormant recollections flashed through her mind that she thought were completely forgotten.

Chapter 5

It was harvest time. Jana had just turned sixteen and her father had asked her to spend the day watching the children of the neighboring Mench family while both sets of adults hurried to bring in the barley before an approaching storm system moved in and damaged it.

"But, Dad," she protested, "I think I should help you. We've got to get our crop in too."

"Don't worry," her father replied. "Mother and your brother, Kye, will help me. That gives us three. Aleph Mench only has himself and his wife. If you don't help them out, that would give us four. Mrs. Mench has never been very good at handling machinery, so her husband will probably have to do most of the work by himself. Letting that happen is neither kind nor neighborly."

"But why can't Kye watch the Mench kids?"

"You're much better with the children," her father replied. "And even though your brother is younger he's very good at operating the combined harvester."

"I'm as good as he is," she shot back.

"Yes, but, as I said, you're also better with the children."

"Please, Jana, let's not argue," her mother said, emerging from the bedroom while zipping up her dark blue work coveralls. "Just trust your father's judgment. He is well aware of both you and your brother's skills and he knows how we can best work together. When you help the Menches, you're helping the community—which means you're helping us."

"Oh, all right," she finally agreed. "It still doesn't seem fair."

"Fair or not," her father shrugged, "it's just the way it is. Remember that life is hard, and God is good. Don't get the two confused."

"I don't want to be preached at, Dad!"

His flashing eyes met hers. "Your attitude, young lady, is in serious need of adjustment."

"Kantin!" Jana's mother broke in and stepped forward. Her gaze alternated between her daughter and her husband. "I'll talk with her."

Jana's father broke the stare to look at his wife. "Karis, I don't think I should tolerate many more of these outbursts. Whatever you talk about, make sure she understands that."

Karis nodded.

"You heard me?" He directed the question to Jana.

Jana raised her chin. Her nostrils flared and her mouth remained in a tight line.

Her father ignored her defiant posture. "Kye and I almost have the equipment ready. We don't have a lot of time. *Each* of us needs to do our job."

"Of course, dear," Mrs. Maines said.

"Jana?"

"I'll do my job."

"Part of your job is to have a good attitude. I'm not just saying that for my benefit. I'm saying that for yours."

Jana inhaled and opened her mouth as if to speak but her mother quickly touched her hand. The girl bit her lip and nodded.

"Karis, I know this is important, but it can't take too long."

"Yes, dear. I know. It won't."

The man nodded. The two women watched in silence as he turned and left the room. His footsteps retreated through the house and the back door closed with a solid thud of heavy steel that faintly carried through the concrete shell of the house.

Jana's protest broke the silence. "It's not fair, Mom!"

The woman took a seat on the granite ledge of the large bay window. Beyond her, the cloudless sky bloomed pink and purple in the early dawn. "And what *would* be fair?"

The girl spread her hands. "Kye can baby-sit."

"Honey, you're better with the children. Kye is a twelve-year-old boy. Having to play with little children is hard for him."

"Oh, and like it's easy for me?"

Her mother closed her eyes before speaking again. "I'm not saying that. But it makes more sense. You are very capable of operating the machines—and your father and I are both very proud of you. But you know how adventurous boys are—especially when they are twelve! I think the Mench children are safer with you. But in any case, someday you will need to take care of your own children. This is good practice."

"*That's* what I mean!" Her finger stabbed the air.

"Honey, *what* do you mean?"

"Everyone acts like I should just take care of kids—like that's all I'll ever want to do."

"Sweetheart, being a mother is the most wonderful gift the Creator has given to women. You should be thankful, not resentful."

"Mom, I am thankful that I might be a mother—*someday*. But I'm not a mother now. And sometimes it seems that its all people think that I can do. Especially Dad."

Jana's mother shook her head. "That's not true."

"It seems that way to me."

Mrs. Maines placed her hands on her knees as she regarded her daughter. "You didn't used to talk like this. In fact, I'm sure this didn't start until the co-op hired that new educator, Mr. Winrad. What has he been telling you?"

"Mr. Winrad is a good teacher. He knows a lot—about some things, more than Dad."

The older woman took a breath. "I'm sure he does. That's why the co-op hired him. But he isn't a member of our faith fellowship. I don't believe he is a member of any fellowship."

"The Menches aren't members, and Dad wants me to help them."

"We might not agree on matters of faith or education, but we can still be kind. Even though they tend to isolate themselves, they are still our neighbors. Mr. Winrad is different—he's in a leadership position. You have to be careful about some of the things he says."

"He has nothing to do with what I feel."

"You may not realize his influence."

"I'm not a little kid, Mother. I understand what people say."

"It's not just what people say. It's how they live. That has more effect than you might realize."

The girl crossed her arms and stared past her mother out the window.

"Look," her mother continued, "whatever you're feeling right now, remember that your father and I love you very much. We only want the best for you. Dad works very hard, but he can't do it alone. We all need to do our part."

"But he gets to give all the orders."

"That's not as easy as you imagine. You are concerned only about your own future. Your father has to be thinking about *all* of ours. That's a heavy responsibility."

Jana sighed. "All right, but I'd still rather help with the harvesters."

"I know," her mother nodded. "But sometimes we have to do what we don't want to do."

The girl looked at her mother. "What do you have to do that you don't want to?"

Mrs. Maines flashed a smile. "I'd rather take care of babies!"

"Then why don't *you* help Mrs. Mench?"

Her mother's brow creased. "Dad wouldn't like that. Working together is a bonding experience. You'll understand better when you're married."

The younger woman raised a skeptical brow.

Mrs. Maines rose and extended her arms. Jana made a face but she moved into the embrace.

"I love you, Jana," Mrs. Maines whispered as she hugged her daughter.

"I love you too, Mom."

After a moment, they moved apart. "Now, you better get going."

"I'm going! I'm going!" Jana said, but there was no longer much heat in her tone. She headed out into the bright harvest morning sunshine and gently closed the heavy steel storm door behind her.

The Mench farm was a good kilometer to the west, marked by an island of trees that formed a natural wind barrier for their house and yard. Jana glanced eastward over her shoulder toward the brightening blue sky. She turned back to the west, noted the high, thin film of cirrus clouds spreading from the southwest and involuntarily shuddered. The high clouds indicated that another, potentially violent weather system was approaching.

Crickets sang morning choruses in the dry stalks of thresh on the sides of the dirt track. Jana's bare feet sent up little puffs of dust from bone-dry ground with each footfall.

The gentle sound of the crickets disappeared in the sudden double thud of a sonic boom and the following rumble. Her head shot upward to track a deep space transport as it thundered across the sky. Its distant, shiny metal sides reflected the morning sun, a bright, star-like object falling slowly toward Port Saint John more than a hundred kilometers to the north. Her eyes followed the ship intently and tried to catch the sapphire flash of its engines.

You can tell how good the pilot is by the number of engine flashes, her father had informed her. *The fewer flashes you see, the less he needs to correct his descent. So, the fewer the flashes, the better the pilot.*

"Good pilot," she muttered at the single flash that winked before the ship dimmed and sank out of sight below the northern horizon.

She studied the advancing film of high clouds as she resumed her walk, then the barking of a dog caught her attention and she smiled at the brown and white mutt that bounded up to her, pink tongue hanging out and brown eyes bright in anticipation of play.

"Hey, Ras!" she called, scratching him under his chin while looking around for something to throw. "Sorry, boy. I don't have any toys for you."

He barked impatiently and jumped beside her while she continued toward the Mench house. As she passed under a large elm, she stooped and picked up a short piece of broken branch. Ras barked in anticipation and sped away in a flash of brown and white, giving chase even as the stick left her hand.

"Jana! Thank goodness!" Mrs. Mench's voice caught her attention. The young girl smiled at the woman who was approaching with three boys in tow. Her oversized work coveralls were worn and work-stained and her dull, brown hair was tied roughly in a faded bandanna.

"Hello, Mrs. Mench," Jana greeted her, and then she turned her focus to the boys. "Hello, Jaff! Hey, Penn! And how is Korick?"

The oldest, six-year-old Jaff, simply frowned in reply. Penn, the middle boy, licked at a smear of jam across the back of his arm. Additional jam was streaked across his four-year-old face. The youngest had his finger in his mouth and dragged a dirty stuffed toy along the ground behind him. He toddled up to Jana, pulled his finger from his mouth, and raised his arms toward her. She scooped him up and balanced him on her hip while Mrs. Mench knelt and attempted to wipe some of the smeared jam from the middle child's face with her work-reddened fingers.

"I'm afraid I haven't been able to keep up with the children," she confessed. The dog bounced over and attempted to lick at Penn's face. The woman pushed him away impatiently. "No, Ras! Go away!"

"I'll get them cleaned up, Mrs. Mench," Jana offered.

"Thank you," the other woman sighed, rising. Jana knew the woman was barely ten years older than she was, but she had already become the mother of three and could have passed for a much older woman. The bright morning sun revealed a deepening pattern of tiny lines at the outer corners of eyes that Jana remembered had recently been as youthful as her own.

"Mazie, we've got to get a move on!" Aleph Mench's harsh voice echoed across the yard from the side of the large combined harvester.

"I'm coming!" the woman replied. She started toward the machinery while Jana followed with the boys. "We'll be working 'til late," the woman said as they all walked.

"I understand." Jana nodded and then glanced at the western sky. "I could drive and you could watch the children," she offered.

"That would be wonderful!" Mazie Mench brightened. "I'll ask Al!"

The man looked up impatiently from his work on the grease fittings as the group approached.

"Al," the woman began tentatively, "Jana has offered to drive the grain transporter while I watch the children."

He grunted, raised a dark, bushy brow and regarded the young woman skeptically.

"I asked your pa to send you here to watch kids, not drive transport."

"He sent me here to help you and your wife. I don't think he meant that I *had* to mind the children."

"Mazie can handle the transport," the man insisted as he looked at his wife. The woman looked down.

Jana shifted Korick from one hip to the other. "I'd be happy to drive, Mr. Mench."

He shook his head. "I don't need my neighbor's little girl driving my equipment."

"Call Dad," she offered. "He'll tell you how capable I am."

"No doubt he will." The man nodded, swiped his chin with the back of a greasy hand, and then slid the hand down the side of his stained coveralls. "I know your pa sets great store by you. Maybe too much. But that's *his* business. In any case, I can only afford to pay you for watching the kids. I can't afford to pay you for driving. That's *my* business."

"Pay me the same."

"Please, Al," Mrs. Mench pleaded. "I just don't feel confident enough—"

"You can handle it, woman. And if you can't then you gotta learn."

"But Aleph—"

"We're wasting daylight, here," he said with a scowl at the sky before dropping the look to his wife. "Now, everything's charged up. I've indicated the fields and bins on the transport's display. All you need to do is drive. It can't be no simpler, Mazie."

"All right, Al," she sighed.

He swung up the ladder into the harvester's cab and then glanced down. "Thanks for the offer, missy, but we do things our way here. I 'spect your pa understands that."

Jana nodded wordlessly.

"I'm heading to field bravo five," he said to his wife. "The hopper'll be full in twenty minutes. I 'spect you there when it is."

"Yes, Al."

"Good. Now, missy, get them kids back so they don't get run over."

"Yes, sir. Come on, children. Your daddy's going to move the big machine. Back away. Danger! Danger!" She still held the youngest, and now she grasped the dirty hand of four-year-old Penn as they moved away from the large machine. Ras barked excitedly and ran in circles as Mrs. Mench helped Jana herd the children back. The harvester's electric drive engaged, and it whined away in a cloud of dust.

"I'm sorry," Mazie Mench said as they stared at the retreating harvester.

"It's all right," Jana assured her. "I'm sure you will do fine."

"I can drive it forward well enough, but I have so much trouble backing it up at the storage bins. It seems to take forever to get it lined up right." She sighed. "We used to be able to afford a work crew."

"I can help," Jana offered.

"How?"

"You drive the transport to and from the field. When you get back to the bins, I'll teach you how to back up."

"Oh, thank you!" Mrs. Mench exclaimed, embracing the girl in a hug. The two-year-old perched on Jana's hip giggled and laid his head on his mother's shoulder. "All right, kids," she said, addressing the children. "Mommy is going to help Daddy. I want you to be good boys and listen to what Jana tells you."

"Are you going to tell stories?" six-year-old Jaff asked.

"'Tories!" repeated Penn, the four-year-old, in a raspy voice.

"Yes, but only if you mind me," Jana warned.

"Yes'm."

"All right, I'd better get going," Mrs. Mench said, nervously running her hands down the sides of her coveralls.

"Don't worry, Mrs. Mench. I'll be here."

"Believe me, Jana, I don't worry when you're here."

They walked to the huge transport truck, and the older woman gave Jana and her children each a hug before she climbed up into the cab of the grain transport. Jana moved the children back and Mrs. Mench waved good-bye as the vehicle growled slowly out of the yard. Ras barked furiously at the wheels, giving up the chase only when the truck cleared the trees and sped away down the same dusty track that the harvester had taken. The dog returned, panting, and flopped down on the ground where the small group stood in the shade of a tree.

Jaff dropped to his knees and started patting the dog's head and flipping his ears. Suddenly he looked up. "Tell me a story."

"I will. But first, you boys need to get cleaned up. I also want you to clean your rooms—and I probably have some dishes to wash."

"Aw," the boy grumbled, but he got to his feet and started toward the house; the dog frolicked beside him.

"'Tory," the four-year-old repeated to Jana as he held her hand and they started toward the house.

The two-year-old looked down at Penn, removed his fingers from his mouth so he could grasp Jana's blouse, and then swung his stuffed toy at his sibling's head. Jana caught the maneuver and quickly pulled him back before the toy could connect with the other child.

"No, Korick!" she said firmly to the little one. The child put his fingers back in his mouth and laid his head on her shoulder. *Driving transport would have been so much easier!*

The children had put away a few things in their room, and Jana had cleaned their faces by the time Ras's barking and the whine of the heavily loaded transport signaled Mrs. Mench's return. Jana hurriedly put some crackers on the table as a snack for the two older boys.

"You two stay here," she instructed as she picked up the littlest one. "I'm going to help your mother for a few minutes. I'll be right back. Watch your little brother," she addressed to the six-year-old. "Make sure he stays inside."

Jaff nodded. "Sit down!" she heard him order his brother, Penn, as she left the house.

Mrs. Mench had driven up to the grain storage bins and was attempting to back the transport up to the grain elevator receiving chute. When properly lined up, a small door at the back of the transport's storage tank could be opened to allow the grain to spill out into the chute. The grain elevator would then lift the grain to the top of the bin and drop it inside. But the woman was having difficulty maneuvering the huge transport in reverse accurately enough to make the unloading possible.

"Thank goodness!" she cried from the window of the cab when she saw Jana run up.

"Come down," Jana said and motioned with her hand. "I'll show you a trick I use."

The woman left the cab and joined Jana. The two-year-old reached for his mother, who eagerly took him while Jana led her to the rear of the vehicle.

"It's difficult to see exactly where the chute is while backing up," Jana said, "so I use a marker … " Her voice trailed off as she glanced around. She spied a few pieces of scrap metal at the base of the bin and retrieved several meter-long pieces. Eyeing the chute, she laid the first piece a short distance from it, perpendicular to the transport's track.

"This is about how far you need to back up," she explained. "As long as you don't cross this marker, you won't go too far." Mrs. Mench nodded as Jana laid the next piece perpendicular to the first piece and parallel to the transport's track.

"This is about where your rear wheel should be. We can adjust it if we need to when we get everything lined up. You stand clear while I do it the first time."

Holding her child, Mrs. Mench moved back, and Jana scrambled into the transport's cab. She pulled forward and then reversed toward the metal markers—the two-meter wheels coming within centimeters of the metal before she stopped. She climbed out to inspect the results.

"My goodness!" said Mrs. Mench admiringly. "You did that perfectly!"

"I was a little off," Jana observed, critical of her work, "but it's close enough for now. We'll adjust the markers for next time." She turned to the other woman. "Start the elevator, and I'll open the chute."

The older woman twisted on the control knobs using one hand until the elevator whined and rattled to life. Jana operated the mechanical crank that opened the transport's dump hatch. The golden grain poured like water into the receiving chute in a billowing cloud of dust and chaff. She quickly stepped out of the dust plume to the side of the woman and her child.

"You're a lifesaver, Jana. You made that look easy."

"It's not hard—you just need to know what to do. I'm surprised your husband never showed you the technique."

"Al's not a … well … he's not what I would call a natural teacher," the woman confessed, and hugged the child. She suddenly looked up. "What are the boys doing?"

"They are having a snack."

Mrs. Mench nodded and watched the grain.

The transport was soon emptied, and Jana shut down the rattling elevator.

"When you back up next time, just guide off of the markers," Jana said as Mrs. Mench handed Korick back to her and climbed into the cab.

"I will. See you soon!" the woman said, smiled, and drove off with Ras barking in pursuit.

Jana returned to the house to find the two boys laughing and shouting while chasing each other around the table.

"What's going on here?" she demanded.

"Penn wouldn't sit down," the older boy explained.

"*You* sit down," the younger child rasped.

"Jana told me to make *you* sit down."

"You sit down," the younger boy rasped again, sticking out his chin.

"Well actually, Jaff, I told you to keep him in the house," Jana said. "I suppose having him sit down would accomplish that, but it wasn't necessary to be that restrictive. Thank you, though, for keeping him inside."

"He should have sat down. I told him to."

"How about we all sit down," Jana suggested. She set the littlest boy in his chair, pulled a chair out for herself, and sat. The six-year-old glared at his brother but slowly took his seat. Last of all, the four-year-old climbed into his chair and made an exaggerated grin, his grimace exposing a set of small, crooked teeth.

"Very good, boys!" Jana encouraged. "Now, would you like another snack?"

"Yeah! 'Nack!" four-year-old Penn rasped in agreement.

The older boy narrowed his brown eyes in thought. "I want a story."

"Yeah! 'Tory!" Penn again agreed. "An', uh, 'nack too!"

Jana opened her mouth to speak but suddenly gasped in surprise as the smallest boy kicked her in the elbow. Despite the fingers in his mouth, she could see his mischievous grin. Her quick reflexes saved her from a second blow as she caught the foot in midstrike during his second attempt.

"No!" she said firmly as she squeezed the heel of Korick's bare foot. Her quick and firm reaction stunned him, and in that brief moment of his surprise, she released his foot. He quickly pulled it back under his chair. "Do not kick," she instructed in a firm voice, her blue eyes flashing directly at the child.

"He bites too," Jaff advised.

"He'd better not," Jana warned, rising. "I might bite back."

This struck the oldest boy as very funny and he started to laugh. The four-year-old began to copy his brother. Soon they both were making faces at each other while they continued the exaggerated laughter. Even the little one took his fingers out of his mouth to join in. Their immaturity amused Jana and she shook her head and laughed quietly as well.

She found a package of dried apricots in the cupboard. She sliced the golden, leathery disks into thin strips and scooped them into a small bowl while the boys continued to entertain each other with their forced laughter.

"How about we go out under the trees?" suggested Jana. "We can have our snack, I'll tell you a story, and you can build stick houses."

The two older boys sprang from their chairs and shouted as they ran out the door. Jana watched the door swing closed behind them and then turned, placed her hands on her hips, and gave the smallest boy a commanding look. "No biting. No kicking. Be nice."

He regarded her, wide-eyed and somber.

"Good!" she said, then smiled and picked him up. He laid his head on her shoulder.

The shouts of the boys led her to a clearing beneath the trees behind the house, where they were breaking small branches and leaves from the trees with sticks. Ras was barking and running in circles.

"Come sit down, boys!" she called, settling herself and the littlest boy at the base of a spreading ash. She gave Korick a sliver of apricot.

He pulled his fingers from his mouth, took the treat, and then put both fingers and fruit into his mouth.

The older boys came running and threw themselves on the ground at Jana's feet. Ras flopped down between them; his panting joined with theirs in a breathy chorus while Jana passed out a few apricot slivers. The sound of gnashing, open-mouthed chewing replaced the panting.

"And now the shtory!" Jaff said past the wad in his cheek.

"Please close your mouth as you chew your food, first," Jana instructed them. "It's not polite to show everyone what you are eating."

"Everyone sees what you put it in your mouth," Jaff countered. "Why can't they see you chew it?"

"Well," Jana replied, and she held up a bright yellow piece of apricot to study while her fine brows creased, "the food looks pretty before you eat it, but when you start chewing it, it gets all mashed up and looks messy. And sometimes when you chew with your mouth open, some pieces of chewed-up, messy food can squish out. I'll bet you wouldn't like it if I was chewing my food and some flew out of my mouth and landed on your nose!"

"Bleahh!" the four-year-old shouted. His pink tongue extended, mottled with yellow, masticated blobs of apricot.

Jaff gave him a disgusted look and closed his mouth.

"No, Penn," Jana said firmly. "That was not nice."

"Yeah, keep your mouth closed so she will tell us a story."

Penn glanced questioningly back and forth between his older brother and Jana. At last, he decided they were serious, so he closed his mouth and made exaggerated chewing motions while bobbing his head up and down.

"That's better, Penn," Jana said. "Not perfect, but better." She cleared her throat as she thought of something to tell them.

Chapter 6

"Far away, far to the south," Jana began her story and motioned with her hand as she talked, "there is a great desert. Almost nothing grows there and it is very hot and very dry. Over the years, animals that wandered into the Great Desert have lost their way. Desert explorers occasionally find their remains—just bleached white bones."

Penn's eyes were wide, while Jaff grinned and wiggled in excitement. "Do they find people bones?" the older boy asked.

Jana looked thoughtful. "It's possible. But people usually know better than to try to walk into the Great Desert. I don't think it happens very often."

"Yeah, but if they did, you know what they would find?"

"What?"

"A skull! And all the teeth!"

"Ooh! I suppose so."

"And the … the leg bones, and the hand bones, and the ear bones!"

"You wouldn't find ear bones—at least none that you can see."

"Why not?"

"Your ear—the outside part of the ear—doesn't have any bones," Jana explained, and she wiggled her ear between her fingers. "Your ear is made from **cartilage**, not bone. In the desert, the ear tissue would simply dry up and fall off."

"Wow!" Jaff said, grasping at both his ears.

"And the end of your nose, too," Jana added as touched the child's nose and wrinkled her own. "Your nose would fall off because it's also made from cartilage."

Jaff and his brother were now grasping at their ears and noses and laughing at each other. Jana waited until they settled down and directed their attention back to her. "Beyond the Great Desert are mountains—huge mountains that are so high that there is always snow on them, even in the summer. They are called the White Mountains because they are always white.

"A great sea lies beyond the mountains. The land between the mountains and the sea is green and moist. It's called the Emerald Plain. Many trees of all kinds grow there, including many fruit trees. And it rains almost every day.

"The ripe fruit is shipped from the Emerald Plain, through passes in the White Mountains and to the edge of the Great Desert. There, the hot winds dry the fruit so it will not spoil before it is sent to all sorts of different places."

"What different places?" Jaff asked.

Jana shrugged. "It's distributed to communities all over this planet," she replied. "I am sure some of it even goes to other worlds on the deep-space transports."

"The boom ships!" the boy grinned.

"Boom!" his little brother rasped an echo.

Jana nodded and smiled.

Jaff said, "We saw one just this morning. Did you see it?"

"Oh, yes."

"Have you ever been on a boom ship?"

"No," Jana laughed. "My parents were on one, but that was a long time ago. I don't know of anyone who has been on one recently."

"Do you think you ever will?"

"Will I ever what?"

"Go on a boom ship."

Her long ponytail shook. "I don't think so. I'll probably always stay here."

"Good," Jaff said.

She chuckled. "Why do you say that?"

"Because *I* want to go."

"Hmm. You will have to study *very* hard. But what does that have to do with me going or not?"

"You'll be here to take care of my brothers."

"That's very sweet, Jaff, but don't you think your mommy and daddy will do that?"

The boy said nothing, just looked away as Ras roused himself and ran barking toward the transport that rumbed in from the field.

A short time later, Jana noticed that the two younger boys had fallen asleep. "Here, Jaff, help me," she said, and handed him the empty fruit bowl. He took it while she carefully picked up the younger of the two sleeping boys. "I'll take him inside and come back for Penn. You stay here and watch him."

Jaff nodded and looked down, then he kicked some leaves on the sleeping form.

"Be nice, Jaff," Jana warned sharply.

"He's asleep. He doesn't care."

"If you were sleeping, would you want him to kick leaves on you?"

The boy looked down uncertainly and then slid to the ground with his back to the trunk of a tree. "All right," he sighed.

"Good! I'm sure your mother and father would be proud to see you act responsibly."

He dug the heels of his bare feet into the grass. "Are you proud of me?"

"When you do what you should, then you have a right to be proud of yourself."

He looked up. "I won't do anything bad. I promise."

Jana gave him an encouraging smile before she took the sleeping toddler into the house and quickly returned. Jaff was still standing guard, his hand on Ras's head as the dog lay next to him.

"Good job, Jaff!" she said. He smiled, got up, and looked down as he stroked the dog's head.

Jana lifted the sleeping four-year-old, and Jaff and the dog followed her to the house. The boy opened the door for her and held it while she carried Penn inside and deposited him on his bed. Then she covered each sleeping child with a light blanket.

She emerged from the children's bedroom and found Jaff at the table sorting through a small pile of books. She remembered listening as her mother and father discussed the Mench parents' refusal to contribute to the education co-op and whether this indicated a lack of financial resources or indifference to scholarship. Jana's parents had taught her a great deal and inculcated her with a love of learning, so she was relieved at the sight of the children's library on the table. She was glad, for their sakes, that there was at least some effort being made to educate them.

"Did your mom and dad teach you to read, Jaff?"

He looked at the books and then looked down. "No."

"Then, do you want to take a nap?"

"No. I think I better study."

"But if you can't read, then how will you study?"

He looked up at Jana and frowned. "I can read the pictures."

"Oh, I see." She liked his determination. "What are you going to study?"

"Everything."

"That will be difficult, don't you think?"

"Yes, but I have to."

"Why?"

"Because I have to know everything."

She pulled up a chair, sat beside him, and laid her hand softly on his small shoulder. "No, Jaff. You don't need to know everything."

"I don't?" His tone seemed uncertain.

She shook her head. "Only God knows everything. All you need to know is just enough to learn more."

"How much is that?"

"Whatever you know is enough to start."

"But I don't *know* what I know," Jaff protested with a note of desperation.

"I see your problem," Jana agreed and nodded. "You need someone to help you get started—a teacher."

"Mom shows me stuff sometimes. But she's awfully busy."

"There are other people who can teach," Jana suggested, thinking of the educational co-op.

"Could *you* teach me?"

"I guess I can for a little bit."

The boy wiggled and looked at her expectantly.

"We will begin with some arithmetic," she said. "Arithmetic is all about numbers. So to start, I want to hear you count as far as you can."

The boy quickly rattled off the numbers one through twenty before he became confused.

"Very good, Jaff," she said when he stopped. "You know a lot of numbers. Can you write them?"

He took a pencil and scratched some badly formed numerals on a piece of paper, from one through ten.

"That's good," the young woman said. "Now Jaff, can you tell me what each of those numerals means?"

He gave her a worried look and shook his head. She held up two fingers. "How many fingers am I holding up?"

"Two."

"Right. And which figure is also called two?"

He pointed to the scrawled two.

"Correct again. Now, don't say anything. When I hold up some fingers, you write the numeral that means how many fingers. Are you ready?"

He nodded.

She continued the exercise for a few minutes, holding up fingers and nodding approvingly each time as he scratched the correct symbol.

"Now I will ask you again," Jana said. "What do the numerals that you write on the paper mean?"

"They mean how many fingers you hold up!"

"Well, yes, they *can* mean that," she agreed. "But is that the only thing they can mean?"

Jaff looked puzzled.

His teacher jumped up and grabbed some apricots from the cupboard. She placed three on the table in front of him. "How many is that?" she asked.

He scratched a three on his paper.

"How many legs on this chair?" she asked and pulled it back so he had a clear view.

He scratched a four.

"Now, what do those numerals mean?"

He frowned. "I guess they mean how many of ... of ... *anything*," he said slowly.

"Right! You got it!" Jana enthused. "A *number* is the abstract concept of a quantity—four fingers, four legs, four apricots—four of *anything*. The *numeral* is the symbol we use to express that quantity. It's not the number itself, just a symbol for it."

The six-year-old's worried look returned. "I don't know what you mean."

"It's all right," she smiled reassuringly. "The important thing right now is that you know how to count things and which symbol stands for the amount of things that you counted."

He nodded, but the frown remained.

"How many chairs are there?" she asked, hoping he would be encouraged by a few more right answers. The boy pointed to each of the chairs and then scratched a numeral six on his paper. "Six chairs," he said proudly.

Jana nodded, and for a while, he counted pencils, books, buttons, lights, and spoons.

"Numbers are easy," Jaff finally concluded.

"You're right," Jana agreed. "Many basic concepts of arithmetic are easy, but that doesn't mean they aren't very important.

"Let's go do more! I want to learn *everything* about numbers!"

Jana was gratified at his enthusiasm but she realized that the boy's young mind was probably saturated for the time being. She suggested taking a break, escorted him to the main family room, and helped him get into a deep, soft chair. She brought him a warm drink, and although he insisted on looking at a book, he was soon asleep. She covered him with a blanket and quietly retired to the kitchen.

Now that the boys were asleep, Jana quickly completed the domestic chores. She smiled to herself and fantasized that she was married and that she had been caring for her own children and home.

The pleasant daydream continued: Her husband might be the young man, Vannin Foss, who had recently asked her father for permission to see her. She didn't know him that well, but she knew he had two brothers who worked with him. That meant she wouldn't have to work in the fields, but hopefully, he would ask her to come with him occasionally—just so they could be with each other. She smiled as she suddenly remembered what her mother had said about the bonding nature of working together.

No, she didn't know this young man yet, but she could imagine. He would be patient with the children and would take time to listen to her—especially when she was upset or just wanted to talk. He would sing and play music with her for their parents on holidays and at worship. And, of course, he would be very, *very* romantic. He would write little notes to her, and she would often find one on a dish in the cupboard, fastened to the bathroom mirror, or tucked into her folded underwear in her drawer. And they would all say something like, *Just thinking of you …*

A far-off smile played on her youthful face as the grain transport once more thundered across the far end of the yard. She finished the dishes and checked on the children. They were all sleeping soundly, so she decided to let Mrs. Mench know how they had been faring.

Jana leisurely left the house, closed the steel door softly so it wouldn't slam, and started walking across the graveled yard toward the collection of metal grain bins peeking above the trees. She started as Mrs. Mench burst from the trees, running toward her with arms flailing.

"Jana!" the woman called frantically when she saw the girl.

Jana started running toward her. "Mrs. Mench, what happened?"

The older woman's dusty face was tear-streaked and distorted with emotion as she clutched Jana's shoulders. "Where are the boys?" she demanded.

"They're in the house, asleep. I was just coming to tell you."

"Good! Good!" the older woman gasped and let go of Jana to hold her own bowed head in her hands. "Oh, no! Oh, no!"

"Mrs. Mench! What *is* it?"

"I killed him! I'm sure I killed him! Oh, no!"

Jana extended an arm, and the older woman sagged against her, her body shook with sobs. "Did something happen to Mr. Mench?" Jana asked breathlessly.

"No! No! It's Ras! I think I killed him!"

"What? How did it happen?"

Mrs. Mench took several noisy breaths and wiped her running nose with the sleeve of her dusty coverall before she could answer. "He came running toward the transport like he always did—the silly dog. When I turned around, there he was, lying on the ground …" Her voice trailed off as she broke down again.

Tears welled up in Jana's eyes, but she managed to say, "Maybe he's just hurt. Maybe he'll be all right."

"No! No! I looked. He's not moving. And there's blood coming out of his nose and everything!" Once more, Mrs. Mench buried her face in her sleeves and shook with emotion.

The young woman said nothing. She continued to hug Mrs. Mench while tears ran down both of their cheeks.

At last, Mrs. Mench straightened and took deep breaths, fighting to regain control of her emotions. "We'll have to pick him up. Put him in something. I'll have Al bury him in the field."

Jana nodded. "Your husband can tell the boys. I think it would be easier for him to explain what happened."

"No!" Mrs. Mench exclaimed thickly. "The boys must *not* know! They won't understand. I'll—we'll tell them that Ras just … just ran away. Yes, we'll say he was … chasing a bird and … and didn't know how to get back home."

"I don't think that's such a good idea, Mrs. Mench."

"Please, Jana, don't make this more difficult than it already is," the woman insisted. "I can't have the boys knowing I killed their dog." She glanced around the yard and then ran to a shed and emerged with a ragged green tarpaulin. "Please help me," she said, and started back toward the trees.

Jana wiped her eyes with the back of her hand, sniffed, and walked quickly after the distraught mother. They passed under the shade between the arching ash trees, and Jana could see the transport parked well short of the unloading position. Several meters beyond it was a heap of brown and white fur. Jana's eyes filled with new tears as they approached the dog's still body.

The same bundle of energy that had bounded and played with the children an hour earlier was now eerily quiet; its brown nose dipped in a small, darkening red puddle. The tarpaulin rustled as Mrs. Mench threw it over the body. "Help me, Jana! We must wrap him up."

Numbly, the young woman knelt and assisted in the task of rolling the dog's body into the tarp. They continued rolling until the dog was completely inside the sheet. Then the two women grasped the ends of the roll and lifted it clear of the ground.

"To the transport! Hurry!" the older woman said as she started to pull the gruesome package. They reached the vehicle and set it down. Mrs. Mench stared at the transport in confusion. "Jana, where can we put it?"

"In the cab?"

"Does it have to be so close?"

"Where else?"

"What about in the back?"

"That's still full of grain."

The brown-haired woman staggered to the shade of the nearby trees and sank to her knees. Jana followed, knelt, and put an arm around her.

"Can you empty it for me, Jana? I'm shaking so badly I can't drive well enough to back up."

Jana nodded and gave the other woman's back a few comforting pats. She rose and ran to the back of the transport to make sure nothing was in the way. Then she climbed up into the cab and used the markers she had placed earlier to back the great machine slowly to the receiving chute. When the transport was in position, she scrambled from the cab, ran to the back of the machine, started the elevator, and opened the dump chute. Another golden, dusty shower of grain flowed forth and was soon in the safety of the storage bin.

As the last grains tumbled into the receiving chute, Jana secured the elevator. She ran to the transport, climbed up into the cab, and pulled it forward so the dump chute was clear. Mrs. Mench slowly got to her feet and moved to follow Jana to the rolled tarpaulin. They dragged it to the back of the truck, lifted it to the open chute, and pushed it into the open metal box that formed the transport's grain tank.

Jana closed the chute door, and Mrs. Mench leaned against the back of the transport, head back, eyes closed, and exhaled loudly. "Oh, Jana! I don't know what I would have done without you!"

"You would have done what you had to do. I just made it easier."

The other woman roused herself and took several deep breaths. "I have to hurry. Al will wonder what took so long." She gave Jana another quick hug and walked toward the cab.

"Will he be upset?"

"Yes, if I'm late."

"I mean about Ras. Will he be upset that you—that the dog is dead?"

Mrs. Mench reached the cab and paused with one hand on the ladder. She made a short, mirthless laugh. "I think that it might *improve* his mood."

"What do you mean?"

"He really didn't want the dog." She stared at the transport tank and a hard look crossed her face, deepening the shallow lines that already crossed it at her young age. "We only had Ras because he was given to us and the boys insisted we keep him."

"Oh," Jana said shortly.

"So I'm worried for them. They loved that dog and I am afraid they will be very resentful if they found out I killed him—even if it was an accident." She looked up and gave Jana a sharp look. "Promise me you will never tell them what happened."

Jana hesitated. "My father says that honesty is always the best policy."

Mrs. Mench sighed. "Your father is a wonderful man, Jana, but he's not a mother."

"My mother says the same thing."

Mrs. Mench sniffed. "We have our way of doing things, Jana. Life is difficult enough for the children without knowing every bad thing that happens. Now promise me you won't tell. They are my boys and I think I know best how to deal with them."

"I ... I promise," Jana agreed reluctantly. But she thought, *This isn't right!* She wanted to protest further but she said nothing out of respect for the older woman's position as matron.

"Thank you." The voice sounded relieved. "I knew I could count on you. You're my rock."

Jana made no reply. She didn't feel like a rock; she felt like a limp, dirty sponge. She stepped back from the transport and Mrs. Mench drove it away with a whine of its motors and a swirling cloud of dust. It felt odd not seeing Ras bounding after it or hearing him bark furiously. She watched until the transport disappeared behind the trees and its whine and rumble faded. Overhead, the thickening clouds in the western sky presaged the coming storm.

Jana entered the house quietly. She glanced at the deep chair where Jaff had been sleeping and inhaled sharply. The chair was empty! She quickly scanned the kitchen.

"Jaff!" she called in a loud whisper. There was no response.

She hurried to the bedroom of the two younger boys. They had kicked off their blankets in their sleep but were otherwise lying quietly. She covered them again, then she checked the small study in the next room, but it was also empty.

"Jaff!" she called more loudly, but there was no response.

There was one more room in the short hallway—the parents' bedroom. She looked into the room. "Jaff! Where are you?" she called quietly but urgently.

"I'm right here."

Jana jumped at the voice behind her and whirled, breathing hard at the sight of the boy. "Jaff! Where were you?" she demanded.

"I had to use the bathroom," he said.

"Oh."

He studied her face. "What's wrong?" he asked.

Jana swallowed. "What do you mean?"

"Your eyes look funny. Did you cry?"

She flushed and blinked. "Yes. Something happened, but I think your mother and father should tell you," she finally said.

"Why can't you tell me?"

"I … I promised your mother I wouldn't."

"Why not?"

"I said I can't talk about it," Jana insisted.

The boy stared at his feet for a moment and then suddenly looked up. "Can you teach me more number stuff?"

"Um," Jana said, and she shakily exhaled. "Maybe after lunch."

"How about a story? Can you tell me another one?"

"Not right now. I'm not feeling well."

"Are you hurt?" A look of concern crossed the child's small face.

"No. I'm just a bit upset."

He continued to study her, but a small cry from the boys' room ended the conversation. Jana roused both of the younger children and tasked Jaff to help Penn go to the bathroom while she changed the youngest boy's diaper. After everyone had washed, she prepared sandwiches and milk.

The children were in good spirits after their nap. By the end of lunch, Jana had calmed down and almost felt back to normal, although the dog's demise and her promise to Mrs. Mench still weighed heavily upon her heart.

After she cleaned up the lunch dishes, Jana took the boys out to the trees and helped the two older ones to make a village of stick houses. The transport rumbled across the far side of the yard. Jaff looked up. "Where's Ras?" he asked.

Jana pretended not to hear the question; instead, she concentrated on helping Penn arrange his sticks. She blinked back tears, but her vision became so watery she had to wipe her eyes with the back of her hand.

"Here, Ras! Here, boy!" Jaff called, but the only sounds that returned were the wind rustling the leaves and the distant, mechanical rhythm of the grain elevator.

Jana wished she could tell the boys what had happened, but she had promised not to, so she studiously returned her attention to helping Penn make stick teepees. "This can be the central street," she said, indicating a ragged trail between several stick constructions. "This building can be the electrical shop, and next to it can be the agricultural station."

Penn nodded but said nothing as he aligned his sticks. His tongue stuck out sideways in concentration. The youngest boy sat next to Jana. He hugged his toy with one arm while he grasped a small stick in the other, waving it experimentally and striking the ground, her leg, and his own head with equal frequency. Jaff wandered away, found a much larger stick for himself, and began beating at the lower tree branches to knock off autumn leaves. He paused as the transport rumbled out of the yard and disappeared behind the distant trees in a cloud of dust.

"Very good, Penn!" Jana complimented. "That is an excellent stick house. Here, I'll help you make another." She reached down to begin, but at that moment Jaff burst from behind the tree and kicked apart several of the houses.

"Boom!" he shouted. "Atomic war!" Another structure went flying in a shower of sticks.

"Jaff, what are you doing?" Jana cried. "Penn worked hard on those!"

"It's atomic war!" he shouted back, while he continued stomping and kicking.

Jana looked at Penn, expecting him to be distressed, but he was getting to his feet and grinning. "'Tomic!" he shouted and began to kick at the stick houses, as well.

"Now, boys … " Jana protested but she let her voice trail off as she realized they were completely focused on their destructive activity. She picked up Korick and moved beyond the range of the flying twigs.

Their kicking and shouting continued for a frenzied minute. Each boy tried to outdo the other with the speed of his kicks and the distance he could make the twigs fly. Jana sighed and waited for them to tire. Korick wriggled in her arms, seemingly wanting to join in.

"No. Wait," Jana told him, holding him tightly despite his continued struggles.

At last, the boys stopped. They breathed heavily as they looked at each other and surveyed the destruction they had wrought.

"Is the war over?" Jana asked.

Jaff nodded and his chest heaved.

Jana set Korick down and he toddled toward his brothers while he dragged his stuffed toy and tried to kick at the leaves. About the time he reached them, the older boys walked past him and threw themselves on the ground next to Jana's feet, still taking deep breaths.

"What was that all about?" Jana asked.

"I told you—atomic war," Jaff replied.

"'Tomic!" Penn rasped.

"What do you know about atomic war?"

"I know it's got big bombs that blow up stuff. *Boom*!" He threw his arms out from his chest.

"Boom!" the younger boy echoed as he grinned and flailed his small arms.

"What do you think happens when those bombs explode?" Jana asked in a somber tone.

"They knock down buildings. The pieces go flying."

"What about the people in the buildings? What happens to them?"

"They get killed, I guess. I don't know."

"They *do* get killed," Jana said, remembering the description of the devastation of atomic warfare from her history studies. "It's a very horrible thing. I don't think it's a very nice game to play."

"We didn't *really* kill anybody."

"No, but you are playing a game that pretends to kill people. Does that seem nice to you?"

Jaff seemed thoughtful. "Maybe the people were bad enemies. Then it would be good to kill them, right?"

"Emenies *bad!"* Penn mispronounced the word in a serious tone.

"If you knew that everyone in the city you were bombing was bad, perhaps. But what if there were good people too? Would you still want to bomb it?"

"I would tell the good people to leave."

"But suppose the bad people wouldn't *let* the good people leave. Then what would you do?"

"I guess I would still have to bomb it."

"Even if your bombs killed the good people?"

"Well," the boy frowned in thought, "if the bad people were catching good people and not letting them get away, then if I bombed them, then at least they wouldn't be able to catch any *more* good people."

Jana nodded. "But when you're playing, why not just build cities? You don't have to bomb them."

"But I want to bomb 'em!"

"Really? Why?"

"'Cause it's more fun!"

Penn suddenly resumed kicking at the few remaining upright sticks and making explosive noises. Jaff quickly joined in, and Jana scooped up the wriggling Korick and moved him back a few steps to be safely out of range of the flying twigs.

Jaff soon tired of the game and threw himself down on the grass and leaves, breathing hard. Then he sat up and asked, "Where's Ras?"

Jana looked around, pretending to scan for the dog, and then she looked back at the boy. He was watching her intently, his eyes slightly narrowed.

"I don't know where Ras is right now," she said as truthfully as she could. "You should ask your father when he gets back. I believe he will tell you."

The boy's eyes quickly turned away.

Jana checked to see what the other boys were doing and was disappointed to see Penn trying to snatch a twig from his little brother's hand. "Penn! Let Korick have his stick! There are plenty of others for you."

Penn hesitated, but he broke under the girl's hard look. He reluctantly let go of the stick and turned to pick up another. The smallest child soon dropped the contested twig and laboriously reached for another, as well. Jana sighed, relieved that they were playing and not fighting each other.

"How does it work?" Jaff asked.

"How does what work?"

"Atomic bombs. How do they work?"

"It's quite complicated. Are you sure you want to know?"

"I told you, I gotta know this stuff."

"Well," Jana smiled, "I will try to explain but I think it might not be easy to understand. I might use some words you don't know, so just ask if you have a question, all right?"

The boy nodded with an expectant look.

The girl took a deep breath and began. "The basic principle is called atomic fission—that means *splitting*. The atoms of the bomb's explosive material are split, releasing a lot of energy. That energy forms the atomic explosion."

"What are atoms?"

"They are tiny bits of matter. The bomb is made of them. Actually, everything is made from atoms."

Jaff squinted at a leaf that he held to his eye. "I don't see 'em."

"You can't. They are much too small to be seen."

"How do you know they are there if no one can see them?"

"Just because something is invisible doesn't mean it isn't there. For example, when we breathe in or out we can't see the air but we can feel it. We can't see the gravity field around this planet but we feel it pull us downward. Atoms can't be seen but we can do experiments that prove they exist."

"Like what?"

"Hmm." The girl smiled while her brows contracted and she tapped her smooth cheek with a delicate finger. *How to explain atomic theory to a six-year-old? Let me think …* After a moment, her face relaxed, and she turned to the boy.

"We'll do what is called a *gedanken* experiment. That means we'll do the experiment in our heads. We'll just think about it." She held up a clump of dirt. "Imagine we break this clump in half. Then suppose we take one of those half pieces and break *it* in half." At this, she divided the clump of soil. "Now imagine we kept on doing this—breaking one of the remaining pieces in half, and in half, smaller and smaller. What would happen after we did that a few times?"

"We'd get a very tiny piece."

"Right. Suppose we kept doing that. How small would a piece finally be?"

Jaff suddenly grinned. "It would be so small we couldn't see it!"

"Exactly. So just by thinking about it, we can conclude that matter could be made of tiny pieces too small to be seen. That doesn't prove such tiny pieces exist, but it gives us the idea that they *could* exist. We call those tiny bits of matter *atoms*."[24]

The boy picked up a small clod of dirt and crumbled it, watching the small pieces fall to the grass and drift on the breeze. "So why doesn't *everything* explode like an atomic bomb does?"

"Some atoms are more stable than others, just like some of the stick houses you made were stronger than others. But just as some houses are easy to knock down, some atoms, such as ones called uranium or plutonium, are easy to split. Those types of atoms are collected and put into bombs."

"Could we collect some?"

Jana shook her head. "No, it is much too difficult and too dangerous."

"Aw, it would be fun."

"No, it wouldn't," she replied as she looked thoughtfully at the two younger boys busily engaged in reconstructing the stick village. "Atomic bombs might be necessary sometimes, but they are never fun."

A rumble from the west caused them both to flinch, and Jaff shot Jana a worried look.

"It's just thunder," Jana explained calmly as she rose and moved to pick up Korick. She kept her tone casual but she knew the storms on

Ceres could contain dangerously high winds. It would unwise to remain outdoors much longer. "Come on, boys. There's a storm coming and we should get into the house so we are not struck by lightning."

"Lightning!" Jaff yelled as he ran toward the house.

"Light! Light!" Penn hollered, running after his older brother.

Chapter 7

The darkening western sky flickered, and another, closer thunderclap rumbled over Jana and the boys as they reached the protection of the porch. Jana turned and saw the harvester and the transport sweep around the trees and into the yard. Brown dust billowed ahead of them, borne on the storm gusts. She held Korick while she waited for Mr. Mench to park the harvester and Mrs. Mench to unload the transport into the storage bin behind the trees. She smiled in satisfaction as she heard the tiny rattle of the grain elevator above the rumbles of thunder and keening wind, then she turned and entered the house.

The children were washed and enjoying another snack by the time their dust-covered parents entered the house. "Ma! Ma!" they cried, jumping up and running to her. She knelt and, despite the dust, took them into her arms. Mr. Mench was in rare good humor. His soil-darkened face split into a grin at the sight.

He turned to Jana. "She did real good," he said, with a nod toward his wife.

"I'm glad for you," Jana replied, feeling gratified with the success of her assistance.

"Yup," he nodded again. "She used to have a lot of trouble backing the transport, but she told me she figured out how to place markers on the ground, which made it easy for her. Pretty clever, huh?"

Jana felt a flush of indignation that the other woman had taken credit for the idea she had given to her. She nodded and looked at

Mazie, who was holding her youngest and trying to listen to the older boys while they both talked over each other. If she heard what her husband had said she gave no outward sign.

"So, the yield was good?" Jana asked in an attempt to take her mind off her resentment.

Mr. Mench nodded. "Real good. And thanks to Mazie, we got it in just in time. You ought to have 'er show you how she did it." He motioned toward his wife over his shoulder. "You might learn something."

"I can handle a transport," Jana replied quietly.

"Oh, yeah. You said that earlier." His dirt-covered face broke into another grin. "Just trying to be helpful."

"Thanks."

"You'll stay for supper, won't you, Jana?" Mrs. Mench suddenly asked above the noise of her children.

"Um, I hadn't expected to—"

"It's storming out there," Aleph cut in from his position near the door. He cracked it open to let the sounds of the crashing thunder and pounding downpour prove his point.

"You really ought to wait it out," Mazie agreed. "I must insist you stay a while."

"All right. You and Mr. Mench can clean up while I have the boys help me set the table."

"Thanks!" Mazie smiled. "There's soup in the keeper and ham and bread in the larder. If you would cut the bread and ham for sandwiches, I'll shower and then flash heat the soup."

"Don't worry, Mrs. Mench. I'll get the soup too."

"You're a dear, Jana," she said and then she turned to follow her husband to wash up.

Jana sighed and helped the boys clear the table of their snack before assigning Jaff to set out the cups and bowls, and Penn to bring out the spoons. Meanwhile, she sliced the bread and cold ham and then put the cold vegetable soup into the flash heater. By the time the boys' parents returned the table was ready and the kitchen was filled with the rich smell of warm bread, meat, spices, and onions. Jana nodded to the two older boys and they took their seats while she sat Korick in his chair.

"I can sure tell you're in *your* element," Mr. Mench commented as he took his seat. "You got the table looking real nice and the way you handle those kids I 'spect you'll be having your own before too long."

"It looks wonderful, Jana," Mrs. Mench agreed, and she sat down, smiling.

"Thank you, Mrs. Mench," Jana replied. "I'm glad I could help you out. You've had a long, busy day."

"Are we going to talk or eat?" Mr. Mench asked.

"Oh, Aleph." Mrs. Mench shot him a look of exasperation as she passed the plate of sandwiches to him. "The food is right here."

"Jana sometimes says that at her house they pray before they eat," Jaff commented.

"Your ma is a good enough cook so we don't need to pray," the man replied and he guffawed at his own joke.

Mrs. Mench pointedly cleared her throat. "Honestly," she muttered.

The conversation lapsed while Jana passed the sandwiches to the children and Mrs. Mench ladled the soup. The older woman finally broke the silence. "Has that handsome Vannin Foss seen you yet?"

Jana blushed. "My father has been talking to him."

"Oh, yeah," Mr. Mench grunted. He reached for another sandwich. "I heard that your pa does a hard interview with the young men who want to spark you. What's he trying to do—scare 'em off?"

"He's just looking out for me. He says that if a young man is too afraid to talk to him then he probably wouldn't make a very good son-in-law, anyway."

"You can be *too* careful," the man argued. "If he was really looking out for you, he'd get you married off right quick. You got your looks now but they'll be gone before you know it."

"Oh, Aleph!" Mrs. Mench chided. "Don't be rude."

"Mazie, now you know I didn't mean anything rude. I was just speakin' my mind. I reckon I can do that in my own house."

"It's all right, Mrs. Mench," Jana said. "Mr. Mench is what my father calls a plain speaker. You never have to guess what he thinks—he'll tell you straight out."

"Your pa's got that right," Aleph Mench nodded and grinned as he took in what he considered high praise. "And as far as the Foss kid goes, your pa'd be foolish to turn him down. He's set up to be one of the biggest operators this side of the White Mountains. Why, Old Man Foss even has holdings on the coast. Can't see why he don't just slap him on the back, call him son, and set the date."

"For goodness sake, Aleph, you make it sound like some sort of … some sort of business transaction. Perhaps Mr. Maines is thinking about more than his prospective son-in-law's cash flow."

The man raised a bushy brow. "Like what?"

His wife pressed a red hand against the base of her throat. "Like … like love and consideration and sensitivity."

"Nice things—in their own ways," he nodded. "But all the sensitivity in the world won't buy you a single energy credit. Maines would do his daughter better if he was more practical." He turned to Jana and added, "After all, he'd not only be setting *you* up for life, he'd be setting *himself* up too."

"Oh, Aleph! A girl wants to marry for love, not for money."

The man raised a brow and looked at his wife. "Don't you think a young man feels the same way?"

She blinked and straightened. "I would think so. I would *hope* so."

"Of course he does," Aleph Mench nodded. "I 'spect just about every young fellow that ever took the plunge figures it the same way—all he needs is love. Well, at some point, he comes to the realization that most all those romantic notions are just moonshine. Sooner or later, he wakes up and realizes that love can't feed his family or repair his machinery. It takes work—and money. An' generally speaking, the less a man can supply of one the more he's gonna need of the other.

"The young missy here might feel that she wants to marry for love. I'm just sayin' that's fine as far as it goes but you need to think a season or two ahead. Women go to seed before you know it—and it don't stay summer forever."

A moment of uncomfortable silence followed but Jana broke it by saying, "Dad says Mom is more beautiful to him today than when they married."

The man grinned sardonically. "Your pa is good with words. And your ma has kept herself up, I have to admit." He shot a brief glance at his wife and then looked down at his soup. "Most women just let themselves go. Or maybe it don't make no difference what they do."

Mazie Mench's eyes were brimming with tears as she looked at Jana. The older woman attempted to speak but then blinked and looked downward.

The man sat back, cleared his throat, and ran a callused hand through his dark but thinning hair. "So," he began to ask, and his eyes narrowed, "you figurin' on hitchin' up with the Foss boy?"

"Perhaps. It all depends."

"On what?" He rubbed the back of his hand across the dark stubble on his chin.

"On love."

The man started. "Now just a minute, missy. You know I just said that was romantic moonshine. If you're trying to fun with me, I don't much appreciate it."

"I'm not trying to joke with you, Mr. Mench."

"But Jana, then what *do* you mean?" Mrs. Mench asked with a puzzled frown.

"My father," began Jana, "says that humanity often behaves like a drunkard trying to get on a horse. He'll fall off one side of the horse then try to get back on and fall off the other side."

Mr. Mench emitted an amused grunt at the word picture but said nothing as Jana continued. "You correctly pointed out, Mr. Mench, that many people think that marriage is all about the feeling of love and they fall off the romantic side of the horse, so to speak. But in an attempt to correct that mistake, I think you are falling off the practical side. The place to be is not on one side or the other, but in the saddle."

"So how does that play out?" the man asked. "You gettin' hitched or not?"

"Like I said, that depends upon love."

"Moonshine!" he snorted. "How can you figure love?"

The girl stared at her glass and ran a finger thoughtfully around its rim. "My father would agree with you that you can't feed a family on romantic feelings, but those feelings aren't love—they're just feelings. And like all feelings, they come and go on their own. We can't control them.

"On the other hand, he would say that love, by contrast, *does* feed a family, because the motivation for a man to work to provide for his family is rightly his love for them. Harvesting grain or repairing broken machinery might not involve romantic feelings about your wife, but that's how you prove you really love her. I'm sure your wife didn't have romantic feelings about driving the transport but she did it because she loves her family—and she loves you."

Mr. Mench cleared his throat, sat back, and scratched his head. His wife rose quickly and hurried from the table toward her bedroom, one hand half-covering her face.

"Ma?" Jaff asked and rose.

"Sit down, boy," his father said. "She'll be all right."

The child glanced at his father's stern face and slowly slid back into his seat.

Jana glanced down and saw that Korick had fallen asleep in his chair. Penn fidgeted and pensively looked back and forth between her and his father.

"I think the children have finished eating," Jana said. "Perhaps they would like to help me clear the table?"

"Get this stuff cleaned up," Mr. Mench said with a nod to the children and a short wave of his callused hand.

The two older boys left their seats and picked up their dishes. Jana rose and gently lifted Korick from his chair.

"I'll put Korick in bed and be right back," she told them.

Meanwhile, Mr. Mench had slid his chair back, stood up, and sauntered to the front door, opening it to observe the weather. "Rain's lettin' up," he announced, and then he stepped out onto the covered porch and closed the door behind him.

"Is Ma all right?" Jaff asked Jana with a worried look.

"I think so," she replied. "I'll check on her after I lay your brother down. You boys finish clearing the table. I'll wash the dishes when I get back."

She hurried to the children's room, laid the toddler in his bed, and covered him with a small blanket. She left the boy's room and tapped on the parents' bedroom door. Mazie Mench emerged, red-eyed but composed.

"Are you all right?" asked Jana.

The woman nodded and looked past the girl. "What are the boys doing?"

"Korick is asleep in his bed, and the two older ones are cleaning up the kitchen."

Mrs. Mench shot her a doubtful look and moved to the kitchen while Jana followed. The kitchen was empty, the dirty dishes stacked in unstable piles in the sink. Mrs. Mench sighed. "I better get started."

"I'll do them." Jana moved past her.

"Jana, you've done enough."

"I told the boys I would do them."

"They won't notice. It's late. You should be heading home before it's completely dark."

"You might be surprised at how much they notice," Jana replied.

"For goodness sake, Jana!" The older woman shook her head. "They are just *children*."

"I said I would do them."

"Very well," she finally relented. "But I'll wipe the table."

The two women set to their tasks. They were almost done when the door opened. Mr. Mench and the boys entered, looking very grave.

"Mazie, the boys was askin' about the dog."

"Oh?" Jana heard her catch her breath. "And what did you tell them?"

"I told 'em you'd tell 'em."

The woman's mouth tightened and she shot a glance at Jana before she absently set aside the damp wiping cloth and knelt in front of the boys. "I'm afraid I have some bad news, children," she said. Once more, she looked toward Jana. The girl found it impossible to meet the woman's gaze and quickly looked away.

"What happened, Ma?" Jaff pressed.

"Ras, well … Ras … ran away."

"No! Not Ras! He wouldn't!" Jaff protested. His lower lip trembled. "He was a *good* dog!"

"I'm … I'm sorry, Jaff. But he followed me out to the field and … and then saw a bird or something and just ran away after it."

"He's lost! Maybe we should be looking for him!" the boy cried.

"We can't," Mrs. Mench said with a shake of her head. "It's too muddy and dark."

Jana could see the boy was trying not to cry. His eyes brimmed but he kept his face pinched to keep his lower lip from trembling. His gaze quickly shifted to his father, who gave a shrug and spread his hands. The boy then turned to Jana. She felt her face flush and once more dropped her burning eyes downward.

"Maybe … maybe he'll come back," Jaff finally said and his voice cracked as it rose in hope.

"Yes. Maybe he'll come back," his mother agreed.

"Wouldn't count on it," Mr. Mench commented. "Dogs sometimes just take off and you never see 'em again."

"Oh, Al! You're taking away all of our son's hope," Mrs. Mench chided before turning to Jana. "He might come back, don't you think?"

The young woman turned away as a hot tear rolled down her cheek. She wiped it quickly and cleared her throat as she turned back to face the family. She resented this crude attempt to force her into the tiny conspiracy. "I wouldn't know. We never had a dog run away."

"Oh," Mrs. Mench said, and her face and voice fell.

"I think I should be heading back home."

Mrs. Mench rose. "Of course, Jana. I'll see you to the door."

"Thanks for mindin' the boys, missy," Aleph Mench said with a small nod. "And thanks for offering to help drive, but we done all right."

"I'm glad I could help in some way," Jana replied. She looked at Mrs. Mench who suddenly seemed to notice an overlooked crumb that needed to be removed from the table.

"Ras will come back, don't you think, Jana?" Jaff suddenly asked.

The girl found herself looking down at him, at a loss for what to say. She glanced up and saw that both of the adults were watching her intently. Her tongue went dry as she struggled for the right words.

"Ras is …" she started to say. Mrs. Mench's eyes widened and then narrowed. "Ras is … I think he's all right, wherever he is," she finally managed, and from the corner of her eye, Jana could see the woman relax.

"So you think he'll come back?" the boy asked hopefully.

"He might not. Your father said that sometimes dogs don't come back."

"You think he won't come back?" His voice dropped.

Jana knelt and looked at him closely as she put a hand gently on his shoulder. "It's something you—it's something we have to be prepared for. Even if Ras were still here, there would always be the chance that something could happen to him. One of the most important lessons in life is to learn to let go of the things we want to hold on to the most."

The six-year-old looked down and then looked up. "Why would he go away?"

"Animals can make mistakes—like the animals that wander into the Great Desert and get lost."

"Maybe it wasn't a mistake. Maybe he didn't he like me anymore."

Jana smiled and shook her head. "I'm sure Ras liked you and would come back if he could."

The boy sighed and shoved his hands into his pockets. "I sure wish he would come back."

"Yes," Jana whispered. "I wish he could too."

Penn suddenly let go of his mother's leg, dropped on all fours, and pretended to bark. "Gog. Raf!" he said. He grinned and then stuck out his tongue and pretended to pant.

Mr. and Mrs. Mench laughed loudly and even Jana found herself smiling as she hugged the boys, rose, moved to the door, and bid them good-night. She stepped into the cool, damp darkness, and Mrs. Mench followed her.

"You handled that wonderfully, Jana," the woman complimented.

"It didn't feel wonderful," she said flatly. She turned and faced the other woman in the soft, purple light. "I feel awful. Please don't ask me to lie for you again."

The woman's smile fell into a look of surprise. "I didn't ask you to lie. I simply asked you not to tell what happened. And you *didn't* lie. Everything you said was completely true."

"Yes, but it implied something that wasn't true. Some day Jaff will find out that we all knew Ras was dead and that I went along with not telling him. He won't want to trust anybody. He may even find it impossible to trust."

"I don't think he'll even remember it," Mrs. Mench countered. "He's just a child. And anyway, he doesn't ever need to find out any different." Her voice had a hard, defensive edge.

"My father says that the only thing harder to keep than money is a secret."

"I hadn't figured you for a chattermouth."

"I'm not a chattermouth."

"Then there's no problem, is there?"

"No. No problem. Except …"

"What?" Again, the older woman sounded defensive.

"It doesn't matter, I guess."

A few fireflies emitted tiny flashes of light in the darkness of the yard. Low in the southeastern sky, shadowing clouds flashed mightily with electrical discharges, eerily silent because of the distance. Behind the clouds, a steady yellow-white glow indicated the rising moon. A cricket started to sing in the grass just beyond the porch.

"Thanks for your help, Jana," Mrs. Mench said, breaking the uncomfortable silence.

"Do you mean with the children, or with the transport?"

"I mean … with … both—with everything."

"Mr. Mench seems to think I didn't help with the transport."

"He just got the wrong impression."

"You didn't care to give him the right impression?"

"Look, Jana." Mazie Mench took a deep breath. "I never *said* I came up with the idea. I just told him what I had done and he assumed I had thought it up myself."

"Convenient."

"Look, if it's about getting paid less for watching the boys—"

"That's *not* it," Jana interrupted with uncharacteristic force.

The other woman raised a hand to her mouth and blinked at the outburst. "Aleph doesn't—I don't get many opportunities to hear him say nice things about me. Today, when he actually said something nice, I just couldn't bear to spoil it. You don't begrudge me that, do you?"

"No. I said it's all right."

"Good. I really didn't think you'd care."

"I suppose I ought to go." Jana stepped off the porch. "Good-night, Mrs. Mench."

"Good-night, Jana."

The girl had only taken a few steps when the woman called after her. "I'll tell him if you want me to."

Jana stopped and exhaled a long, slow breath. She tried to sort out her tumbling thoughts and feelings. "I … don't care," she managed to say.

"Oh. Well. Good-night."

"Good-night."

Jana walked through the wet grass and then left the yard for the soggy dirt track that led back toward her home. Cool mud oozed up between her toes while hot tears started to flow down her cheeks. The nearly full moon floated above the ragged cloud deck to the east, golden and serene above the silent storm.

Chapter 8

Aboard the derelict ship, the old woman's lips twitched and parted. Jana was unsure if she was observing an attempted smile, nervous apprehension, or a grimace of discomfort on the ancient features.

"You soon to be waking the crew?"

I have to tell her the truth. "I'm sorry. Your ship has malfunctioned and is adrift in deep space. The cryonic systems for the crew have failed. You are the only one left and … and have little time."

The old woman frowned in confusion before pain filled her eyes as she comprehended.

"The crew be dead?"

Jana strained to hear the whisper through her helmet. "Yes," she nodded. "I am sorry." She reached out to cradle the thin form that shook with sobs in her arms.

"Why?" the woman uttered at last.

Jana remained silent as she held her. She assumed the other woman wanted to know why her crewmates had died. It seemed unnecessarily harsh to say that the crew had probably succumbed to old age. But the woman's next words indicated that she had a different question in mind.

"Why did I … not … die too?"

Jana continued to hold the frail body until the weak convulsions ceased. Though her skeletal system had deteriorated considerably during the extended stay in cryonic hibernation, it was obvious that she had been very beautiful as a young woman. The fact that her body had survived such an ordeal meant that she must have entered the chamber in exceedingly robust health. Three centuries of hibernation, however, had reduced that body to a frail husk.

Jana glanced at the medical cuff, expecting to see it flatline, but the withered woman still clung to life. She eased her down and studied the aged face. The dark orbs rolled, rheumy and moist, before they fastened again on Jana with a painful, questioning intensity. The young woman breathed a prayer for the right words.

"What is your name?" Jana asked.

"Maia. It *did be* Maia." The voice cracked and the eyes closed.

"That's a pretty name," Jana said.

"It done be a name. Now it be useless—as I be useless."

"No, that is not true. You still have the breath of life—and that means you have as much value as *any* human being. Our worth is not based on our feelings but on the Creator's love for each one of us."

"Creator? Do you mean the Maker?" the old woman asked.

Jana's nod moved her helmet up and down. "Your speech is somewhat different from mine but I think they have the same meaning."

The woman made a slight shake of her head. "Maker. A word also that be of little use."

Jana said nothing as she continued gently to stroke the old woman's head.

"I be of no worth," Maia finally said. "I have nothing. I *be* nothing."

"No." Jana shook her head inside her helmet. "You have life, and as long as you have life, you have hope."

"Hope? In what? My life be soon ending. Then there be nothing. There be no hoping."

"Humanly speaking, yes. But the Creator—the Maker—offers a life beyond this life. As long as you have the breath of life you have an opportunity to receive that."

The parchment lips twitched. "You do speak as my grandmother did speak."

"Tell me about her."

The woman took a deep breath and her vital signs steadied. "She did good. She did good to me."

"What do you remember most about her?"

"Stories … she did tell me … stories."

"What kind of stories?"

The leathery lips pulled back. "Fabulous tales of the beginning of the worlds, of talking animals, and … and of a final day when all things we know will be ending. Then will be coming a new beginning. She said I did be known to the Maker—that he did put within us a spirit that will be living beyond this beginning into the next beginning."

"And you believed her?"

"I did believe. And then I did not believe."

"Why did you stop?"

The rheumy eyes opened and then closed. The wrinkled face took on a bitter look. "I did stop being a child."

"Your grandmother was not a child and yet she believed."

"Such beliefs only do meet the need of the young, the old, and the weak."

"We have all been young and we are all becoming old."

Another faint, bitter smile moved the ancient's lips and she nodded. Then her eyes opened slightly once more. "You be young and strong. You do believe?"

"Yes."

"Why?"

"I became aware of an emptiness—a desire for a purpose and meaning beyond this life. I was troubled by the existence of evil and of suffering. I could not explain the desire for ultimate justice without the possibility that some day, all wrongs will be made right—that nothing happens without a good purpose."

The woman coughed weakly. "Emptiness. We do all know it."

Jana nodded. "I came to realize that this was the Creator speaking to me—almost like a whisper from *inside* that made me look *outside.* Now I see his handiwork in nature and in the stars. In the quiet stillness, I hear his voice in my heart."

"There do be many voices," the woman objected. "Which do be the voice of the Maker?"

"The Canon says that the Maker knows us and cares for each of us personally. He gives us this life to prepare us for the next. We can choose a path that leads toward the Creator or one that leads away from him—to desire to find his will or to do our own."

"You would have me be returning to childhood?"

"My father would say that when you realize that you've taken the wrong path, then the shortest way home is to go back the way you came."

The woman settled back and her wrinkled brow contracted before she broke into a fit of weak coughing. Jana held her and gently patted her, offering what comfort she could through her gloved hands.

The paroxysm passed. The woman relaxed and stared into Jana's eyes. "Your ship be large?"

Jana nodded.

The woman's mouth twitched. "You be a great crew? Many weapons?"

Jana shook her head. "We have no weapons. The crew is only the captain and I."

"You do conquest, not?"

"The last war ended almost three centuries ago."

"Which system did be victor?"

"Everybody lost."

The woman closed her eyes. "You did say the Maker permits nothing into our lives that cannot be serving a good purpose." Her eyes opened, and she rolled them questioningly about the shattered ship and then at her withered body. "What good purpose be there in *this*?"

Jana was thoughtful. "Was there ever a time," she finally replied, "when you would have even asked that question before? Did you *ever* question your path?"

The woman shook her head weakly and narrowed wrinkled lids in deep sockets.

"Then I think that you have your answer," Jana said. She studied the medical cuff. The vital signs were dropping.

"My path … be …" the old woman mumbled.

She relaxed and closed her eyes. Jana watched the curves sag on the tiny screen. They stabilized briefly and the woman's lids slowly opened. She looked at Jana and her cracked lips twitched into a faint smile. "I be thanking to you," she mumbled thickly. "I be hearing …"

Her voice trailed off but her eyes widened as if seeing something beyond Jana. The faint smile once more crossed her face. Her eyes softened, then they rolled back, still open, but sightless. Her body convulsed weakly and then relaxed. Her jaw slackened open to reveal mottled, gray teeth. The cuff registered a precipitous drop in all vital signs and the small screen went dark.

Jana placed the body gently into the cryonic chamber and her gloved fingers pulled the eyelids closed. She lowered the cover of the tank and clicked the seals. *In his time*, she hummed, thinking the words to an ancient hymn. *He makes all things beautiful in his time.*

Chapter 9

Jana scrambled up the crawl tube toward the airlock as she attempted to sort out the mixture of feelings that moved like restless waves across the surface of her consciousness.

She was both relieved and proud of her discovery but also disappointed that she had found nothing of value that she could take back with her. She felt privileged by the providential discovery and her conversation with the ancient woman, but she had to fight back bitterness that her find would only be of medical interest and provide no financial reward.

Am I being petty by wanting to make a lucrative discovery? Or am I letting my family down by not trying harder? I just don't know.

The equipment she had seen was archaic and bulky—and, for the most part, firmly bolted in place. Data storage or other records must have been kept farther forward, but the centrifugal forces that far from the center of gravity would have made movement difficult and far more dangerous. And she was almost out of time.

I want to get off this ship! The thought kept going through her mind and no other part of her mind argued. Her chronometer indicated that she had just enough time to cycle the airlock, clear the ship, and return to the *Phoenix*. She did not want to give Captain Larkin anything more about which to complain. She hoped he would express some satisfaction at her prompt and safe return. *At least the derelict is marked and perhaps it won't be long before a salvage crew arrives.*

The inner door of the airlock clanged shut behind her with the somber sound of a temple gong. She spun the wheel closed and mashed the button with the inverted triangle, signaling decrease in pressure. As the atmosphere in the airlock began to evacuate, the external sounds—the scrape of her boots, the squeak of her suit, and the clicks of the harness on her maneuvering pack—faded as she fastened herself into the unit. She was soon once more in a world of silence except for the sound of her own harsh breathing and the faint hiss of static from her earphones.

The routine of connecting up to the pack relaxed her slightly and she found she could smile to herself at humanity's capacity to adapt. The simple confines of the airlock almost seemed familiar compared to the strange warren of crawl tubes and rooms she had just explored.

It's amazing how familiarity is comforting! Is that why people don't leave toxic relationships?

This momentary calm evaporated in a flash as a red indicator light winked on and then fluttered to darkness. Fear propelled her hand immediately to try the outer hatch but it would not budge despite repeated efforts to pull it open. *I'm stuck!*

It was all Jana could do to control the panic that surged from the pit of her stomach as she realized that the evacuation pump had quit prematurely. The airlock was not completely devoid of air and the remaining pressure pressed the outer door closed with the force of a giant fist. If she could not get the hatch open she would join the forgotten crew in death—the ship her tomb, this airlock her sarcophagus. Moments before she had been disappointed she had found nothing of value to take back. Now all she wanted was to be able to open this final hatch.

Did the ancient designers neglect to include an emergency valve? They couldn't have!

Frantically she scanned the hatch for something that would allow the remaining air to vent into space. Her breath came fast and shallow;

her heartbeat thudded loudly in her ears. Gloved hands trembled as she rapidly felt about the hatch in the narrow beam of light from her headlamps, desperately searching for a valve, lever, or other release mechanism, but the scan was fruitless.

She made another futile attempt to manually pull the hatch open and then fell back and pounded her fists on her thighs, fighting to control her emotions. Eventually she forced herself to be still and breathe another prayer for guidance.

Creator, help me!

The simple prayer gave her enough presence of mind to make a more studied examination of the airlock. She moved the focus of her lamps away from the hatch itself. Scanning the darkened walls of the chamber, she found a small, knurled, red knob half a meter to the side. She reached for it and twisted it. Though it turned, there seemed to be no effect. Jana maintained her calm by rationalizing that this was to be expected. If it really were a safety-evacuation device it was logical that it would require many turns to open it to prevent accidental decompression. Grimly, she kept turning it, determined to keep going until the knob hit the stops.

She felt a slight vibration through her fingers on the knob—the inaudible hiss of escaping gas! When she once more reached for the outer airlock hatch, it rose easily, swinging up and open. There would be no need to close it.

Shaking with relief, she gripped the edge of the hatchway and allowed her body to "fall" outside, while maintaining a firm grip on the handholds. Beneath her feet, the galaxy swirled as before, the bright band still resembling wisps of fog over the surface of a calm lake at sunrise.

"Captain Larkin, this is Jana. I'm outside," she called as she hung from the open hatch.

"Roger, Lieutenant," Larkin's relieved voice sounded in her ear. "Are you ready to come home?"

"Affirmative. Very ready, Captain. Standing by for your mark."

"Roger. Calculating. Stand by."

The computer determined the optimum time for her to let go to avoid striking the ship as it pitched and rolled. The exact moment of release needed not only to allow her to safely escape the dangers of the derelict's movements, but it must also return her in the general direction of the *Phoenix* in order to minimize the consumption of reaction mass in her pack. The maneuvering pack's supplies were generous but not limitless. They both knew, as every spacer knew, that survival was maximized when waste of any sort was minimized.

"Unable to call a mark for launch, Jana," Larkin finally said. "You will still be in the radio shadow at the release point. I'll give you a release time minus one-zero-zero seconds. On my mark."

He paused to allow Jana to set her chronometer. The universe continued its slow, silent spin.

"Five seconds from the mark … three, two, one, mark!" he intoned.

Jana watched the clock begin to count down. She glanced from the clock to the glowing band of the galaxy, marveling again at the silent and awesome grandeur. A minute and a half later the clock read zero seconds. She let go and fell away from the ship at a velocity equal to the tangential speed of rotation at her launch point.

"I'm in free-fall," she announced as she emerged from the radio shadow and stared back at the ship as it tumbled silently away.

"Roger. Data link on channel one," Larkin responded.

"Maneuver. Data link. Channel one," Jana instructed the computer. She felt the maneuvering pack turn and accelerate her. She scanned ahead and tried to pick out her ship visually, but the spinning encounter with the derelict had so disoriented her that she didn't know where to look. Her stomach involuntarily tightened, even though she knew that the pack's navigation system was guiding her back to the *Phoenix* more efficiently than she could have managed by herself.

"Guidance, visual," she instructed, and a faint green line flashed on her faceplate. At the end of the line, she stared to try to make out the strobes of the *Phoenix*, winking against the star field.

"Your flight path is nominal," the captain's calm voice reassured her.

"Roger, tally ho!" she replied as the *Phoenix* at last became visible in the dim, ancient starlight. It was a relief once more to see the graceful lines that curved from the bow, around the cargo section, and tapered to the *n*-space generator at the stern. The tail swept out to three fins, each tipped with magneto-hydrodynamic generators.

The red light from the airlock near the bow reminded her of the warm, welcome glow of a hearth, beckoning the weary traveler in from the cold winter night of space.

The pack slowed her and eased her toward the massive bulk of the ship as delicately as a butterfly might land on a petal. She had almost come to a full stop a half-meter from the airlock hatch, when she reached out, grabbed a handhold, and pulled herself inside.

She closed the outer door, spun the lock closed, and then pressed the cycle button to pressurize the chamber. While she removed her maneuvering pack, she could hear the atmosphere whistling in.

She touched the button labeled *Decontaminate* and a spray of surfactant fluid shot out of several nozzles until her suit was thoroughly soaked. Globules of various sizes quivered and jiggled around the chamber. She reached out to touch them. The liquid's surface tension immediately pulled the fluid onto the surface of her suit where it destroyed any microbes that might remain from the ancient ship.

The next cycle vented the chamber's atmosphere directly into space and the sterilizing liquid flashed into a momentary fog as it boiled away.[25] The chamber cleared as it bled to the hard vacuum of deep space.

The chamber was once more pressurized, her suit and equipment were rinsed with pure water, and once more, the atmosphere in the chamber was vented to hard vacuum where most of the water boiled off at just a few degrees above freezing. A burst of infrared **sublimated** the ice crystals that had formed on her suit and the chamber walls from the rapid, low-pressure boil. Then a blast of intense ultraviolet light bathed the chamber. Jana maneuvered her equipment and herself about the chamber, exposing every fold and crease of the gear to the antibacterial rays. After several minutes, the light cycled off and new air whistled into the chamber. When an indicator showed the pressure had equalized to the ship's interior atmosphere she opened the inner lock.

"Welcome aboard, Lieutenant," Captain Larkin greeted her with a relieved smile as she emerged through the hatch. "I'm glad you made it back." He secured the hatch while she released her helmet catches, pulled the dome off, breathed deeply, and exhaled slowly.

"Thank you, sir. I'm very glad to be back."

"I expect a full report after you've cleaned up," he continued and glanced at her empty storage pockets. "Did you find *anything* of value over there?"

For a moment, she was uncertain how to answer. She was undeniably disappointed that she had found nothing of tangible value—nothing she could turn into immediate credit that might have provided financial security to her family. But she also felt a measure of peace that what she had done *was* of eternal value—the old woman hadn't died hopeless and alone.

"It was an old cryonic hibernation ship. All but one of the life units had failed," Jana finally replied as she wiped her damp forehead. "I found only one survivor. She seemed to have been revived about the time we dropped into 3-space, but she died in my arms shortly after I found her."

The man regarded her as he stowed the maneuvering pack in its compartment. "You found the only survivor in a three-century-old sleeper ship just minutes before she expired? I'd call that an amazing coincidence."

Jana shook her head as she secured her helmet in its rack. "I think the presence of our own ship or our radar signal probably triggered the revival sequence. What is beyond remarkable is that we dropped into 3-space so close to it."

"Beyond remarkable," the captain agreed.

"So except for that miracle, everything was pretty much normal," she concluded weakly.

Larkin ignored her attempted humor. "Their automated detection equipment probably interpreted the broadband electrical noise of our jump as another ship's signal and tried to wake up what was left of the crew—in this case, the only person left."

"That is my thinking, sir," Jana agreed as she placed the life support unit back in its cabinet.

"Could she communicate?" he asked.

"Yes."

"Well, what did she say to you?"

Jana remained thoughtful for a moment. "She thanked me for coming."

The Prophecy

Those that think faith is best when simply believed are prone to being self-deceived.

But whatever one's faith, this fact must be faced: faith's only as good as in what it is placed.

—*Meditations on the Canon*, Book LXI:I:XVI

Chapter 1

Jana had been told that she and Captain Tred Lowe were heading for a sinkhole of a planet. An earlier check of the ship's library had confirmed that Tachon III, the planet a hundred kilometers below them, was hot and dry with only basic industrial development—barely a two on the IFS, the Irwin-Flyger Scale. Jana studied the monitor screen. The slowly moving image of the surface confirmed the negative reports, indicating a vast desert landscape cut by multiple twisted and ragged mountain ranges. West of the high country lay a small, shallow sea. To the north a band of thin, high-level clouds spread across what the ship's library generously referred to as the planet's **temperate zone**.

"Mind your hull temperature, Lieutenant," Captain Lowe's voice rumbled next to her and punched through her thoughts. "Steady on course. You don't want to miss the beam."

"Aye, sir," she replied, quickly turned her attention from the external vid screen, and resumed diligent scanning of the instruments.

As the large deep-space transport, the *Pride of Europa* encountered the atmosphere its outer hull began to heat from friction. This was normal, and if the ship maintained the proper approach path, they would soon intercept the contra-grav beam from the surface, which would slow their descent. A deep, moaning rumble from outside the ship grew as it left the vacuum of space, nearly drowning out the high-pitched cacophony from the hydraulic pumps, electric servos, and control motors that surrounded the flight station. The bass note grew in intensity as they fell deeper into the ever-thickening layer of life-sustaining gases that had been produced through terraforming over the past several centuries.

The ship was still too high to experience any significant atmospheric turbulence, but the increasing growl of the thickening atmosphere on the hull, compared to the previous absolute silence of space, made it seem as if they were entering the heart of a storm. Weightlessness gradually gave way to the stubborn tug of Tachon III's gravitational field, atmospheric resistance increased, and the golden corona of Jana's short, blonde hair slowly sagged. She gently tested the aerodynamic controls to see if they would respond and the ship sluggishly acknowledged her commands.

"You're doing well, Jana," Lowe's voice rasped in her ear set. "Contact approach and request the beam."

Jana checked the frequency indicator. Her light pink thumbnail tapped the transmit sensor. "Tachon Approach, this is *Europa*. Request the beam, over." Tension had raised and pinched her normally mellow voice.

"*Europa*, Tachon Approach," the controller's voice crackled back in her ear. "Radar contact. Vectors to final. Continue on present heading. Five-eight-two kilometers on line from the marker. Cleared pad one approach. Report the marker."

"Roger. Report the marker," Jana acknowledged.

"One lousy pad and we're probably the only traffic he's had all week," Lowe commented with a deep chuckle. "But he's doing the right thing by following the correct procedure." His wrinkled countenance grew serious. "If you don't develop good habits in the slow and easy times, you can't expect those good habits to be there to help you out when things get hot and heavy."

"Yes, sir," Jana replied with a renewed scrutiny of her instrument board. She wasn't sure if she had been reprimanded or not, but in any case, Captain Lowe's reputation as an excellent instructor made her take his advice seriously. As the junior officer of the ship, she not only wanted, but also needed his approval. She could never hope to obtain a command of her own without his endorsement, and she knew she would need the benefit of his experience whenever that day arrived.

The ship was now thumping though the stratosphere at supersonic speed, bleeding kinetic energy away to atmospheric friction. Somewhere far below, a sonic shock wave boomed across the empty, arid landscape. The elegant, tubular transport with its sweeping, aerodynamic surfaces rolled slowly as Jana S-turned it to reduce velocity and to cross the radio marker at the correct speed and altitude.

"*Europa*, you are five-zero kilometers from the marker. Continue inbound," the approach controller announced.

"Roger, Approach," Jana replied, and she glanced at her position indicator to verify the report. She felt sweat beginning to bead on her back under the thin pressure suit. Her concern wasn't about making a safe landing; Captain Lowe was watching the panels closely, and she knew he wouldn't allow her to stray off course. But she wanted very badly to demonstrate her proficiency by making the landing correctly and without assistance.

An amber indicator light on her panel winked and a chime pinged. Jana tapped the transmit button. "*Europa* over the marker."

"Roger, *Europa*. Report landing beam intercept."

The large ship's descent had slowed below the speed of sound, and the vessel was responding smartly to the aerodynamic controls. If Jana kept the ship on the correct heading and rate of descent, they would continue into the high-intensity portion of the contra-grav beam, which would slow them even more for the final landing to the planet's surface. If she drifted off the beam, she would have to initiate a go-around, which required the use of the ship's fusion engines. This was an expensive and noisy maneuver and one not looked upon favorably by instructors, Space Trading Coalition stockholders, or the citizenry living within many kilometers of the landing area. Jana was determined not to irritate any of them. Her delicate eyebrows furrowed in concentration.

The creaks, groans, whines, and rumbles of the ship became a sonic background merely indicating normalcy. Jana's concentration on the approach indicators shrank her world to a yellow pip on a screen that crept along a white dotted line toward a green triangle. The ship's computers, of course, were doing most of the work. It would have been impossible for a human being to fly such a complex craft without their help. Nevertheless, computers weren't perfect, and it remained her responsibility to monitor the machines and to be prepared to override them. An override didn't happen often, but the pilot had to be ready for anything. With an instructor sitting in the next seat, "anything" could include a simulated failure.

"This is a simulated failure, Jana," Lowe said, and she felt herself tense as if in anticipation of a physical effort. "The smoke detector indicates fire in the cargo bay. What is your first action?"

"Scan fire sensors." She tapped the screen to demonstrate her ability to bring up the correct display. All indications were normal, of course. This was, after all, a simulation.

"Cargo bay section twenty-three lima shows positive. What is your next action?

"I would advise approach control of my status and continue the descent."

"Why not initiate a go-around?" the senior man asked sharply, no doubt attempting to rattle her and break her concentration.

"We're only, uh—" Jana paused as she glanced at the pip on the screen, "twenty seconds from the contra-grav beam final lock-on. If we have an onboard fire I'd rather be coasting down on the pad's beam than trying to stay up on my own engines."

There was a momentary pause and Jana wondered whether Lowe was satisfied with her answer or was pondering another trap to spring. "I agree," the man finally said. Jana didn't take her eyes off her screens but her peripheral vision caught the slight motion of him settling back in his chair and she thought she detected a satisfied grunt despite the noises of the ship. "Now set this tub down on the dirt—gently, of course, Lieutenant. Gently."

Chapter 2

The hot desert wind spit occasional grains of fine sand and dust into the space pilots' faces as Jana and Lowe departed the ship. They strode across the concrete ramp toward the port authority office a half-kilometer ahead of them. The sun above them beat down on their heads, and Jana began to feel uncomfortably warm in her pressure suit. The beige sand effectively reflected the heat of the bloated orange-yellow orb that hung halfway from the **zenith**, and the few bands of high cirrus clouds did little to alleviate its burning rays. A quick tap on the suit's wrist control panel increased the suit's cooling effect and soon provided some relief. She sighed and glanced up at a deep blue sky directly overhead that faded to a silvery-brown horizon, colored by a large amount of suspended dust particles.

"What a God-forsaken hellhole," Lowe muttered as he glanced at a stark landscape that was relieved intermittently by a few tough desert plants. "And to think this is as good as they can get it after three centuries of terraforming."

Jana's eyes studied the gently rolling dunes and then the hard, concrete angles of the support buildings and the indistinct outline of a city several kilometers distant. "I suppose at least some of the people who live here call it home," she commented.

"Huh," the senior officer grunted derisively. Beads of moisture had formed near the edges of his close-cropped, graying hairline. "People don't live here—they survive. The only reason for anyone to stay is the siliconium mines." He paused to wipe his hand across his face and then resumed his scowl at the scenery. "From what I've seen, those who can afford to get out of here have gotten. Those who stay behind are the ones who lack sufficient money, good sense, or both."

"You've been here before, Captain?" Jana asked, glancing at him.

"Yeah. About ten years ago," he affirmed. "Doesn't look like it has improved any."

They walked on, accompanied by the soft crunches and scrapes of their boots on the concrete apron and the intermittent hiss of the tiny sand grains blowing in from the desert across the open concrete surface of the ramp. Jana glanced back behind them, toward the distant shouts of the **lading** crew that surrounded the ship, gleaming silver and white on the gray landing pad. The sun's orange glow gave the ship a faint tangerine hue.

Jana made a slow visual survey of the bleak, arid surroundings. "What's in town?" she asked with a wave of her hand toward the distant structures.

The man made a short, mirthless laugh. "Basically all the economic machinery needed to separate the miners from their credits." He glanced at her svelte form, poorly concealed by her thin pressure suit. "You command a certain amount of respect because you're STC, but nothing is certain. Don't take that respect for granted. People aren't always rational. I strongly suggest you not travel alone. And, just so you know, your conduct on shore leave is also part of your evaluation."

"Don't worry, sir. I plan to stick close to you."

The man nodded. "Good. I'm glad you have enough sense so that an order wasn't necessary."

"So, are there many women on this world?" she asked to change the subject.

"Of course. It would be difficult to keep the men here otherwise."

"Don't the crews receive a bonus to compensate for the adverse living conditions?"

"Yes, but there's not much point in having more credits if you can't spend them on something."

"Oh," Jana said shortly, and she quirked her mouth as if she had tasted something foul.

The captain noticed her reaction and the furrows above his heavy brows deepened. "You can't allow yourself to be too critical, Lieutenant."

She looked up sharply, her mouth a tight line as she held her tongue.

"If you hope to be a captain, you've got to be more than a good rocket jockey. You must be prepared to function as a diplomat."

"What do you mean, sir?"

"Look, Lieutenant." The man stopped and faced her. He paused to wipe away the sweat that had formed on the creases over his eyes. "Most of these outposts are as close to a pure free-market system as you can get. They have to be—it's the only system that works in these primitive, hardscrabble hellholes. If a woman can turn a wrench or drive a hauler, then there's no one stopping her. If a woman comes to a place like this and decides she'd rather work with something other than her hands, feet, or brain—then that's her choice."

"The policy of the STC does not promote prostitution, sir."

"The STC generally doesn't interfere with local economies. A trade contract has to be honored by both sides."

"I understand that. But I am also concerned that some of these girls might be forced into that life out of economic necessity. Perhaps they don't have enough physical strength to turn a wrench or the training to drive a hauler. It's not really much of a choice if it's the only thing you *can* do."

"It *is* a choice, Lieutenant. These outposts can't afford any freeloaders. You produce a product or service of value or you don't last. We're not here to right wrongs or rescue victims from their own incompetence. We're here to bring manufactured stuff in and take siliconium out. All we can demand is that the local company honors the STC contract."

"I was trying to think more like a diplomat and not simply like a rocket jockey, sir. We can use diplomacy to encourage improvements on the planets we serve."

Lowe shook his head. "There are limits to diplomacy, Lieutenant. A good diplomat keeps that in mind. It's not our place to micromanage our ports of call. "

"Aye, sir." Jana nodded and looked thoughtfully toward the city.

They resumed walking and soon reached the large concrete box of a building that held the port authority office. The door hissed open to a welcome coolness.

The office was a small corner of a larger maintenance building. Because of the light traffic, there was only a single stationmaster and this one had projected his personal interests liberally about the office in the form of old-style printed posters of exotic vacation spots. They had a common theme—copious amounts of water in various liquid and frozen states.

The captain eyed the posters and then the empty chair at the dispatcher's desk. "Is this a port authority or a travel agency?" he muttered.

Jana hid her smile at her senior's irritation. She liked the colorful arrangement of the displays that brightened up an otherwise drab area. It was a small act of defiance against the ubiquitous and oppressive dullness.

A side door suddenly hissed open to a large hangar beyond. A man entered the office, and the door swished closed.

He was of medium height and good-looking, though a languid expression played over his dusky features. A shock of dark hair sprang up at odd angles on his head, and a few days' growth of beard covered his still-youthful face. He wore sandals, a light-fiber shirt, and shorts in a rainbow of colors. He nonchalantly studied the databoard in his hand, paying the visitors scant attention as he ambled to his desk and slid into his seat behind the counter.

"Excuse me, Mr. Cruise Director," Lowe greeted him. "Where might we find the port authority?"

"Cool your jets, Captain," the man replied without looking up as he began touching commands on the screen. "Let's see the lading record."

Lowe shot Jana an exasperated look and tossed the memory chip onto the counter. His eyes narrowed as he searched in vain to find the worker's identification badge. He finally spied a nameplate setting askew on the desk. "How long you been here Mister … Herzog?"

Herzog continued his work. "Long enough to know that a ship captain's authority generally ends at his airlock, and that I'm in charge of loading, unloading, and departure approvals." He finished his computer work and finally looked up, giving the captain a smirk. "Did you have a nice trip?"

"The trip was delightful," Lowe rumbled.

Herzog pulled the chip from the coding programmer and handed it back to the captain. "Here are your orders, authorization for departure, and bill of lading for tomorrow. If you have any questions …" he paused and scanned his screen before continuing, " … you or Lieutenant Maines can reach me by vid whenever—"

Herzog stopped in midsentence the moment he finally noticed Jana standing beyond the captain. He did a double take, then quickly returned his attention to his computer screen and cleared his throat. "As I was saying, you and Lieutenant Maines should stop back at the office before leaving to … uh … to verify any last-minute changes," he finished weakly as his focus returned to the woman.

Lowe made a sour expression toward Jana. She nodded slightly, but otherwise remained impassive.

"Nice posters," she said, flicking her pink nails in a short, circular motion.

"Thanks," Herzog grinned. He quickly turned back to his computer and studied it with a look of concern. "Hmm," he repeated several times.

"Is there some sort of problem?" Lowe growled.

"Uh, yeah," the young man said, stroking the stubble on his chin. "I was just going to say that I think I just found an error on your accommodations chit."

"What?" Lowe asked with narrowing eyelids.

Herzog glanced quickly at Jana, then to Lowe, and then back to the screen. "Yeah, well, usually the flight crews are put up at the Tetragon, but they are undergoing repairs, and I don't think I changed the chit to the Aurora." He held out his hand. "I'll make the changes for you."

"Mighty lucky you caught the mistake in time," Lowe muttered as he slowly passed the chit back.

"Yeah!" Herzog agreed enthusiastically, repeatedly flicking his eyes to the other officer. "And I can even give your lieutenant a ride since I just happen to live at the Aurora myself!"

"*We* will take you up on that offer," Lowe commented dryly. He turned to Jana. "Would you mind heading back to the ship, Lieutenant? I want to have a few words with the port authority, here."

"Aye, sir!" Jana acknowledged, and she turned for the door. "Thank you, Mr. Herzog!" she called over her shoulder as the door swished open and she stepped back into the heat.

"You're welcome, Lieutenant!" he called back, rising out of his chair and leaning onto the counter. "And it's Harlin! I'm looking forward to seeing more of you!"

The door had barely hissed shut when Captain Lowe leveled a steely gaze straight into the dispatcher's face. He dropped his normally low voice even lower and his dark green eyes became boring, black pits. "Let's get one thing straight, Mr. Cruise Director," he rumbled, bringing his head scant centimeters from the sneer on Herzog's face. "I think you are unprofessional and don't know your limits. Well, the lieutenant is one limit you'd better not cross. She's not one of your town dollies or mech girls. She's STC, which means strictly hands off."

"I don't think your authority includes my personal life—" Herzog started to say, but Lowe cut him off with a blunt finger raised to the other man's face.

"I don't care if you stuff your personal life where the sun doesn't shine—it's of no interest to me. The lieutenant, on the other hand, *is* my responsibility. I will not tolerate harassment, and I consider excessive fraternization an unacceptable distraction. Save yourself a load of grief and chart a wide course. Are you reading me, mister?"

Herzog tried to match the captain's eyes, but the older man's gaze did not waver. An angry flush spread up his face.

"Yes, Captain," the dispatcher finally said, and he dropped his attention back to his computer. He rapped the touch pad fiercely. "You've made yourself perfectly clear."

Chapter 3

The portmaster swung the yellow ramp tug wide of the lines of transports that hauled supplies from the space freighter. His dark hair tousled in the hot wind, and though he was already squinting from the sun and the dust, his eyes narrowed even further and his brows beetled as he studied the silver ship. He resented the frequently peremptory attitudes of the space crews, but he found Captain Lowe's criticism and admonitions especially irritating.

Cruise Director! Harlin felt he had earned both the title and the privileges of being Port Authority. The captain's disparaging remarks wounded his pride, but even more irksome was the man's blunt intrusion into his personal life.

The man calls me unprofessional and then threatens me—what a hypocritical blowhard! His frown remained deep until he managed to push the glowering face of Captain Lowe from the forefront of his consciousness and replace it with the far more pleasant image of the captain's fetching lieutenant. His angry expression became more thoughtful. *Captain Blowhard seems very protective of her. She's probably some admiral's daughter out for experience. Well, if she's looking for experience, I can give her some!*

The shrill whine of the tug dropped to a low hum as it pulled into the great ship's shadow and rolled to a stop behind the massive front landing skid. The portmaster leaned back, braced his head with his hands, and propped his sandaled feet up over the front of the tug while he casually observed the lading and contemplated the junior officer.

She had barely spoken to him, but Harlin considered himself an expert with women, and he felt he had detected a subtle softness in those few words that he took as encouragement—perhaps even a flirtation. Whether they admitted it or not, he reminded himself, most women enjoyed being noticed, but they could be particular about who was doing the noticing. The trick was to engage in pursuit without coming across as threatening. The easiest way to do that was to listen carefully to whatever a woman said and act interested—without making it too obvious, of course. He broke into a grin as he considered the pleasant possibilities, but the smile faded almost as quickly when the dark visage of Captain Lowe once more imposed itself between Herzog and his daydream. He grunted.

There are ways to deal with Old Starch-and-Polish too.

Amid the noise and activity of the loading crew, Harlin occasionally impatiently honked the tug's collision alarm. When Jana finally emerged from the forward airlock, behind the tug, she went unnoticed by the dispatcher and Harlin was interrupted in midhonk when she tossed her sea bag onto the back of the machine.

"Lieutenant Maines!" he turned, greeted her, and rose out of his seat. He tried carefully not to stare as he observed that she had changed from the light blue pressure suit to a fabric khaki jumpsuit, which, while not formfitting, nevertheless fit her form.

"Hello, Mr. Herzog," she said. "Thank you for offering to give us a lift."

"Absolutely my pleasure, Lieutenant," he replied with complete sincerity. He gestured to the passenger's side of the tug. "Please have a seat—"

"Nice of you to help us out, Herzog," Captain Lowe's voice boomed from behind them and cut the man off. The senior officer, now also in a khaki jumpsuit, strode to the tug, tossed his sea bag into the cargo box, and plopped into the front passenger seat. "I'll ride shotgun,

Lieutenant," he said. He jerked his thumb over his shoulder to indicate she should ride in the back.

Herzog glared at the captain but managed to restrain himself from any outburst. Instead, he moved to assist Jana onto the tug.

"Thank you," she said politely as she took his hand and climbed aboard.

"You're welcome, Lieutenant," he said and reluctantly loosened his grip on her small, delicate fingers. A shift in the desert breeze brought an intoxicating odor of mixed perspiration and perfume so heady that he had to grab the side of the tug to steady himself.

"Let's go, Cruise Director! You're wasting our time!" Lowe rasped from the front like an angry bullfrog. Harlin found himself gripped in alternating paroxysms of anger and pleasure so confounding that it was all he could do to control himself. He took the driver's seat, dumbly buckled in, and steered a reasonably straight line across the sun-soaked apron while his knuckles flexed on the steering wheel. The ramp around them shimmered under the orange sun in the western sky as they drove toward the distant cluster of buildings that made up what was called Tachon City.

Conversation remained muted while the electric tug whined across the scorching ramp, trailing a thin column of dust that tumbled and dissipated in the warm wind. Jana surveyed the escarpments to the west and northwest. The wind was coming from that direction and she could see traces of white snow lacing the black, rugged tops of the highest elevations.

She leaned forward. "What do they call those mountains?" she asked above the noise and gestured to the distant peaks.

"They're called the Ghost Range," Harlin called back, relieved that she had broken the silence and given him an opportunity to interact with her. Just the sound of her voice had both an exciting and a calming effect on him—and he wanted to hear that voice as much as possible.

"That sounds mysterious," Jana observed.

Captain Lowe flicked a quick glance at the mountains and then resumed his forward stare.

"The westerly flow of the atmosphere at this latitude encounters the Ghost Range. What little moisture is in the air rains out on the western slopes when it is forced upward by the mountains."

"I believe the process is called orographic lifting,"[1] Jana commented with a nod.

"Yes, I think you're right," Herzog agreed, trying to sound agreeable and confident. "Anyway, the geography is such that we have a desert here and the snow on the mountains remains a phantom—something that we see but never touch down here—like a ghost. Hence, the Ghost Range."

The captain snorted. "Your water comes from those mountains."

"A pipeline isn't my idea of recreation, Captain," the portmaster replied peevishly.

"Have you ever been to the mountains?" Jana interjected.

"No."

"Why not? There's probably enough snow in some of those canyons that you might be able to ski—just like in one of your posters."

"The Ghost Range is off limits." Harlin shot a quick look at the captain, as if bracing for an outburst, but the other man remained seemingly indifferent.

"What do you mean?" Jana asked. "I would think that the more exploration, the better. Why would the mining company set the mountains off limits?"

"It's not the mining company," he explained. "It's the Prophet."

“Who is the Prophet?” Jana asked.

Harlin had just started to open his mouth when Lowe cut in. “Watch it, Herzog.” He nodded toward the woman. “The lieutenant here is a serious devotee of an ancient faith called the Way. She’s up on religion. You’re wasting your time blowing smoke in her direction.”

The younger man could not hide a smile of satisfaction that the captain’s jibe had inadvertently given him insight into the woman’s interests. *The old windbag is making this easy! Thank you, Captain Blowhard!*

“The Prophet,” the young man began with a serious expression and renewed self-confidence, “is the son of a wealthy **entrepreneur** who died and left a massive fortune to him. He hasn't exactly purchased the Ghost Range, but he and his followers claim some kind of spiritual privilege—that the Ghost Range is sacred to them. They won't allow trespassing on what they call the Consecrated Slopes. Skiing and other 'irreverent behavior' is … well … they won't grant permission."

"What about the local civil authority? Can't anyone take some legal action against them?" Jana asked.

Harlin shook his head. "The local civil authority is the mining company board. The local police force is the mining security service. Since the Prophet is the major shareholder in the company, and since there's no great financial incentive to open the mountains up for recreation, it's not likely that any kind of legal action could prevail against him."

Jana's eyes narrowed. "What is it about having financial resources that makes some people think they can order everyone else around?"

Harlin shrugged. "My understanding is that the Prophet's control over his followers has more to do with his religion based on some sort of prophecy rather than his finances."

"Prophecy?" Jana asked.

"It's more involved than I can explain now," the man replied with a quick sideways glance at the captain. "Perhaps we could discuss it later?" He turned far enough to catch Jana's eyes.

Lowe's head jerked sharply toward Herzog but the dispatcher ignored him. He and Jana traded smiles and then he resumed looking forward.

Discussion ended as they left the landing pad area. They made their way along a bumpy, dusty track that approached the edge of the cluster of buildings surrounding their hotel.

"It's rustic but the place isn't that bad inside," Harlin offered. "They've even got a swimming pool, a cabaret of sorts—local talent, of course—and there's gaming if you're into that. It's pretty cutthroat, though."

The dust swirled around the tug as Harlin brought it to a stop in the sandy parking area. A few attempts to enliven the gray concrete with paint had been made but the chipped and weathered colors only emphasized its industrial ruggedness.

"Goodness! A pool, you say?" Jana asked. "That sounds very nice right now." She hopped from the tug's box, while Lowe swung their sea bags over his shoulder and shook his head.

"Yeah," Harlin grinned eagerly. "I'm sure I could reserve it for the two of us."

"Well," Jana replied thoughtfully, "I think I'll just take a nice cool shower or a soak in the tub."

"I was hoping we could get together to discuss your faith," Herzog suggested hopefully.

Lowe cleared his throat.

She shot a quick look at him and then returned her attention to the port authority. "I think the captain and I need some time to get settled in."

Harlin's face tightened but he managed a nod to hide his annoyance. *Act interested, not desperate*, he advised himself.

"But," Jana added, "perhaps you would care to join us for coffee? At say, 2030?"

"Yeah!" Harlin brightened in genuine relief and pleasure. "I'll be there!" He hopped back into the tug. "Captain. Lieutenant." He bid farewell and the tug whined and pulled away in a swirling cloud of dust.

Lowe studied the retreating vehicle then turned to his junior officer. "Why in the world did you invite *him*?"

She shrugged. "He *is* a fellow member of the Space Trading Coalition and his stories were interesting. I thought it would be a good opportunity to expand my knowledge of this system."

"You won't learn much of anything useful from that poser." He shook his head. "We had a guy in my undergraduate intake named Shub Piffen who simply couldn't stop telling completely bogus stories. He would claim his uncle had been an admiral or he had aced the entrance exam. He washed out halfway through the first year, of course, but before he was gone, the rest of the class had created a word to describe what was always coming out of his mouth. We called it *piffdrivel*." The captain looked back toward the spaceport. "Herzog is a piffdriveler. You can't believe half of what he says. As far as being STC goes, he's a disgrace."

"He's probably just a lonely guy. The chance to spend a bit of time with other professionals will be good for his morale."

"Lieutenant, I think I understand the male mind well enough to know he's hound-dogging you. Morale building has its place but remember the order of your responsibilities: the mission, the ship, the space service, and yourself. Don't allow your concern for Mr. Herzog—or his interest in you—to distract you from your primary duties."

She flushed. "I was only trying to think diplomatically, sir."

"As I said earlier, diplomacy has its limits."

"At least you're here to look out for me."

"I have my limits, too, Lieutenant."

Chapter 4

Despite the captain's doubts, Jana found that the dispatcher had been truthful about the hotel. The Aurora looked better on the inside than on the outside. The interior decorator had utilized natural earth tones in a manner that Jana found pleasing and restful. An unsung artisan had even carefully arranged many small, flat, pastel rock chips into a mosaic in the bathroom floor to create a seascape. There were spiraled nautili, starfish, seaweed, and even a few cavorting seahorses. Jana smiled as she lay in the soothing suds of her bath and contemplated the irony of the seascape in the desert. *I wonder if desert scenes decorate homes and offices on watery worlds.*

Because of storage limitations, her wardrobe was quite small. She had carefully sandwiched a few outfits, her dress uniform, shoes, and accessories into her sea bag without squashing them too tightly. The fabrics were very wrinkle resistant, but even they—like diplomacy—had their limits.

She bit her lip as she held up a simple white shift with spaghetti straps. Her gaze lingered a moment on the white slingback sandals with eight-centimeter heels, and she sighed. There really wasn't anyone for whom she wanted to dress up. In order to draw the least attention to herself, and to maintain some personal social protection, she reluctantly chose to don her uniform—a white dress shirt and slacks in a military cut with small, gold stripes on the shoulder tabs to indicate her rank. Gold star pilot wings were pinned above her left breast. Low white pumps completed the outfit. She brushed her short, blonde hair and deftly applied a minimum of makeup before inspecting herself in the full-length mirror.

"Hmm. I could use longer hair—and another stripe would be nice," she muttered to herself as she scanned the gold braid on her shoulders. "But for now, this will have to do."

She picked up the intercom and tapped the code for the captain.

"Yes?" His voice and picture popped into view on the tiny hand vid.

"Are you ready for dinner, Captain?" she asked.

"Well, you sure took *your* time," he commented in reply. "I got tired of waiting, so I already ate lunch. But I'll go down with you and have a little something. The salad wasn't bad," he added, "and they have a great wine selection, as well. These miners may look rough, but some of them must be real gourmands."

"Life is full of surprises, sir."

"I know. I hate that part. I'll meet you at the **mess,**" he said shortly and the vid went dark.

There were few other guests in the dining area when Jana arrived. Her entrance created minimal stir as she was shown to Lowe's table across the room from a small stage upon which sat a number of familiar and unfamiliar instruments.

The possibility of music piqued Jana's interest. "Did anyone play earlier, Captain?" she asked after she had been seated. She nodded toward the stage.

He shook his head. "Some guys brought the instruments in but they didn't really play any songs. I wouldn't call them songs, anyway. They sounded to me like random noises."

"They must have been doing the sound check," the woman explained.

The captain shrugged, glanced at the stage, then looked up as the servers arrived with Jana's food and the captain's drink.

"These fellows are certainly jumping to more smartly than they did at lunch," he observed wryly after the servers left.

"Probably a different crew," suggested Jana.

"Same crew," the man retorted. "Different customer."

Their conversation continued in mixed mild banter and professional discussion until 2030 when Herzog entered the dining room. Gone were the rainbow casual wear, worn sandals, and three-day beard. The dispatcher appeared in official dress blues—from spit-shined patent leather shoes to white gloves and service cap with its thin, gold braid. Jana and Lowe both rose as he approached the table.

Herzog extended his hand and met the other man's gaze. "Good evening, Captain Lowe," he said solemnly.

"Good evening, Mr. Herzog," Lowe replied, taking his hand. He eyed the younger man carefully but did nothing to continue his earlier antagonism.

Herzog turned to Jana. "It is my distinct pleasure, Lieutenant Maines," he said without dropping his eyes, "to join you for coffee."

"Thank you, Mr. Herzog." She smiled and took his hand firmly. "I am glad that you could come. Please, be seated." She motioned to the empty chair.

They all took their seats. The dispatcher removed his hat and gloves while they placed their coffee orders on the table's pad. Jana ordered mocha and Harlin ordered cappuccino, but Lowe said he would wait, since he still had half of a glass of claret.

"So, where are you from, Lieutenant Maines?" the dispatcher asked and leaned slightly forward with a genuine smile of interest.

"Ceres," she answered. "It's an ag world. You've probably never heard of it."

"Actually, I have," he replied and raised his brows. "I regularly process inbound grain shipments—some from Ceres. I'm told the grain from Ceres is of the highest quality."

"My father grows that grain," she said proudly.

"I imagine he must have a big operation."

"Not really. We farmed several thousand **hectares**. That might sound like a lot, but it's not large compared to some of the other farms—" she stopped herself, but not before a note of bitterness had crept into her voice.

Herzog cleared his throat. "We?" he asked. "You must mean your family owned the farm and your father directed the work crews. You didn't actually do any of the farming yourself, did you?"

"I did," she replied matter-of-factly. "We couldn't afford work crews, so I operated the tractors, the combined harvesters, the transports—everything."

"What did you think, Herzog?" Lowe broke in. "The lieutenant here was some sort of debutante?"

"No sir. I just assumed—"

"Maines is a star pilot because she knows how to *work*," Lowe cut him off. "We're not on a pleasure cruise."

"No, sir," the dispatcher reddened and straightened in his chair. "I was only going to say that I knew Ceres produced high-quality grain. I wasn't aware that they also produced such attractive … star pilots."

Jana smiled at the compliment. Lowe growled and took a sip of wine.

There was a brief, awkward pause, but at that moment, their coffee arrived. Jana thanked the server and Harlin cleared his throat.

"Captain Lowe," he began, "I wish to apologize for my behavior earlier today. I believe I was out of line and lacked professionalism. I offer no excuses. Simply an apology."

"Apology accepted," Lowe acknowledged. "And it's good of you not to waste your excuses—on me or anyone else."

"Well, Harlin, you seem to have had quite a transformation," Jana commented with another smile. "What brought about the change of heart?"

Harlin looked thoughtful. "I guess that after talking with you earlier today, I realized that I had lost touch with the STC and a lot of what I was supposed to represent. Tachon is rather isolated. **Ennui** is a more insidious enemy than I realized."

Lowe grunted assent, nodded, and took another sip of wine.

Jana motioned toward the other officer. "Captain Lowe is my instructor. He emphasizes following the right procedure at all times so that the habits are established and ingrained to the point that we automatically do the right thing—even when we can't remember what it is."

"It's simple human psychology," Lowe added. "When you have time, you can ponder and decide your course of action. But when events develop quickly, you don't have time to think. Your mind will automatically revert to habit, or it will simply freeze. You will either respond automatically or sit with your brain spinning madly without mental traction. You either sweat now, or bleed later."

"In a word, *discipline*," offered Herzog.

"Yes," Lowe said slowly. He looked at his glass and gently rocked it from side to side.

Jana noted this subtle move, then dismissed it and turned to Herzog.

"You were going to tell us something about a prophecy?" she asked with a smile.

"Yes, of course." Harlin grinned in satisfaction that he had correctly anticipated her topic of interest. He took a sip of cappuccino before he began. "As I remember it, the prophecy is about finding truth, knowing truth, and being truth. It says that if you believe hard enough in what the Prophet teaches, nothing can kill you. Sounds pretty crazy, huh? I mean, everybody dies, right?"

"I told Jana that people stayed on this planet if they lacked either the money or the good sense to get off it," Lowe interjected. "You're proving my point."

Herzog set down his coffee and raised a finger. "Some of us are here to do our duty, sir."

Lowe leaned back and raised a heavy, skeptical brow. "I've noticed that."

The portmaster reddened slightly but managed a smile. "I *have* acknowledged my mistakes, Captain."

"That doesn't erase the fact that you made them."

Herzog attempted a small, uncomfortable laugh. "Reversing the flow of time is a scientific impossibility. What has been done can't be undone."

"And that's why you usually need to get it right the first time."

The portmaster's jaw tightened, but he held his peace. He dropped his eyes to his coffee and nodded.

"But what about this man's followers?" Jana asked, breaking the tense silence. "I can understand one man with a god complex, but what's in it for the others?"

Harlin flipped his hands in a helpless gesture. "Do people ever need a reason to believe in their god?"

"Have you given that question much thought?" Jana asked.

The young man shrugged and tilted his head. "I've never seen the need. I've always considered it just one of the many instinctive human reflexes, I guess. People *want* to believe in something and they simply choose to believe it. It's a leap of faith—just a blind leap of faith."

He hoped his honesty would overcome any perceived antagonism. Lowe was blunt, but honest. If he had said the lieutenant was devout, Harlin assumed she would put some effort into proselytizing him. He suppressed an anticipatory grin. *She'll want to convert me. All I need to do is act interested and she'll be willing to spend time with me—and then we'll see who is converted!*

"Would you say then," Jana responded, "that there seems to be a genuine need for God—some deep desire for a spiritual aspect to our existence?" She took a sip of mocha and waited.

"Yeah," Harlin agreed. "I'd say it appears to be pretty common."

"Very well," Jana said. "Now, we feel thirst and there is water, or," she held up her cup and smiled, "better yet, mocha."

Harlin returned the smile easily. This was more interesting than he had anticipated and despite his cynicism, he was curious to see how the woman would defend her beliefs.

"We experience hunger," she gestured around the dining area, "and we meet that need with food."

Herzog shook his head. "The things you've mentioned are real, physical needs that can be met with real, physical remedies. What does any of that have to do with a nonphysical god? By definition, if a god is non-physical, then it can't be real."

"Would you say the same about love or loneliness?" Jana asked.

"Look, you're talking about phenomena that happen when certain chemicals are present or absent in the brain. The sensations produced don't have an independent existence," Herzog insisted. "You can't fill a bottle with happiness. If I could, I'd keep a case of it handy, myself!"

"So, you maintain that something without a material existence cannot be real?"

"There are different kinds of reality. A dream, for example, like the emotions you mentioned, is real in some sense. It was a genuine experience within the brain."

"Then let's consider something that doesn't need a brain," Jana suggested, "such as momentum. The momentum of an object is the product of its mass and its velocity. If the mass is zero, then there can be no momentum. Are you saying that the principle of momentum itself ceases to exist when matter is not present?"

"The concept of momentum is still a brain function."

"Our *understanding* of the concept is a brain function," Jana corrected. "The principle or property of momentum existed as a real thing before anyone thought of it and the principle exists whether matter is present or not. It's a real thing *without* a physical existence."

"All right," conceded Herzog with a downward-pushing motion of his palms, unwilling to carry his objections too far. "I agree, at least for the sake of argument, that something can be real without needing a physical existence. But it still needs something physical to become manifest. If it didn't interact with the physical world, we could never detect it."

"I agree," Jana nodded, "and I contend that God does interact with us—both in his call to us and in our need for him. The desire for God spans all of recorded time and every known culture, so it seems to indicate a truly fundamental human need. The claim that its fulfillment is a nonphysical entity is entirely rational. What is the basis for your assumption that God is not real simply because God is understood to not require a physical existence?"

Herzog exhaled and leaned back. "The basis is …" He paused while he searched for words. "It just doesn't make sense. Believing in God means having simply to believe without reason. I can't accept the existence of God without some kind of proof."

"Oh, but you already *do* believe," Jana countered. "It's just that your leap of faith is in the *nonexistence* of God. We *both* have faith, Mr. Herzog. The only difference is where we have placed it."

"What?" Herzog seemed puzzled.

"In a court of law, the jury is presented evidence. Their decision whether the accused is innocent or guilty depends upon their faith that the evidence is valid or their faith that the evidence is in error. *Either* decision requires faith. I have given you proof in the form of a pattern of need and something that meets that need. This pattern is evidence that God is real. I've also demonstrated that something can be real and yet not have a material existence. You can decide to reject or accept the evidence—but you cannot proceed either way without faith."

"But even if I accept that conclusion," Herzog objected, "it still leaves it a toss-up. Whichever way you decide, you are still just making a guess. There's no way to determine who is right."

Lowe made a small grunt. Jana quickly looked to him but it seemed his focus was on his near-empty glass, so she continued.

"Let's suppose that God exists," she began. "The theistic position in general, and the teaching of the Way in particular, is that he created us with a desire to have a personal and loving relationship with him. And this is exactly what we find—people everywhere—at all times and in all places—desire to have a relationship with the Creator."

Herzog frowned but nodded.

"Now on the other hand, if we suppose there is no Creator—that we came to exist without any supernatural influence—is there any reason to expect people to have a need for such a mythical being?"

"Yes. Easily. They could simply imagine such a being," Herzog said and snapped his fingers, "and you would still find people believing in his existence."

"But would we expect this belief to be so nearly universal? Would we expect it to fill a deep-seated need in so many?" Jana asked. "You mentioned that the Prophet has only a few followers. That supports your argument that a few people might believe just about anything. On the other hand, it supports *my* argument that such a delusion has limited appeal—the spiritual need for the Prophet obviously doesn't carry very far. But it does demonstrate the desire for a spiritual component in people's lives—a desire to connect with the Creator—and hence argues for his existence."

"That seems incredibly subtle to me," Harlin declared. "After all, if there is a Creator out there who has designed people with a need to know about him, then why doesn't he do something to make his existence obvious?"

"I've just pointed out the almost universal desire for God."

"I was thinking of something less indirect. I would think God would be capable of doing more spectacular feats."

"Do you mean miracles—like raining fire from the sky and turning water into wine?" Jana asked.

"That could come in handy," Lowe commented quietly at his empty glass.

Harlin nodded.

"But he does," Jana countered with a gesture toward Lowe. "Water turns into wine at any winery. Millions of moons and planets are constantly subjected to meteor bombardment—fire from heaven, if you will. The Creator does exactly the things you asked for. But because they happen with regularity, they are considered natural phenomena. A miracle that happens every day is no less a miracle."

"If something has a natural explanation, then it's simply the result of the operation of natural laws—not a miracle."

"That's incorrect for two reasons," the woman countered. "In the first place, the *timing* of an event is sometimes the miraculous part—not the process that brought it about. Secondly, so-called *natural laws* are simply descriptions of what *usually* happens. They don't explain *why* things happen."

"*Coincidence* answers your timing objection," the dispatcher quickly replied. "There's nothing miraculous about a coincidence."

"Really? How would you know? Suppose a person prays for something and then it happens. How do you determine that it's a coincidence and not an answer to that prayer?"

"People pray for things all the time and nothing happens. Just because circumstances line up once in a while doesn't prove anybody's listening."

"Hmm," Jana frowned. "On one hand, you claim that the predictability of natural laws eliminates the possibility of miracles. But on the other hand, you object to the unpredictability of answered prayer. That's inconsistent."

Herzog forced a smile and shifted uncomfortably in his seat. "Look, if you want to talk about consistency, then you can't call things miracles when they have a natural explanations. By definition, miracles are *violations* of natural laws."

Jana shook her head. "Unless you are prepared to claim you know how every natural law applies in every possible situation, then you can't honestly claim a natural law has been violated. At best, you can say a natural law has been *superceded*."

"Superceded by what? Divine intervention?"

"Not necessarily. A natural law can be superceded by another natural law. For example, the law of density states that iron sinks in water. But if that iron is formed into a boat, it floats. The law of density has not been violated—the law of buoyancy has superceded it. In the same way, a miracle doesn't necessarily violate of any law."

"All right. I'll agree with you—and point out that you've just defined miracles out of existence. What you are calling a miracle is simply something for which our technology doesn't yet have a good explanation. Space flight—even air flight, for that matter—once seemed miraculous. It doesn't seem like a miracle anymore because our technology enables us to understand it. As our knowledge grows, the gaps in our understanding shrink. Eventually, the need for the miraculous will disappear—except for those who cling to such an outdated, unnecessary concept for emotional reasons."

Jana took a sip of mocha and leaned back thoughtfully. "Have you ever seen a rainbow, Mr. Herzog?"

He shook his head. "Not here. It's too dry. But yes, I've seen one. They are beautiful."

"Yes, they are. Have you ever wondered *why* a rainbow looks beautiful?

He shrugged. "It has something to do with the way light is bent when it passes through drops of water, I think."

"You're on the right track in terms of explaining what happens," Jana agreed. "The light rays that enter a droplet of water are bent[2] as they cross the air-water boundary. The blue rays have a shorter wavelength. They bend, or **refract**, more than the longer-wavelength red rays. The waves reflect off the back of the droplet and exit at slightly different angles from the direction at which they entered. This splits the light into the different colors that we see as a beautiful rainbow."

"There. No miracles—just physics."

"No, Mr. Herzog. The question remains entirely unanswered."

"What?" He sat up, frowned, and spread his hands. "You just explained it—the whole refraction thing. The blue rays bend more than the red rays. All of that explains a rainbow completely."

"No," Jana shook her head. "It explains *what happened* with the light rays. It says nothing at all about *why* the result is generally considered beautiful, or why we spend so much time thinking about beauty and trying to define it."

Harlin raised his hands. "Social conditioning and the chemical reactions in the brain—"

"Another 'what happens' answer," the woman insisted. "It's not a 'why' answer. We encounter miracles every day—from the beauty of a sunrise, to the intricate and complex operation of the cosmos—even the gift of life itself is a miracle. Any description that limits reality to the exchange of energy and the movement of matter in space is necessarily incomplete. It can only explain *what* happens; it can say nothing about *why* anything happens. Explanations of the 'what happens' variety can only move the cause further back: this event results from that event which is the result of a previous event. Everything is contingent upon a preceding event. Eventually your string of contingent events must take you back to the beginning of the physical universe. Before the first event—before the beginning—nothing physical existed. A physical universe that does not yet exist can't create itself. It had to have been created by something *outside*—something completely independent from the natural, physical universe. The universe itself is therefore a miracle since there can be no natural explanation for it.

"On the other hand, if we assume some external but impersonal creative force brought the universe into existence, then there can be no purpose for it. You spoke of the destructive danger of ennui. Ennui is inevitable in a purposeless universe. Yet without purpose, we die. There can be no purpose in survival if survival itself is meaningless."

"I'll acknowledge you have reasons for your faith," the portmaster conceded, "but that still doesn't establish it as true."

"No," Jana admitted, "but I hope I did demonstrate that faith in the Creator's existence is not necessarily a blind leap."

"You've given me much to think about."

Lowe cleared his throat and Jana observed his raised brows. "Captain, you've been very quiet. Is there something you want to contribute?"

He shook his head. "I'm not taking sides in this war. It's been going on for thousands of years and there's never a winner—only casualties."

Jana blinked. "I wasn't trying to fight with Mr. Herzog, sir. I was just trying to answer his question."

"Well, you answered him. Any more is just jaw flap. Proselytizing is not one of your duties."

"Aye, sir," she said quietly, and her face colored slightly at the reprimand.

"I don't mind, Captain," Harlin put in. "I found the discussion stimulating."

"I'm sure you did. I was just reminding the lieutenant that we're never completely off duty when we're on a **sortie**. Whatever her personal convictions, she should remember that she represents the STC. Religious arguments solve nothing and often bring out the worst in people. You two have been at it long enough. I think she should let it go."

The portmaster studied Jana's attempt at a stoic face and exulted inwardly at the excess of moisture in her eyes. *Thank you, Captain Blowhard! Keep giving her reasons to look for a sympathetic shoulder to cry on!* He leaned across the table and smiled. "Thank you for taking time to talk with me, Jana." He felt a flush of satisfaction when she smiled in return.

"You're welcome, Mr. Herzog."

The sound of music drew their attention to the small stage at the far side of the room. The opening chords provided a welcome diversion from the moment's tension, and everyone at the table took advantage of it. Several musicians had arrived and taken up their instruments as their female singer began to croon. The trio at the table quietly watched as additional customers arrived while the music progressed. The musicians expertly coaxed music from their instruments while the singer did her best to sustain the melody.

"This is local talent?" Lowe asked Herzog.

He nodded. "The guys in the band play a lot of gigs all around town. They are **eclectic** and really quite good. Seems to me they haven't been so fortunate with their latest vocalist."

Lowe quirked his mouth and studied the miners around the room. "I doubt these guys would care if she was using a bucket to carry a tune."

"Well, I can see she's really trying," Jana came to the woman's defense. "It takes courage to stand up and sing in front of a crowd."

"Then why don't you get up there and help her out, Lieutenant?" the captain asked.

Herzog shot Jana a questioning glance. "You sing?"

"You bet she does," Lowe answered for her. "She has quite a reputation from the academy. Sings like a lark."

"I know the manager," Herzog said as he snapped his fingers. "I'm sure he'd let you sing if I asked."

"They probably wouldn't know any of my stuff," Jana demurred.

"Lieutenant, the coalition charges us with the responsibility to maintain good public relations. You expressed a desire earlier to improve morale. I think this is a fine opportunity to do just that. Remember, diplomacy is a part of your duties." Captain Lowe nodded toward the small stage. "I'm not going to give you a direct order, but I think you'd be doing both the coalition and everyone in this room a huge favor if you could end that noise over there for a while. Besides, I've heard you sing in your quarters on the ship. You were practicing on the clock, so you may as well put that practice to good use in public relations."

"Well, I'll try a song, sir—if the band can play it," she finally agreed.

"Good!" Lowe stated and sat back.

Herzog stood and gestured over his shoulder. "I'll talk to the manager and he'll introduce you to the band." He snapped his fingers, turned, and left.

Jana looked at Captain Lowe, whose face was flushed as he leaned back in his chair with arms folded across his chest, grinning from ear to ear.

How much claret has he had?

Chapter 5

Herzog returned with the manager, Leni Grai, to the table and introduced him to Jana and Captain Lowe. Mr. Grai gave Jana a gap-toothed smile as the captain briefly recounted her singing experience.

Grai's dark face with its thin mustache remained creased in permanent worry lines, and the long strands of dark hair combed over the top of his head failed to cover the shine of his scalp where beads of perspiration had formed. He took a red fabric handkerchief from his breast pocket and wiped his face before addressing Jana.

"It is certainly not that I doubt you can sing," he said and patted his brow. "But you must realize that, for the most part, our clientele are somewhat unsophisticated—provincial, you might say. You're from off-world so I must make you aware that they are unreserved and tend to hesitate very little when it comes to self-expression."

"He means they can be a rough crowd," Harlin translated.

Leni shot a nervous glance at the captain. "I certainly can't take the responsibility for any repercussions if there is an incident. I don't want any trouble with the STC."

Jana looked at Lowe, dropped her mouth, and made a helpless gesture with her hands.

"Diplomacy, Lieutenant," he responded, "always carries an element of risk." He turned to the manager. "There won't be any trouble with the STC."

Jana pursed her lips and listened to the dark-haired woman on stage. "She's singing a ballad," she observed, and motioned around the room. "Do they like ballads and love songs?"

"Oh, yes," Leni responded quickly. "Generally, the sadder, the better."

Jana took a deep breath and let it out slowly. She noticed that at least one of the miners at the next table seemed to be staring at her wings—or at least in their vicinity. She ignored him.

"All right, Mr. Grai," she said. "I've got a song in mind. When the band finishes this set, will you please introduce me?"

"Certainly!" the man replied. "Excellent! This should at least be a little bit interesting."

I think I'm better than that! Jana silently protested.

The band finished the set, and during the break that followed, the manager led Jana to the stage. There was a rising murmur as she strode forward, and many heads turned and tracked her progress. The sound of voices died down to a low hum while Jana was introduced and talked to the musicians.

The band consisted of a percussionist on a synth pad, a bassist with a four-string, a keyboard artist with an optical symphonium, and a lead musician playing an ancient six-string. The chanteuse, dressed in a purple low-cut evening dress with what looked like vestigial wings of stiff, sheer fabric rising out of the shoulder straps, sat atop a stool and observed the introductions with brows raised skeptically. Jana gave her a smile, but the other woman's look was more questioning than welcoming.

"I like your shoes," Jana said to her.

The woman extended a foot and rocked the jeweled pump a few times. "Thanks," she said, and Jana was gratified to see a faint smile cross her face.

"Nice instrument," Jana commented as she turned to the lead player and with a motion to his six-string.

He seemed surprised by her apparent familiarity. "You play?" he asked.

Jana nodded. "They are quite common on Ceres. My father played, and I learned from him."

"Are you any good?" he asked.

"I know a few **licks**. I am told the men here like a ballad. Do you know 'Even If'?"

"Not sure. Might. Hum a few bars."

The space pilot quietly voiced a few measures of the chorus and looked at the other musicians expectantly.

The string player frowned and shook his head. "No, it's not familiar. But they like a ballad well enough—especially if someone dies in it. Anyway, I never heard of that one."

"Since you're playing the guitar, you must be using the classic twelve-tone **chromatic** scale,"[3] Jana thought aloud while she studied the fret board. "Is that right?"

"Yeah," the player nodded. He jerked his head to the symphonium. "Rantee here does amazing stuff in twenty-four tones. You do any of that?"

"Sorry, I'm only used to either **pentatonic** scale or the twelve-tone chromatic scale," she admitted.

"Well, if you sing ballads you just might do real well with this crowd." He paused and his eyes narrowed slightly in thought as he studied the dim outlines of the audience before he continued. "Say, if you play," he suddenly looked at her and nudged his instrument, "why don't you accompany yourself? Less prep time that way."

"All right. I'll go solo. Is that thing in tune?"

He snorted and feigned insult but then smiled broadly and patted the instrument. "Oh yeah!" he said as he passed the old guitar to her. She took it carefully, ran her fingers along the worn fret board, and then glanced at the vocalist.

"May I borrow your perch?" she asked with a nod to the singer on the barstool.

"Sure," the woman shrugged. She stood and stepped aside.

Jana sat and played a few **arpeggios** to get a feel for the instrument while the ensemble retreated from the stage. The audience's murmurs dropped at their departure.

"I'm ready, Mr. Grai." she said to the manager.

He stepped forward, raised his hands, and the buzz of conversation dropped. The relative dimness of the house and the bright lights of the small stage area made it difficult for Jana to see the audience clearly, but she sensed that the room was far more occupied than when she'd come forward. There seemed to be more men than tables and chairs, as a fair number were sitting or kneeling on the floor close to the front. Jana noted that most had a drink in their hands—no doubt a factor that helped explain the reported lack of inhibition to self-expression.

"Tonight we have a special treat for you," Leni announced to the accompaniment of a few whistles and murmurs of approval. "Appearing for a very limited engagement," he said with a smile and hand motion toward the space pilot, "I present Lieutenant Jana Maines of the *Pride of Europa*!" His red kerchief swiped his brow and then, with a final gesture toward Jana, he stepped back out of the light.

There was another ripple of noise, but Jana didn't wait for it to die completely before she spoke. "Thank you, Mr. Grai," she said, smiling in the general direction in which he had disappeared. "And thank you, gentlemen," she nodded toward her audience.

The noise level went up a notch, with a few snickers and derisive repetitions of the term *gentlemen*. She paused a few seconds to pluck a lick of her song's opening chord, to set a musical mood and to find her pitch. Experience had taught her that regardless of her technical performance, it would be deemed a failure if she failed to connect emotionally. If that connection could be established early, the crowd would be more forgiving. Otherwise, an audience tended to become very critical.

"I'm sure many of you miss your families," she continued while gently plucking the strings. There was another ripple of snickers. "And I would expect many of your families miss you too." There were fewer laughs, now, and Jana hoped she was beginning to connect.

"My home world is Ceres," she announced to scattered claps of applause and one hoot. "I haven't been back to see my family for quite some time, so I miss them and know how it must be for you guys, who I'm sure have sacrificed time with your family and friends to work here."

There were murmurs of agreement.

"Music encourages me when *I* feel alone," Jana continued.

"Call *me*, next time you feel that way!" a voice from the front called out.

Jana glanced in the direction of the voice, grinned, and shot back, "I've never been *that* lonely!"

There was a hearty burst of laughter, and the poor fellow received a number of good-natured shoves from the other men near him.

"So, to perhaps brighten your day just a little bit," she flashed a smile to a considerable increase in approval noises, "I would like to share an old song that I learned on Ceres that dates back to the beginning of the Third Age. It's about some of those pioneers of space who rediscovered worlds lost after the war. It takes place right when travel to the stars resumed, and it's about loss, death, and separation." At this, the room became very quiet. "It is called 'Even If,' and it goes like this." Her plucking fell into a rhythmic cadence, and she began her story in song.

They were young and full of life and love, but their world had grown old.
It could no longer sustain them—their sun itself would soon grow cold.
So, with a crew of brave and hardy souls, he set out to explore n-*space.*
One last kiss before he left, she sang this song as she held his face.

Even if the winds will not blow;
Even if the grass will not grow;
Even if the sun and moon together will not shine anymore;
Even if the tides will not rise and all the stars fall from the skies;
I'll love you 'til forever and forever, and ever again.

He was tired, worn, and lonely, and the voyage was so long.
His only comfort was the memory of the words of her song.
He would do his best without complaint as each day was slowly done.
Remembering her faithfulness gave him the strength to carry on.

Even if the winds will not blow;
Even if the grass will not grow;
Even if the sun and moon together will not shine anymore;
Even if the tides will not rise and all the stars fall from the skies;
I'll love you 'til forever and forever, and ever again.

Their search was long and fruitless—not a world did they find.
It seemed their task was hopeless, and they were running out of time.
A final scan of the sector—a faint star with a planet green!
Her song rose up within him as he stared into the screen.

Even if the winds will not blow;
Even if the grass will not grow;
Even if the sun and moon together will not shine anymore;
Even if the tides will not rise and all the stars fall from the skies;
I'll love you 'til forever and forever, and ever again.

They returned to celebration; the cheers were long and loud.
But he looked in vain to see her—she was missing from the crowd.
At a lonely grave he found her. A simple cross marked her final bed.
And on that cross was written the last words that she had said.

Even if the winds will not blow;
Even if the grass will not grow;
Even if the sun and moon together will not shine anymore;
Even if the tides will not rise and all the stars fall from the skies;
I'll love you 'til forever and forever, and ever again.
I'll love you 'til forever and forever, and ever again.

The last notes faded amid a cacophony of whistles, hoots, clapping, and stomping.

Jana rose as the manager hurried from stage right while the band returned from stage left.

"You were wonderful, Lieutenant Maines!" Leni gushed. "They liked you—I had no doubt but that they would!"

"Not bad," the string player commented thoughtfully as he studied the crowd. "Simple, but effective."

She carefully passed the instrument back to him. "You have a very nice machine," she commented. "Thank you for letting me use it."

The vocalist gave her a quick hug. "You sounded real good, Admiral," she said.

"So," the string player asked and dropped his eyes before looking up again, "will you be doing one with us?

Jana glanced at the expectant audience and the hopeful Mr. Grai.

"Would you please, Lieutenant Maines?" he asked as he mopped his brow.

Jana smiled but shook her head.

"Why not?" the musician asked.

Jana grew serious. "A wise and experienced performer once told me that you should never give the crowd all they want. 'Always quit before they get tired of you, and they will be far more likely to invite you back.' I've always followed his advice."

He nodded thoughtfully.

Jana turned, intending to rejoin Captain Lowe, but found her path blocked by her new and enthusiastic fans. She spied an exit and headed for it. Leni followed her in an effort to get her to change her mind.

"I will certainly make it worth your while, Lieutenant," he offered. "I certainly appreciate your wonderful effort—and believe me, this is certainly unprecedented in my memory. I have no doubt that you could do an entire show by yourself, if you wished. It would be wonderful if you would extend your stay at least a few days. Won't you please consider it, Lieutenant?"

Jana shook her head with small smile. "I am sorry, Mr. Grai, but I have orders. My ship will be leaving tomorrow."

"In that case," he mopped his brow with his red kerchief, shrugged, and made a resigned smile. "If you're ever back on the planet and I have anything to say about it," he gestured, "that stage is certainly yours."

"Jana!" The dispatcher's voice called to her. He had finally made it part way through the overfilled room near the side exit. A few of the miners scowled as he pushed past them, but his uniform silenced any direct objection.

"Mr. Herzog!" she greeted, with the relief of seeing a familiar face. "Where's Captain Lowe? Can you help me get out of here? It's great to be popular, but this is getting to be a little too much for me!"

"Give way!" he called out and led her toward the door. "Official business! Stand aside! Coming through!"

Jana breathed easier when they left the crowd behind them and they were finally outside the cabaret.

"My goodness!" she exclaimed quietly to Herzog. "They certainly are an expressive crew, aren't they?"

"They like what they like," agreed Herzog, "and they like you. Did you see how many vids they were holding up? You made a citywide broadcast at least, and I wouldn't be surprised if many of those calls went to Farside. Half the planet's probably seen you by now!"

"My goodness!" Jana repeated. "Captain Lowe wanted me to make a good impression, but this has to be more than he expected. Do you know where he is?"

"He's indisposed," Herzog replied shortly.

"What happened to him?" Jana asked. Her voice rose in concern.

"He's fine, just unavailable right now. I'll escort you."

"Oh? Where?"

He stopped and faced her. "Where do you want to go?"

"To my room, please. I think that would be best."

He looked at her and smiled as disarmingly as he could. "I asked where you *wanted* to go, not where you thought you *ought* to go."

"I want to go to my room."

Harlin shrugged, turned, and they began to walk in silence. Within a few turns, they stood before Jana's door. Herzog made a flourish with his hand and stepped back.

"Thank you, Mr. Herzog."

He shrugged, crossed his arms, and leaned against the wall. "I can't believe you really want to hide out in your room. Don't you get enough confinement on the ship?"

"Of course I'd like to get out, but I would risk a bad fitness report if the captain found me in violation of the code of conduct."

"I'm not asking you to violate the code—and he's not here, anyway."

"He expects good discipline at all times."

"I don't think you need to concern yourself about him for a while."

"What do you mean?"

"I'm afraid the man has his own weakness for liquid cheer. As soon as you left the table, he started slamming them down. At the rate he was going, by now he's got to be somewhere sleeping it off."

Jana's mouth fell in surprise.

"So much for good discipline," Harlin sniffed.

Jana's brow wrinkled, and she shook her head. She felt unnerved at the dispatcher's negative report of someone she considered as supremely self-disciplined as Captain Lowe, and it shook her deeply.

The man straightened and took a step toward her. "On the other hand, I think I've demonstrated *my* trustworthiness."

She nodded.

"So how about a little of your time?"

"Won't we violate the code?"

He grinned. "Only if you insist."

"What did you have in mind?"

He motioned with his head. "There's a central court with a fountain and some real plants over that way. It's like a little oasis. We could relax. Have a conversation."

"And what would we talk about?"

"It doesn't matter. I would just like to get to know the *real* Jana—not the prim and proper STC marionette that's been on display so far."

"Maybe that *is* the real me."

He laughed. "I certainly hope not. Come on," he urged gently, "let's find out who we really are." He stepped close and gently took her hand. "You might find out I'm just who you've been looking for."

The handsome man's touch was light—bold, but not threatening. The thought crossed her mind that she should pull back, but the soft warmth of tender human contact felt good—and it had been a long time since she had experienced it. She knew Lowe was correct, and that the man was "hound-dogging," but the attention of someone so courteous was nice. She hesitated, and he dropped her hand. She was relieved and yet wished the contact hadn't ended. "Mr. Herzog—"

"Please, call me Harlin," he broke in softly.

She smiled

His laugh was quiet and low. "We can drop formality with its ritual politeness and ceremonial deception," he said. "I don't want pretenses, I want honesty."

"I want honesty, too, Harlin. And I want to trust you—but how can I? I hardly know you!"

"Then *get* to know me! Give me the chance. Let me prove it." He took a small step back. As the space between them opened, she found herself feeling less defensive.

He looked down and then gave her a steady look. "I'm not ashamed to admit that I feel lonely and isolated here." He caught a sympathetic softening in her eyes and was encouraged to go on. "You mentioned that we all need to have a relationship with the Creator. But we also have a need for human relationships. Shouldn't a person's relationship with his or her Creator show itself in how he or she relates to others?"

"Yes, of course. That is what the Teacher of the Way said, 'As you have treated the least of these others, so you have treated me.'"

"I was completely honest when I said you gave me much to think about. I've learned so much from you already. I hope you would give me opportunity to learn even more."

"I suppose there's no harm in talking. That doesn't violate the code."

"No," he grinned.

"But still, if the captain doesn't want me to—"

"Forget about the captain. He has removed himself as a factor. You can do what you want—not what you think he wants."

He does have a nice smile. "All right, Harlin, I'll go—"

"Mr. Herzog, are you lost?" Captain Lowe's voice growled, cutting off her next words. Herzog spun, and Jana looked up to see the captain, arms akimbo, standing a few meters down the hallway.

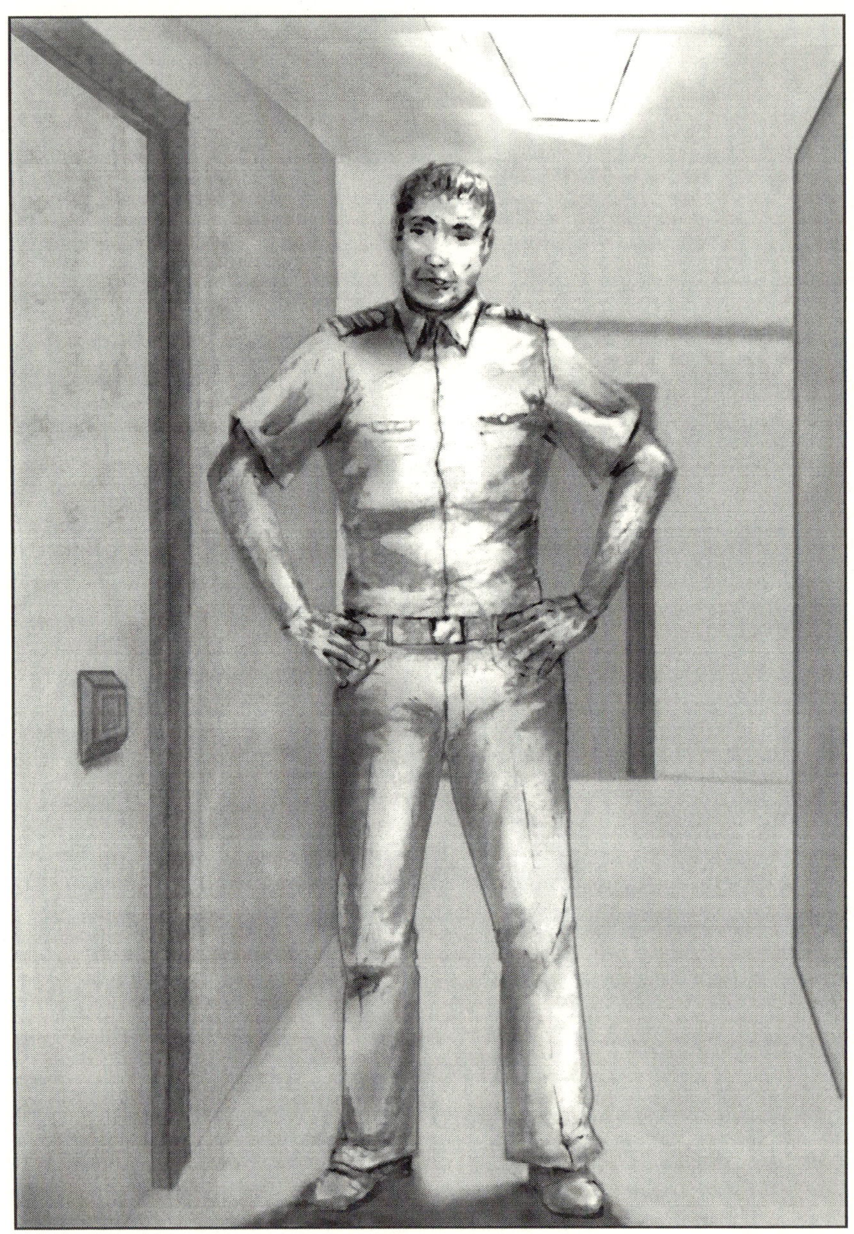

"No, sir," the portmaster struggled to find his voice. "I was just showing the lieutenant to her room."

"Well, you've showed her. Mission accomplished."

Jana's eyes alternated between the two men, her face a mask of puzzlement. "Sir, what happened to you at the cabaret? Mr. Herzog said you were indisposed."

Lowe's brow went up, and his lined face broke into a crooked smile. "The portmaster bought me a few drinks. I didn't want to be rude and pass up his generous hospitality." His tone was sarcastic, and he ended his explanation with his heavy gaze on the other man.

Herzog's jaw tightened. He glared through narrowed lids, frustrated by the older man's return.

"I'm glad you didn't have too much to drink, sir," Jana offered hesitantly.

Lowe straightened and slowly turned his head toward her. "Lieutenant, I *never* have too much to drink."

"No, sir."

His head rotated back to the other man. "Good-night, Mr. Herzog."

The portmaster scowled and turned to the lieutenant. "Jana, we could still—"

"*Herzog!* I said it's time to shove off!"

"Excuse us, Captain," the younger man hissed, "but *we* were having a conversation."

"Your conversation's over, sonny."

Herzog returned the glower for a moment before he broke the stare, turned, and gave Jana a questioning look.

Her mouth tightened, her eyes narrowed, and her chin went up. She said nothing, but her thoughts were riotous: *Forget it, mister! Captain Lowe warned me, but instead I gave you the benefit of a doubt—and you lied to my face! Why didn't I see it?*

"Jana, this isn't fair!" Herzog protested at her silence. "You aren't even giving me a chance!" He took a small step toward her. She fell back and Lowe quickly positioned himself between them.

Herzog's frowning gaze flashed back and forth between them several times. "This is ridiculous!" he concluded. He suddenly turned on his heel and departed in scowling anger.

"You all right, Lieutenant?" Lowe asked after the other man was gone.

"Yes, sir."

He gave her a careful look. "Better get some shut-eye. I need you alert tomorrow morning."

"I will."

"By the way, you did well on the song. I'll note it in my report."

"Thank you, sir."

"Preflight is at 0600. I've arranged for a ride at 0530."

"I'd like to walk, sir."

"Very well, but dress warmly. The desert will be quite cold by morning. Don't be late."

"I know, sir. I won't be late."

"Good-night, Lieutenant."

"Good-night, sir."

Lowe turned down the hall. Jana pressed a finger against the sensor lock on the door. It slid open, she went inside, and the door closed silently behind her.

Chapter 6

Jana walked through the quiet coolness of the dying Tachon night. Overhead, a dazzling display of unfamiliar constellations wheeled and turned, their rays brilliant and undimmed by their brief passage through the dry and cold desert air. Ahead of her, still a kilometer away, the *Pride of Europa* lay bathed in a pool of harsh, artificial light.

These moments of solitude were a time of renewal for her—welcome breaks from the demands of the schedule. Times like this reminded her that it was good to be alive, to be grateful for the little things—to listen to the crunch of sand beneath her shoes and feel the comfortable pressure of her feet against the padded soles in her boots. She studied the colors of the stars overhead and the way her breath formed temporary halos around the lights when she exhaled in their direction. Her mind had remained unsettled through the night, and her sleep had been fitful. She appreciated the calming silence and the exercise of this morning walk, and hoped the desert coolness would help to clear the cobwebs of sleep from her head. She breathed deeply and exhaled another cloud of vapor as she raised her eyes to the blazing stars above.

"When I consider the works of thy hands—" she mentally began to recite, but her meditation was interrupted by the whine of an electric tug and the bobbing of a headlight coming toward her from the direction of the landing pad.

Harlin Herzog screeched to a halt in a cloud of dust illuminated in the tug's lights, and greeted her. "Good morning!" His face peeked from the depths of a hooded snorkel parka.

"Mr. Herzog," she replied with a cough from the dust. She was not happy to see him, and irritated for this interruption of her quiet time.

"The captain said you'd be out here, so I figured I'd give you a lift," he explained.

"I really don't care for a ride, thank you," she replied, and resumed her walk.

The tug whined quietly as he matched her pace. "I'm just trying to be nice."

"You're not nice. You're bothering me."

"Why are *you* so upset? I was the one given the boot last night."

"You deserved it!"

"Oh? What did I do?"

"You lied to me about the captain."

"What? How?"

She stopped, and the tug went silent and still. She turned to face the man sitting on the far side of the machine. "You said the captain had gotten drunk, when he hadn't. You implied he drank too much, when *you* were the one who bought him those drinks. And all this while asking *me* to be honest and drop all pretenses! Upset doesn't even *begin* to describe how angry I am with you, Mr. Herzog!" Her explanation ended in a fierce glare.

Harlin slowly pulled his hood back. At another time, Jana might have found herself admiring his features, but not now.

"I'm sorry," he said.

"I don't believe you." She turned and once more continued her walk. An elongated shadow moved ahead of her as she put distance between herself and the tug's headlights.

"Captain Lowe asked where you were," he called after her.

Jana stopped and turned slightly. "Did he ask you to pick me up?"

"No, not exactly. But he seemed impatient to get started. I wouldn't want you to get into trouble."

She glanced at her thumbnail chronometer and noted that she had less than fifteen minutes to make it to the ship. There was just enough time if she walked quickly. On the other hand, Lowe would appreciate her being early, and tardiness would be inexcusable. As much as she hated to admit it, Herzog was doing her a favor.

She wordlessly returned to the tug, slid into the passenger seat, and fastened the belt.

"Hang on!" Herzog called out. Gravel flew from the tires as he accelerated toward the ship.

"Thanks for the warning," Jana muttered to herself, determined to ignore any of his further pleasantries. *Piffdriveler!*

The fact that the man had lied to her was bad enough, but that she had been so easily and willingly deceived—betrayed by her own loneliness and his charming smile—bothered her even more. She was as angry with herself as with him, and so she maintained a stony silence behind an emotional wall—a wall designed as much to keep her own feelings in check as to repel his periodic attempts at conversation.

The pool of harsh light that turned night into day around the *Europa* revealed a dwindling level of activity from the lading crew as the tug and its two passengers approached across the concrete ramp. Most of the twenty-four great side hatches were already closed, as the lading had been proceeding since the ship had landed the previous day. The diverse supplies that they had brought in yesterday were already in the process of distribution. The majority of outbound cargo—refined blocks of siliconium stored in shipping containers—was already loaded. All that remained was the last miscellany of special-order items and ships stores to be put aboard to make the ship ready for launch.

Jana idly recognized many of the familiar support vehicles and personnel that always swarmed around the great ships after they'd landed and before they departed. A few were transport vehicles—some for long-distance hauling and some for the short trip to a storage facility on the spaceport grounds. There was also a maintenance platform, a provision truck, and the all-important sanitation tank. She glanced about for the small, squat, deuterium fuel truck, but it apparently had already departed.

They neared one of the forward hatches that remained open, and Jana motioned with her hand for Harlin to stop the tug. The lighted interior of the bay revealed the loaded **stanchions**. Each marked container was locked into position on these stanchions to prevent the slightest shifting of the cargo.

Jana braced as Herzog slammed the brakes and brought the tug to a screeching stop.

"Thanks," she said flatly, as the seat belt clinked and she swung easily and quickly from the seat—too quickly for Herzog even to make the offer to assist her. Her boots rang on the tread plate of the short ladder as she entered the forward airlock.

"Jana!" Herzog called from where he was now standing beside the tug. He looked up, and the hood again slid back around his neck. Jana turned and paused, looking sideways and down, her face impassive.

"Will you be stopping by the office before you leave?"

"I don't think so. Why?"

"I wanted to say good-bye."

"You just did."

"I mean, I would like to say good-bye, again."

"You fooled me once, Mr. Herzog. I don't intend to repeat that mistake."

"I didn't say anything that you didn't *want* to hear!"

The truth of his accusation stung her inwardly, but she would not allow herself an outward sign.

"I'm sorry," he repeated his apology.

"I don't like being played, Mr. Herzog."

He stepped around the tug and spread his hands. "Look, it's my office. Nothing will happen. I promise."

Jana's silhouetted head looked away briefly then turned back. "We'll see." Then she turned and was gone.

Harlin Herzog took a deep breath, slowly let it out, and then resumed his place in the driver's seat of the tug. He turned it toward the port authority office and continued at a moderate pace across the ramp.

He was about halfway to the office when a series of lights in the western sky caught his attention. They appeared to be a line of descending, high-speed aircraft. Harlin was familiar with the regular air transports that made many shuttle runs to the spaceport, but this squadron did not appear to be following a typical flight path. *Something's not right, here!* He wrinkled his brow and gunned the tug to its limit.

The whine and rumble of the aircrafts' turbines increased with their approach. The tug squealed to a stop in front of the office. Harlin jumped from it and ran inside, shed his parka on the floor beside his chair, and scanned his computer for any message traffic. But his message windows were empty of any notifications. He grabbed the vid and punched the code for the air traffic office.

"Welcome to the Tachon Consolidated Air and Space Traffic Control Facility," the recorded greeting began. The menu screen had hardly flashed on before Harlin accessed a special code to speak directly to the air traffic control officer.

The vid changed to that of a man in a dimly lit room. An indistinct pattern of equipment lights glowed in the background of the tiny image. The controller seemed to be concentrating on something out of the vid frame. He looked up, obviously irritated at the distraction of the call, but he relaxed slightly when he recognized the caller.

"Harl," he said, "I was just about to notify you. You've got traffic."

"Yeah, I figured that," Herzog agreed above the noise of the landing aircraft. "What's it all about?"

"This is weird," the controller answered. "It looks like a flight of three jumper jets must have departed from a private 'port in the range. They air-filed just before entering Tachon Spaceport airspace."

"Are you sending me a copy?" Herzog asked. The sound of the turbines dropped in pitch as they spooled down to a low rumble.

"You should have it now," the controller replied. "Sorry for the no heads-up, but we were all taken by surprise."

"Thanks," Herzog said shortly, and he clicked the vid off. He turned to his computer screen and tapped it for inbound traffic that now displayed a flight strip for a flight of three jump jets going under the call sign PROPHET. He studied the displayed information briefly and then headed for the door. Seconds later, his tug screeched and shot toward the flashing red anti-collision strobes of the parked jets.

A small security team dressed in black leather skullcaps, jackets, and boots moved to form a phalanx between the tug and the aircraft as Herzog pulled up. He noted the men were armed and grunted derisively at the unnecessary show of force.

From the size of those weapons, they must be sonic blasters, he thought as he approached the group, but he was more irritated than intimidated. As the port authority, he was responsible for the port's proper use. He was not about to risk losing his position due to the laxity of the air traffic team.

One of the security men stepped forward and held up a gloved hand. Several of his men stood behind him, weapons at the ready.

"That's close enough. Display your identification and state your business," the dark-clothed figure ordered.

Herzog bristled. "I am the port authority. You display *your* identification and state *your* business," he demanded in return.

"Where is the woman singer, Jana Maines?" the security member asked in a low voice.

Harlin said nothing but held out his hand, palm up. The security man walked slowly forward and stopped a half-meter in front of him.

"The Prophet has sent us. Where is Jana Maines?" he asked again.

"Well, that's half of it," Herzog retorted. "I know your business; now let's see some identifica—*oowf!*"

His order was truncated into a cry of pain as the other man slapped a small baton across his open palm. Harlin staggered backward, clutching his throbbing hand. The pain quickly subsided into a tingling numbness that left his whole arm as unresponsive as if he had slept on it the entire night. The man in black took a step toward him, and Herzog stumbled back against the side of the tug.

"Your attitude was irreverent," the guard informed him soberly. "By the grace of the Prophet, you are unharmed. Where is Jana Maines?"

"I … I don't know," Harlin stalled. He used his good arm to pull up his deadened hand and examined it in the fitful illumination from the flashes of the jets' lights.

"Repentance is not optional," the guard said, taking another step forward. He brought the wand into full view.

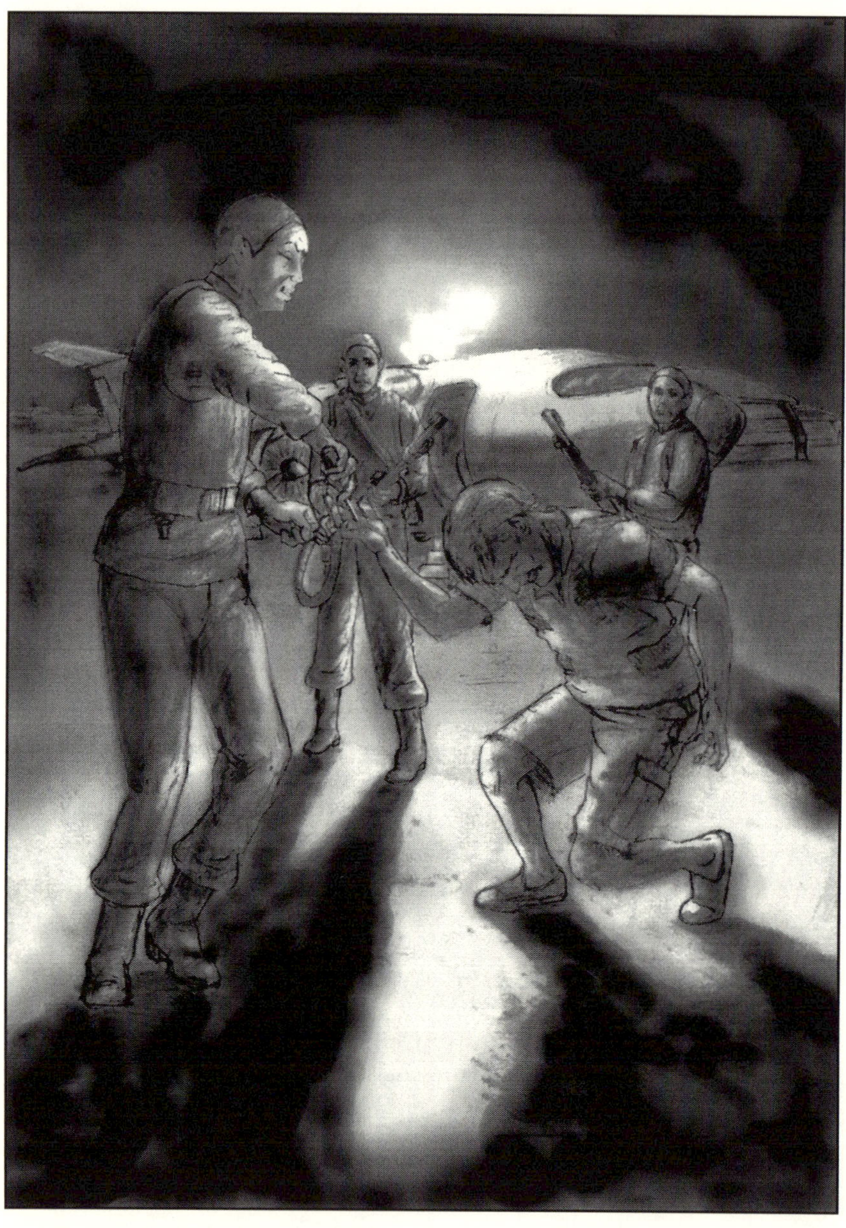

"She's somewhere. In the ship," Harlin admitted reluctantly with a glance toward the *Europa*, gleaming in the arc lights.

"Summon her."

"I can't!" Harlin spat, and the man raised the wand. "Not here, anyway. But she will be coming to my office—at least I think she will."

The black jacket turned to his men. "Squads one and two, maintain security here. Squad three, on the tug!" The security team immediately shifted their positions or climbed aboard the tug as instructed. The officer turned his attention back to Herzog. "You will take us there," he ordered quietly.

Harlin made a face but slowly maneuvered himself into the driver's position. The chief security officer walked around the tug and wordlessly took the passenger seat. Harlin let his numb arm drop and took a trembling grasp on the steering wheel with his other hand. The tug bumped forward. He turned it and headed toward the port authority office.

Chapter 7

Jana moved through the familiar confines of the ship. Her eyes scanned the stanchions, the containers, and their fastenings, checking them for any damage, discoloration, or leakage. Her ears listened for any irregularity or change in the normal hums and whines of the ship. She sniffed through the mixed smells of **ozone**, hydraulic fluid, and human odors until she was satisfied that she did not detect the distinctive, pungent smell of overheated electronics.

She climbed another short ladder to another airlock and finally reached her small stateroom. She slipped off her jacket and stored it. Then she unpacked and stored the contents of her sea bag that the captain had already delivered. She debated between remaining in the looser jumpsuit or switching to the warmer pressure suit, and finally decided to change. The walk had been pleasant, but the high-speed drive on the tug had given her a chill. The heating elements in her pressure suit would quickly warm her.

She slid out of her khaki jumpsuit, moved to her small lavatory, and splashed her face with warm water to freshen up, then paused to stare into the small mirror above the metal sink and examined her face critically.

"Too much excitement," she sighed to herself.

Moments later, she emerged from her room dressed in the flexible pressure suit and made her way to the flight station, where she found Captain Lowe still in his khakis, already engaged in completing one of the many pre-launch checklists. Completion of the checklists could take several hours before they would finally be considered ready for departure.

"Good morning, Captain," she greeted him as she slid into the seat on the right.

He glanced up from his screen, grunted, and handed her the datapad that listed the current checklist. She took it wordlessly, knowing it was a time-honored tradition that whoever held the datapad was the one required to get up and move about the ship whenever a physical check was needed. Of course, the junior officer usually held the datapad.

The pilots reviewed hundreds of items while the computers reviewed thousands more. Each item the pilots checked was called out and verbally verified in a tedious routine that had been the hallmark of flying machines since humanity had first taken to the air. This was no empty ritual. The interplay was one of the last bulwarks protecting the pilots from themselves and the human tendency to forget, overlook, and cut short.

"Main bus circuit breaker," the captain called out.

"Reset and on," Jana responded after she physically checked it.

They continued in this manner through the checklists for nearly an hour, as Jana fought the urge to yawn. It was a relief when Lowe occasionally yawned, which informally allowed her to follow suit, blinking and covering her mouth with her hand or the datapad.

"You get enough sleep?" Lowe asked after a particularly extended yawn.

"I tried, sir," she explained, "but I didn't sleep as well as I usually do. I guess too much happened yesterday."

He grunted and continued with the checklist until the ship's communicator chimed.

Lowe glanced up from the list with a look of irritation. "What?" he muttered as he checked the transmit ident. "It's the port authority," he announced, shooting a quizzical look at Jana. "And on radio. Why not use the vid?"

She shrugged and shook her head.

Lowe selected the frequency and flipped the transmit button. "*Europa*'s on, over," he said.

"Uh, Captain Lowe." Herzog's voice sounded dull. "Is Lieutenant Maines there?"

Jana reached for the transmit button on her side of the console, but the captain held up a hand.

"She is working on the checklists and is around here, somewhere," he replied. "What do you need?"

There was a pause before Herzog came back on. "She said she was going to stop by before she left. Do you know if she still plans to do that?"

"We are rather busy here, Mr. Herzog," Lowe responded with irritation. "I will ask her if she can fit you into her social calendar. And I would suggest you stay off the frequency with personal chatter."

"It's kind of important," Herzog responded meekly. "I kind of need to see her."

"Well, I'll kind of try to get through the checklist in order to kind of make our launch window, and then we'll kind of see," Lowe shot back. He turned to Jana and shook his head.

"Well, your launch time is … is somewhat in dispute."

The radio made a faint hiss.

"You are making precious little sense, Herzog," Lowe said, and he would have continued, but Jana laid a hand on his arm and made a cutting motion with her other hand.

"I'll talk to her. *Europa* out." Lowe ended the transmission.

"Yes, Lieutenant?" the captain turned to her and asked.

"Sir, something is wrong with that man," she said.

Lowe nodded. "I've been trying to tell you that for some time. I'm glad you're finally seeing the light."

"No," Jana objected. "I mean, yes, he has his problems, but that didn't sound like the man I met this morning. Just now he sounded like he had—it sounded like something has happened to him."

Lowe coughed. "*You* happened to him, Jana," he said. "If he sounds down and depressed it's because he knows that you'll soon be gone. This is just a lame excuse to see you one more time."

"Well, he did ask me to say good-bye. I didn't exactly say that I wouldn't."

"That was foolish."

"Maybe so, but it might be good diplomacy. It is his office, sir. I can't imagine too much could go wrong."

Lowe considered for a time before he spoke. "Hurrying through a checklist is like kissing a hologram. You're only going through the motions."

Jana rose with a swish and quiet squeak from the seat. "He also said our proposed launch time was in dispute. We need to find out what that means."

"Yeah," Lowe frowned and nodded. "That was odd."

She handed the datapad to the captain and moved aft.

"Give me a report after you speak with him," Lowe called over his shoulder as she left the flight station. The sound of her steps on the deck plate faded.

"Piffdriveler," Lowe muttered.

Jana left the ship through the forward airlock and stepped into in the cold darkness that still prevailed beyond the pool of light surrounding the *Europa*. She could see a trio of jump jets at the western end of the ramp. Their anti-collision beacons flashed as if they were ready to depart. She recalled that she had heard them rumble in when they landed a short time earlier.

A special shipment, perhaps? But there are no transport vehicles! I'll ask Herzog—whether he will tell me the truth or not is another matter!

She turned and walked backward to look behind her. The great ship was almost completely sealed. The arc lamps fully illuminated it, making it stand out against the thin but growing band of pinkish eastern sky. A few cirrus wisps glowed orange-red.

Red sun in morning, sailors take warning she recited mentally. *But in this dusty climate, I suppose every morning has a red sun!* She turned and continued to the port office. Shortly thereafter, she stepped into the small pool of yellow light that shone from above the office door. The door hissed open and the cool interior light spilled out. Jana wondered how Harlin would take the farewell, and the explanation for his cryptic remarks regarding their departure. She saw him studying his computer screen at his desk behind the small counter and stepped toward him. Then she noticed the large, dark shape of a man dressed in black move forward from behind the counter.

She stopped just as the door closed behind her. Harlin looked up from his console and stared at her helplessly. The large man in black waited beside the console, but the scrape of boots from behind her as well as motion in her peripheral vision informed her that there were others in the room.

"Jana," Herzog said weakly. His eyes flicked to the men in black, and then he looked down.

The tall man stepped forward from behind the console and extended an empty, gloved hand. "Welcome, Lieutenant Maines," he said in a deep and commanding voice. Despite the gravity of the situation, the thought crossed her mind that he would have excellent prospects as an operatic **basso profundo**, should a career change become necessary.

"Hello," she replied, ignored the hand, and turned to Mr. Herzog. "What's this all about?"

He rose. His right arm dangled uselessly.

Jana's eyes widened. "Are you all right?" she asked as she took a step in his direction.

"He is unharmed," the tall black-robed figure said.

Jana gave the stranger a hard look and stood as straight and tall as she could. Her small chin rose slightly. Though fear tingled in her back, she summoned as much authority as she could and demanded, "Who are you and what do you want?"

"Good luck," muttered Herzog, and he grimaced as he touched his injured right hand.

The tall man bowed his black skull-capped head slightly and clasped his hands together. His short-bearded face smiled, revealing a fine set of white teeth.

"Dear lady," he began, "I first wish to assure you that you are in no danger. My fellow servants and I wish you only peace and good health." He finished his statement with a brief motion of his hand to the three other men in black.

Jana looked at the imposing, dark figures and then at Herzog, holding his useless arm. "Forgive me if I don't find that very comforting," she responded. "I still want to know who you are and what you want."

"I am Rogebrae, First Acolyte and servant of the Prophet, the Seeker of Truth, the Speaker of Truth, and the Destroyer of Ignorance. Do you know of him?" he asked with another flash of flawless white teeth.

Herzog's mouth dropped.

Jana raised a brow. "I've heard of him," she said. "What does he want of me?"

Rogebrae smiled again in an attempt to appear reassuring. "He merely desires to converse with you on spiritual matters."

She glanced at her thumbnail chronometer. "My ship is scheduled to leave shortly. I'm sorry, but I don't think I have the time."

The man in black looked at Herzog. The port authority jerked as if he'd been poked with a prod.

"Oh!" he said sharply. He blinked and looked at the computer screen. "I meant to tell you. Um, your departure clearance is on hold."

Jana's face fell. "For how long?"

Herzog shrugged his good shoulder and waved his good hand. "There's no proposed time. It's suspended."

"Well, it seems your Prophet has quite a bit of influence with Air and Space Traffic Control, at least," Jana admitted to Rogebrae. "But this has to be costing somebody a lot of credits."

"The Prophet, the Seeker of Truth, the Speaker of Truth, and the Destroyer of Ignorance, is little concerned with credits," the messenger replied, waving a gloved hand in a small, dismissive gesture.

"Fine for him, but STC stockholders expect us to maintain a schedule. They tend to be unhappy with the crew that they think let them down. If we fall behind schedule, the stockholders lose credits. If the stockholders lose credits, the flight crew loses credits."

"You and your STC stockholders will lose no credits," Rogebrae assured her. "All expenses will be made aright by the Generous One—after he has had an opportunity to speak with you."

"Just a moment, please," Jana said, and she reached for her vid. She tapped the captain's code.

"Yes, Lieutenant?" The tiny image squinted at her from the flight deck.

"Sir, we have a situation … "

Chapter 8

Some time later, the three huddled behind the portmaster's desk in his office and quietly discussed the Prophet's demand. Rogebrae and his men stood near both exits while Herzog sat silently and massaged his arm.

"They might legally be able to do this, but I still don't like it," Lowe growled. "I've checked the Tachon Company's charter with the STC. It authorizes the mining company to initiate delays if they provide compensation."

Jana eyed the dark figures guarding the doorways. "The way they treated Mr. Herzog, I wonder if they care much about the charter."

Lowe shook his head. "You better hope that they do. That charter is the only thing right now that could protect your safety if you go with them. But at this point, we can't even refuse and threaten to lodge an official complaint. An investigation would show that the charter is on *their* side."

"If they intend to hold *us* to it, then we'll have to hold *them* to it," Jana concluded.

"I am also bothered by the nature of Mr. Herzog's injury," Lowe whispered. "What he described sounds like a completely unfamiliar weapon. The Prophet seems to have access to some unusual technology. That makes me nervous."

"I don't like it either, sir," Jana agreed, "but what other choice do we have? The Prophet has agreed to pay for any losses due to this delay.

The longer we wait, the more difficult and more expensive it becomes for everybody. I think it likely that he will give us what we want when he gets what he wants."

"Yes," Lowe growled. He lowered his heavy brows while he stroked his chin. "And that is the rub. What exactly does he want?" He looked pointedly at Jana. She blushed when she caught his meaning.

"Sir, I doubt that a man who has enough credits to rent a fully loaded star transport for several hours or more needs to send a dozen men and three jump jets simply to procure brief female companionship. I'm flattered that you think I'm worth it, but by your own account, there are less expensive women at his disposal."

Lowe made a dour face. "Jana, you don't know men like I do. Sometimes it's not the object of desire itself that creates its value to a man, but the difficulty in obtaining it."

"Forbidden fruit? The stolen apple tastes the sweetest?"

"Sometimes it's that," agreed Lowe, "but not always. Sometimes it's just being able to have the satisfaction of knowing you did something that few others could do. That might be climbing a treacherous mountain, navigating a ship through a storm, or obtaining a certain woman. Men can fixate on things like that." His attention shifted to Rogebrae, and he studied the First Acolyte through lowered lids. "And his intentions for you might not be brief."

"That seems unlikely to me, sir," she disagreed. "If I simply 'disappeared,' the negative repercussions to the Tachon Company would be huge. I don't think they would allow him risk their entire trade status on his personal whim."

Lowe's brows contracted as he thoughtfully stroked his chin. "Herzog seemed to think that the Prophet tells the company what to do—not the other way around."

"That might very well be," Jana agreed. "But I believe it's possible that this could be an opportunity given for our advantage. According to Mr. Rogebrae, we might actually earn a larger profit *because* of this delay. The pragmatic thing to do is to make the most reasonable decision we can—and then trust that Providence has put us in the situation for a purpose—that he has some good outcome in mind."

"Are you asking me to make a command decision based on faith in your religious convictions?" Lowe asked.

"No," Jana replied. "I'm asking you to make the most logical decision. What will enable me to carry it out will be my trust in Providence."

Lowe shook his head and ran his hand over the short crop on his graying scalp. "Even if we win the battle, we lose the war. I can keep you from seeing the Prophet, but I can't make him release the ship."

"They wouldn't risk harming me," Jana assured him despite her own apprehension.

Lowe worked his tightly clamped mouth as he studied her. "You have that much faith that the Prophet will abide by the agreement?"

"No, sir. As I said, my faith is in the hand of Providence—not the Prophet, the agreement, or even myself. Besides, sir, what's the alternative?"

Lowe looked away.

Jana took a deep, shaky breath, stood, and turned to the messenger in black. "I am ready, Mr. Rogebrae."

Rogebrae bowed slightly and gestured toward the door. Two of his men took a position abreast and led the way through the doors of the port authority office. Jana followed with Rogebrae at her side. The remaining man fell in behind them.

Herzog and Lowe watched wordlessly as the tiny procession filed out and the door hissed closed. Neither of them spoke or moved.

Outside, the jump jets spooled up from a high whine to a deep, thunderous rumble that the men felt with their feet as well as heard with their ears. The rumble lifted and faded westward until it was gone.

Lowe took a deep breath and let it out slowly. Finally, he looked at Herzog.

"Well, what do you know?" Herzog said and lifted his right arm. "The feeling is coming back! I think it's almost normal!"

"Amazing," commented Lowe.

"You know," Herzog said with renewed energy, "if I had recovered just a bit sooner, why, I bet between you and me and Jana, we could have taken those four guys. I really think we could have."

Lowe closed his eyes and shook his head in disgust. "Piffdrivel!" he muttered.

Chapter 9

On board the air transport, the inertia of Jana's own body pushed her downward into a plush, maroon velvet seat, and through the large circular side window, she watched the grounds of the spaceport fall away. The sun was just rising, so the flatlands remained in purple shadow punctuated by the lights of the spaceport and surrounding buildings.

At an altitude of about a hundred meters, the jump jet accelerated forward, and Jana was thrown back against the cushioned softness of the seat. She looked ahead past the pilots out the cockpit windshield and toward the Ghost Range, now mottled dark purple and deep red at the base of the mountains to orange and pink at their tops, and all set against a deep lavender sky. Somewhere in the depths of those escarpments, the Prophet had built a palace, a monastery—or something else.

"What a beautiful setting," she murmured, despite the ominous implication of what might lie ahead. Then she glanced around the interior of the jet and noticed how fine woods, rare metals, and expensive fabrics combined tastefully to convert this aircraft into an elegant virtual flying carpet. Rogebrae sat to her left across the narrow aisle. He leaned forward to look at her; a half-smile played at the corners of his mouth. He met her gaze, and his lips parted.

"You are impressed?"

She nodded and cast another look around at the rich interior. "Very swank."

"Ah!" The man nodded and settled back.

Jana turned forward and took a deep breath when she saw that the mountains, now completely pink and gold had filled the front windshield. "My goodness!" she said silently, and wished for a better view.

The eastern edge of the range of the mountain chain topped only about four thousand meters. But it was very rough and jagged, for even though the atmosphere had been thickening over the past few centuries, rain and erosion were still rare. The jump jets climbed most of the way to the summits, and their forward speed increased as they began level flight.

Jana turned to Rogebrae. "May I go forward?" she inquired over the rumble of the jets.

He nodded and motioned with his hand. Jana unfastened her seat belt with a soft click and took the few steps toward the flight station. The pilots glanced up apprehensively, but Jana flashed a smile. "Is it all right if I watch?"

"No, it's fine," the pilot in the left seat replied.

The copilot in the right seat reached back and unlatched a small, padded platform from the bulkhead, and a seat flopped down with a clunk. "Take the jump seat," he offered. Jana positioned herself on the seat and fastened the lap belt. She leaned forward, with her head between the shoulders of the two men, and was surprised by the sudden drop in the rumble of the engine noise. She leaned back, and the sound of the jets returned.

The pilot glanced up and grinned at the puzzled look on her face. "Sound cancellation," he explained simply, and motioned to a series of tiny speakers on the **overhead** above him.[4]

Jana studied the small speakers, nodded, and then leaned forward again into the quiet zone. She scanned the instruments and mentally compared their relative simplicity to her own complex panels. Rogebrae had come forward as well and stood quietly behind them.

The pilot noticed her space pilot's pressure suit. "What do you fly?" he asked.

"Deep-space transports," Jana replied. "I'm right seat on the *Europa*."

The pilot's brows went up.

"That's what I'd like to do!" the copilot suddenly spoke up. "This atmospheric stuff is *sooo* boring." He yawned and stretched one arm and then the other.

"We sure don't see much scenery between the strip and Tachon City," the pilot agreed.

Jana gestured at the magnificent mountains ahead and below. "You don't call this scenery?" she asked.

"I meant, we don't see much new scenery," the pilot corrected himself.

The copilot turned and gave Jana a frank look and grinned. "The mountains we call obstacles," he informed her. "*You* we call scenery!"

"Mr. Fee! Attend to your duties!" Rogebrae's peremptory tone sobered the man instantly and he returned eyes forward to his instruments with no sign of protest.

Jana observed this and felt a growing sense of dismay at the unnatural, animal-like obedience that the copilot displayed. Even after the black-robed acolyte returned to his seat moments later the copilot studiously ignored her, and her earlier confidence that she could deal rationally with the Prophet began to falter. But she was committed. There was no turning back now.

"Are you using fusion generators?" she asked, hoping to divert her disquieting thoughts.

The pilot nodded. "We have two micro-fusion units—each one cross-connected to the fan motors. At full flow, we can crank out four megawatts,[5] although two meg are usually enough for our loads."

Jana nodded, but her main attention was now drawn to a line of strobe lights ahead that flashed like tiny sparks in the purple shadow of the mountains. The mapping screen between the pilots changed to an approach mode. The jet descended in a shallow dive toward a short landing strip cut from the side of the mountain. Buildings constructed from cut rock and concrete were visible on the plateau. Additional buildings were under construction on the slopes above the strip. Since they were built from the native rock, they blended well with the surrounding terrain and were almost invisible except for the shadows they cast in the ruddy sunrise.

The ship settled with a soft jar, and the pilots cut the engines. Jana unbuckled, rose from the seat, and placed it back into position. "Thank you, gentlemen," she said and smiled at the pilots. The man in the left seat looked up and nodded in reply, but the copilot ventured only a glance in her direction before he quickly resumed staring at his hands.

The poor man! What sort of control does Rogebrae have? Jana shook her head and struggled to remember everything she had ever read or heard about mind-control techniques. A mental review of the gruesome list, from **lobotomies** to **cranial** implants, did nothing to put her at ease until she remembered a psychology lecture on the subject at the academy. The instructor had pointed out that invasive methods caused considerable **cerebral** damage. Victims were rendered controllable, but listless—a description that didn't fit the copilot's behavior. She was not completely reassured; however, as the same lecture had included a short discussion on sketchy pre-war reports of some unknown mental influence device that might have used sound. The actual methodology was not known, and the report was unclear whether such a machine had ever been produced or to what degree of success it had been employed.

"This way, please, my lady."

Jana started at Rogebrae's deep voice and felt weakness in her knees, but determination and self-discipline moved her aft, toward the man in black who gestured to the open side hatch.

A cold mountain wind swept across the tiny ramp, stung Jana's nose, and ruffled her short, blonde hair as she stepped across it. She shivered despite the warmth of her pressure suit.

Stay alert! Stay cautious!

She slowed to look eastward to the great red-orange Tachon sun, now just above the horizon. The mountains had gone from pink to copper-gold and the eastern sky from lavender to blue and orange. Far below, through a narrow gap between the mountains, the distant lights of the spaceport and the city were fading in the growing brightness of dawn.

"Mr. Rogebrae," Jana observed as they made their way through a massive doorway cut into the side of the mountain, "you have been quiet on this trip."

"In many words there is foolishness," he replied.

"Yes, but I was wondering if you could at least tell me what to expect."

"The Prophet, the Seeker of Truth, the Speaker of Truth, and the Destroyer of Ignorance will reveal himself in his own time and way. Such is not my place."

"And what of you, Mr. Rogebrae?" the woman asked as they passed through a rock hallway and into a large foyer.

"I know my place," the deep-voiced man said simply as he led the way through thick, transparent doors into a large reception hall. Once inside, her escort held up his gloved hand. "Please remain here. The

Prophet will meet you shortly." He made a small gesture around the room. "Consider this room and everything in it as your own. It is the Prophet's wish that you should have a few moments to relax and be comfortable."

Jana nodded, and Rogebrae retreated through another door across the room. She watched him go and apprehensively began to evaluate her surroundings.

The room was well appointed with brass or gold sconce lights, woven tapestries, and potted plants. The bit of greenery added an element of luxury and relief from the oppressively barren landscape outside. The granite, mirror-finished floor reflected the morning light coming through the huge siliconium plate windows framed in brass that formed the east wall.

Jana's eye caught a shining rainbow from a clear cube of crystal near the center of the room and she moved closer to study it. The crystal was a full half-meter on a side, with intense sparkle and fire where it caught the light at a corner or edge.

A cube of diamond—a half-meter on each side? She caught her breath at the thought.

The crystal cube held a gold tray, upon which were two crystal glasses holding a dark, wine-colored liquid. She sniffed unappreciatively. She was fatigued enough from her fitful night. Wine would do nothing to clear her head. She had also picked up a chill, and despite the heat from her suit, she would have preferred something warm to drink, like a mug of hot chocolate or café mocha.

The décor of the chamber, like that of the air transport, seemed designed to express a masculine sort of luxury. Jana quirked her mouth as she studied the ornamentation. Evidence of a softening, feminine touch was absent. Despite the elements of comfort, underneath that pleasant veneer—much like the rock walls behind the tapestry—there was a hardness and immutability that was unyielding, heavy, and onerous. This trip had clearly been designed to impress her with the sheer wealth, influence, and power of the Prophet.

Despite earlier reminders to herself to remain vigilant, Jana was experiencing a slowly growing mental fatigue—a sense of dullness bordering on indifference. The shock of this realization gave her a burst of adrenaline that brought her back to a more alert state. It reminded her of the jolt she experienced whenever she was fighting sleep on watch and suddenly realized she had almost dozed off. She could remain alert, but only for as long as the adrenaline lasted. *I wish I had slept better!*

To keep her mind active, she pondered the Prophet himself. If Herzog had been truthful that the Prophet was the child of a wealthy entrepreneur who had died and left everything to him, then it seemed more likely for the man to be older rather than younger. The construction she had seen would have taken years to complete, so that also argued for an older man. The choices of furnishings and decorations were tasteful and generally spoke of quiet strength, which also suggested someone with more mature tastes. And yet the heavy-handed approach to bring her to this place was more characteristic of the impulsiveness and impatience of youth.

She stood at the central, large window and looked down on the city in the early morning. The only sounds were her breath in her nostrils and a faint hum that seemed to be everywhere. She couldn't locate it. It reminded her of a ship's background noise, but it had a much more relaxing quality to it. *Whatever that thing is, I would not want it on during a long, quiet midwatch.*

"Lieutenant Jana Maines."

The sound of her name once more temporarily jolted her from the fog of her reverie. She turned and started at the sight of a man in a black jumpsuit. A dark, wine-colored cape covered his shoulders, held together near his throat by a fist-sized gold clasp. He stood by the door through which Rogebrae had departed several minutes earlier. The man walked toward Jana, his soft black boots falling almost noiselessly on the stone floor.

He moved purposefully, his steps measured, uniform, firm, and steady. His thick, dark hair was shot with gray and was white at the temples, and dark eyes sparkled with probing intensity from a lined, brown face. Prominent cheekbones stood out above a gray-streaked Vandyke beard. Jana found him an attractive example of a fully mature man.

"I am glad that you have come," he said in a firm and pleasant voice that carried the edge of command. "I trust you had a pleasant trip."

"Pleasant enough," she admitted, "considering it was demanded of me. You are aware that your man, Rogebrae, promised payment for the delay of the *Europa*'s departure?"

"I apologize for the inconvenience," he said with a nod and an attempt at a warm smile, "but it was unavoidable. It was, in fact, the imminence of your departure that required the somewhat forceful and direct intervention on my part. I desired your complete attention and thought it best to bring you here to conduct this interview. I hope you realize how much I value your goodwill and desire your cooperation. Please, do not trouble yourself about such mundane matters as expenses. And I assure you that you are in no danger. Simply relax and enjoy my hospitality. That's all I ask." He gestured to the glasses of wine on the crystal cube, but Jana declined with a brief smile and a small shake of her head.

He moved past her and stood next to the window, the red sun lighting his face and hair so that it looked to Jana like a flaming halo. He studied the view a moment and then turned. The halo effect remained as the sun backlighted his head. He struck a proud pose, his feet well apart and his chest out. His left hand rested easily on his hip, and his strong chin was only slightly raised.

"Are you impressed, Jana? I hope so." His tone indicated that this was not a plea for approval, but a statement of pride. He made a sweeping gesture with his right hand, and the wine-colored robe fell from his right arm in graceful folds. "All of this *I* have made. All of this is a work of faith—a testament to the power of belief."

His eyes roamed the room briefly, before they returned to her face. They slipped downward for a fraction of a second, but he caught himself and held her returning gaze. "I am told you are a woman of faith. My hope—no, my expectation—is that you are someone with the ability to truly appreciate the successful application of faith."

The man's borderline arrogance put her off, but she found herself mentally acknowledging that he had a dramatic and powerful way of presenting himself. Despite her misgivings, she found his air of certainty and self-confidence somehow attractive. There was something about him that seemed almost more than merely human. He was only one man, and she his only audience, but the strength of his convictions seemed to radiate from him like an invisible energy field.

She became dimly aware that the strange mental fogginess was again growing, and she tried to remain focused, to keep her wits about her. She breathed deeply and hoped some mental exercise would help to keep her mind alert. *I must ask him some questions.*

"Faith," Jana said, and she cleared her throat, "needs to be placed in something. You say you have shown me an impressive display of faith—but faith in what?"

He threw his head back, laughed, and then dropped his gaze to her. "Why, faith in *myself!*" He had placed his hand against his chest and now brought it out once more in a grand, sweeping motion. "To be truly liberated, one cannot live in timidity and fear, but with confidence and boldness. I did not shrink from risk, for each opportunity is a risk, and each risk is an opportunity. A risk taken and lost is better than an opportunity passed by, for we at least learn in our trying. An opportunity that is passed up is cold and dead. It is worth nothing."

He was not shouting—he didn't need to. The smooth tones of his voice were captivating. His demeanor was persuasive. His voice carried a tone of authority and inspiration that, despite its low volume, still rang in Jana's ears and filled her mind with a tantalizing sense of limitless potential.

She took a small step back.

"Do not be afraid." The man who called himself the Prophet relaxed his brows, and his face became gentle. "I would be disappointed to find that you are given to fear."

"I ... am not ... afraid," Jana replied slowly. "But I am careful."

He chuckled. "*Careful* can be another word for *timid*."

She bit her lip. "We have a saying: 'There are old pilots and there are bold pilots, but there are no old, bold pilots.'"

He laughed appreciatively and nodded. "You are a victim of your training. Of course, when dealing with the harsh dangers of space you must be careful. I compliment your instructors for their thoroughness—and you, for taking their lessons to heart."

"Thank you," was all she could manage from the edge of the strange fuzziness that clouded her mind. Strangely, the encroaching dullness seemed to diminish whenever he approached. It was as if all else was darkness, and he was the source of light. To move in any other direction except toward the light seemed madness.

"You would like to live up to your potential, wouldn't you, Jana?"

"Yes, of course," she said slowly.

"Good! Everyone is special, but you are *very* special. Grant me just a few moments to show you just how special you are."

She found herself smiling shyly.

He focused his dark, bright eyes on her and extended his hand. "When I saw you on the vid last night, I sensed that within you was that rare spirit of power—of confidence and expectancy which, if properly directed and developed, can be used for tremendous benefit—mine as well as yours."

"Benefit? In what way?" She heard her own voice as if listening to someone else's.

"Look about you," he smiled as he gestured. "All you see is but a fraction of what I am willing to share. But all that I have now is *nothing* compared to what is yet to be grasped—unlimited wealth, unlimited power, unlimited pleasure." He stepped toward her, smiled, and extended both hands. "Join me. Strength to strength. Equal to equal. Partner with me, and all of this—and more—will be yours."

A vague sense of unease tugged at the pit of her stomach, but only the smallest portion of her mind seemed able to think of anything but the images of wealth and power the figure before her had conjured in her mind.

Wealth and power! Clearly, it was no idle boast. If she were given access to it, her problems and those of her family would vanish! Images of her parents appeared in her mind. They were calling to her, but she couldn't hear what they were saying. Their faces were fuzzy, and their voices were indistinct. *Are they urging me to grasp this opportunity, or are they warning me to refuse?*

But this man was so persuasive, so sure of himself, that Jana found it difficult to find the strength to resist him. Indeed, it was almost impossible to find a *reason* to resist. Her normal cool objectivity seemed to have fled to some tiny closet in her mind, hiding from the charismatic presence that stood before her.

"This is happening so fast," she managed to say, "I need time to think."

"Hesitation is a bad habit," the Prophet urged gently but insistently. "Each moment is an opportunity that passes and is gone. *This* is your moment. Seize it! *Live* it!"

He took her hand. His was strong and cool. She felt weak and unguarded before his dark, glittering, compelling eyes. She opened her mouth to speak, but she had no idea what she wanted to say. Another wave of confusion engulfed her before she felt him drawing her closer to him, folding her against his solid chest, his cloak covering him like the tapestries covering the rock walls surrounding them. She felt the cold metal clasp of his cape against the hair above her temple, she caught the faint odor of exotic, spicy cologne, and her mind grew clearer.

"Come, Jana," he said, and his voice had deepened and grown husky. "Let us pleasure ourselves—a mere foretaste of all that awaits us!"

He drew her toward a side door that whispered open for them. Though her mind cleared slightly, it still seemed as if she was in a dream and merely watching herself move toward the door.

Chapter 10

Pleasure ourselves! Lowe was right! This man thinks I am for sale—that I can be bought! The faces of her father and mother flashed into her mind. *How can I bring this shame to the family? How can I let them down?*

"You must speak … with my father," she struggled to say aloud.

"There's no need for that. Don't fight the opportunity of the moment," the Prophet whispered. "Wealth, power, pleasure—all are yours for the taking! Relax and enjoy yourself!" She felt his hand through her suit gently pressing the small of her back, urging her forward.

"I don't want to … do this," she managed to say. As the doorway came closer, somehow, despite the difficulty, she was finding the words. She pulled away from him.

"Oh, but you do," he insisted.

She was once more rapidly losing all ability to protest—even to think using words. Her mental processes seemed to be devolving into wordless bursts of emotion. *Help … me …* were the last words that remained in her vocabulary—and somehow, they gave her enough control to stop her feet.

"Jana, what is it?" the Prophet asked in surprise and irritation at her resistance. "Do not fear. No harm will come to you. This is no mere dalliance, but rather an act to seal our commitment."

She continued to back away and to bring her arms up in a weak defensive gesture. The mental fog once more pressed down on her, but she struggled against it. "Let me make sure I understand this," she said with great effort. "You said you wanted me to join you, 'Strength to strength and equal to equal.' Is that right?"

He smiled, nodded, and took a step forward.

The pitiful image of the cringing and obsequious copilot flashed into Jana's mind. *That's going to be you! That's what he does to people! But how is he doing it?*

The latent image created a fear and anger that bubbled up like lava bursting from a volcano and released a torrent of adrenaline. The rush brought the reality of her situation back into sharper focus. *Adrenaline!* The realization came in a burst of insight. *Adrenaline counters it! That's why he keeps urging me to relax!* This knowledge fueled another surge, and for a few seconds, the mind fog lifted further. *The pre-war device! He must have somehow obtained a pre-war sonic sedation device!*

The luxurious apartment became, in Jana's mind, a simple stone cave with a few rags tacked up. The refined brass fixtures became industrial appliances, and the ageless, charming, persuasive spiritual guide became a foolish old man, goat-like in his technique and repulsive in his eagerness.

The Prophet's smile faded into a hard look of frustration. His hand went to the clasp near his throat, and he fiddled with it for a second, then his expression melted into a controlled and calculated softness. "Have I been misunderstood?" he asked.

"No!" Jana screamed. "I understand perfectly! Turn it off!"

His eyes widened, and he stepped back at her unexpected outburst. "What do you mean?"

She moved forward aggressively in a final, desperate effort of resistance, energized by the fear that her capacity to resist would dwindle as the adrenaline rush faded. Her small finger jabbed centimeters from his face. Whether it was the adrenaline or her proximity to him, she didn't know, but once more, her mind seemed to clear. "You're doing something! That hum—that machine—turn it off! Turn it off *now*!"

He wavered. His hand moved for his robe, but then he stopped himself and his eyes narrowed, no doubt doing the same mental calculation as she had done: trying to determine how long before she succumbed to the influence of the device.

"Do you think you can get away with this?" Jana renewed her desperate verbal attack. "The STC charter *demands* my safety. Captain Lowe knows where I am. He knows I'm with you. And he's *very* suspicious. If anything happens to me, the STC will cut Tachon off like a malignant growth. There will be *no* trade. They'll slap an embargo on the entire planet. Your credits won't be worth *anything!*" She forced her voice so hard that it hurt, but the pain helped keep her mind focused.

The man turned back to the large window. If those panes had been simple glass, the sun would have been uncomfortably warm, but the variable transmissivity of the siliconium reduced its heat to a comfortable level—one of the many useful applications of the versatile mineral.

There was a small motion of his robe as he fumbled for something. The low hum ceased, and Jana's clarity of thought returned with the suddenness of a face full of ice water. She was left gasping and shaking from her mental exertions. Her chest heaved, and her breath whistled hard and fast through her flared nostrils. Her mouth was set in a determined grimace, and her gaze was unblinking at the Prophet's back.

"I want to go," she said weakly between breaths.

"I cannot begin to express my disappointment. I really thought you were different, Jana," he said regretfully as he studied the desert below. He slowly turned, leaned back against the stone sill and made a small gesture around the room. "I offer you wealth, power, security—more than you could ever hope to attain as a star captain—even as a star admiral."

"Yes, but at what price? Would I even be *me* anymore?"

His eyelids dropped. His mouth took on a subtle twist. "It is unfortunate that you have been taught to fear your own sexuality."

"No." She shook her head slightly and her face tightened. "I honor it."

He made a dismissive gesture with his hand.

"That machine of yours—it's some kind of mind-bender—sub-sonic sedator or psychotrope.[6] That's pre-war stuff. Where did you get it?"

He shrugged. "I found it."

"It's horrible!"

"No," he shook his head. "It's a simple a tool. A harmless device."

"I said I want to get out of here."

He clasped his hands behind his back and slowly walked from the window. "I would have made you the mistress of an entire planet, with the wealth and technology that could, in time, go far beyond even that. Whatever you ever wanted would have been yours. And that would have been—and still can be—a very good thing, wouldn't it?"

"If it's such a good thing, then why did you feel the need to use your 'harmless device' on me?"

"A miscalculation on my part," he said, and he spread his hands. "Perhaps the result of wanting something too much." He took a seat on the block of crystal next to the wineglasses. "You would at least permit me a few moments to converse without its influence?"

She was too weary to protest and too wary to give him permission, so she said nothing. He waited for her to respond, and then finally shrugged at her silence.

"I sensed you were special." He crossed his arms as he regarded her. "I was certain that you would see the most important opportunity of a lifetime when it was offered."

"I did," Jana said.

"Then you must join me."

She shook her head. "No. Yours was not the most important offer of a lifetime."

The man's face darkened. "Do not toy with me, woman. Speak plainly." His voice took on a brittle edge. "Or do you suffer the confusion of speech so common to your sex?"

An insult? I must have really rattled him! She forced her face to remain impassive and took a deep breath before she spoke. "What you have offered is, by ordinary human standards, an opportunity of sorts. You are right that part of me wants to take hold of it. The lure of wealth and power is undeniable."

The other raised his brows but otherwise did not move.

"The part of me that desires your offer is my spirit of self," Jana continued. "But the offer of a lifetime was when I accepted the Spirit of the Creator, given as a gift, and became a follower of the Way. It is that Spirit which assures me of a purpose beyond this life and a hope of possessing more than what I can see with my eyes or hold with my hands."

The Prophet shook his head. "The existence of the metaphysical world is an ancient and useless belief. I am both surprised and disappointed to find that you are so primitive in your thinking."

"The ancients believed that water was wet and that love was a mystery," she replied. "Were they wrong?"

"No," he admitted with a shrug. "They simply guessed right about some things, but wrong about many others. What is your point?"

"Assume, for a moment, the truth of metaphysical reality. If that was the case, we would *expect* it to be an ancient belief."

"Error is also an ancient concept," the Prophet said with a grimace. "Antiquity is no guarantor of truth. I am very familiar with many religions—which is why I created my own—but without a mindless reliance upon some imagined outside source of spiritual energy and insight." He made a derisive shake of his head. "No, my creed is clear, logical, and based upon what works—a religion based upon truths. These are real, demonstrable truths, not merely a supposition, or yet another's interpretation of that supposition. And a religion because it recognizes the only supreme authority that really exists—the one within each of us."

Even without the device, the man remained persuasive. His dark eyes took on a faraway look as he continued. "I had a dream. I was walking on a beach. The sand was pure white, and the sea was as smooth as polished glass. I could discern no sun, but the sky was bright gray, as if I was under a thin, but solid overcast. I walked to the edge of the water and struck it with my foot. But as the ripples began to spread out on the surface, something rose out of the sea and stood before me. It was an image of me, except this image was clear, like the water in the glassy sea! The image spoke in a voice that was mine—and yet it was not mine. I can still see it and hear it as clearly as the night I dreamed it."

The hair on the back of Jana's neck rose. The Prophet's eyes grew dark and unfocused. She wondered if he even saw her anymore. His voice was also taking on another tone, as if he now spoke with two voices. *The voice is his—and yet not his!* She swallowed hard and listened for the sound of the mind-control machine, but its hum was absent. Her thoughts remained clear. The only sounds were his peculiar voice and the thudding rush of blood in her ears. Whatever was happening, it didn't seem to be happening to her, but to *him*!

"I spoke of faith in myself," he continued in the altered voice. "I am but an archetype of what is available for everyone. The first foundational truth is: 'I alone am the ultimate reality.'" He brought his left arm up and extended the first finger. "The second foundational statement is: 'Whatever will be is up to me.'"

He raised his right arm and extended the first finger in the same manner as the other. He slowly brought the two fingers together so that his hands were above his head and the first fingers of each hand touched side by side. Now he slowly lowered the fingers so that they stood together before his face. "The mind and the will together," he said, "are bounded and limited only by self-imposed constraints. Once the mind is made aware of this fact, the will can be freed from the untruths that keep it constrained by the wills of others. As this constraint is removed, self-knowledge becomes without bound, and the human potential is limitless!"

He completed his statement, slowly raised his hands, spread his fingers, and brought his arms up until they extended above his head. He closed his eyes, tipped his head back slightly, and intoned:

The past that is gone
And the future to be
Are less than what is presently.
With will and mind
Together entwined
No other's limit let you bind.
But be strong and brave
Yourself to save.
Then nothing past and nothing to be
Nothing—nothing can destroy thee.

The Prophet dropped his arms, and his gaze came to rest upon the woman's face. "No assumptions, no lies, no myths—just the simple, pragmatic truth of methods of what is and what works." His voice returned to normal as he finished his soliloquy, and his eyes once more became clear and focused.

Jana remained very uneasy, unsure if she might very well be in the presence of a maniac. "Of course, inheriting a fortune didn't hurt, either," she remarked in an attempt at nonchalance.

The Prophet sniffed. "What I chose to do with that fortune was up to me. It was an opportunity of which I took advantage. The fact that it made my life easier and gave me influence more quickly simply makes my point that opportunities must be seized—and if done so, the reward is even greater opportunities."

Jana cleared her throat nervously. "Two fundamental questions that every faith tries to answer are, '*Where did I come from?*' and '*Why am I here?*' How can your creed answer these questions?"

He chuckled and ran his hand along the fringe of a tapestry. "It doesn't," he said. "I can think of no more useless questions than that of ultimate origin and purpose. Does it matter where we came from or where we are going? No. The first foundational truth is that I am here, and that is *all* that matters. The fact that many religions have attempted to answer the questions of ultimate origin and destiny—and have done so in dramatically different ways—demonstrates the impossibility and futility of the attempt. The past is gone. It cannot touch us. All that we have is the present, which we can use to touch the future."

Jana spread her palms. "But to what end? You propose an endless growth to nowhere."

"No!" The man turned and wagged a finger. "Not nowhere, but *everywhere*—anywhere that the mind and will wish to go." He dropped his hand. "The purpose of other religions is to provide unproven answers to unanswerable questions. The price exacted for these answers is to be bound by the religious leaders' visions of the past and future—as if they could somehow know both what was and what is to be."

"And what is your alternative—a compass that points in all directions at the same time?"

He shook his head. "You set your own course with your own mind and will. Why surrender your will to the religious professionals? And religious leaders are indeed professionals, because religion is a business, Jana. Religious organizations sell speculative answers to unanswerable questions and provide eternal security to nonexistent souls. In exchange for these metaphysical benefits, they collect very real, very tangible goods and services from the gullible faithful, who are simply the slaves to another's will."

"You have your machine. Are your followers truly free?"

He waved his hand as if to dismiss her question. "You overestimate its power. It is not capable of controlling the masses. It was a mistake to experiment on you, and once more, I apologize." He relaxed and stood proudly. "I have built a following based upon the fundamental knowledge that each one of my followers is ultimately responsible only to their own self. When people cooperate and combine their minds and wills, their potential is multiplied. That is not some speculation from a dusty book—it is a fact. It is truth, and I, the Prophet, speak only truth."

"So you say," Jana remarked. "I am yet to be convinced."

The Prophet raised his brows as if amused. "And, no doubt, you will attempt to correct me."

Jana crossed her arms and looked away from him.

"Oh ho!" he laughed. "And how would you do so? Recite supposedly sacred and inspired verses from some long-dead ancients? Quote doctrines and creeds that are mere archaic interpretations of those same dead ancients? Perhaps you would allege a miracle or relate some personal experience that I cannot gainsay but you cannot prove. Is that what you would do?" His voice had lost its humor and become hard. He stared coldly at her, his silver brows contracted with contempt and scorn.

She shook her head slightly. "No."

There was a long, tense pause. The Prophet did not drop his glare. Jana held her own expressionless stare in return.

"I think I should go now," she said at last.

"I'm waiting for my miracle," he said.

"Would a miracle convince you?"

The Prophet laughed. "Why should it? So-called miracles are simply processes too advanced for our current technology to explain. Even if you were able to do something that I could not account for, it would prove neither the existence of the divine[7] nor that you are its spokesperson. It would only mean that you know something that I don't. Given enough time, I'd figure it out."

Jana raised her brows. "That's quite a neat claim; it can never be proven false. No matter how inadequate your explanation, you can always say, 'But one day I'll figure it out.' That's a statement of faith, not a demonstrable truth."

The Prophet shook his head. "You disappoint me, Jana. You have so much potential within you and yet you are hobbling yourself. I offer you limitless freedom in self-expression, passion, and pleasure in the great depths of imagination—and even beyond." His lower lip protruded slightly. "And yet you persist in splashing childishly in the shallows near the shores of experience."

"You're doing it, again," Jana said.

The man twisted his lip and beetled his brow in irritation. "Doing *what* again?"

"Take some time and figure it out."

"Ha!" the older man scoffed. "I know what you are up to. You are using your feminine wiles and spiraled logic to pretend as if I did something wrong to … to unsettle me and cause confusion. I am far too mature and immune to such primitive tactics, little theist. I am too well acquainted with the female mind to succumb to such weak attempts."

"You can't help it, can you?" Once more, she shook her head.

Despite his claim to the contrary, the Prophet's nostrils flared, and his eyes narrowed. "Jana, this is pure silliness, and you should be ashamed of yourself for such cheap emotional tricks and attempted manipulation. Can't you see that I am far more capable than you to see beyond your droll ploys?"

She raised her brows slightly and sniffed. "Evidently not."

Color rose in the man's face, highlighting the white hair at his temples. He was breathing deeply and rapidly through his nose.

"I really think I should go," Jana insisted quietly. "No matter how much more of my time you take, I could never give you the answer you want. Your philosophy is the **antithesis** of everything I believe in and hold as valuable."

"*Rogebrae*!" The man's voice cracked with the strain of his shout, and he seemed to age before her eyes. "Rogebrae! Attend!"

There was the faint sound of feet, and the door ahead opened. Rogebrae and his assistants aggressively burst into the room and fanned out from the door.

"Yes, All-Knowing One?" Rogebrae asked with a questioning look at Jana and then at the Prophet.

Jana found the irony of his address amusing, and her silver laugh tinkled through the stone chamber.

"Uh, Rogebrae," the flushed Prophet said quietly as he approached the group of attendants, "spare all the titles for the moment. And send the men out. I don't—we don't need them."

The acolyte nodded and motioned to the men. Their concentration vanished immediately, and they left without even a single curious glance. Jana's face fell as she watched them.

Robot people? How awful! Indignation and pity drove her to speak rather than to be pragmatically silent and quickly escape this place. "How can you *do* this to them?"

"What do you mean?" The Prophet's dark look deepened, and Jana feared another outburst, but she pressed on.

"You've used your machine to turn them into mindless slaves!"

The Prophet's face quirked and he made another dismissive gesture.

"Nonsense. The machine is not capable of such a feat. All you are seeing is the result of training and good discipline."

"Why don't I believe you?"

He shrugged. "If the machine could be used as you say, then why have I not taken over the planet already? I've had it for years. No, the truth is that it is of limited value. It merely encourages a willingness that is already present. The subject must be calm and compliant. Strong emotions render it almost useless, and its effects are temporary in any case."

"It's still wrong."

His dark brows rose, and his mouth twisted. "Wrong? How do you determine such a thing? *Every* religion is coercive. The entire premise of theism is the surrender of the will to some supposed greater being—which is, as I have already pointed out, actually the surrender of the will to the religious hierarchy. Even if I was using the machine exactly as you accuse me of doing, how would it be any different from what has been done for centuries in the name of any number of gods?"

"Those that did it were wrong too."

"Oh? And how are *you* any different? I neither know nor care if your particular brand of theism is virulent or insipid. All I am certain of is that it contains a threat—implied or expressed—of punishment, should I assert my will contrary to the will of the imagined deity."

"That isn't the only way to understand the Creator."

"What other way is there?"

"You frame it as reward and punishment. I see it as choice and consequence."

"You're parsing. It's the same thing."

"Only in outward appearance. If you choose to touch a flame, the resulting burn is not a punishment, but a consequence. If a person refuses the Creator's invitation to enter into a relationship with him, the absence of that relationship is not a punishment, but a consequence. You get what you want."

"Enough of these word games," he said, turning to his acolyte. "Take the lieutenant back to Tachon Spaceport, Rogebrae. Let her play with her toys."

Jana deliberately rolled her eyes.

"Get her out of here, Rogebrae!" the Prophet shouted.

"Come, my lady." The man gestured toward the door that led through the long stone hallway. Jana stepped forward without looking back.

The rap of their boots on the stone floor and the swish of Jana's suit were the only sounds until the Prophet loudly cleared his throat behind them. "Wait!" His peremptory shout came to them just as they were about to cross the threshold.

Jana turned slowly and faced him as he approached with a slight scrape of his boots and a faint rustle of his robe.

"What … what was it that I was doing?"

"Why do you want to know?" she asked.

A look of irritation shot across his face, but he controlled it and remained calm. He closed his eyes briefly, took a breath, and then reopened them before speaking. "I want to know because I meant it when I said I wanted your cooperation and valued your goodwill. And while it appears that I shall have little of your cooperation, I still desire your good will—at least, as much of it as you choose to give."

"I see," said Jana. "What you did," she began, "was to insist upon name-calling rather than answering the logic of the argument."

"I was merely using derisive terms to describe how I felt."

"Describing how you feel is not an intelligent argument. Name-calling and derision are almost always tacit admissions that one has run out of ideas."

The Prophet grimaced, and nodded. "Socrates,"[8] he muttered in a barely audible voice. He pursed his lips and looked down, then back up. "You said you could correct me. How would you do it?"

She glanced beyond him before she began. "I would point out the logical errors you have made."

His smile was condescending. "I have made no logical errors, Jana."

"Do you want to hear this or not?"

"Yes, of course," he said, and he clasped his hands behind him. "Please continue."

"Now, you said that you built your religion on what was real—no assumptions and no reliance on secondhand experiences."

The Prophet nodded, once more.

"Then you said the first fundamental truth was 'I alone am the ultimate reality.' How can you be sure? How do you know there is no reality outside of yourself? The fact is, you *don't* know. For a belief system that claims to have no assumptions, it is logically inconsistent that the first tenet is an assumption!

"Then the second fundamental truth makes an even greater assumption: 'Whatever will be is up to me.' This is nothing but a statement of faith; you can't know what will be. You said it yourself: 'All we have is the present.' The past is gone and cannot be changed.

The future is always out of our reach. We possess only the thinnest sliver of time—the moment *now.* It is only a hope that the mind and will can combine to create a desired outcome. There is a lot of future out there over which we have no knowledge whatsoever."

"But you don't know that it couldn't happen," objected the Prophet. "We are limited by ignorance. Should we obtain all knowledge and a perfectly focused will, then the desired outcome wouldn't be just a hope. It would be a certainty."

"You have just described what sounds very much like an omniscient Creator," Jana said. "By your own admission, you have acknowledged the possibility of his existence—something outside of you that is the real, ultimate reality."

The man opened his mouth as if to make an objection but then closed it. His brow creased in concentration before he let it relax into a rueful smile. "Almost you persuade me," he said, "but I must have overlooked something. There is a flaw in *your* logic, although at the moment, I am at a loss to find it. Give me some time. I'll figure it out."

Jana raised a brow. "Let me know when you do."

The Prophet studied the woman thoughtfully.

After a moment, he cleared his throat and motioned for them to continue. They left the room and proceeded down the stone hallway. The Prophet fell in beside Jana, and the sound of their feet on the stone floor echoed in the long, hollow corridor. Jana took a deep breath and noticed that the air seemed somehow stale and dead. *This is,* she thought, *the smell of loneliness.*

"Well, Jana," the Prophet finally said, "you shall be much in my thoughts."

"And you shall be in my prayers," she replied.

His eyebrows rose. "And what will you pray for?"

Jana looked at him. "I shall be praying that you find the wholeness that you seek."

A surprised look crossed his face, and he quickly turned away.

They reached the landing strip in the bright yellow-orange light of midmorning. Wind still whistled across the flat area, ruffled Jana's blonde hair and flapped the Prophet's maroon cloak. A signal had apparently been sent ahead, as the jump jet pilots were already at their stations. At the sight of the group's approach, one of the jets began to spool up.

The three of them stood next to the jump jet as the sound of its engines increased. Rogebrae opened the hatch and stood beside it.

The Prophet extended his hand. Jana took it and, despite the smallness of her hand, she responded with firm pressure.

The man gave her one more intense look. "Pray hard, Jana Maines," he said. "Pray very hard." Then he stepped back and walked to the entrance to the stone hallway, where he stopped, turned, wrapped his cloak tightly against the chill, and waited for the jet to depart.

Jana stood on the small ladder leading into the aircraft and watched him. When he had taken his position, Jana raised her hand. He raised and dropped his in return and then again pulled the cloak about him.

Jana entered the jet. Rogebrae followed her and the hatch closed. She strapped into her seat across the narrow walkway from him. The pilot pushed a lever forward that increased the flow of deuterium into the micro-fusion reactors. The turbines thundered, and the jump jet leaped skyward, turned, and sped eastward toward the rising sun.

The Prophet watched it shrink to a black dot, flash brightly as the sun reflected off a wing, and drop and bank toward the city in the desert far below.

Chapter 11

The pilot of the jump jet invited Jana forward. Although she was emotionally exhausted from her experience with the powerful religious leader, she welcomed the distraction to chat about lighter topics, such as motor thrust profiles and maximum lift capacities. The effort was only partially successful. The pilot conversed easily enough, but the copilot's clipped responses reminded her of her own frightening experience with the Prophet. She hoped his demeanor was simply an act of amazing self-discipline, but she could not shake the chill from her heart that it was not, and it left her feeling despondent.

The morning sun was warming the eastern slopes of the Ghost Range and the intensity of the rays on these angled surfaces created rising bubbles of warm air that rocked and bumped the tiny aircraft on its descent. Jana was feeling slightly queasy by the time they were on final approach to the spaceport.

The pilot noticed her swallowing hard and asked, "Are you all right, Lieutenant Maines?"

"I'm sorry," she confessed. "I think I'm a bit airsick. I'm not quite used to this. We don't have turbulence like this in space."

"Hang on. We're almost there. You'll make it." The pilot flashed an encouraging grin.

Jana managed a smile in return. "A small deed of kindness is never small," her mother had said. *You were right, Mom*, she thought, and fought back the tears.

The jump jet settled gently on the spaceport apron. To her relief, Jana's stomach quickly settled as well.

The crew gave her a thumbs-up, and the hatch was opened. A warm blast of dusty desert air swirled into the cabin.

Rogebrae stood by the entrance. "Farewell, my lady," he said, with a hand extended toward the hatch.

"Before we bid our fond good-byes, Mr. Rogebrae," Jana said as she approached him, "I would be more comfortable verifying that the appropriate credit transfers have been made, and that our departure time is not in dispute." She extended her own hand toward the hatch.

The man smiled humorlessly and hopped down the short ladder, Jana on his heels. They had only started for the port authority office when Herzog and Lowe approached in the tug that whined toward them over the ramp at full speed. The tug screeched to a stop, and the men jumped out and ran toward them.

"Lieutenant!" Lowe shouted.

"Jana!" Harlin called. Her mouth quirked as she noted that he carefully kept the captain between Rogebrae and himself.

"Are you all right, Lieutenant?" the captain asked while eyeing the Prophet's acolyte coldly. The man-in-black's expression remained bland and inscrutable.

"Yes, sir," she replied. "I am unharmed."

Lowe's eyes flicked back and forth between Jana and Rogebrae, seeking subtle clues that would verify or deny the verbal report. Jana appeared to be unhurt, though subdued and thoughtful. The only change in Rogebrae as he studied the acolyte was a subtle lift of his eyebrows as if to say, *I told you so.*

"So, what happened?" Herzog asked.

"I will submit a full report to Captain Lowe," she said coolly, casting a glance at Rogebrae. "The first thing I'd like to confirm is that the captain and I aren't in hock over this delay and that we have a solid proposed time of departure." She ended this with a look at Herzog.

The port authority shot an apprehensive look at Rogebrae and shook his head. "We didn't even try to reschedule a departure time while you were gone, and since the delay was indefinite, I didn't check on the status of the *Europa*'s account."

"All will be in order," Rogebrae said confidently.

Lowe gave Jana a questioning look. She studied Rogebrae for a moment. He seemed completely undisturbed by the captain's skepticism. The gaze he returned to Jana did not waver.

"Shall we walk or ride, Mr. Rogebrae?" Jana asked with a gesture toward the port authority office.

He gave a short laugh. "In this heat? Let's ride."

They climbed aboard the tug, and Jana braced for the jerk as Herzog squealed away from the jump jet and sped over the ramp. Within moments, they were gathered around the port authority's console while Herzog tapped the screen to make the necessary inquiries.

"Well," he said, "you are authorized for departure at your discretion. The *Europa*'s account has been credited to cover any expenses due to this delay plus six more hours. If you get off in less time than that then you'll be making a lot of money." He glanced at Rogebrae, then back at the screen, and shook his head. "Somebody has a lot of pull," he added, "and isn't afraid to use it."

Lowe wiped a hand over his mouth and took a thoughtful breath. "It will take about an hour to get all the systems back online," he thought aloud. "Are you up to it, Lieutenant?"

She nodded. "Yes, Captain Lowe, If you permit me, I will see Mr. Rogebrae back to his jump jet and be back momentarily."

"Very well," the senior officer agreed. "I will be at the ship."

Jana returned her attention to the acolyte and motioned toward the door.

Once outside, the man and woman climbed aboard the tug and Jana eased it in the direction of the jump jet, the hot desert wind in their faces and the yellow-orange Tachon sun on their backs. The tug hummed quietly.

Jana glanced at the man next to her. "Thank you, Mr. Rogebrae," she said.

"If you are thinking of the credits," he replied, "your gratitude is misplaced. I had little to do with it. I am but a conduit and not the source; however, I shall convey your thanks as appropriate."

"Then thank you for that, at least," Jana replied. "By the way, you never did answer my question."

"Your question?" he responded.

"Yes. When you said it wasn't your place to tell me about the Prophet, I asked you to tell me about yourself. I would still like to know." She gave him a reassuring smile and waited for him to reply.

"I see no reason why I should be of any interest to you." His voice carried a scornful edge, and he looked at her askance.

The negativity of his tone took her by surprise, and Jana swallowed down the surge of emotions. She had been tense and on edge ever since the confrontation with the Prophet. Herzog's announcement that she and Captain Lowe had been generously rewarded had lifted her spirits, and it was natural for her to respond to the acolyte with gratitude and kindness. Now her expression of interest was returned with hostility. She looked away, blinking back tears of anger and indignation. Then the image of the copilot returned, and she wondered if Rogebrae himself was as much a victim. Her compassion made her anger more manageable.

"Well," she finally said, staring ahead at the jump jet slowly drawing closer, "I really would like to know about you as a person. Even if you don't want to talk about yourself, I would at least be interested in knowing why you follow the Prophet."

"He pays well," Rogebrae replied flatly.

"But that isn't the entire reason, is it?" she asked.

Rogebrae said nothing for a beat and then replied, "I agree with his teaching."

"Doesn't the weight of that teaching get awfully heavy at times?" she asked.

"What do you mean? He teaches freedom."

"Sort of," agreed Jana as they pulled up to the jet. The pilots saw them, and the turbines began to turn with a low rumble.

Jana stopped the tug, rested both hands on the steering wheel, and turned to Rogebrae. "It's a fine philosophy to have when everything seems to be going your way and you can take all the credit for your success. But suppose you work for something, apply all your will and mind to it, and you are still unsuccessful. You only have yourself to blame, right?"

His returning gaze remained unperturbed.

"You're exhausted. Completely spent. You want to rest. You want to admit that maybe somebody else has let you down, but you can't. You can only blame yourself and spur yourself on to ever-greater effort. That doesn't sound much like freedom to me, Mr. Rogebrae. It sounds like an endless, striving servitude—a heavy weight to carry, indeed."

The man gave a short, mirthless laugh and stood, his hands on his hips, his imposing black mass towering above the tug. "Nevertheless, my lady, it is *my* weight. If it is a burden, then it is the load I carry on the path *I* have chosen."

"Even if you find that it is destroying you?" she asked.

He looked down on her with a half-smile and recited the last lines of the prophecy:

But be strong and brave

Yourself to save.

Then nothing past and nothing to be

Nothing—nothing can destroy thee."

The whine of the jet's turbines climbed higher as they spooled up. Jana rose to her feet, turned and faced the man across the tug.

"Is loneliness a real thing, Mr. Rogebrae?"

"The mind and will are all that count, my lady," he asserted. "Loneliness, and all the other human emotions that occur due to the chemical processes within the **cerebral cortex**, are mere mental abstractions. They don't really exist. They are nothing."

Jana cocked her head and raised her small chin slightly. "Then *nothing* might very well destroy you—and your prophet."

Rogebrae raised his brows, pursed his lips in a half-smile. He regarded the woman briefly and then turned abruptly and went into the jet. The hatch closed, and the pilot saluted her. She returned the salute, climbed aboard the tug, and pulled away from the increasing thunder coming from behind. She didn't look back as the howl increased, rose, and faded westward.

The Two Hundred Million that Almost Got Away

We pen our lifesong every day, each note a thought, deed, or word we say.

And whether angel or demon those notes one day sings, our lives are made of little things.

—*Meditations on the Canon*, Book XX:XIV:XIV

Chapter 1

Jana Maines, the lithe first officer of the interstellar transport *Aegis*, casually reached up to scratch her ear under the short golden strands of her coiffure. Though most of her attention was on the ship's manifest, she remained aware that the middle-aged man behind the dispatcher's counter was observing her.

"Fish eggs?" she asked with a questioning look at the dispatcher who quickly returned his attention to the manifest. She noticed his nametag read, "BO NYLEN, DISP."

"Uh, yes," he replied and cleared his throat. "We're loading up a couple hundred million tilapia eggs raised here on Oceanus. They have been in frozen storage waiting for a ship heading in the right direction to come though."

"Tilapia," Jana murmured. "What type of fish are they, Mr. Nylen?"

The dispatcher ran a hand through his thinning hair, then tapped the computer screen and observed the readout. "Let's see … genus[1] *Tillapiini* … family *Cichlidae* … primarily a freshwater food fish … widely used in aquaculture … they were produced for … um … Blueworld," he answered as he scanned the data. "According to the invoice, the eggs must be kept in **cryogenic** status below 120 Kelvin until final delivery."

"Seems easy enough," the woman remarked. "We just have to keep them cold. I don't have any fish stories, but if I ever need one, I will be able to say I once brought in a couple hundred million tilapia!"

"That would be *quite* the fish story," the dispatcher agreed with an amiable chuckle.

Jana glanced about the small, windowless dispatcher's office. Various memory boards hung from their hooks. An old-style marking board containing a few notes in Nylen's neat print took up one corner of wall space next to the door. The institutional white ceiling and beige walls made the room seem not much more than a tasteful prison cell. The only ambient sound was the whisper of the air conditioning—a distinct luxury on this backwater planet.

"I read the planetary summary on Oceanus before we landed," Jana offered. "It's only a level two on the IFS, but it mentioned some very nice beaches. The report was not very current, but based on your tan, it looks like it was right."

"It is," the dispatcher confirmed with a nod. "The beaches here on Oceanus are superb."

"How far away are they from where we will be staying?"

"We put the crews up at 'the Z'—the Hotel Zephyr. They have a very nice bistro, and the beach is within easy walking distance—just a few kilometers."

"Could I get a map for my datapad?"

"I can do better than that. I spend a lot of my time at the beach, and my shift is just about over. I'd be happy to take you there myself so you wouldn't have to be alone."

"Lawlessness is a problem here?" Her brow creased in concern.

"No, not really. The local company is very good at maintaining the social order—it has to be. This is a frontier world. Since scofflaws and rule breakers threaten everyone's survival, the local company simply won't tolerate them. And, like most frontier worlds, they don't have the money to spend on prisons."

"I see."

The dispatcher cleared his throat. "I was only thinking that it's generally not a good idea for a person to swim alone."

"Thank you for your offer, Mr. Nylen," Jana replied as she tried to think of a polite way to decline. The man seemed pleasant enough, but her previous experience in morale boosting had gone badly and she preferred not to repeat the mistake. "I think I should first ask the captain."

"I understand," he acquiesced with a nod and returned his attention to his work.

Jana studied him with curiosity. He seemed older than the typical, adventurous young man or woman who lacked seniority and who generally staffed the hardscrabble frontier **billets**. She wondered why someone old enough to be in the prime of his career held a position with the pay and status of a novice. "Have you served on any other world?" she asked casually, hoping to discretely solve the mystery.

"Yes," the man replied quietly.

"Where?" she asked. "Perhaps I've been there."

"Tronheim. Bachman III. Dulcet."

"You were stationed on *Dulcet*? That's a dream assignment! Why would you leave the most perfect planet ever for a frontier level two outpost like Oceanus?"

He smiled ruefully. "How much time do you have?"

"I'm sorry," she apologized, noting his embarrassment. "I didn't mean to pry."

"It's all right," he shrugged. "I screwed up, plain and simple. I feel fortunate I ended up here. Oceanus is what Dulcet used to be like, anyway—a long time ago—before all the people and development."

"I'm so sorry," Jana apologized again.

He shook his head. "It's not that bad. I've accepted the situation, and it was for the best. I think of it now as just part of the plan."

"The plan?"

"The ultimate plan, you know," he motioned upward. "Providence."

Jana eyed him with increased interest. "You hold to the **tenets** of the Canon?"

He nodded. "As much of them as I understand—and I have to admit there is a lot I don't."

She smiled. "Any honest person will agree. How long have you been on the Way?"

"Since Dulcet. The experience was painful, but it was what I needed. Looking back, I'm glad that it happened."

Jana nodded and gave a quick smile despite the twinge of her own bruised memories.

The man caught her subtle expression and seemed to sense her own discomfiture. He grinned and his voice took on an understanding tone. "It gets better. Time has a way of changing your perspective. Then it doesn't hurt so bad."

She smiled more easily. "Thanks, Mr. Nylen. That's encouraging—and I could use some encouragement."

He spread his hands. "We all do."

"I—" she started to say, but was interrupted before she could continue.

"Lieutenant Maines!" a nasal male voice sounded from the doorway of the office. She and the dispatcher quickly turned to see another space pilot standing at the entrance, as straight and rigid as his dark, close-clipped hair. His gaze was intense, and his jaw muscles worked so that his temples wriggled as if something just below the surface were attempting to emerge.

"Yes, Captain Fesner?" Jana answered as she straightened from the dispatcher's console.

He raised an accusing finger and took a few slow steps. "You failed to notify me that you had already coordinated replenishment with the fixed base operator."

"I logged it while you were aft with the maintenance crew. Is there a problem with my entry?"

"No," Fesner's voice and hand dropped. "I didn't check the log," he admitted, slightly deflated.

From his seat, the dispatcher grunted quietly and tapped slowly at his computer console.

"However," the captain continued as he approached the desk, "it is considered common courtesy to ensure your superior is kept informed." He paused as he stood before her, his eyes a centimeter lower than hers. "You could have spared me needless, excessive redundancy," he concluded.

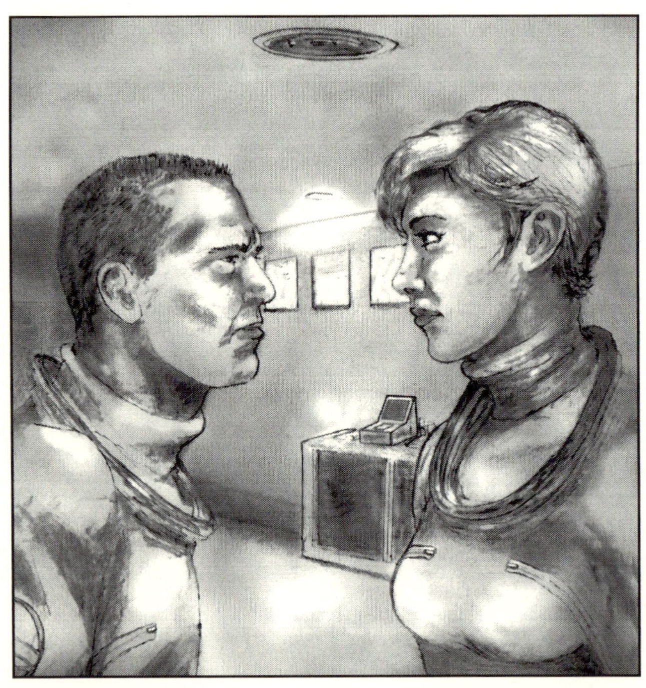

"I am sorry you made an unnecessary call," Jana explained. "Captain Lowe taught that the log should be reviewed before any request or offer for service is made outside the ship."

Fesner snorted and made a dismissive wave of his hand. "That is the minimum effort. I was hoping for more than that. There's too much minimalism these days. We have to strive to maintain a higher standard."

"I will keep that in mind, sir."

"Well," the captain shrugged, "I won't be too hard on you this time. I suppose I do bear some of the blame myself, but I was expecting more of a natural rapport between us—a sort of *instinct* for communication," he flipped his hands back and forth, "that would be more efficient than the more formal procedures." His attempted smile was too toothy to be attractive.

Jana took a breath. "I guess I'm not much of a mind reader."

"Oh, come, come," Fesner snickered and lightly tapped her shoulder. "I'm not expecting you to read my mind. Don't get crazy on me here. I just think that we need to become a bit more familiar with each other. It always takes a bit of time to figure out how a captain skippers his ship, so I don't blame you for not realizing my expectations. We'll just let it go this time and chalk it up as a learning experience."

"I will do my best, sir," Jana promised.

There was another pause. Jana was embarrassed that Captain Fesner had accused her in public of committing an error that was actually his own. His actions reflected poorly on them both. In the relatively brief time they had worked together, she had already found that he could be mercurial in his moods. She was not comfortable initiating the next move, so she said nothing while she waited for him to continue.

"Well, Lieutenant," the captain finally broke the silence, "I was thinking, if you had no other plans, that you and I could get a tour of the place. I hear Port Oceana is quite developed—especially considering it was built entirely within the last century. There are a lot of restaurants and seafood shops and a beautiful coastline. Maybe we could work on our … communication. You ready for a bit of sightseeing? I'll even write it up as local familiarization!" He ended with another toothy grin.

Jana forced a weak smile. Part of her acknowledged that additional time together in a more casual setting might improve their professional relationship, but another part of her bristled at playing his toady. She did not relish the thought of spending her off-duty hours being the potential target of Fesner's moodiness and short temper. She quickly tried to think of a way to avoid that unpleasant possibility and glanced at the dispatcher who continued to stare at his console.

"Well, sir," Jana said, turning back to the captain, "Mr. Nylen has offered to accompany me to the beach. I'm sure he would show us around."

"Oh?" the captain responded flatly.

She hoped that another man's presence would moderate the captain's caustic behavior. She turned to the dispatcher. "Would you be willing to be our tour guide, Mr. Nylen?"

The man looked up at the mention of his name. "Certainly," he nodded. "As I just told the lieutenant, my shift will be over soon. We could spend what's left of the day out there and be back by 1800."

"Would you join us, Captain?" Jana asked as invitingly as she could manage.

The jaw muscles in the captain's temples made another brief escape attempt while his intense gaze alternated back and forth between his junior officer and the dispatcher.

"No," he finally said, shortly. "I don't think so. I was planning something more along the lines of a nice restaurant. If I meet a fish, I want it on my plate—not lurking behind some stalk of seaweed. I don't much care for the beach."

He started to turn away but stopped himself and his eyes flashed back and forth between the pair. "I will be at the hotel, Lieutenant. Check at the desk, since I don't know yet what room I will have. I expect you to be ready tomorrow morning at 0530—and I caution you that I will not be sympathetic if you complain of sunburn or injury from some sea animal. You are supposed to be resting and recuperating for the next flight, not partying and carrying on to the point of exhaustion."

"I'll be sure to get her some protection for sunburn," the dispatcher offered quickly as he got to his feet. "And I will have her back around sunset, so she won't be out too late."

The captain sniffed and raised his chin and his dark eyebrows. "Very well. See that you do," he said with a disparaging look at the dispatcher, who simply grinned and raised a thumb.

Fesner's temples worked again as he shot one more look back and forth between them. He clasped his hands behind his back, made a slight bob of his head, turned on his heel, and left. The door hummed closed behind him.

Nylen leaned across the counter, and then glanced at the door and then back to Jana with a low whistle and a questioning look. "Is he always like that?"

She shrugged. "I really don't know him that well. We were assigned together just prior to this flight."

"I see what you mean about needing encouragement."

She nodded.

"I was a bit surprised when you mentioned going with me to the beach," he said. "I was getting the distinct impression that you were about to refuse."

"Well," Jana cleared her throat, "I did think the captain would be coming with us."

Nylen's face showed disbelief. "You want to spend time with *him*?" He gestured at the doors through which the captain had departed.

"To be honest, no."

He chuckled. "I didn't think so. He's not a nice guy. I am."

"I'll hold you to that, Mr. Nylen."

"You can call me Bo."

"I'll hold you to that, Bo."

He placed his hand over his heart. "Promise," he said.

Chapter 2

Jana returned to the ship and obtained some more casual clothing from the small selection in her tiny stateroom. She then made her way to the Hotel Zephyr, or "the Z," as Bo Nylen had called it. There she checked in and obtained Fesner's room number, but she did not call him for fear he might change his mind about going to the beach. She had convinced herself that his presence was unnecessary and likely to be unpleasant. *Bo is right. I really don't want to spend any more time with him than necessary.*

She tossed her bag onto the bed and took a quick shower before donning a black maillot. She selected a pair of khaki shorts and a loose, white shirt as a swimsuit cover, but her ensemble ran into a problem—she had no appropriate beach shoes. Her available footwear consisted of fabric ship's slippers, a set of heels, and her boots. She made a face while she considered the lack of options, then broke into a smile. *I'll wear the slippers and go shopping!*

She brushed her short, golden hair into place and applied a small amount of waterproof makeup. Then she clipped her identification and credit badge onto the waist of her shorts and left the room to wait for Mr. Nylen on the covered veranda at the front of the hotel just above the street that bustled with activity.

A broken line of shops flanked the street. The open spaces contained makeshift booths and displays of local products that had been laid out on mats under the trees. As she studied the scene, something soft brushed her leg. She started and looked down to see a small, striped cat rub against her.

"Hello, kitty!" she said. The cat looked up, the black pupils in its yellow eyes mere vertical slits in the bright afternoon sunlight. As she watched, it gathered itself and sprang lightly in the relatively weak gravity of Oceanus to the balustrade in front of her. It arched its back and purred as she stroked the soft, gray fur. She moved closer, and the cat placed its forepaws on her chest and rubbed its head against her chin. "My goodness, you're a lovey-dovey!" she laughed and continued to pet the animal.

"I see you made a friend," Bo Nylen's voice announced from the street below. She smiled at the grinning dispatcher, now out of his STC blues and sporting a faded, loose gray shirt, frayed, cut-off dungarees, sandals, and a well-used floppy hat woven from palm leaves. A mesh bag of swim equipment hung over one shoulder.

"Yes, and isn't he a little darling?" Jana replied as the cat climbed onto her arm. She turned and held it to show to Nylen as he came up the veranda's short set of stairs.

He grinned broadly and scratched it behind its ears, which caused the cat to repeatedly extend and retract its claws in enjoyment.

"Ouch!" Jana said with a laugh, and she quickly set the cat back on the balustrade. She was pleased to see that the man continued to be gentle with the animal, and though he didn't notice, she smiled warmly at him.

"I was surprised to see a cat," Jana admitted.

Bo shrugged as he idly stroked the animal. "These terraformed worlds are just mimics of Old Terra. They require a wide selection of flora and fauna to remain self-sustaining—plants, birds, insects—this little fellow is here because he fits into an ecological niche like every other living thing brought to Oceanus." He looked at the cat and stroked it. "You got a job to do like the rest of us, don't you, little fella?" The cat's only response was to push his head against the man's hand.

The faint, deep, thrumming sound of the contra-grav beam came from the direction of the spaceport and diverted their attention. They turned to watch a space transport drop slowly toward the surface. Jana shielded her eyes to get a better view and possibly identify the vessel. There were so many ships in the space trading fleet that it seemed unlikely she would identify it by sight, but she still had a professional curiosity and couldn't help but wonder about the ship and crew.

"That's the *Joy of Candide*," Bo announced. "Almost a megaton of industrial metal, manufactured goods, and **logistical** supplies under Captain Parnell and First Officer Jaxon."

"You have remarkable eyesight, Mr. Nylen," Jana joked as the ship sank below the skyline.

"Not really," he smiled, "unless you mean how well I can read the inbound manifest."

"Anyone else coming in today?"

He shook his head. "Two star freighters in one day is heavy traffic for us, Lieutenant. Our lading and support facilities are going to be pushed to the limit as it is. A third ship would have to park in orbit—and I know how much you rocket jockeys hate doing that."

"There's a lot of pressure on the flight crew to maintain the schedule, and our percentage is reduced if we're late—whether it's our fault or not," Jana explained. "A delay on the ground is bad enough, but spinning in orbit is worse."

"There's a lot of pressure on the ground crews too," the dispatcher countered. "Logistics are difficult on these frontier worlds, and the maintenance types are usually scrambling for spares. Not every spacer seems to appreciate that."

"Well, I appreciate it, Mr. Nylen."

He grinned. "I thought so."

"Speaking of logistics," Jana said, looking at her feet, "could we go shopping for some sandals?" She squinted up in the direction of the orange-yellow Oceanus sun. "And a hat?"

The man nodded and gestured down the street. "I planned to take you to a beach shop to rent some snorkel gear. I think the owner might have a hat or sandals. We also might find a shoe vendor on the way." He motioned toward the market area and then extended his arm. She took it just to be polite, but she was surprised at how much she enjoyed the feeling of having a friendly companion and the sense of security the man provided.

"Good-bye, kitty!" Jana called to the cat, which watched them from the balcony as they moved down the steps from the hotel and into the flow of pedestrian traffic typical of a frontier town. A mixture of farmers, fishermen, craftsmen, and artisans surrounded them, as well as fellow customers all busily engaged in the trade and commerce of locally produced goods. Light, two-wheeled, man-drawn carts seemed to be the most common transportation device for these items, although a heavy transport vehicle from the spaceport occasionally whined and rumbled slowly past on the unpaved street.

While they looked for a seller of footwear, Bo assured her that hot food was safe to eat, so they sampled steaming grilled fish cooked over a smoking fire of coconut husks, as well as deep-fried breadfruit-on-a-stick. They nibbled on their morsels as they made slow progress through the market area, surrounded by the cries of hawkers, the barking of dogs, and the smells of smoke and hot cooking oil.

"Look!" Jana pointed to a large mat laid out in the shade of a tree. Several rows of woven sandals lined the mat. "A pair of those would be perfect for the day." Bo nodded, and they moved closer.

A woman sat behind a small booth weaving palm leaves. She could not have been much older than Jana, but her hands were callused from her labor of expertly twisting the long, green, narrow leaves. Her olive-tone face still appeared young, and she looked up at Jana and smiled.

"I would like to purchase a pair of sandals, please," Jana said.

The woman leaned over the counter, eyed Jana's feet, and then grinned and nodded. "I have some—just for you," she said. She rose, moved around the counter, and picked up a pair among the many lined up on the mat. Jana saw she wore a soft mesh sling over her shoulder that held a sleeping infant to her side.

"What a cute baby!" she complimented. "What is the name?"

The woman smiled, and she set the sandals on the counter so she could pull the sling forward to give Jana a better view of the sleeping child. "His name is Teek. He's a good baby."

Jana peered into the sling. "Can I touch him?"

The young mother pulled the mesh opening of the sling wider, and Jana carefully stroked the baby's dark hair. "I haven't held one in years."

"Would you like to hold him?" the woman asked.

"Yes, but wouldn't I wake him?"

The woman's answer was to lift the child from the sling and carefully lay him on Jana's shoulder. Jana held him and cradled his head with practiced ease from taking care of her younger brother and the neighbor children, and she pressed her nose against the back of the tiny head to catch his baby scent. "He *is* a good baby!" she said.

The woman's dark green eyes moved to the dispatcher. "Mista Bo, is this your new lady?"

Bo shot Jana a look of embarrassment, laughed, and shook his head. "No, Tareze. She's one of the star pilots. I'm just showing her around."

The woman's dark brows rose, and her eyes moved back to Jana. "You're a *sky toucher*?"

Jana nodded as she gently rocked the child on her shoulder.

Tareze gave Jana a studied look as she held the child, and her brows contracted. "You don't want to be a sky toucher," she declared.

Jana glanced up at her and then at the dispatcher before her eyes went back to the baby on her shoulder. "I enjoy my job," she insisted. "It's a challenge and I am proud of what I do."

The other woman's head shook and she tapped the center of her forehead. "I have the third eye. I know."

It was Jana's turn to raise her eyebrows.

The woman looked at Bo and then back to Jana. "Mista Bo is a nice fella. There are lots of nice fellas here," she said with a sweeping motion of her arm. "You could take your pick."

"Well, that's nice to know. But all I really wanted right now was a pair of sandals."

The woman shrugged and motioned to the pair on the counter.

"They're cute!" Jana exclaimed as she looked at them and then carefully handed the child back to its mother. "Thank you for letting me hold him," she said. She then held up the shoes and ran her finger over the intricately woven design on the instep. "Look—a star! Like me! Star pilot!"

The woman shook her head. "No. That's a star*fish!*"

"It's still very pretty," Jana said. She knelt and pulled off her cloth ship slipper, slid the sandal on, and tied the two strings that ran from the heel around her ankle. "And it's a perfect fit! I like them." She pulled her STC credit chit from her waist and held it out to the woman, who frowned and looked at Bo, then shook her head.

"I'm sorry, star lady. I only take real coin. The price is three."

Jana looked at Bo in embarrassment. "I'm sorry, Bo. I just assumed a credit chit would be good here."

"It's good at the major establishments," he shrugged and dug into the pocket of his dungarees, "but a lot of the small operators only use the local coinage." He pulled out a small handful of metal disks and gave the woman the asking price. She deposited them in a pocket on the baby sling and smiled.

"Thanks, Bo. I'll pay you back when we return to the hotel."

"Don't worry about it."

"I said I'll pay," she insisted as she fastened on the second sandal.

"Fine."

"Thank you, Tareze," Jana said to the woman as she stood and tucked her space slippers into Bo's equipment bag.

The woman nodded and smiled in return, and then she touched her forehead and motioned to Bo. "Think about it. Sky touching is not what you want." She motioned downward to the child on her shoulder. "Maybe someday Teek will touch the sky."

"Yes," Jana agreed with a nod and a final, gentle stroke on the infant's head. "When he is old enough, Mister Bo—or anyone at the spaceport—will be able to help him. He's such a beautiful baby," she added wistfully.

The woman smiled warmly and patted her baby as they took their leave. Jana looked down to admire the new shoes on her feet as they walked away. "That was interesting," she commented. "Is everyone so free with career and marriage advice around here?"

Bo laughed. "That's the way it is on the frontier. Growing a family is often the first crop."

"I'm almost afraid what will happen when I ask about buying a hat!" she said, and Bo laughed.

"Maybe we just ought to head for the beach," he suggested, eyeing the sun. "I'm sure the surf shop has hats, and the old guy there won't give you as much grief."

Jana nodded, and they left the relatively congested market area near the hotel and followed a palm-lined white coral track. She found herself feeling more and more relaxed. Bo Nylen was more like a genial uncle than an STC dispatcher. His easy manners were a very pleasant contrast to the harsh conduct of her acerbic captain. The yellow sun of Oceanus shone brightly overhead between the palms, and the sea breeze was cool and refreshing. She inhaled deeply and caught the salty tang.

"Mmm," she murmured. "I love the smell of the sea. It makes me think of faraway and mysterious places."

"The sea is mysterious, all right," Bo nodded in agreement. "So many things are predictable about it—like the tides—and then a storm that you never see forms a thousand kilometers away and changes everything. Just when you think you've got it figured out, it does the unexpected."

"Sounds like life," Jana remarked.

He looked at her. "Yes, the sea is a good metaphor for life. All we see is the surface, but all of the important stuff is hidden in the depths. You just never know what will happen next. All you can do is trust that all things work together for good."

"That's hard to do, sometimes. How do you deal with doubt?" She gave him a questioning look.

"I put thoughts like that aside."

"I usually find that difficult," the woman admitted.

Her companion's brow wrinkled in concern. "Doubt is the opposite of faith—the first step to disbelief."

"My father said, 'It's all right to question your faith—as long as you also question your doubts.'"

Bo frowned. "No disrespect to your father, but I don't see how encouraging doubt is beneficial. When you listen to your doubts, your mind becomes like a wave moving back and forth. It never settles. No, you have to simply say, 'This is what I believe,' and stick with it."

"But does that really work? How long have you been able to deal with your doubts that way?"

"Since Dulcet, when I hit bottom."

"What happened?"

He glanced at the stately palms arching above them into the blue sky mottled with scattered, puffy cumulus clouds that were forming over the coastline. "I was sitting on a great career. But despite all the credits I was racking up, it seemed meaningless. To try to fill that sense of emptiness, I let my life become a nonstop party. Being stationed on Dulcet made the party pretty big. I lost control—and I almost lost everything else. But thanks to the kindness and understanding of one of my supervisors—and what I now believe to be the hand of Providence—I came to the realization that I was wasting my life. By grace, I ended up here and not on the street. The experience literally sobered me up. I gave up alcohol and any other substances that distort reality. My days of mindlessly chasing the mirage of pleasure are done."

"What do you do now?"

"Mostly I work on being thankful for each day—for all the little things. Life is quiet here. Not much changes. I like it."

"The contemplative life."

"You could call it that."

The crunch of their footsteps on the coral sand was the only sound for a few moments as they each thought about what had just been said. Bo Nylen at last cleared his throat. "So, what about you? Care to share anything about yourself?"

Jana shrugged and took a breath before she began. "I grew up on the agricultural world of Ceres." She gestured to the sky. "We had to work hard, especially during the planting and harvest seasons, to beat the weather or dodge the fierce summer vortices that often swept through."

"Summer vortices?"

"The arrangement of seas and continents on Ceres creates a weather environment where a summer storm on the plains can contain a violent wind vortex. Only structures made of steel or concrete can withstand them. The storms also contain powerful electrical discharges and hail."

"How does anyone manage to survive there?"

"It isn't that way all the time—just during the spring and early summer. Mostly the weather is quite mild, but we always had to be prepared for the worst. You didn't want to be caught in the open when a weather system moved through. Besides, we needed the rain for the crops. Growing up there, I really didn't think much about it. It seemed perfectly normal to me."

"This sounds like a silly question in light of what you've just told me about vortices and electrical storms, but why did you leave?"

Jana chuckled and then grew serious. "I had everything planned out. I was pledged to be married to a handsome man who I loved deeply and who I thought loved me—and who happened to be the son of one of the most successful farmers on the planet. I was set to live a life where all I had to do was have my babies and take care of them."

"And then he dumped you?" Bo guessed.

"No. I dumped him."

"Oh. I'm sorry—I think. There's *got* to be a story there."

"Yes, a sad and confusing one. I won't bore you with details, but the man didn't really care about me. I found out that he wanted a wife simply to provide cover for his indiscretions—of various kinds. I was young and naïve—but not so naïve that I didn't realize that if he would deceive one person, he would deceive others, including me. I refused to honor the marriage pledge. In our culture, that brought shame to him and his family. He vowed vengeance against us all. The space service was the only way to get away from him and to earn enough credits possibly to protect the ones I loved. My world had fallen apart, and I was hurt and desperate. It was one of the lowest times of my life."

Bo nodded sympathetically and patted the back of her hand, which remained hooked around his arm.

"As you said," she continued, "hitting bottom made me evaluate my priorities, as well. I realized I had been able to fill the emptiness in my own soul with farm work and the love and presence of my family. When they were torn from me, I was forced to deal with the void. I finally understood what my father and mother had been trying to teach me all those years. I found I needed a relationship with the Creator."

"Love is the flower that grows in the soil of pain," the dispatcher recited.

"Poetry?" Jana asked.

"I believe it is, but I don't know from where. I read it a long time ago, and it stuck in my head."

"What does it mean to you?"

He took a breath, and his tanned brow creased under the wide brim of his palm hat. "I think it means that good results come out of difficult circumstances—in fact, the difficult circumstances are absolutely *necessary* in order to obtain the good result. A flower cannot grow without soil—whether it's real dirt or a hydroponic media."

Jana sighed and nodded.

"You must be thinking of something," Bo surmised.

"I'm thinking of a *lot* of things."

"Can I hear about one of those things?"

She looked at him and then at her new sandals before she spoke. "I found a ship once, a derelict. I was so *sure* it was a sign—an answer to my prayers, a gift from Providence to provide a way to secure my family's finances and allow me to resign as soon as my obligated time was up."

"What happened?"

"Nothing. The ship has yet to be claimed. Other than a good report from my captain at that time, I haven't received *anything*. It's almost as if it never happened."

"Somebody will eventually claim it. You'll get your percentage, then."

"Yes, but that could take years! If my father and brother have a bad crop year, they will need those credits right away."

"You still have your pay, right?"

"Yes, but being junior officer doesn't pay nearly as well as being a captain and it's a probationary position, as well. I need good reports from *every* instructor captain I fly with in order to make command grade as soon as possible. A single bad report could push that back a year or more. And more than one bad report could wash me out."

The man nodded and frowned. "I don't know what to say, other than you just have to trust the promises in the Canon that whatever happens is for the best."

"I know," Jana sighed. "Intellectually, I agree, but sometimes my head is one place and my heart is in another."

"Ah! Following your heart is usually the short cut to disaster."

"Yes," she agreed quietly.

After a pause he continued. "Well, I've had plenty of experience with space crews, and in my professional opinion, anyone with your level of motivation has to be doing a fine job," he said with an encouraging smile. "But anyway, at the moment, your duty is to enjoy yourself. Tomorrow you're going to jump into your ship and take some fish eggs to Blueworld. That's a safe cargo. What can go wrong?"

She threw up her hands. "Everything!"

"Besides that."

"Well, nothing."

"There you go," he grinned.

The humor was weak, but Jana felt tremendous relief to have someone with whom to share her concerns. Even though her life situation remained the same, she felt better, and she found herself smiling. She thought of her family at home and breathed a prayer for them, followed by one of thanks for the encouraging and unguarded conversation. *Bo is right. I should have a good time. Tomorrow will have to take care of itself.*

She grinned and then looked up at the orange-yellow sun. "I need that hat."

"The shop is just ahead." Nylen motioned to a shack nestled under the palms and junipers.

It was a tiny store, typical of those on many pioneer worlds, which catered to a small but dedicated clientele. The economy of scale didn't favor such entrepreneurial enterprises, but they survived because their owners had a personal interest in their businesses and had faith that there was at least a chance that, with economic and population growth, commerce would eventually pick up.

The shop's selection wasn't large, but it represented the essentials needed for swimming and other beach activities. Most of the items were local, but a few were expensive manufactured imports. Jana glanced at the walls covered in swim fins, harpoons, and swim masks, and attempted to locate a hat.

"Hey, good looking! Welcome to my shop and to Oceanus!" the dark and grizzled man behind the small counter greeted them.

"Come on, Fram," Nylen pretended to protest. "You know I've been in here before!"

The other man guffawed. "I know—and you ain't the good-looking one, either!" He gestured toward the woman. "I was talking to your spacer *palix*, there."

Jana smiled questioningly. "How did you know I was space crew?"

"Well," the man leaned back and chuckled deeply as he rubbed a nut-brown, paw-like hand over several days' growth of gray stubble. "Seems rather obvious. You've got no tan, your clothes are almost new," he paused and motioned to Nylen, "and you're hanging around with *this* beached jellyfish."

"It does seem rather obvious," Jana agreed with a mischievous smile at her guide, "when you put it that way."

"Hey!" Bo shouted in mock protest.

The shop owner chuckled and leaned forward. "So, are you going to snorkel or scuba?"

"Oh, just snorkel," Jana replied, and she handed him her credit chit.

"What ship you with?" he asked as he examined the chit.

"The *Aegis*," Jana answered, "and I would like a hat, too, please."

The shopkeeper nodded and motioned to a small selection of hats displayed on the far wall. He pursed his lips, made a sucking noise on his tooth, and once Jana had stepped away from the men, he turned and looked at his friend. "Sort of out of your league, don't you think?"

Bo Nylen chuckled and made a good-natured but dismissive wave of his arm. "I'm too old for that sort of thing, you barnacle. I'm just showing her around."

"Too old, huh?" The shopkeeper eyed Bo and made another sucking noise on his tooth. Then he focused on Jana, who was trying on a hat in front of a small mirror at the back of the store, and shook his head. "The day I'm too old for *that* is the day I'm fish bait," he said quietly.

Chapter 3

The cool sea breeze freshened as they neared the coastline and provided relief from the tree-sheltered warmth of the trail. Jana heard the breakers through the palms long before they reached the white dunes.

The ridge of dunes contained enough salt grass to make good footing as they climbed several meters to the crest. A tree had taken root in the dune and provided an island of shade for the pair while they took in the grand view of the shoreline spread out before them.

A half kilometer to the west, the surf pounded a coral reef that arced across the broad bay from north to south. The farthest edges of the bay were dimly visible through the hazy, salty air as low, dark lines on the horizons to the northwest and southwest. The sun to their left sparkled on the blue-green waters. To the north, the towers, cranes, and tall storage buildings of the seaport of Oceana peeked above the ragged tree line. They watched a large seagoing vessel silently make its way from the port, a slow-motion shadow driving into the wind and trailing a glimmering wake. Water foamed off its prow and slowly settled around it. At the shoreline, gulls cried overhead and dipped to the beach as each retreating wave deposited hapless, small sea creatures on the sand. The beach was not desolate; a few homes clustered behind the dunes among the palms and breadfruit trees.

They were in the midst of the visual survey when the loud double thud of a sonic boom pulled their attention overhead. Jana pointed to the silver glint of a craft moving rapidly southward with a deep and powerful rumble that overpowered the hiss of the surf and wind noise in her ears. "What ship is that, Mr. Nylen?" She asked above the noise.

"It's the **hypersonic** air transport," he shouted back. "It makes a run every other day from Boreal Station to Southland Station and back."

"What are they carrying?"

"Active biologics," the dispatcher replied. "The two main research sites are completely sealed, but even so, they are also isolated near the poles to reduce the possibility of local contamination if something got out. They don't work on anything that can survive the cold."

"Genetic research?" she questioned.

He nodded. "We call them the Monster Factories. All the conventional breeding programs are in the temperate or tropical zones—that's where your load of tilapia came from."

Jana nodded and stared thoughtfully at the southern patch of blue sky, where the silver speck had disappeared.

The air transport's rumble faded to the sound of the wind, waves, and screeches of the gulls. It seemed that the waves were moving more slowly[2] than she had remembered from other seascapes that she had seen. Then Jana recalled that the gravity of Oceanus was only 85 percent normal gravity, so waves would move more slowly. Even the birds seemed to soar and dip with greater ease than those she'd seen on other worlds with stronger gravitational fields.

They moved back under the large, spreading breadfruit tree and dropped their equipment bags in the shade.

"Are you sure this beach is open to the public?" Jana asked as she eyed the homes. The few swimmers and walkers along the beach could easily have been the homeowners. As an STC officer, she did not fear the harsh justice of the local legal system, but she dared not create an incident with the locals that would reflect poorly on her performance report.

"Yes," Bo assured her. "The north side is more heavily populated, and there are some restrictions. But this area is open. I come here all the time. The Consortium has little concern with the land. Most of their rules apply to the sea."

"The Consortium is the group of companies involved in fishing, transport, and fish processing?" Jana asked.

"Yes, that's right."

"And those homes?" Jana indicated the scattered houses down the shoreline.

"Probably owned by Consortium execs," Bo surmised. "One of the only things Oceanus has to offer for recreation is the coast, so they are pretty free with it."

Satisfied with his explanation, Jana pulled off her shirt and shorts. They both laid their outer clothing on the white sand between the dark gray roots under the spreading branches of the breadfruit tree and carefully anchored their hats with pieces of driftwood so they wouldn't blow away in the stiff sea breeze. They kept their sandals on at Bo's suggestion to protect their feet from sharp coral and spiny urchins.

"So, Mr. Nylen," Jana asked as they straightened up, "you're the official tour guide. What do we do first?"

He fished in his bag and pulled out a tube of sunscreen. "You'd better put some of this on." He tossed her the tube. "The captain warned you not to get sunburned."

"Don't even remind me of him," Jana said as she caught the tube. "It's been so pleasant being able to forget that he was even on this planet."

She popped the top, squirted a glob into her hand, and began smearing it generously over her shoulders.

"Don't forget your nose and ears," Bo suggested. "They are the first to get it, you know."

"Thanks," she said, and she dabbed her nose and ears with the protective gel.

"The backs of your legs will be exposed when we snorkel," he added.

She nodded and smeared her legs.

"Your back is vulnerable too."

She regarded him a moment, but he simply shrugged. She tossed him the tube and turned around.

He caught it, and while she was turned away from him, grinned as he applied a thick layer of gel over her back and shoulders.

"I think that should do it," he said after a moment.

"Thanks," Jana said. She stepped away and grabbed the mesh bag of snorkel equipment. "Are we ready?"

He touched his ears and nose with sunscreen, and nodded. They left the shade of the tree and started to cross the stretch of white sand littered with shells, coconuts, driftwood, and seaweed.

"I'm going to check out the water," Jana said as she dropped the equipment above the ragged row of sea wrack that marked the waterline. Bo dropped his bag next to hers and followed her into the waves. They waded out until they were about waist deep. The clear water rose and fell about them as each foamy wave rippled by. The sandy bottom was littered with pebbles and many varieties of broken shells. Most were variegated shades of mottled brown and white, although some had faint pink streaks.

"Pretty nice, huh?" Bo grinned.

"This is *very* nice," agreed Jana. She plunged in and made a few vigorous strokes seaward before turning and treading water while she waited for the man. Bo eased forward into a sidestroke and soon was bobbing beside her.

"The bottom shelves about here," he advised when he had wiped the saltwater from his face. "It drops to a depth of about six meters very quickly. The coral starts right around here, as well." He flipped his hand, and a spray of water shot from his fingertips, catching her in the face with a few drops.

An impish sparkle entered Jana's blue eyes, which had taken on a slight sea-green tint. Her short, blonde hair was now dark, wet, and pasted against her head. "Are you trying to start a water fight?" she asked playfully.

The man looked surprised. "Water fight?"

"Yeah," she retorted with a flick of her own fingers that sent a few drops in his direction.

"Whatever gave you that idea?" he asked with a quick motion that sent a fair amount of spray toward her.

"Water in my face," she answered with another, more directed splash in return.

"Like this?" he asked, and his hand swept a well-placed spray that drenched her.

She sputtered and retaliated with a broad sweep that soaked him, then she immediately made several strong strokes back toward shore to be out of range.

"Retreat, huh? Are you surrendering?" Bo shouted after her.

"Just come a little closer and you'll find out!" she shouted back.

"We'll just see!" He sent a powerful spray toward her that fell short as she pulled farther back to shore.

He followed, and soon they were standing in the shallows, splashing each other, and laughing like children.

Though they both scored plenty of direct hits, Bo was stronger, and his efforts soon overwhelmed Jana. She turned away for a moment to shield her face. On impulse, he grabbed her so that he pinned her arms to her waist. "I win!" he shouted.

Jana struggled for a moment, then she stiffened, and her fists clenched. "Let go of me, Mr. Nylen!" Her tone was commanding.

He immediately released her with a laugh.

She spun in a half crouch. Anger distorted her face, and she pointed an accusing finger. "You were out of line, *mister*!"

Bo's smile faded in surprise, and he raised his arms. Water dripped from his elbows. "Hey! I let you go. It was just a game."

Her eyes narrowed. "I'm not so sure."

"I think you're kind of blowing this out of proportion."

"I trusted you, and then you go and act like a jerk—like everyone else does at the first opportunity."

He shook his head, turned, and started wading back to the shore. "You started it," he called back. "I was just playing along. Someone's being a jerk here, all right—and it's not me!" He slogged out of the water and dropped next to his equipment bag. Then he yanked out his fins and snorkel mask. One fin was on before he glanced up and noticed the woman watching him. "You still here?" he asked as he pulled on the second fin.

"I'm sorry, Bo," she said.

He reached for his mask and then looked up, taken aback by the look of remorse on the woman's face. The hellcat of a few moments earlier had become a young girl who bit her lip, hugged herself, and watched him with big, sad eyes.

"Well," he said, and he cleared his throat. "I *was* out of line."

"No, it was *my* fault," Jana said, looking down at the water that rose and fell around her waist. A wave caught her, and she had to shift her feet to keep her balance.

"Why don't we just forget it and do what we came here to do?" Bo asked. He attempted an encouraging smile.

She tried to return it, but her face quickly fell. She looked down and blinked, then she looked up. "Can we talk?"

"Sure." The man motioned to the spot of sand next to him. She waded out of the water, sat, and continued to hug herself.

"Do you want your shirt?" he asked.

She nodded.

"Hold on." He pulled the fins from his feet, trotted to the breadfruit tree, and returned with her shirt.

"Thank you," she said, draped it over her shoulders, and pulled it close.

"So, what happened a few minutes ago?" Bo asked quietly.

Jana shook her head. "I don't know. I think the pressure is getting to me. I unfairly took it out on you."

"Pressure?"

"Yes!" she exclaimed, letting her head drop. She sighed, shook her head, and finally looked up. "Have you any idea how many subsystems are on a star transport?"

"A jillion?" Bo suggested the fanciful number in an attempt to be humorous.

"No! *Two* jillion!" she insisted with a wag of her fingers. "And Captain Fesner expects me to know all of them! He treats me like some kind of machine that should be able to instantly spit out the answer to any question he asks."

"Well, you knew when you signed up that being a star pilot is hard. Fesner just wants to make sure you know what he thinks you need to know."

"But he doesn't!" she insisted. "He asks me stuff that I know *he* doesn't know! It's so unfair!"

"But you're learning, right?"

Her hands gestured repeatedly as she spoke. "Yes, but I have to teach *myself!* He's *not* training me—just keeps asking me a bunch of stupid questions!"

"Well, that might be his style. And anyway, you won't be flying with him that much longer, will you? My understanding is that you spacers rotate crews frequently."

She managed a nod and then covered her face with her hands and buried it in her knees while her shoulders occasionally shook.

"It's all right," Bo said gently as he patted her back, and she slowly leaned against him. He kept patting her shoulders for a few moments, until the shaking stopped, but his hand remained on her shoulder.

She finally raised her head, sniffed, and wiped her nose with the back of her hand. "I'm sorry. That wasn't very professional."

"It was human. I've felt the same way."

She turned to him in surprise.

"Yeah," he nodded. "My last days on Dulcet weren't pretty. I was a wreck. Cried like a baby."

She managed a smile. "That's hard for me to imagine. You seem so sure of yourself."

"I've grown up a bit. And maybe I've just learned how to put on a better show."

"I don't think you're putting on a show," she said. "In fact, you remind me of Captain Lowe. He was a wonderful instructor. I learned so much and he gave me a great report—not like what's-his-name. *Ugh!*"

The man's brows went up, and deep wrinkles formed on his forehead. "Captain Lowe? Captain Tred Lowe?"

"I think there's only one."

"If you got a good report from Captain Lowe," Bo grinned, "then I don't think you have much to worry about."

"What do you mean?"

"Back in my wild and crazy days, I partied with a lot of crews on Dulcet—not with Lowe, of course; he was too formal for that. But all his junior officers complained how tight a ship he ran." He sighed and looked to sea. "I actually thought I was doing them a favor by helping them unwind." He shook his head then turned back to Jana. "If you got a good write-up from Lowe, you ought to do fine. He was as tough as they come. Fesner can't be half as bad."

Jana made a face and shook her head. "Lowe was tough, but fair. Fesner is mean."

"The vetting process to become a captain is very thorough. He must have his reasons."

Jana's head shook. "I don't want to talk about him anymore."

Bo nodded, pulled his hand back, and gestured to the water. "Then let's go snorkel."

Jana nodded and forced a smile. They donned their gear and eased out into the swells.

For the next several hours, they explored the little corner of the bay. Colorful fish darted in formation from their path as they dived and surfaced among the schools. Sometimes they simply floated on the surface, allowing the swells to lift and drop them above the green, gray, and lavender coral branches. Occasionally they would dive down to the cooler depths to the sea floor to watch the surface dance a few meters above them and listen to the thumping rumble of the surf.

After a while, Jana's throat felt raw from breathing the salty air through the snorkel in her mouth. Eventually she stopped using it and simply swam with fins and mask, enjoying the exertion and the view and realizing that soon she would leave—possibly never to see this place again. The life of a star pilot brought many new and fascinating sights, but few of them were repeated.

During their time, Bo had pointed out various species of fish and coral. He'd found horseshoe crabs hiding in the sands of the shallows, narrow silver trumpet fish, and spiny urchins that slowly tumbled along the bottom on their long, dark needles.

"I was hoping to see a sea horse," Jana sighed wistfully as they floated between dives.

"We might find some closer to the reef," Bo suggested.

Jana squinted at the sun dipping toward the western horizon and shook her head. "The reef is too far out. I think we'd better head back."

"You're right," Bo agreed.

They slowly swam to shore. Jana savored the last few moments in the warm sea, the sounds of the surf, and the smell of the kelp, now coming toward them as the day sea breeze became an evening land breeze.

They removed their flippers in the shallows so that they could more easily wade through the waves that now broke a few meters higher on the shore with the incoming tide. They reached their sandals, put them on after rinsing the sand from them in the surf, and returned to the tree to pack their gear into the mesh equipment bags.

"It's been a wonderful afternoon, Bo," Jana said as they put their outer clothes on and organized their equipment for the walk back.

"Yes, I've enjoyed myself thoroughly," he agreed, then he leaned back on his heels and studied the beach through narrowed lids. "I wish—" he started to say, but stopped himself.

"You wish what, Bo?"

"I wish there was some way to hold on to a moment. Memories fade, and sometimes you wonder if a thing really happened." He looked up. "Does that happen to you?"

She nodded. "Sometimes. But I'm glad when some of the memories fade—the bad ones, anyway. A keepsake can help you hold on to the pleasant ones, though."

"Do you have anything?"

She looked at her equipment bag and shook her head.

"I have an idea," Bo said suddenly.

She gave him a questioning look. He rose, stood next to the tree, and pointed to a distinctive pattern on the smooth bark. "Put your hand right there."

She stood uncertainly and put her hand on the tree. "Now what?" she asked and smiled.

"That's it. You can drop your hand."

He stepped forward and placed his hand over the pattern. "Whenever I come back to the beach, all I have to do is put my hand on this spot, and I will touch your memory."

"That's sweet, Bo."

"Thanks," he said quietly and he stared at his hand.

Chapter 4

Jana and Bo walked with the setting sun to their backs. The bright evening star of Oceanus IV hung overhead in the darkening sky. Low in the east, a buildup of towering cumulus clouds flickered with internal lightning. At this low latitude and in the presence of so much available moisture, evening thunderstorms were common. From this distance, however, the only effect the lightning had on the two walkers was to alert them to the clouds' presence.

"What a light show!" Jana commented as she observed the distant blue flashes. "And look!" she exclaimed, pointing higher up to a brilliant blue-white streak that shot across the maroon eastern sky and briefly left a glowing trail of faint yellow-green. "A falling star! You get to make a wish!"

"I already did," Bo chuckled.

"What did you wish for?"

He studied the distant sparks with a shrug. "Just something impossible."

Jana's mind tumbled in a multitude of thoughts. His behavior had subtly telegraphed that he was attracted to her. He had been very nice, and she really liked him. Academically, she knew that a romance was out of the question, but she couldn't help feeling a certain satisfaction that someone of his quality had found her desirable. She felt safe with him and able to let down her emotional guard more than she had in a long while. But at the same time, she didn't want to hurt his feelings.

Of course, she might be making more of this than she should. He had just hinted that he knew anything more than a casual relationship was impossible. By the next week, she would probably be forgotten. On the other hand, he had said at the tree that he wanted to remember her. Being overly nice to him might make it worse. But she did enjoy his company, and he had done nothing to deserve anything other than kindness from her in return. She felt badly that she had over-reacted at the beach, and was loath prematurely to give up their time together. She realized she needed some time to sort out her feelings.

"What did *you* wish for?" his voice interrupted her thoughts.

"I wished for a quiet, pleasant evening with a friend."

"That's not impossible, is it?"

She shook her head and smiled. "No, it's very possible."

He laughed, and for a moment, they walked in the silence of their thoughts.

Soon Jana lifted her gaze to the darkened sky, now liberally sprinkled with stars. "On some worlds," she said, "the people imagine pictures, called *constellations*, in the sky." She turned to the man. "Do you know of any such constellations here on Oceanus?"

He shook his upturned head. "I don't know of any sky pictures, and I don't recall anyone mentioning them, either."

"Well then, let's discover some!" Jana grinned and scanned the sky for an interesting pattern.

"I see a triangle," offered Bo.

"Which triangle were you thinking of?"

"That bright little one over there," he said and pointed.

"Why, that *is* a distinctive pattern," Jana admitted. "It is a perfect equilateral—and all about magnitude three brightness. And look! One star is a bit red, another slightly blue, and I see green in the third.

Those are the three primary colors. Now we have to give it a name. We could call it Bo's Triangle."

"How about The Celestial Triangle of Color?" Bo suggested.

"Well, since it is a constellation, the word *celestial* may be redundant," Jana commented. "Let's just call it The Triangle of Color."

"I like that," Bo said. "What do you see?"

"My goodness! There are so many to choose from," she replied, her eyes roaming back and forth. "But I will show you my favorite." She turned her body toward the man, placed her left hand on his shoulder, and leaned her head close to his while she pointed with her right. "See that bright red star?"

He nodded.

"That's the fiery eye of a dragon. And those two dimmer stars are his nostrils. Below them is a jagged line of stars that are his huge, ugly fangs. Behind those stars, you can see that kind of dark area where his leathery wings would be. And then his bumpy, grotesque, scaly body kind of curls to a pointed tail of those faint little stars up there." By the time she finished pointing, her finger had traveled halfway across the sky.

"What are you going to call it?" Bo asked.

"Bo."

"Oh, quit it!" he exclaimed. "You were not!"

Her laugh tinkled through the night above the peeping sounds of the tiny frogs and the quiet sighing of the breeze in the palm trees around them. "You're right," she admitted. "I was going to call it The Great Dragon of Oceanus."

"That's much better," Bo acknowledged, although what concerned him more was that she had removed her hand when he had protested, and now he missed the warm pressure of her touch. "What's another one?" he asked.

"I suppose we really better get back to the hotel," Jana demurred with a sigh. "It is already past sunset."

"We're almost there."

"And I'm getting a little cold." Jana crossed her arms and rubbed them a few times.

"All right. We'd better get going then."

They walked without speaking their thoughts. After a moment, Jana began quietly to hum.

"What song is that?" Bo asked.

"It's an old song," she replied. "It's called 'Everyday Miracles.'"

"I'd like to hear it. Would you sing it for me?" he asked.

She nodded, cleared her throat, and her **mezzo-soprano** voice rose quietly above the sound of the evening peepers:

Every day
As we make our way
Through this maze of life with its twists and turnings,
We experience many gifts from God.
Some things that we know
And some things to be learning.

Everyday miracles.
Look beyond the commonness that just can't quite disguise it.
Everyday miracles.
They're really all around if we just would recognize it!

The way an eagle glides,

Or a reptile slides,
Or the tiny ships that float upon the mighty ocean.
And the gift of love—
A glimpse of heaven above,
The wondrous and amazing way it puts our hearts in motion!

Everyday miracles.
Look beyond the commonness that just can't quite disguise it.
Everyday miracles.
They're really all around if we just would recognize it!

Oh! We look for signs and wonders
And greatness to inspire.
And I guess it's only natural that we do.
But God is in the little things—
Not just the storm and fire.
The still, small, quiet voice that daily
Calls to me and you.

Everyday miracles.
Look beyond the commonness that just can't quite disguise it.
Everyday miracles.
They're really all around if we just would recognize it!

The heavens declare the glory of God!

Her voice faded into the night sounds, and both of them found themselves looking upward at the star-spangled sky, still visible despite the now nearby lights of the hotel and the obstruction of the palms that arched overhead.

"That was a beautiful song," Bo said as he looked up. "'The heavens declare the glory of God.' Thank you."

"You're welcome," Jana replied as they both dropped their gaze and turned back toward the hotel. They soon topped the steps of the veranda.

"Oh, look!" Jana exclaimed. "Our little friend is waiting for us!" The striped tiger cat paced the railing, turning and purring in anticipation as they approached. "Who owns it, and what is its name?" she wondered aloud as she stroked the cat's head.

"I'm not sure, but I've seen it around. He's friendly and seems quite healthy—someone must be taking care of him," Bo observed. "But that doesn't mean you can't give him a name."

"Hmm, how about Aegis?"

"Ah! For the ship, right?"

"Yes. But *aegis* also means something like, *protection*, or *shield*, in an ancient Terran language," she explained as she felt the cat's short, smooth fur, "and this little guy protects us."

"Protects us? Oh, he's a fierce watch cat, all right!" the man teased.

"No, silly! I mean he protects us from vermin, like mice. The ecological niche, remember?"

"Oh, of course," Bo nodded and grinned.

"Would you make sure that nothing bad happens to him?"

"Well, I'll do what I can," the man promised. "If he ever looks mistreated, I'm sure I could make him the station mascot."

"That would be so nice. Thank you, Bo!" she said, and she gave him a quick hug. But just as he started to respond, Jana cleared her throat and stepped back. They faced each other for a moment. Then Jana exclaimed, "Oh, no!"

"What's wrong?" Bo asked with concern.

Jana pulled the snorkel bag from her shoulder and made a face. "I forgot to return my rented equipment!"

Bo's look shifted from concern to relief. "Don't worry about that. I'll take it back for you."

"Well, thanks, but I feel responsible—"

"Don't worry," he insisted, taking the bag. "I know the old guy, and it won't be any problem. I won't even charge you much."

"Oh?" she asked with raised brows. "And what will you charge?"

He grinned. "You have to have dinner with me here at the bistro."

She smiled and crossed her arms. "I don't know, Mr. Nylen. This sounds like extortion."

"It is," he admitted.

"I suppose I have no choice."

"You don't."

"Then I guess you've got me right where you want me."

He gave her a sideways look and grinned broadly. "Not quite."

She pretended to give him a scolding look but then relaxed, and the smile quickly returned.

"Neither the snorkel shop nor my apartment are that far," Bo said. His thumbs were hooked under the bags' shoulder straps. "See you in the bistro in a half hour."

"But Bo, I can't get ready that fast. I'm a mess!"

"Really? I hadn't noticed."

"I need some time to clean up. My hair feels like straw." She ran a hand through the salt-encrusted strands. "And I smell of seaweed. I really need some time to soak—and time to dress up."

"How long will that take?"

She shrugged. "An hour?"

"I'll be back in an hour," he grinned. Then, burdened by the two bags over his shoulders, he turned and disappeared into the darkness toward the surf shop.

Jana watched him depart, then she smiled to herself and turned slowly to go into the hotel. She was tired but at the same time refreshed from the day's activities. She planned to have a nice, long, bubbly, scented bath and then take a little extra time to make herself presentable. If she was going to be remembered, she was determined to make the memory as nice as possible.

Chapter 5

Jana entered the hotel through the large, transparent sliding doors into the arching, spacious foyer decoratively filled with potted palms and tropical flowers spaced about the tiled floor. She looked forward to the long soak in the tub, a quiet dinner, and continued pleasant conversation with her new friend. He was so nice, and she wondered why he wasn't married. Speculations tumbled through her mind, and she decided to try to discreetly find out from him at dinner. *This is going to be fun!*

"Lieutenant!"

Captain Fesner's nasal voice broke into her pleasant thoughts. She looked up to see him sitting in his dress whites on a small bench by a palmetto a few meters away. He rose and slowly crossed the distance as he critically inspected her. "That's quite a get-up for an STC officer, Maines."

"I was at the beach, sir."

"I know. It was just an observation. There's no need to be so defensive."

She took a breath and tried to smile even though she fumed at his remark. "You wanted something, sir?"

"Yeah," he nodded. He motioned with his hand toward the bench. "Sit down. We need to talk."

Jana took another deep breath and sat stiffly at the far end of the bench. She placed her hands on her lap while the man seated himself at the other end. He turned sideways, crossed his legs, and hooked his right arm over the back of the bench, intertwining his stubby fingers as he studied her. She waited, outwardly maintaining an impassive façade, while inwardly she was impatient and apprehensive of the criticism that she was sure to come.

"Will this take long, sir?" she finally asked with forced politeness. *Why did I have to run into him?*

"You were going somewhere?"

"I need to use the head."

"Oh. I thought you might be planning to continue your escapades with that dirtballer." He nodded his head toward the transparent doors.

"Actually, I was planning to have *dinner* with Mr. Nylen."

He shook his head. "Not a good idea, Lieutenant."

"Why not?"

He shrugged. "I did a little research in the personnel file of Mr. Bo Nylen. He's had quite an interesting history—not a very good one, I'm afraid."

"He told me about some of his difficulties in the past, sir."

"*Difficulties?* Dereliction of duty, absent without leave, malingering, public intoxication—these aren't difficulties, they are serious infractions indicative of dangerous character flaws." He shook his head. "He should have been canned a long time ago."

"People change, sir."

Fesner snorted. "A tiger doesn't change its spots, Lieutenant. You spent an entire afternoon with a scoundrel and apparently did not realize it. That calls into question your ability to judge character—a vital skill in the command role. I'm also not so sure that being seen with him reflects well on the space service."

"He is a member of the STC," she countered, letting the misstated metaphor pass. "As far as we know, his work record here at Port Oceana has been exemplary."

Fesner raised a finger. "Exactly. *As far as we know.*" He looked away and then back at her. "Everyone is hiding *something*, Lieutenant. A good captain must be able to peel away the masks."

Jana shifted uncomfortably.

"I can tell, for example," he continued, "that you'd rather not be sitting here talking to me."

She cleared her throat. "No, sir, I wouldn't. I really *do* have to use the head."

"Oh, that's right. Well, just remember, Lieutenant, my job is to evaluate your fitness for command—not just your piloting skills. Your conduct, including the people with whom you choose to associate, is a factor in that evaluation."

She stood. "Is that all, sir?"

He got to his feet, and his eyes narrowed slightly. "One more thing. You received excellent ratings from your previous instructors. Based on your behavior today, I wonder how much those ratings were possibly influenced by you batting your eyes and shaking your derriere. Just so you know—my evaluation will not be influenced by anything like *that*."

Her nostrils flared, and her blue eyes blazed as they met his steely, gray gaze without a single blink. *I cannot believe this!* Despite the roiling of her thoughts, she managed to keep her voice level. "Actually, sir, it has never occurred to me to shake my derriere in front of you."

His brows shot up and he sniffed. "Good." He made a crooked smile that faded to a frown as she walked past him and left.

Meanwhile, Bo Nylen returned the snorkel equipment. Then he walked quickly to his apartment, where he showered and changed into casual eveningwear, consisting of dark slacks, a light yellow shirt, and fabric deck shoes. This took far less time than the hour Jana had asked for to prepare. He was back at "the "Z" and in the bistro a half hour early.

The room held about a dozen tables, several of which were unoccupied. He took a seat at an empty side table, leaned forward on his elbows, clasped his hands, and glanced idly around the room as he waited. Although flight crews were usually put up at the Zephyr, they constituted only a small fraction of the hotel's business. Local commerce and trade drove the economies of the vast majority of the colonized worlds, and the mechanism to meet the basic human needs for food, clothing, and shelter formed their cores. Successful worlds, such as Oceanus, more than met those demands, and consequently, endeavors in science, art, and entertainment became viable occupations.

Bo didn't recognize all of the men and women in the room this evening, but his role as dispatcher had given him a passing familiarity with many of the local officials and business leaders. He recognized at least one fishing magnate, a lawyer, a ship builder, and an engineer. He smiled in satisfaction at the wide variety of successful businesses represented and felt both proud and grateful at the important role he played in maintaining the planet's economic system. One of the executives caught his eye, and Bo felt gratified that the other man smiled and nodded in recognition of him. Bo returned the smile, happily content with his place in the society of Oceanus, and yet acutely sensitive to the near loss of his career on Dulcet. *What an ingrate I was!*

He noted, too, that reasonably attractive women accompanied most of the men in the room. He grinned in anticipation. Jana was sure to turn heads, and *he* would be the lucky guy sitting next to her!

Settle down, Bo! You are just going to have dinner. She will be gone tomorrow. You are casual friends—if even that. But his mental admonitions were useless. His original offer to show Jana around had been a simple act of kindness, and her appearance had created no particular effect on him at the time. She was just another in the long string of pretty faces that he had worked with over the years.

But something had happened during their time together—something he was both reluctant to admit or deny. Passions had stirred that he'd thought long dead, and it troubled him even as it excited him. *Stop thinking like an old fool! You are going to embarrass yourself!* While part of his mind warned him to be cautious, another part answered, *So what?*

A server inquired as to his wishes. Bo explained that he was waiting for someone and simply took a glass of water.

Minutes later, he was toying with the near-empty glass when a figure approached his table. Nylen looked up and recognized the dark, clipped crew cut and diminutive stature of the captain of the *Aegis*. He half-rose to extend his hand, but the officer waved him back down, so Bo let his hand become a gesture to sit—which the captain was already in the process of doing.

"Captain Fesner," Bo said and greeted him with a smile.

The newcomer returned a quick smile and glanced around the room. He clasped and unclasped his hands a few times. "Where's my lieutenant?" he finally asked.

"In her room, I believe," Bo replied.

"Planning on having dinner?"

"Yes. I'm expecting her in about a half hour."

A look of irritation shot across Fesner's face, but then he mellowed. "Can I get you a drink?"

"I don't really care for anything, thank you," Bo declined politely.

"Oh, don't be that way," the captain insisted with a dismissive wave of his hand. "I'm going to get you something." He straightened in his chair and turned to look across the room. "Waiter! We need some service here!" he called loudly. Bo inwardly cringed as several of the business figures cast disapproving glances toward their table.

The server approached, and Fesner adopted a thoughtful look. "I'll take a rum swizzle. And my friend here will have the same."

"Very good, sir," the waiter nodded and left.

"I understand that rum is a local product. You must be pretty familiar with it."

"I told you I'm not interested in drinking," Bo repeated with notably decreased humor.

"Oh, it will relax you," the captain insisted with a toothy grin. "You seem tense. Didn't things go well today?"

"Things went very well."

Fesner's heavy brows went up, and he seemed surprised. "Well. Good. I'm very glad to hear that."

"I'm sure you are," the dispatcher agreed with little enthusiasm.

They sat in uncomfortable silence. Their drinks arrived, and Fesner wagged his finger vigorously. "Come on, buddy, drink up!" He grabbed his tumbler and took a stiff swallow, exhaled, and nodded thoughtfully.

Bo's rum remained untouched.

"I'm going to take it as a personal insult if you refuse that drink, my friend," Fesner warned.

"I don't use alcohol, sir."

"Really?" The captain took a sip and set his glass down. "That's not what your personnel file says."

Nylen's eyes narrowed, and his face flushed. "What were you doing in my personnel file?"

Fesner spread his hands. "I'm authorized. If my first officer chooses to go gallivanting off with someone, it's my responsibility as captain to know who the gallivantee is. The safety and fitness of my crew are of utmost importance to me, Mr. Nylen. I don't take my duties lightly—as you have done."

"That was a long time ago."

"Yeah? Well maybe you just learned to cover your tracks a bit better."

Bo's fists briefly worked under the table. He closed his eyes and took a deep breath. "My work record speaks for itself."

Fesner's brows went up. "Paper trails are notoriously inaccurate. Anyone who trusts them completely is a fool."

"I don't mean to be rude, Captain, but you are being *very* rude," Bo returned.

"No." Fesner made a face and shook his head. "I'm just speaking what we both know is the truth." He paused and took another sip. "And the truth hurts, doesn't it?"

Bo said nothing but just stared at the rum.

"It'll relax you," Fesner urged.

The dispatcher looked away. "There's an empty table, Captain," he indicated with a flip of his hand. He slid the glass toward the other man. "And take your friend with you."

At that moment, another couple entered the dining area and took the table.

Fesner shrugged. "I'm not going anywhere," he said, and he slid the drink back.

Bo wiped his hand over his face, crossed his arms and legs, and stared at a distant wall with a hard and angry expression. He continued to avoid the captain's gaze as they sat in stony silence for several minutes.

"So, how was she?" the captain finally asked.

Bo's head shot toward Fesner, and he frowned. "What are you talking about?"

Fesner rolled his eyes and shrugged deeply. "A lonely old guy like you with a comely young lady on a deserted beach—I think you know what I mean."

"You are disgusting! I can't believe you would speak so disrespectfully about your own first officer." Bo shook his head. "This is unreal."

Fesner broke into a guffaw, which turned into a hacking laugh. "Don't be such a nitwit!" he finally managed to say. "Did you think I was *serious*?" Once more, he submitted to the hacking laugh.

"I fail to see any humor here, Captain."

"Well," the other man continued as he wiped his eyes with the back of his hand, "the idea that Lieutenant Maines would have *anything* to do with you is laughable enough. But to think that you thought that I thought she would actually—" he interrupted himself to chortle. "That's beyond ridiculous—especially with *her* reputation!"

"Her reputation?" Bo asked flatly.

Fesner grinned, gave another shrug, and flipped his hands. "She's an ice queen."

"I don't know what that means. And it doesn't matter. What I do know is that she was a model of decorum. The space service is fortunate to have her. You insult yourself to make such crude jokes."

Fesner lifted his hands. "There's always a first time. I was just checking to see if what turns her on is a pathetic loser."

Bo's chair skittered back and he was on his feet, his face red and angry as he leaned over the table and glared at Fesner, who remained seated. "Insult *me* all day long—I don't care," he hissed. "But I have *had* it with the way you talk about the lieutenant! Keep it up and I will pound that smirk off your ugly face!"

"Do it!" Fesner urged quietly, and he let his eyes roam meaningfully about the room toward several upturned heads. "Plant one on me. Go ahead!"

Nylen shook with helpless rage. He had made a scene by making an empty threat on an angry impulse. He didn't dare strike the captain. To do so would seriously jeopardize his position. Fesner could goad him with impunity, and they both knew it.

"You're not worth it," Bo finally managed to say. He straightened and recovered his chair. He sat down and closed his eyes while his chest heaved.

"Sad," Fesner said.

Bo opened his eyes to mere slits. "You're the Devil!" he growled.

Fesner's brows went up again. "Was that an insult?"

"Crawl back into your stinking hole, you lying piece of filth!"

"Lying? No. I may be a piece of filth, but I'm not lying."

"You're lying now."

Fesner shook his head. "You've totally misread me. I was trying to spare you."

"Why am I listening to you? Spare me? You've done nothing but lie about Lieutenant Maines and insult us both. If this is how you spare someone, I wonder what it would be like to be on your bad side."

Fesner sat back, crossed his arms, and shook his head. "All I did was point out the truth. Your work history is far from perfect. In fact, it's abysmal, and it's only by some fluke that you weren't canned. Everyone but you knows that Maines is an outrageous flirt and that she is playing you for a fool. You are her *entertainment,* I guess. If you don't mind being the day's jape, then who am I to interfere?"

"By the time she comes down, I expect you to have slithered out of here."

"She's not coming down."

"Liar."

"Well, I guess we'll just see, won't we?"

The tense, uncomfortable minutes crept by as Fesner sat, sipped his drink, and smirked. Bo fidgeted and frequently looked anxiously at his thumbnail chronometer and then toward the entrance.

The appointed time came and went. Bo was crestfallen. "I was sure she would come," he mumbled with a furrowed brow.

"Tried to tell you, chum."

"Don't call me that, fiend!"

Fesner threw up his hands and shook his head.

Bo brightened and stood up. "I'll go to her room. Maybe something has happened."

Fesner jumped to his feet. "There will be *no* harassment of my crew, mister!"

Bo's face fell, and he slumped back into his chair. He placed his elbows on the table and held his head in his hands.

Fesner sat and slid the still-untouched glass of rum so it rested between the other man's elbows. "You're *tense*."

Bo straightened and glared at the captain, who gestured to the drink with his hand.

Bo looked at it and then, very deliberately, bent over the glass and expectorated a glob of frothy spittle into the drink. He straightened and resumed his glare.

Fesner shook his head. "That has to be one of the most crude and disgusting displays of boorishness I have ever seen, Nylen. Congratulations on being the worst-mannered employee in the entire STC."

"I believe," Bo growled quietly, "that title is held by another at this table."

Fesner's eyes narrowed. "Your ridiculous performance doesn't convince me, Nylen. You haven't given up alcohol—you've been staring at that drink far too much for that. Like they say, 'Once an addict, always an addict.'"

"You're the one who's drinking."

"Oh, this?" the captain held up his half-empty glass. "I drink in moderation. Moderation is healthy." He set the glass down, leaned forward, and continued in a lower tone. "I'm not the one who showed up at my place of work so completely wasted that I passed out facedown in my own vomit."

Bo's face expressed a look of pain, as if he had taken a physical blow. He looked at his thumbnail chronometer once more before urgently scanning the entrance and the room. Not seeing Jana, he sagged back in the chair. After a moment, he slowly got to his feet and looked down at the captain, who sat and regarded him with a single raised brow, casually holding his drink up with one elbow on the table.

"Do us all a favor," Bo said thickly. "Go back to the hell where you came from—and where you belong."

Fesner sniffed, nodded, and smiled crookedly. "And a pleasant evening to you, too, Mr. Nylen."

Bo checked the time once more and then dejectedly shambled to the entrance as Fesner shook his head and watched him depart. After he was gone, the captain repositioned himself and the chairs so he could easily watch the entrance, then he settled back and took an occasional sip.

Chapter 6

While Captain Fesner was conducting his inquisition on Bo Nylen, Jana was in her room trying to get ready.

You're late! Jana grimaced as she glanced at her thumbnail chronometer. She slipped into the knee-length white sheath dress and adjusted the spaghetti straps. *Too long in the tub—you should have been keeping an eye on the time!* She stepped into her white, peep-toe pumps and fought with her earrings until a tiny gold star on a delicate chain dangled from each ear. *Why am I on time for things I don't want to do and late for things I enjoy?*

She frowned at the reflection of her hair in the hotel mirror and then took a few moments to utilize the de-ionizing brush to smooth and polish her golden strands. *I wish they had some modern hair-styling tools in these frontier hotels.* She sighed and dropped the brush into her kit then clipped a flower from the table bouquet and tucked it over her ear. She stepped back and looked herself over, turning several times to make sure her dress had no marks or wrinkles, but the synthetic material had delivered on its wrinkle-free promise.

She nodded in satisfaction, took a deep breath, then headed for the door. *Bo will understand even if I'm late. He' a great guy. I'm sure he won't be upset.* She smiled in anticipation as her heels clicked on the tiles. His eyes would widen when he saw her. She hoped they would, anyway. *But I don't want him to stare.* She shook her head. *No, Bo won't stare.*

Jana entered the dining area and scanned the room expectantly. Her face fell slightly when she spied the captain, but after a last look around the room, she approached the table and made a small smile in greeting. “Good evening, Captain.”

He remained seated but nodded slightly. “Looking for someone, Lieutenant?”

“Yes.” She cast another look around the room.

“The dispatcher?”

She nodded.

“He was here and left.”

The woman turned her head sharply back to him, eyes wide. “He *left*?”

Fesner shrugged. “Something was bothering him. He didn’t look like he felt very well.”

Jana frowned in concern. “Did he say what was wrong?”

“I’m not his medical doctor or his psychologist. He didn’t tell me, and I didn’t ask.”

“This is very strange,” Jana said softly. She shook her head. The tiny gold stars of her earrings danced on the ends of the thin, gold chains.

“Not really,” Fesner said.

“What do you mean, sir?”

He took a breath and looked up. “I assume you’ve used the head recently?”

She quirked her mouth. “Yes.”

He gestured to the empty chair. “Then have a seat.”

Her brows contracted. She looked away and remained standing.

"Please, Lieutenant. I'm not ordering. I'm asking."

She slowly settled into the chair and crossed her legs. *He's staring! Ick!*

"Quite frankly, I'm surprised you're here. I thought I made it clear to you that it was a bad idea to be seen in that man's company."

"I recognize your professional authority, sir. I was not aware that you were authorized to pick my friends and influence my personal life."

"*Your* personal life is *your* business only as long as it remains personal. But if I think a private decision is likely to negatively impact your professional performance, then it becomes *my* business."

Jana tilted her head questioningly and raised a brow slightly.

"You defended your association with Mr. Nylen based on his employment status. But by his work history, he shouldn't *be* employed. Your willingness to place yourself at personal risk by recreating with him—unaccompanied on a remote beach on a frontier world, no less—suggests an unsuitable level of naïveté for command rank."

"I asked you to go with us."

"I had my suspicions about Mr. Nylen, and so I refused. That was an additional clue that you missed."

"Your objections at the time were directed at the sea life, not Bo's work history."

Fesner snorted. "I've got more finesse than to insult the man to his face, Lieutenant. Please!"

"But what was the basis for your suspicions?"

"Command instinct."

"You mean you had a hunch?"

"No, I said *instinct*. The subconscious analyzes sensory inputs and reaches a conclusion long before the conscious mind is fully aware of it. That ability is an important tool that you can't afford to ignore. Did you sleep through the psychology lectures at the academy?"

You jerk! Jana thought bitterly. Aloud she said, "With all due respect, sir, I spent the entire afternoon with the man and, for the most part, he was professional. Your brain's subconscious evaluation ability is not infallible."

"For the most part?"

Ooh! I said too much! She looked down, then looked up, angry with herself—and at her superior officer. "He was *entirely* professional."

Fesner emitted a single, mirthless laugh and shook his head. "You don't lie very well, Maines."

She raised her chin and held her face tight. *I bet this is what you did to Bo! You twist everything a person says!* "What is the point of this conversation, sir?"

"I'm trying to *teach* you something, Maines. That's my job."

"I'm listening."

Fesner leaned back and took a breath. "All right. Everybody makes mistakes, and everybody has lapses in good judgment. That's understandable, especially in a novice."

You're obviously the expert on mistakes went through her mind, but outwardly, she simply nodded.

"Your choice of the day's activities was unwise, but that is not what really troubles me. It's your attitude. I sense a lot of resistance. You don't say it out loud, but I know you're questioning everything I say."

Jana's eyes widened in surprise.

"Like *that*!" Fesner jabbed a finger toward her, and Jana started. "Playing innocent. Don't think I haven't noticed the eye rolls and sighs. You don't fool me, Lieutenant. I know what's going on."

She took a deep breath to maintain her calm despite the riot of thoughts and feelings. "I'm sorry, sir. I shall make every effort to comport myself in a professional manner."

His look was skeptical, but he simply flipped his hands. "Competence and professionalism in the command **cadre** are not simply desirable, Lieutenant. They're mandatory. Flight crews represent the space service at all times—on duty or off. A ship's captain can be called upon to negotiate a treaty or arbitrate a contract with an entire system. That responsibility can't be handed out willy-nilly. Competence can't be assumed."

"I understand, sir."

"I hope I start seeing evidence of that fact."

"What are you looking for?"

"I told you—good judgment."

"Anything more specific?"

Fesner shook his head. "Our next leg is a three-day run of fish eggs to Blueworld. I'm sure there will be plenty of opportunities for you to demonstrate your abilities between then and now."

"I thought I did everything on the first leg that you required of me. If I haven't been meeting your expectations, can I at least ask that, when we reach one of those decision points, you provide a bit more direction?"

"How much of your load do you expect me to carry for you, Maines?"

"None, sir. I'm just requesting faster feedback when I make a bad call—or a good call."

He shrugged.

"Was that it, sir?"

He looked around the dining area and at several of the couples that remained. "You were planning on having dinner. I was as well. Do you care to join me?"

"No, sir."

His brows went up at her frank refusal, and he once more studied one of the other couples before he finally said, "Preflight is at 0530. Tardiness will not be tolerated."

She nodded, turned, and walked carefully and stiffly in her heels toward the dining area's exit. When she'd said she did not intend to shake her derriere in front of the captain, she'd meant it.

Outside the dining area, the hotel foyer was deserted. She relaxed, and her heels once more clicked rhythmically as she made her way toward the broad staircase. She was halfway across the chamber when two STC officers in dress whites appeared at the top of the staircase and started down. She approached them just as they neared the bottom.

Just because Fesner is a jerk is no reason to be unpleasant to these guys, she thought. "Good evening, Captain Parnell. Mr. Jaxon," she greeted them with a small smile and nod.

The men's eyebrows rose and they looked at each other and then back at her.

"Well, hello," the senior officer said, grinning and spreading his hands. "No complaint, young lady, but how is it that you know us?"

"I'm Lieutenant Jana Maines with the *Aegis*." She extended her hand and shook theirs each in turn. "I was talking with the dispatcher when you landed, and he informed me of your arrival."

Captain Parnell nodded. "Who's your skipper this run?"

"Captain Fesner, sir."

A look of concern flashed across the other captain's face and Jana heard his first officer exhale quietly. "How's it going with Fesner, Lieutenant?"

"He's not—he's not what I expected."

The captain of the *Candide* studied her face. "Fesner's a little unorthodox, but his bark is usually worse than his bite. Just do your job and *don't* let him get to you."

"I won't, sir—I mean, I will. I mean, I'll do my job."

"I'm confident of that, Lieutenant. I've heard you're one of the best. Keep up the good work."

"Thank you, Captain. I appreciate that—very much!"

"I figured you would," he said with an encouraging smile, and then he looked past her and asked, "Is that the mess area?"

She nodded. "Captain Fesner is having dinner in the bistro right now."

The men once more exchanged glances. "What do you think, Jax? Shall we see what's available downtown?"

"Aye, sir!"

"You're welcome to join us, Lieutenant."

"Thank you, Captain Parnell, but I was just heading for my room. Early preflight tomorrow."

He nodded. "I understand. Good-night then, Lieutenant." He glanced at the dining area entrance and turned to his junior officer. "Let's get out of here, Jax."

"Good-night, Maines! Hope to see you, again!" the other lieutenant said quietly as they took their leave.

Jana smiled in reply. Her smile faded to a look of thoughtful concern as she watched them go through the large, transparent doors and then disappear down the steps of the veranda. Her thoughts and emotions tumbled between encouragement and apprehension over her own situation, and disappointment at the dispatcher's disappearance.

Where are you Bo?

Chapter 7

Jana checked out of her room early, left a message for the captain, and arrived in the dark morning hours at the dispatcher's office wearing her khaki jumpsuit. The door of the dispatcher's office hummed and Jana stepped into the brightly-lit cubicle. She hoped she would have a conversation with Bo, but remained apprehensive since she had been unable to communicate with him since his disappearance the evening before.

After she'd left the officers of the *Candide*, she had attempted to contact him via vid, but there was no response to his code. She then called the dispatcher on duty who assured her that Bo was on the schedule for the following morning. The assurance gave her something to anticipate but did nothing to relieve her disappointment over the ruined evening.

"Good morning, ma'am," the young man behind the counter greeted her with an uncertain smile and brows raised in a look of surprise as she approached his desk. He glanced at the chronometer. "You're here rather early."

"Good morning," she smiled back. "I couldn't sleep anyway, so I thought I might as well get started. We had some maintenance issues on the way in and I wanted to check on them."

The dispatcher nodded and touched his screen. "Looks like most of the gripes have been signed off. There is still an issue with the **portside** electrical bus," he paused to study the maintenance report, "but there's nothing noted here that indicates you'll miss your launch time." He tapped a few more commands onto the screen and commented, "Fish eggs, huh?"

Jana nodded. "Tilapia in cryo."

The dispatcher nodded again as he scanned the screen. "Well, they're already on board and ready to go," he confirmed. "That's one big boatload of caviar."

Jana made a face. "Tilapia *caviar*?"

The dispatcher shrugged and grinned.

The woman glanced around the room. "I was expecting Mr. Nylen. When will he report on duty?"

"He's not coming in," the dispatcher replied simply. "Sick leave."

"What's wrong?" Jana asked with concern.

"I'm not sure," the man replied with a shrug, then he looked at her curiously. "You know him?" He seemed surprised and a little doubtful.

"We've … met," Jana replied. "He was on duty when we made planetfall. I was told he would be here this morning."

"I can check on him if you'd like," the dispatcher offered, his curiosity piqued that the attractive space pilot was expressing interest in his co-worker.

"I've already tried his vid code," Jana reported, "but there was no response."

"Yeah, Bo can be like that," the man replied knowingly. "I think I might be able to figure out which rock he's crawled under, though."

"Thanks." Jana flashed a smile.

"Glad to help," he replied.

"I'll be at the ship." Jana tossed her blonde head as she picked up her bags. "If you find him, please let him know I would like to talk with him."

"Sure thing," the man assured her.

"Thank you!" she called over her shoulder and the door hummed closed.

The dispatcher stared after her for a moment and then slowly shook his head. "If I hadn't seen it, I wouldn't have believed it," he finally muttered slowly. Then he grinned. "Way to go, Bo!"

The breezes of the previous evening had died, and now a cool, damp stillness lay over the ramp as Jana entered the brilliant pool of light surrounding the *Aegis.* Swarms of moths fluttered near each of the lights while a small contingent of support personnel loaded the last of the cargo. Only a few of the huge cargo bay doors remained open.

An extra knot of vehicles and men down the aft **port** side near the engine nacelle attracted Jana's attention, and she decided to check out the situation promptly after stowing her gear.

The hum of the ship's four-hundred-hertz electrical system and the smells of lubricant and plastic and human **effluvia** combined to create a sense of welcome familiarity every time she returned from some new experience outside the ship. The lighting was sometimes harsh, the decor utilitarian metal, plastic, and glass, but the ship was functional and generally comfortable—though by no means luxurious. Her boots rang on the metal rungs of the ladder leading up the crawl tube to the habitation section near the bow of the ship. The crawl tube penetrated the layers of plastic, water, and lead that were necessary to protect the crew and cargo from the deadly ionizing radiation of deep space.[4]

Jana quickly stowed her clothes in the small locker of her tiny stateroom and glanced at her space suit in its narrow locker. There was no need for the suit on this planet's surface. She would be living in the suit for the next three days, anyway, so she elected to remain in her comfortable jumpsuit for as long as possible.

She went forward to the flight station and began a preliminary inspection of the ship's log and self-diagnostics programs. She noted the same problem that the dispatcher had pointed out in the port aft electrical subsystem. She carefully logged her activities and then left the ship to begin the walk-around.

This ancient ritual, with its roots in flying tradition extended far back from before the First Age when humanity first took to the air in machines of wood, cloth, and iron. It was, for Jana, the most personal part of the preflight. Its primary utility was that she provided another set of eyes in addition to the ground crew that might pick up something out of place, and the activity increased her psychological sense of ownership and connection with the ship.

The soaring expanse of its main hull, the ruggedness of its graceful, aerodynamic surfaces, and the cavernous throats of its fusion nozzles were both inspiring and sobering. How much she depended upon the proper functioning of these massive systems! And yet how dependent they were on the intricate support network of command and control systems hidden inside! She knew that many pilots took automation for granted and relied entirely upon either the self-diagnostics of the ship or maintenance reports from support personnel to satisfy themselves as to the quality of their craft. It wasn't that Jana didn't trust these sources of information, but she didn't want to lose touch with what she was doing—trusting her life to a huge pile of metal that protected her from the freezing vacuum and radiation of space and the heat of reentry.

And while at times it was occasionally tasked to fuse heavy hydrogen fuel to release thousands of megawatts of power, the ship spent most of its time coasting. During these quiescent times, its energy built up enormous field potentials that would be unleashed suddenly and in such a way as to translineate the ship through the fourth, fifth, or higher dimensions. The *n*-drive allowed the ship to cross the vast distances between the stars quickly and inexpensively—and without the limiting time-dilation effects of normal relativistic translation through three-dimensional space.

Jana found herself awed to consider the tremendous energy at her disposal and the huge responsibility this entailed. The walk-around was just another way she reminded herself of another everyday miracle.

The ship's silvery **ti-alum** skin glinted under the arc lamps. Jana noted the conditions of various blade antenna, static tube intakes, and vents as she made her way down the port side toward the cluster of maintenance crew vehicles.

"G'mornin', ma'am," the supervisor greeted her with a glance at her lapel stripes and a tap of his hand to his white helmet.

Jana nodded and smiled with a glance at his nametag. "Good morning, Mr. Swix. How's that electrical bus problem?"

"The night crew is still trying to finish up. They think they've almost got it, but these intermittent bugs are the hardest ones to solve."

"Do you anticipate a delay?" she asked.

Swix swiped a hand across his mouth. "I don't think so, but I can't be sure. A lot of problems often have a simple solution. This could be just a poor connection or an incorrectly set switch. We'll eventually shoot it down to the right **nexus**. There's no substitute for taking time to carefully look at things."

"But it's working now. And you can't find it if it doesn't manifest itself?"

The supervisor nodded and fidgeted. "Right. And that's what makes it a wild card," he admitted.

"If it's a joker, I'd rather we draw it on the ground."

"We'll do our best to give you a winning hand, Lieutenant," he grinned.

"I hope you do," Jana replied as she started to leave. "I'm lousy at poker."

Jana completed the rest of the walk-around inspection without incident and returned to the flight station. She had worked on the checklists for several minutes before Captain Fesner arrived.

"Good morning, Lieutenant," he greeted her pleasantly enough, then sat and thoughtfully observed her activity.

"Good morning, Captain," she replied, trying to be courteous, and relieved that he seemed to be in a good mood. She could not erase from her mind a slight undercurrent of tension, however, and she was aware that his mood could change quickly.

"It's good you weren't late. I have little patience with laggards."

"Aye, sir," she replied as casually as she could while she continued to work.

A moment passed, and the fabric of his seat squeaked as he adjusted his position. "Feeling healthy today?" he suddenly asked.

"Yes, quite well, sir."

He raised a dubious brow. "No sunburn or fish bites?"

"No, sir," she shook her head. "I survived the dangers of the beach unscathed."

He scanned the log and grunted when he noted the outstanding problem with the electrical subsystem. "I better get back there and kick some tail," he commented.

"I already spoke to the foreman of the maintenance crew when I did the walk-around," Jana reported.

The captain's dark eyes turned to her, and he paused to digest this information. He looked back to the log. "What was the report?"

"He said that since it was an intermittent problem he couldn't guarantee a sign-off by our proposed departure time." At this, Fesner looked up sharply. She continued, "But he assured me they were doing their best to find the problem as quickly as possible."

Fesner sniffed. "Typical maintenance-type smoke blowing," he remarked. "*They* don't lose a percentage like we do when there's a delay."

He rose. "The local company strikes me as very lax. I have a feeling I will need to provide some serious motivation to their posteriors."

"Yes, sir," Jana said.

Fesner started to leave the flight station but then stopped. "I noticed Mr. Nylen didn't make it to work this morning."

"Oh?" Jana allowed herself to sound only mildly disappointed. "Were he at the desk, I think I would at least owe him a good-bye."

"You're wasting your time," Fesner said in a caustic tone. "I told you. That old coot is a loser." He jerked a thumb over his shoulder. "It couldn't be more obvious if he had it tattooed across his forehead and down his backside."

"Hmm," the woman looked at her hands.

Fesner snorted. "You don't owe him a thing, Lieutenant."

"He was nice," she insisted.

"Look, Maines," he continued and his voice lost little of its edge. "I'm not just a spectator here. As I explained before, I've got a responsibility as your instructor and senior officer to see if you have what it takes to captain your own ship."

Jana looked up with a serious expression.

"One thing a good captain has to be able to do is to determine what's worth doing, what can wait, and what should not be done at all. I was glad to find out we were assigned to be together on this trip. I'd heard good things about your technical abilities, but I'm seeing indications that you tend to be too emotional. Command is a lonely position. When you give a command, you need it obeyed—from respect if possible, but from fear if necessary. But one thing is for certain: if you are hoping for cooperation or obedience because your subordinates like you, then you'd better be prepared to be disappointed. When there is fear, or at least respect, you give commands on *your* terms because you command from a position of strength. If you are liked, then you command on *their* terms. That puts you in a position of weakness."

Jana thought of her father. She respected but never feared him. Though he possessed the strength to harm her, he never had. His eyes would flash when he was angry, but he never seemed to lack self-control. She trusted him. She knew he loved her and wanted her to succeed. And more than anything, she wanted him to be proud of her.

Jana raised her eyes to the captain. "Am I to fear you?"

Fesner shrugged. "If necessary. But I wasn't talking about me as much as about you."

"In what way are you speaking about me, sir?"

"I mean that from you, respect is preferable—mutual respect, of course. At the moment, I am your superior, but if you show sufficient progress, we will one day be equals. That's the goal, anyway."

"Thank you for your concern, sir."

"It's my job," Fesner replied shortly. He paused before he continued. "I am not saying that superiors and subordinates can't like each other, just that it is a poor leadership practice to let that be your motivation."

"I think I understand, sir."

"Good." The captain nodded aft. "I'm going to kick some maintenance butt. We'll get started on the checklists as soon as I get back."

"I'll be ready," Jana promised.

"See that you are," Fesner remarked over his shoulder as he disappeared through the hatch into the habitation section.

Jana frowned after him, sighed, and tried Bo's vid code. There was still no response. She called the dispatcher's office, but he had no new information either.

She sighed again and went to her stateroom, where she quickly freshened up before changing into her flight suit. *This is going to be a very, very long flight.*

Chapter 8

Fesner returned to the flight station red of face and nostrils flared. Jana nodded at his arrival but said nothing. They proceeded through the tedious checklists of their multiple systems and verifications without comment, and the routine seemed to calm the captain down. He called a halt when their checklist reached the portside electrical system.

"Maintenance still has it," he grumbled, and Jana could see he was staring at the chronometer, calculating the cost of a delay.

"Uh, Lieutenant," Fesner finally said after an interval. "Go aft and check on the maintenance crew. If we could speed things up by even a few minutes it would help."

"Aye, sir." Her seat creaked, and she was gone.

The rosy dawn painted the ship pastel-pink as Jana dropped to the concrete ramp and walked under the hulking mass of the ship. The thrum of the spaceport's contra-grav beams attracted her attention, and she saw the *Joy of Candide* lift from the other pad. In the time it took her to walk the length of her ship, the *Candide* had reached an altitude of twenty kilometers. Its fusion engines winked on as a brilliant sapphire star that bloomed and accelerated eastward.[3] It would take almost a minute before the fading rumble of its engines would reach her.

"Mr. Swix," she called to the supervisor, who was pacing at the entrance of the aft equipment bay.

He scowled at the sound of his name and looked up, then he relaxed at the sight of her face. "Yes, Lieutenant?" he asked in greeting.

"Still hunting the elusive glitch?"

"Yeah," he admitted. "And hunting hasn't been good."

She nodded, and her brow furrowed sympathetically.

"And I have been *informed* that any delay costs you personally," Swix said.

Jana nodded again. "That's not my primary concern."

The foreman grunted. "That didn't seem to be the attitude of the other spacer who was here earlier."

The woman made a slight, wordless shrug.

"We're doing our best," the supervisor continued, "but I just can't sign this off unless I'm satisfied that you won't be left choking on vacuum later. I want to sleep at night."

"I greatly appreciate your concern, Mr. Swix," Jana replied. "However, this particular subsystem is not critical for flight or life support. It's for cargo use only."

The man seemed relieved. "I still can't just sign it off," he said.

"And I am not asking you to do that," she affirmed. "I'm not even hinting."

"All right," the supervisor nodded. "But I'm glad to know this isn't serious."

"It *is* serious," the woman corrected him. "Every accident begins with something that is probably unimportant under normal circumstances but which, because of the particular situation, suddenly becomes critical." She gestured toward the ship. "I don't know how badly this bug could bite us, but if it isn't eliminated, no doubt it will try to find a way."

The foreman nodded. "We'll do what we can, Lieutenant. That bug is running out of places to hide."

"You find it, Mr. Swix," Jana pointed toward him, "and you swat it!" She gave him an encouraging smile while she turned to go.

The man nodded seriously and watched her leave.

Jana observed the approaching sunrise; the eastern sky was now pink and golden. Already she could feel the growing warmth, and she dreaded the thought of Fesner's reaction to waiting out the repairs in the sticky heat.

She paused in the entrance of the forward airlock just behind the front landing leg and signaled the flight station on one of the ship's intercom panels. Fesner acknowledged and asked how things had gone with the maintenance crew. Jana reported that they were still working on the problem and then asked if she could take a short walk back to the dispatch office. She could hear reluctance in his voice. He agreed, though he asked her to check back within ten minutes.

"Aye, sir." She snapped off the switch on the communications panel and stepped briskly across the ramp.

The dispatcher on duty recognized her immediately and greeted her with a broad grin. "I was just about to call the ship, Lieutenant Maines. I have something for you." He slid a message chit across the desk and carefully studied the woman's face as she read it.

She activated her vid and dialed the code indicated on the chit. A tiny image of Bo's face appeared on the screen. He looked haggard, though he smiled weakly.

"Hello, Jana," he said.

"Bo!" Jana replied. "What happened last night? Where *were* you?"

"Where were *you*?"

His hurt tone cut Jana to the heart. "I'm so sorry, Bo. I just forgot the time. I was late, but I did come to see you!"

Bo grimaced and shook its head.

"Bo! I'm sorry I was late. I'm so sorry!"

"It was my fault, too, Jana. I was stupid enough to listen to Fesner."

"What did the captain say?"

"He said you weren't coming."

"I said I was coming. You shouldn't have listened to him!"

The man shrugged and shook his head.

"What did you do last night?"

"I went out to the tree."

"All night?"

He shrugged again. "Most of the night. I came back to my room this morning. That's when I got your message."

"You were out all night by yourself. Oh, Bo!"

"I had company."

"Really?" A surge of emotions—surprise, curiosity, jealously—flooded upward. *This is silly—you can't be jealous! You just can't!* "With whom?" she found herself asking in a small voice.

"Aegis," he grinned. After a pause, the nose of the cat filled the tiny screen as the animal sniffed at the vid in Bo's hand.

"That's so sad—and so sweet!"

"Yeah, well, like your song last night said, life is a maze with twists and turns. There are some things we know and some things we still need to learn. That's why things happen."

"Do you forgive me, Bo?"

"Of course, Jana! Do you forgive me?"

"Yes, Bo. With all my heart."

Jana's vid chimed, and Fesner's face and voice replaced Bo.

"Jana, we've been given an *up* on electrical. Get back here, and let's get back on schedule!" He signed off before she could respond.

"Bo, I have to go."

He nodded. "I know. I wish I had been there."

She nodded in reply.

The vid chimed, and once again, Fesner broke in. "Come on, Lieutenant!" he urged. "Maintenance has things just about buttoned up. Let's go!" His image blinked off.

"I'll see you in forever, Jana."

"I'll see you in forever, Bo."

"I'll be at the tree," he promised.

She managed a small smile. "I'll wave."

"Me too," he said, and then his image was gone.

Jana lifted her eyes from the vid, and the dispatcher, who had been watching intently, immediately looked away.

"Thank you," she said to him.

He looked up. "For what?" he asked.

"For taking the message," she replied.

"Sure. No problem. Is everything all right?"

Jana smiled thinly. "No, not at the moment. But I believe everything will be all right."

"Good," he replied, and he gave her a curious look. Jana left, and the dispatcher stared at the door as it closed automatically behind her. He shook his head. "Well, I'll be dipped," he muttered.

Chapter 9

Less than a half hour later, the crew of the *Aegis* strapped themselves into their command seats, sealed the ship, and began decontamination procedures. They were behind schedule, but not so much that it couldn't be made up if they performed at optimum efficiency, so both Jana and the captain allowed nothing to distract their focus from their preparations for launch. Conversation was terse and limited to required phraseology as the ship lurched upward. The contra-grav beam stabilized, and it began a rapid and smooth acceleration. Because of the nature of the beam, there was no feel of inertia pulling back; rather, the sensation was that of falling—an impression rocket jockeys usually called *falling off the planet.*

At an altitude of about twenty kilometers, the effect from the surface-based beam waned. At this point, the fusion engines erupted in a sapphire glow and the ship accelerated from the reaction motors. The crew were pushed back into their padded seats and reached escape velocity[5] in less than twenty minutes after launch and at a distance of about five thousand kilometers from the surface.[6]

The ship could have completed its escape from the planetary gravity well at this point by coasting alone, but the planet's remaining tug would slow the ship so that almost forty hours would be required to coast far enough from the planet to activate the *n*-drive. Maintaining an acceleration of ten meters per second per second for an additional thirty minutes enabled the ship to travel most of the required million kilometers in about eight hours.[7]

Captain Fesner shifted into an ebullient mood. "I don't know what you said to those maintenance types," he chortled, "but within ten minutes of your little chat with them, they signed off on the gripe sheet."

Jana made a quick smile but was not feeling nearly so buoyant. She wondered what Fesner had said to Bo—and she knew he had said *something.* The captain said Bo claimed not to be feeling well, but Bo hadn't mentioned any illness. She was sure the captain had done something to upset him

On the other hand, perhaps she wasn't reading the captain right. She had read people incorrectly before. Fesner had expressed concern, albeit in a rough sort of way. Some people were spiky like that. It was so confusing. She needed to put it out of her mind for a while.

"What was that hand-wave thing you did back there?" Fesner asked suddenly.

"Hand-wave thing?" Jana repeated.

"Yeah," the other nodded. "Just after takeoff you waved at the planetside monitor. Was there a problem?"

"No," she replied. "I was waving good-bye."

Fesner snorted. "That's not rational, Lieutenant. You were looking at a monitor—no one on the planet could see you. You're not going crackers on me, are you?"

She smiled weakly. "No, sir. I just felt sentimental."

"Well, I'll cut you a little slack, Lieutenant," he replied. "I realize that, as a woman, you probably look at the world a little differently than I do."

"I'm sure I do."

"But that's not to say it's a bad thing." Fesner held up a finger. "Even I have benefited, from time to time, from a different viewpoint or perspective."

"I'm sure you have," she agreed.

The captain gave her a studied gaze, but Jana continued working smoothly. She appeared to be making no subsequent point.

The rumble of the fusion engines, the whines of pumps and gyros, and the hisses from the gaspers filled the gaps in conversation. During the launch and initial boost phase, the crew tuned in a "breather" frequency, and comm chatter consisted of control instructions for aircraft that operated within the planetary atmosphere. As the spacecraft rose above the blanket of air, they switched to a frequency set aside for deep-space communications only—a "spacer" frequency—and the radio fell almost silent.

While the ship was under acceleration, the pilots felt pushed backward, as if their seats were fastened to a vertical wall. During this time, they carefully monitored the ship status and reported to Departure Control at regular intervals. At a distance of almost forty-one thousand kilometers from the planet, the main engines were shut down, and the ship continued coasting at over twenty-eight thousand meters per second. Fesner then fired the ship's small maneuvering thrusters in order to initiate a roll that would create a sense of artificial gravity.

"Set condition two," Fesner instructed when the roll had been established.

Jana unfastened her harness and gratefully left the flight station. Condition two was a visual inspection of the ship. Periodically she would call back to the flight station and advise the captain on the results of her inspection. A typical report would be a simple statement of the location and condition, such as, "**starboard** stations, nominal," or, "capacitor bank two, nominal." The cargo stanchions were given an especially careful look. A loose container could cause considerable damage if it broke free under acceleration and piled into other containers. The damage could be disastrous if the freed container struck the ship's hull or equipment bays, and the crew could not afford either contingency.

The major components of the current cargo consisted of numerous Peltier[8] containers of fish eggs frozen in liquid nitrogen. These eggs were planned as the seed stock for untold numbers of future generations of fish at their destination planet, Blueworld. Each container maintained a temperature of seventy-seven degrees absolute[9] by means of insulation and an electrically active Peltier-effect cooling unit. Jana's inspection of the cargo revealed row upon row of green indicator lights glowing among the dimly lighted stanchions that indicated the proper operation of each container.

Some containers had no indicators because they did not require refrigeration. They contained alga spores. Some alga varieties were for food, others for fibers, and still others for cleaning the water. Jana smiled to think that in her own way, she was helping to feed the hungry, clothe the naked, and give water to the thirsty.

The inspection provided a welcome break from Fesner's odious presence. Jana found it difficult to decide whether she found his attempts at pleasantness any more bearable than his normal rudeness. In any case, her present activity provided an excuse to be away from him as well as exercise. It also helped to pass the time needed to wait before the first *n*-space jump.

But the checks were eventually finished and she had to return to the flight station. Fesner announced the normal cruise mode of condition three, and the ship's procedures became more relaxed. Jana requested a few minutes to repair to her stateroom to freshen up.

Fesner nodded. "But don't take too long. I need a break too."

"I won't be long, sir," she replied. "I just need to use the head."

"Figures," he grunted.

She maintained an impassive expression until she was aft of the flight station, and then she grimaced, clenched her fists, and made a quick twisting motion with her hands.

After using the head and freshening up, she returned forward. The seat creaked as she climbed into it and made the harness fast. The captain briefed her on the ship's status and when they were both satisfied that she was familiar with all the important conditions, she initialed the log. Fesner left to take his own personal break.

Jana flicked through the various external views available and idly selected a shot of the shrinking sphere of Oceanus—now a blue-white crescent with no discernable landmasses, even under high magnification. It was a warm and wet island in the vast, cold ocean of space—a mere grain of sand in the huge desert of the cosmos, but one that was being successfully modified for human habitation. In addition, the success of this world was helping to create another success on another world-in-the-making.

Like a scaffold maker, humanity was building upon previous constructions, clawing its way back from the cataclysmic fall of the Second Age. Occasionally a world would be rediscovered, sometimes inhabited by descendents with only a dim memory of their star-traveling ancestors. Often there were only the remains of failed societies that, through mismanagement or misfortune, did not survive. Jana couldn't help but wonder if, should the Day of Judgment be delayed, some future pilot would one day look upon Oceanus from the perspective of a Fourth Age and wonder who its inhabitants had been.

Hours later, Jana was once more on watch as the ship coasted closer to the point where it could make the first jump. She idly watched her instrument panels while the main capacitors charged. Suddenly, an alarm jerked her away from her reverie, and her heart skipped a beat as she studied the indicator. She made several taps upon the control screen while her brows knitted. The electrical subsystem for the cargo bays was experiencing the transient power flutter that had been observed by the maintenance crew before takeoff. Apparently, they had not solved the problem, after all. She anxiously scanned the data screens, but the electrical systems had quickly returned to normal and she tried to force herself to relax. *No need to panic over a transient flutter. Everything looks good—but keep your eyes open!*

The Peltier containers in the cargo bays were dependent upon a steady electrical supply to maintain their temperature. The trip to Blueworld would take several days. If the power supply failed, the insulation for the containers could not maintain the super cold and the valuable cargo of fish eggs could be lost. But all indicators had returned to normal. Jana reset the system and made an entry in the log.

She was about to page the captain when another indicator caught her attention. A further series of small corrections followed this and Fesner returned to the flight station before she could call him.

"Steady as she goes?" he asked, and his harness clinked.

She reviewed the checklist items, briefly mentioning the power bump in the cargo subsystem.

He frowned. "But the system appears normal now?" he questioned her for confirmation as he initialed the log and took the watch.

Jana nodded and brought up the trace. "The power supply has generally been perfect—except for that transient dip."

"You know, I wonder if it isn't the power supply at all," Fesner muttered. He looked at his first officer, and his face split into a toothy grin. "I'll bet it's the sensor itself! Yes," he concluded, "that would explain why the maintenance crew couldn't find it back there." He jerked a thumb aft, indicating the planet they'd left far behind. "The problem must be between the cargo bay and the readout up here in the flight station."

Jana nodded. "That would explain the problem, all right," she agreed. "There is a data terminal in the cargo maintenance bay. I wonder if it will show the same dropout."

"Depends upon if it's getting input directly from the cargo or if it is first processed through the flight station," Fesner pointed out. "And I don't have the entire wiring schematic of this ship committed to memory."

"But we can look it up," Jana suggested.

"We?" His tone was instantly caustic.

"*I* can look it up," Jana corrected herself.

Fesner nodded. "But before you do that, get down to the maintenance terminal and check it out. If it doesn't show anything, then we'll know it's a false alarm. If it does show it, then I'll handle the watch while you study the manual and trace the signal. It's tedious, I know, but good practice for you."

"Aye, sir," she acknowledged, and since he had assumed his position at the console, she left the flight station without further comment and went aft.

Jana inspected the data recorder in the maintenance bay. It had recorded the same power fluctuation as she'd seen in the cockpit. Despite this, Fesner predicted that an analysis of the signal path would show that the maintenance recorder received its data from the flight station. They hadn't proven the problem was a bad sensor, but it was still not certain that the glitch was in the power supply itself.

Fesner expected Jana to continue to study the schematics, but her efforts were interrupted when she was needed to help prepare the ship for the first jump. The more rigid environment of condition four replaced the relative calm of condition three as they prepared to create a crack in the sky, the execution of the *n*-space transition.

No one, from the mathematicians who had derived the calculations of multidimensions to the engineers who built the drive, understood the *n*-space drive completely. But humanity had learned how to use it, and while the theoreticians puzzled over the explanations, the engineers built ships following the ancient credo of their craft: First find a way to exploit it, and then figure out why it works.

The *Aegis* entered the fourth dimension at a point and on a vector that would take it to another favorable point along the space lane. Their voyage to Blueworld would require a series of such jumps that were each carefully selected and plotted to take them along the four-dimensional path to the next destination.

Human comprehension of *n*-space was more theoretical and mathematical than practical. The human brain simply lacks the capacity to properly process spatial sensory inputs with more than three dimensions. Because of this, the hyperspace world was quite literally indescribable.

So, like an insect nibbling its way through a stack of folded sheets, the *Aegis* proceeded slowly in terms of 4-space, but it flashed through layers of 3-space. They had a fleeting existence at wide intervals, many light-years apart. During these brief 3-space episodes, the ship's navigational computers updated their position and provided the pilots with the information necessary to determine any course corrections.

After the jump, Captain Fesner returned the ship to condition three, and he and Jana settled into the standard routine of alternating watches. During her off-watch periods, Jana ate, slept, exercised ferociously, and studied the ship's electrical schematics in order to trace the bus monitor's signal path. She looked longingly at her guitar, Sebastian, when she was in her stateroom, but because of the issue with the electrical system, she didn't want to risk Fesner's ire or ridicule if she took the opportunity to play.

While on watch, Jana monitored the status of the ship, verified the navigational computer's output, and worked on the data terminal's signal path—even though except for the occasional transient flutter, the electrical problem continued to be nothing more than a nuisance.

But about twenty hours into the voyage, near the quarter-way point en route to Blueworld, the nuisance developed into a serious problem.

Jana was on watch when the power monitor went into alarm. But this warning signal had become a familiar routine, so she thought little of it until she found that the system would not reset. The power monitors indicated an electrical power failure in the portside cargo bay—the location of a large portion of the tilapia eggs.

She signaled the captain, who was on his sleep period at the time. Rarely in an upbeat mood, being awakened to the information of a power failure—and one that portended the ruin of a significant portion of their cargo—did little to improve his attitude.

"Is there any chance it's a bogus alarm and not a legitimate failure?" Fesner asked.

"One of us will have to go aft and verify the status on the containers themselves," Jana replied.

Fesner's next words were mumbled and indistinct but there was no mistaking a tone of extreme displeasure. "I'll be right up," was all Jana finally made out.

When the captain arrived, he was more collected. He slid into the seat and quickly reviewed the information Jana had recorded in the log. Finally, he sat back and rubbed the dark stubble on his chin thoughtfully with one hand. "I'll go aft and have a look," he said. "If the units have lost power, they'll start to warm up, and we lose a couple hundred million tilapia—whatever the blazes they are."

"Some kind of fish," Jana offered.

"I knew that," Fesner said with irritation. "I meant I was not certain just what kind of fish."

"I'm not sure, either," Jana replied.

Fesner scowled darkly. "It looks like there are several things you're not sure of, Lieutenant."

The woman felt a rising flush but remained silent.

Fesner grunted, then he rose and went aft. A few minutes later, his voice crackled over the squawk box. "Stone dead," he announced. "The temperature is up a degree to seventy-eight absolute."

"Aye," Jana replied, at a loss of what else she could say.

Chapter 10

"So what *did* you say to those maintenance techs?" Fesner demanded after an hour of repeated attempts to restore power to the fish-filled Peltiers had proven unsuccessful. The loss of the majority of their cargo now seemed inevitable and the search for a solution had quickly deteriorated into a search for someone to blame.

Jana felt the intensity of the captain's gaze upon her almost as an additional weight. *He's going to try to twist whatever I say.* But she had to say something. She took a deep breath, determined to carefully avoid making any statement that could be construed to mean that she had somehow encouraged the maintenance crew to be less than thorough.

"I said that we needed the system operational."

Fesner's eyes narrowed. "That's it? *We need the system operational.* That's *exactly* what you said?"

"Well, of course, I said a few other things," Jana admitted. She immediately regretted it.

"Don't be coy, Lieutenant," the man snapped. "Did you say *anything* that one of those wrench benders might have taken as permission to sign off without really solving the problem?"

Jana shook her head. "Exactly the opposite. I pointed out that, while this problem might not appear critical, such apparently minor problems have a way of growing into big problems. I told him that we wanted the problem solved."

"You told him this was a *minor* problem?" Fesner exploded.

Jana reddened but fought to remain in control. "I didn't say it was a minor problem. I said it was an *apparently* minor problem." *I knew the jerk would twist my words! I just knew it!*

"What's the difference?" he snarled. "You've got to remember who you're dealing with when you talk to support personnel. Have I not made this clear, or you are you just not capable of getting it?"

"You've been clear, sir," Jana admitted. "I just don't agree with you."

"Yes, I know you don't agree," the captain sniffed. "That's been obvious for some time. I pointed out my concern with your contentious attitude on Oceanus. So far, despite your promises to do better, nothing seems to have changed." His temples worked a few times while he considered his next words. "I have gone out of my way to instruct you and to otherwise give you every possible benefit of the doubt. But if we lose this cargo, I do not see how I can give you a positive endorsement."

"But sir! I *need* that endorsement!"

"What you need is of absolutely *no* importance! Your performance report will be based on your *performance*—not on what you want. Losing an entire shipment is hardly the basis for a good evaluation. My recommendation must be based entirely on whether you have demonstrated the skills necessary to be a ship's captain."

"But I have!"

"Really? By your own admission, you downplayed the importance of solving our electrical problem to the maintenance personnel. And I distinctly remember needing to call you back to the ship to continue your duties because you were at the portmaster's office conducting personal business."

"Sir, that's entirely bogus!" she protested hotly.

"Mind your tongue, Lieutenant!" he added, looking up sharply. "Your attitude borders on insubordination. You *will* maintain good self-discipline, or I will not only fail to give you a positive report, I will recommend that you be terminated from the flight program!"

No! You can't do this to me! Jana screamed inside her head, but outwardly, she simply nodded. "Sir, I request to be relieved."

Fesner gave her a hard look and sniffed. "How long? I was on my sleep cycle and since there appears to be no immediate remedy to our problem, I should like to get back to it, if you please."

"Just a few minutes, sir," Jana replied with forced calmness.

"Very well," he agreed reluctantly, and his voice dropped in resignation. "Proceed with the watch checklist. Then you can go." He sighed as if he had been called upon to do heroic service.

The familiarity of the phraseology and the brevity of the checklist routine helped in some small measure to get Jana through the ordeal. Within moments, she was proceeding to her stateroom, tears silently flowing.

She buried her face in a towel, flopped on her bunk, and silently permitted herself to sob for a few moments, opening the emotional floodgates wide and letting the salty headwaters spill out while her body racked and shuddered. After this brief period, she sat up, her feet on the deck but her face still buried in the damp towel, and tried to collect her thoughts.

Why is this happening? What good can there be in this?

She was hurt, angry, and confused. Despite her best efforts to be polite and accommodating, the captain remained demanding, displeased, and accusatory. She *hadn't* encouraged the maintenance crew to sign off the gripe without fixing it. She had tried to trace the signal path, but the manuals were written for maintenance people who were familiar with the systems, not for the flight crew. The captain must know this, but he acted as if she wasn't even trying.

Her experience with the other officers, however, had been far more positive. *I'm so glad Captain Parnell said something encouraging to me on*

Oceanus! I must remember to be positive when I get the chance—especially if I ever become captain.

But self-doubt still plagued her. After all, she *had* told Mr. Swix that the subsystem was noncritical, even though she had also qualified it and emphasized that she wanted the system repaired. *Why did I even mention that?* And could she have tried harder to understand the schematics? Granted, the point was moot now, since most of the Peltiers had lost all power.

But Fesner still uses that to say I can't do the job. I wish Bo were here so I could talk with him. She took a deep breath and made a final wipe of her face with the towel. *You've got to stop this blubbering and get back out there.* She closed her eyes and took several deep breaths as she prayed. *Clear mind. Calm heart. Wisdom. Patience.*

Slowly she opened her eyes. The flood of emotion, though still present, had at last begun to ebb. She was done crying—determined to hold to the conviction that nothing happened without some greater purpose. But looking at the reflection of her red nose and puffy eyes in her small mirror made that particularly difficult to believe at the moment.

She splashed her face with cool water, patted herself dry with a clean towel, and then brushed her hair. She set her brush down and looked herself in the eye. "Don't let him get to you," Captain Parnell had advised her.

“I won't!” she addressed her reflection forcefully. With resolution, she headed back to the flight station.

Captain Fesner looked up and noted the redness of her eyes. “Feeling better after your little cry?”

She slid into her seat and buckled the harness before she answered, surprised and relieved at her own sense of calmness and unusual lack of urgency to speak. “Yes, quite better,” she said quietly after a moment. “I am ready to resume the watch.”

"All right," the captain replied slowly, "if you think you can handle it."

"I have, I can, and I will," Jana replied flatly. "If you have reason to believe otherwise, then put it in the log, relieve me from all duties, and stand the watch yourself. I leave you to explain it to the Board of Inquiry." She turned her head and looked directly into the man's dark eyes.

He held the gaze briefly but then looked aside, and his brows contracted. "I have never said you were incapable of standing the watch, Lieutenant. I said I had reason to believe you may lack the prerequisite good judgment of command. You are an adequate subordinate." He gave her a sideways look, as if expecting a strong reaction.

But there was no outburst. Instead, she studied her readouts. "Thank you, Captain Fesner. I am gratified you think I can pilot the ship. I am ready to resume the watch."

His temples worked for an instant then he punched up the checklist and mechanically went through each item. Jana carefully replied according to the standard phraseology.

"I have the watch," she said when the list was completed and initialed. She returned her attention to the instruments, her face impassive.

Fesner unbuckled but did not leave immediately. He studied Jana for a moment before speaking. "You're mighty calm for the trouble you could be in," he commented. "You don't know the ship's schematics, and I'm not at all happy with your cavalier attitude toward maintenance."

Jana turned her gaze to the captain. "I eagerly await your review of the schematics so that I might learn how to do it."

He sniffed and waved a hand. "At this point, the schematics are irrelevant. But even if you had figured the schematic out, you would still have the problem of loose lips."

"Perhaps I should have gone back and *kicked their butts*, like you did."

Fesner colored. "I did no such thing! I treat *all* personnel with respect and courtesy."

"If we did go before the board, I wonder what would be contained in the maintenance crew deposition," Jana speculated aloud.

The man pursed his lips, and his eyes became mere slits below the dark bushiness of his eyebrows. "Perhaps I may have … underestimated you," he finally said.

"You have," Jana replied, looking straight ahead.

Fesner snorted. He leaned forward and tapped a screen, studying it briefly. "The Peltiers are up to eighty-six degrees. We lose cryonic status at one twenty. At the present rate of heating, we have only about twelve hours before that happens—and we're still nearly fifty hours out from Blueworld. What I wouldn't give if we could get that electrical bus back online!"

"Would you sign off my syllabus if I did?"

The captain regarded her with surprise. "By what miraculous process do you expect to do what the entire Port Oceana maintenance team failed to do?"

"I don't know. But if I save the cargo, will you give me an endorsement?"

The man shrugged. "Sure."

"I'd like it in the log, sir."

He hesitated. "That's hardly necessary, Lieutenant."

She looked up from the instrument panel. "Memories can be disputed, sir. My endorsement is too important to me to jeopardize because of a difference in recollection."

His temples slowly worked a few times as he continued to regard her silently. He crossed his arms, rested his chin lightly on one hand, and looked thoughtful. "I have faulted you for being too soft. I think I need to revise my assessment. You are obviously quite capable of being cold and calculating."

"What about my endorsement?"

His eyes narrowed. "We need to solve the electrical and cooling problems first. Everything else will have to wait."

"Aye, sir."

"Now, I am supposed to be on my sleep cycle, and I intend to get back to it. I need to be mentally fresh. You have the watch. We still have almost twelve hours to fix the problem. I suggest you use the time wisely."

"I will do my best. Good-night, sir."

"Yes. Good-night, Lieutenant." He gave her a last look, and then his footfalls faded aft.

Jana took a deep breath and checked her instruments. The temperature of the Peltiers had crept up another degree. Ever so slowly, the ship's warmth was making its way through the silvered vacuum walls of the containers. Each tiny impingement of molecule upon molecule inexorably carried a bit of thermal energy into a container's interior, seeking to equalize the higher energy outside the container with the low energy of its frozen contents. The waste heat from the fusion generators was more than adequate to keep the entire ship warm, and while this kept the crew comfortable and alive, in this case it seemed it was also going to destroy their cargo.

Jana studied the data traces, noting the rate of the slow rise in container temperature and the time remaining before they reached their destination. She leaned back while her eyes scanned the instrument panel. She crossed her arms and cradled her chin in her hand. Something obvious seemed to be near the surface of her consciousness but the emotional noise in her head drowned out orderly thought.

She attempted to simply ignore the voices of the replayed scenes, but they would not be silenced. She found herself repeatedly stung by Fesner's accusations of incompetence and weakness. She had always sought to be a good example, so these accusations were especially painful. But for someone as empathetic and open as she was, the charge of duplicity hurt the most.

She felt herself color, first in a brief wave of anger and then in the realization that, perhaps, there was some truth in the words.

You are … cold and calculating. The words echoed in her mind. Cold and calculating. Cold. Very cold. Cold as ice. Cold as … cold as … cold as the depths of deep space!

Her emotions suddenly washed back in a flush of excitement. *The solution is so obvious—why didn't I think of it immediately?* An excited smile crossed her face as she flipped the communication chime to the captain's stateroom.

"Yes, Lieutenant?" he sleepily responded.

"Sir! Captain Fesner! I have the answer! I know what we can do to save the cargo!"

Chapter 11

The captain arrived at the flight station looking tired and dour. "Did you really find it necessary to scream, Lieutenant?"

"My apologies, sir," Jana replied. "I just got excited."

The senior officer gave her an exasperated look. "As I said, you are far too emotional, Maines. You need to learn to control yourself." He settled into the left seat. "Well, let's hear what you came up with." He glanced at the instrument panel and muttered, "Nearly ninety-five degrees. The rate of warming seems to be increasing. We don't have much time."

"The containers are absorbing energy from the interior of the ship," she explained. "My solution is to deactivate any heat pumps to the cargo bays, then seal the off the cargo area from the crew area. We'll then pump the air out of the bays to transform the entire cargo section into a giant vacuum bottle. At that point, the only energy transferred to the containers would be from thermal radiation and the physical contact they have with the stanchions—and those heat amounts should be minimal."

Fesner nodded but frowned. "We don't know how the ship might perform with the cargo area at reduced temperature for such an extended period. We can't allow the water jacket to freeze."

"The normal circulation pumps will keep the water jacket from freezing. In any case, we can keep a close watch for any pending failure as the temperature falls."

"This is a risky move, Lieutenant. I can't say that I like it."

She glanced at the temperature trace on the screen. "The only certain thing is that we will lose those tilapia if we do nothing. I think it's worth a try, sir."

His temples worked as he thought. Finally he said, "Get aft and button things up."

"Standing by the watch relief checklist," she replied.

Fesner grunted, and when the checklist was completed, he took the watch. The fasteners on Jana's harness clinked. Her suit made a quiet swish on the seat as she rose.

She moved aft through the habitation section and trotted through the cargo bays to the aft equipment section. All the airtight doors between the aft passage tubes and the cargo area were already sealed, so she returned forward and ensured the seal on all hatches between the forward passage tubes and the cargo area. When she returned to the flight station Fesner started the vacuum pumps. They could have vented the atmosphere into space, but the loss of air would have been considerable and they didn't want to waste it.

The evacuation pumps lost efficiency as the pressure fell to the last few torr. But within an hour, the trace of the containers' temperatures indicated a noticeable reduction in the rate of increase. Thermal radiation trapped in the cargo bay was still causing a slight increase in temperature.

Several hours later, Fesner studied the temperature trace, sniffed and settled back. "We still won't make it," he concluded bluntly.

Jana pursed her pink lips and breathed heavily. The cargo bay was near vacuum, but there was still too much radiant energy in the ship to stop the containers from increasing in temperature.

"Thermal radiation is too high," she thought aloud. "Heat leakage from the water jacket is being trapped in the cargo area and then absorbed by the containers."

"We can't stop that without shutting down the reactors," Fesner pointed out. "And if we do that, we'll join the fish eggs at absolute zero."

"I wasn't thinking of stopping the radiation," Jana replied slowly. "I was thinking we might give it someplace else to go."

The captain looked at his lieutenant. "The only place for the heat to go is *outside*. Are you proposing opening the cargo doors?"

She nodded. "The ship's openings would allow the long-wave heat to radiate out. Each bay opening would behave like a blackbody cavity."[10]

Fesner seemed thoughtful. Jana didn't know if he hesitated out of fear or caution, but she acknowledged that the final decision was his, and so she waited patiently for him to speak.

"What about closing the doors?" he asked at last. "It's not standard procedure to run open ship for so long. If the cargo doors get too cold it's possible some of the door motors might fail, or the seals might freeze. We might not be able to tighten down the ship."

"I could crank them shut manually," Jana offered.

Fesner snorted. "I don't think you'd have time to hand-crank a couple dozen doors. You might not even have time to crank more than one."

"True," Jana agreed, "but we need not open all the doors, and even if we did, it is not certain that all of them will fail."

"Think worst case, Lieutenant, and you will rarely be disappointed."

"We'll open only one door as a test," she suggested. "Then if there is a problem, at least it will be a small one."

"Small problem? The only small problems are those that belong to somebody else," the man remarked.

"All right, small*er* then," Jana conceded. "Let's roll one just part of the way open and see how it operates."

Fesner nodded as he studied the instrument panel. "We're down to just a few torr, so we can open one of the doors."

"Starboard number one," she quickly suggested.

He creased a brow slightly. "Any particular reason for that door, Lieutenant?"

"It's nearest the airlock. If I have to crank it, at least I won't have to go so far."

"You're not exactly inspiring my confidence."

"Just thinking worst case, sir."

The doors operated by opening inward and then sliding upward on rails by means of electrically driven screws. Seal integrity was maintained by a series of mechanical latches around each door's perimeter, connected by rods to a common actuator in the center of each hatch. A single throw of a switch sealed or unsealed all the latches on a door simultaneously in the same way that a manual hatch wheel extended or retracted the hatch dogs. When the ship was on the surface, an open valve to the external atmosphere maintained equal pressure with the interior. But in the vacuum of space, the ship's internal pressure caused the large door to push outward, tightening the seals far more than the mechanical closure devices, but also making it impossible for the screw devices to open the doors until the internal air pressure was zero.

Since most of the air in the cargo area had been pumped out, the remaining step was to equalize the inside pressure to zero torr. To this end, Captain Fesner opened a small valve to vent the remaining pressure in the cargo bay into space. The loss of air was minimal at these pressures and simply could not be avoided. Vacuum pumps would require many days to capture the last air molecules and they couldn't wait that long.

"Zero torr," Jana announced when the pressure in the cargo bay reached perfect vacuum.

"Breaking seal, door one," Fesner replied, and he tapped the instruction on the screen. The actuator slammed open with a distant mechanical sound that traveled through the metal structure of the ship. A tiny light in the middle of two columns of lights on the control panel winked from green to red.

"Setting seal, door one," Fesner quietly said as he attempted to close the large cargo door. The actuator dimly banged again, and the little light winked green.

"The actuators work, at least," Jana observed.

The captain cycled the actuator several times, and each time the light and sound indicated the device was working at the low temperature.

"Opening bay door," the captain said. A distant whine made its way through the ship's ti-alum skeleton. When the door was open, he cycled it closed and then to open.

"Nice to be disappointed once in a while," Jana remarked.

"It's only one door," Fesner cautioned.

The same procedure was followed with the same success until four of the twelve large doors on each side of the ship stood open. The open portals emitted invisible infrared and longer wave thermal radiation to join the sea of cosmic background radiation at three degrees absolute.

The ship's internal temperature began to drop almost immediately, and the containers soon registered a decrease in energy. Jana felt satisfaction that her idea had worked—so far—but she shared the captain's reservations concerning closing the ship back up prior to planetfall. The ship could travel safely with its cargo doors open through the vacuum of deep space, but travel through the atmosphere of Blueworld required the ship to be aerodynamically clean to maintain stability and prevent damage from friction. Hitting the atmosphere with an open cargo door could rip the ship apart.

Fesner studied the temperature traces and nodded slowly. "At this rate, the cargo should remain well below the **cryogenic** limit," he observed.

"Reactor and control functions appear normal," Jana reported as she scanned her indicators.

"Now maybe I can go aft and get some sleep," Fesner said. To Jana's surprise, he didn't leave, but instead he leaned back, stretched, and yawned.

"Sleep well," Jana offered, hoping he would be encouraged to depart.

"Huh. I don't sleep that well, usually," he said as he crossed his arms.

"I'm sorry to hear that, Captain."

Fesner sounded skeptical. "Do you really care, Lieutenant?"

Jana nodded.

"Huh," he grunted. He took a noisy breath. She assumed he was deep in thought and ignored him while the quiet sounds of the ship filled the flight station. The hum of cooling fans and the soft whistle of the gaspers surrounded them like an old blanket, perhaps a bit frayed, but comfortable and familiar. Jana maintained her watch. She glanced at the captain and thought he was staring thoughtfully at the console. She wondered if he wanted to say something. Perhaps he was thinking of a way to apologize for his harsh criticism.

The prospect that he might express remorse gave Jana mixed feelings. On one hand, she would be truly glad if he treated her with more respect and fairness. On the other hand, she couldn't help but have a little malicious glee that he was humbled and perhaps regretful that he had wronged her. She was prepared to be magnanimous and hold no resentment, but part of her couldn't stop savoring the moment—experiencing what an ancient, Old Terran language called *schadenfreude*—a feeling of happiness at another's misfortune. Fesner would make his apologies in due time, and she felt no need to push him. Even if he never apologized, the important thing to her was that it appeared as if her endorsement was as good as signed!

She avoided looking his way, thinking that it might help to keep him from feeling embarrassed. Time went by, however, and he seemed unusually quiet, so she glanced briefly at him. Her face broke into a rueful smile. He wasn't thinking about how he could apologize to her. He was sound asleep!

Chapter 12

"Blueworld Approach, this is the *Aegis*," Jana announced as they neared the planet about a million kilometers ahead. At this distance, it took their radio signal three seconds[11] to reach the surface and another three seconds for a response. She waited patiently for the reply.

"*Aegis*, Blueworld Approach. Continue inbound. Report point five **megaclicks**."

"Roger, report point five meg," Jana acknowledged.

They had departed 3-space before their last jump traveling about twenty-three thousand meters per second on a heading that would put them on an approximate intercept course with Blueworld, about ten hours ahead of them. They would now continue falling toward the planet for almost five hours[12] before their next contact with approach. In the meantime, they would monitor their course and make adjustments. The correct heading and speed would enable the ship to intercept the contra-gravity beam from the Blueworld spaceport as it rotated below them. The necessary precision would be obtained through several course corrections as they approached the planet.

"Let me know when you have the first course correction plotted," Fesner instructed. The edge in his voice indicated his preoccupation with their open cargo bay doors. They had been open for nearly forty hours in the extreme cold of deep space—just a few degrees above absolute zero. It was crucial that they close, but would they? There was no record in their database of anyone else having tried Jana's **unorthodox** solution of running "open ship" to keep the cargo frozen.

"Course plotted, sir," she announced after a few moments.

The captain tapped the holoscreen and studied her solution. "Very well. Stop spin."

"Aye," Jana acknowledged. At her command, thrusters, mounted at various points on the surface of the great ship, winked sapphire-blue as they ejected ionized streams of heavy water. The rotation of the ship slowed and then stopped. Inside, the apparent sense of gravity disappeared, and the crew experienced weightlessness.

"Turn ship," Fesner instructed.

Once more, the thrusters winked, and the ship slowly turned. The thrusters winked again to stop the ship on the required heading.

"Ready to fire main engines," Jana announced.

"Proceed."

The three main engines fired, and brilliant blue streams briefly shot from the tail fin nacelles. Jana and the captain were pushed back into their seats for several seconds from the acceleration on the new bearing to correct their course.

"First firing complete," Jana announced.

"Give us some gravity," Fesner ordered. "It will be several hours before we'll be able to calculate our next correction. We may as well be comfortable."

"Aye. Starting spin." Once more, the thrusters winked, and the ship began to spin, restoring the sense of apparent gravity in the ship.

"All right, Maines, you handled that well enough," Fesner announced when the tasks were completed.

"Thank you, sir." She turned to him. "Do we have time to talk?"

"About what?"

"My performance report."

"We're not on the ground yet."

"We will be in less than ten hours." She glanced at the monitor screen. "And the cargo is holding at less than sixty absolute. I'd say it looks like we're going to make a successful run."

"That is our job, Maines. That's the minimum. So what? You want a medal?"

Jana frowned. "I've done more than the minimal effort to solve this problem, sir. You said if I could figure out how to save the cargo, you would sign me off."

"If the cargo is safely delivered, I'll sign you off."

"Thank you, sir."

"Save it 'til we're on the ground. So far, you've been lucky. We'll see if your luck holds."

"Aye, sir." *Jerk!*

Five hours of coasting passed. Jana made contact with Blueworld Approach at the appointed time and was cleared to point one megaclick, just less than five hours ahead. The planet's gravity this far out was still very weak, so they gained very little speed, but as they drew closer, she knew their speed would rapidly increase. Everything would happen very quickly closer in, but for now the ship's relatively sedate routine continued—except for the remaining issue of worrying about the open cargo doors. Jana endeavored to be thankful that the temperature had stabilized, and she tried to stay optimistic that the fish eggs would be successfully delivered, but the captain remained tense.

"We'd better check the doors before we hit the atmosphere," Fesner said. "If we can't secure them, our emergency plan will be to steer wide of the planet's atmosphere and enter orbit." He looked up from the screens, and Jana noticed a few drops of moisture on his upper lip. "I don't even want to think of what a mess *that* would be."

"We'll make it, sir," Jana said, trying to counteract his negativity. *We have to make it!*

"You better be right, Lieutenant. This is a lousy class-one world—maintenance service doesn't get any more basic. If the servos don't work and we can't crank the doors manually, we could be waiting in orbit for days until they shuttle a tech team up from the surface."

"Port door twelve," Jana announced as calmly as she could, trying not to think about the unpleasant possibility of being stuck in orbit for days with this man. *Please let it work!*

The faint whine of the servos and final thump of the closing actuator came through the metal structure of the ship. They both exhaled in relief when the indicator on their instrument panel went from red to green.

"One down, seven to go," Fesner muttered.

Three more doors were secured in quick succession.

"Portside, secure," Jana announced.

"I can see that," Fesner snapped.

Jana continued the scan of her instruments. "Captain, the temperature is creeping up," she warned.

He frowned as he studied the display. "We'll hold off securing the remaining doors as long as possible. The portside doors worked well enough. We can only hope that the starboard-side functions the same way."

Jana nodded.

The *Aegis* continued falling toward Blueworld, a planet with extensive freshwater seas, carrying a cargo of vital importance to its ongoing development. Jana adjusted their course several times, mindful that the margin of error was very small—and that the captain was watching her every move. A descent from deep space was like the threading of multiple needles: they needed to be at precise points in space, at precise times, and at precise speeds.

Fesner remained in the flight station, nervously checking the cargo and confirming every calculation Jana made. "We're just under an hour from the decision point, where we either enter the atmosphere safely or divert to orbit," he said at last. "I don't want to take any chances. Let's get the starboard side closed up."

Jana nodded and began activating the servos. The first door closed, but starboard door number eight did not.

"Another problem?" the senior officer sputtered in disbelief and frustration. "We're either jinxed or someone stuck us with the junk bird!"

"I'll try cycling it," Jana suggested, but there was no answering whine, and the indicator remained an angry red dot.

"Skip it!" the captain ordered sharply. "Go on to the next door!"

"Aye," Jana acknowledged grimly. She successfully closed the remaining two doors.

Fesner eyed the chronometer, breathed deeply, and ground his hand against his chin as he studied the instrument displays. "I *knew* this was a bad idea! We've *got* to get that door closed, or we'll have to make orbit. We don't dare hit the atmosphere with it open."

"I'll suit up and go into the cargo area," Jana quickly volunteered. "I might see what is wrong or I'll manually crank it closed if I have to."

"We don't have a lot of time, Lieutenant." His eyes flicked to the chronometer. "Fifty minutes at most. You ever crank a cargo hatch?"

"We practiced on my midshipmen's cruise," she replied. "I didn't crank it the whole way because we all took turns, but I remember—"

"I don't want to hear your life story!" he cut her off. "Get aft!"

"Aye, sir," she said past clenched teeth as she punched up the checklist.

"Forget the checklist! I have the watch," Fesner said, cutting short the routine in a surprising break with protocol. "I'll stop the spin as soon as you're suited up. Get going!"

Jana scrambled to her feet. She hurried through the habitation section and down the crawl tube to the airlock. She was already wearing her pressure suit, so she only needed to slide into the oxygen supply harness and make the connection. She pulled her helmet and gloves from the rack and tapped the communication panel.

"I'll be in the airlock. Stop the spin in thirty seconds," she announced.

"Thirty seconds," Fesner repeated curtly.

She entered the airlock between the suit-up chamber and the cargo bay and slammed the door closed. She spun the wheel until the latches hit the stops and braced herself against the bulkhead. The ship slowed as Fesner fired the thrusters to stop the spin and she was held against the bulkhead even as the sensation of gravity decreased. She used this time to pull on and attach the wrist seals of her gloves and to seat her helmet.

She made another check of all the seals once the ship had stopped rotating and then initiated the evacuation of the airlock. External noises faded as the atmosphere decreased until the only sounds that remained were her breathing and the faint hiss of Johnson noise[13] in her earpiece. Readouts in her helmet indicated that the suit was functioning normally and holding pressure. Her heart pounded as the airlock pressure dropped—not from fear of working in the hard vacuum, but from fear she couldn't solve the problem.

Help me get the door closed! The prayer was part of her breath.

"Radio check," she announced.

"Loud and clear," Fesner responded.

A green light flashed to indicate pressure had equalized with the other side of the outer door. She spun the wheel and pulled the door open to complete darkness in the cargo bay. *I forgot we secured the lights! I've got to stay focused!*

"Lights on, please, Captain." A second later, the cargo bay blazed with light, and she pushed off the deck and floated between the stanchions. The power indicators on each portside container remained disappointingly dark.

"Thirty-five minutes is all we have left, Maines. I don't intend to even graze the atmosphere with that hatch open."

"Roger. I'm almost to the door."

Stay calm! Look!

She floated carefully aft between the racks, until the open cargo door gaped from the far side of the stanchions. Jana involuntarily shuddered to think what would happen if she drifted out of the ship. She readied her tether line as she moved between the stanchion frames and emerged near the top of the door. She clipped the thin line to the stanchion and then floated next to the door closure mechanism.

The door moved between cogged tracks that ran from near the top of the ship to the bottom of the door. An electric drive motor mounted on the door drove the cogged drive wheels that moved the door up and down. A serpentine cable, called a traveler, carried power and control instructions to the motor housing from the ship's internal bus.

It might be something simple! Just look!

She tugged on the traveler's connections, but they were secure at both ends. She scanned the large cargo hatch for an obstruction but found nothing blocking it.

"Twenty-five minutes, Maines."

I'll have to crank it!

She braced herself in the footholds and fumbled for the manual crank, which was stowed next to the motor housing. She inserted the crank and started to turn it. The door crept downward at a pace that would have made a snail seem like a speed demon. Her heart sank. *It's so slow! It didn't seem to take this long in training!*

"Twenty minutes, Lieutenant. How's it going back there?"

"I think manual cranking will take too long," she finally announced in a shaken voice. "Send me the schematics. Maybe I can get the door's servos working."

"I'll call them up. Stand by." His tone was brusque with annoyance, but a moment later a hopelessly complex maze of lines flashed onto the heads-up display of Jana's helmet visor. "Isolate door switch circuits," she instructed the computer. Most of the lines disappeared, and she struggled to decipher those that remained.

"I think I see six switches," Jana thought aloud as she studied the diagram. "Two upper limits, two lower limits, and two obstruction sensors."

"Fifteen minutes," Fesner cut into her thoughts.

Jana tried to ignore him and continued thinking aloud. "Logically, the upper limit tells the system to stop the motor when the door is fully open. That shouldn't prevent it from closing. We don't have an obstruction warning, so those switches must be good. But the lower limit switches tell the system to stop the motor when the door is closed. If one of those switches was faulty and part of the system thought the door was already closed, the motor would be disabled."

"The lower limit switches are at the base of the door," the captain offered. "They are simple optical switches. You can find their positions by locating the optical path cutter tabs on the bottom edge of the cargo door."

"Roger. I'll find them," Jana replied as she found handholds in the structural bracing of the door so she could maneuver toward its base.

She grasped the ribbing at the open door's lip and ran her eyes along the door's edge. She spied the two short blades that protruded a few centimeters beyond the rest of the door. This told her where she needed to look to find the optical switches at the base of the door's opening. She quickly pushed off and floated back to the cargo stanchions. Behind her was the serene, star-filled background of space. Blueworld's sun illuminated the brilliant blue-white crescent of the planet, coming ever closer at the rate of over twenty-three thousand meters every second.

Jana reached the stanchion, grasped it, unhooked the tether, and moved it down, then repositioned herself and continued this leapfrog process until she reached the main deck. Once at the base of the stanchions, she left the tether connected to the framework and pushed off toward the base of the door opening.

"Seven minutes," the captain's strained voice announced in her helmet.

"I'm almost to the switches," she replied as she reached the bottom lip of the open hatch and pulled herself to the edge of the abyss.

"Lights on," she ordered her suit, and the helmet beams illuminated the dark recesses of the door seal. The faceplate of her helmet pressed against the seal as she pulled herself as close as possible to examine the optical switches. The first switch showed no obvious flaw.

Only one more!

Just beyond the lip of the open cargo door, now less than forty thousand kilometers above Blueworld, she moved hand over hand to the location of the remaining optical limit switch. Her light beam revealed a receiver notch identical to the other one she'd examined, but there seemed to be something jammed in this one!

"Maines! Get back to the airlock. We're three minutes from the decision point. I'm going to divert. We'll go into orbit, and then you'll have plenty of time to crank it closed."

"No, Captain! Hold off! I think I found something!"

"What did you find?"

"I don't know—I'm checking!"

"This is insanity, Maines! If you don't know what you're looking at, then forget it! We don't have time for fooling around. Get back to the airlock! I can't fire the engines with you back there and the hatch open!"

"Please, Captain! Just another minute! I think I might have discovered the problem!"

"Sixty seconds, Maines! That's it!"

She was unaware of her ragged breath—unaware of the ship around her or of the planet speeding toward them. Her total world was a tiny slot at the base of the great door. She fumbled in her small equipment kit for something with a thin blade, found a small screwdriver, withdrew it, and struggled to manipulate it with her trembling, gloved fingers.

She swept the notch with the screwdriver and was elated to see the dry carapace of a moth float free. She had literally found a bug in the system! The tiny body of the dead insect tumbled slowly away from the ship—a fragment from Oceanus that was now its own organic **planetesimal** on its own collision course with Blueworld.

"Try the door, Captain!"

Jana felt the whine of the motor through the metal deck and looked up to see the door descending into position. She hauled on the tether to move back toward the containers, and was clinging to the stanchions when the great panel settled into position.

"We have a seal!" Fesner announced with relief in his voice.

"Great!" Jana managed to whisper through a throat choked with emotion. She shook in the anticlimax and could hardly see as the tears, in the absence of gravity, filled her eyes instead of rolling down her cheeks. She blinked hard and shook her head to clear them. Several beads of water broke free and floated briefly in her helmet before impacting and disappearing into her hair or clinging to the faceplate.

"I'm turning the ship," Fesner announced. "Are you in a position so I can start a point-one-g burn while you get back into the airlock?"

"Almost, sir," Jana replied as she forced her shaking hands to pull rapidly forward. "I'll be at the airlock momentarily."

The turning of the ship seemed to twist the world, but she was prepared for it and was able to pull into the airlock just as the main thrusters engaged. Suddenly, the cargo hold became a deep pit. The outer door of the lock moved slowly down with the force of acceleration, and Jana spun the wheel to set the hatch dogs. She tapped the control panel and soon could hear air whistling into the chamber.

The inner pressure light winked green. She spun the inner door lock open and pulled herself up against the one-tenth g force into the suit-up room. Because of the acceleration, the aft bulkhead was now the deck. Her feet dangled into the airlock as she sat on the lip, twisted and unseated her helmet, and pulled it off. She gave a great sigh followed by several deep breaths.

Thank you! The simple prayer of gratitude ran repeatedly in her mind.

"Maines, are you almost finished down there?" Fesner's voice came through the communication panel beside her. She tapped the tiny screen.

"Aye, sir. Just catching my breath. I'll be right up."

"Well, don't take too long. We need to start our full retro burn very soon, and you should be up here. If you want me to sign you off, you can't expect me to do *everything*."

Jana broke out in a full laugh, and she didn't care that Fesner could hear her. "No, Captain, I wouldn't dream of it!"

Poetry Section

These poems are sagas—adventures in poetic form. They are supplemental stories of their own, containing background material that describes the universe of Jana Maines and some of the details of her early life.

Poetry possesses a power of expression and beauty that prose lacks. The rhythm, or meter, of poetry seems to activate a different portion of the human mind and can paint a word picture, create a mood, or evoke a feeling with even a single line.

The best way to read poetry is aloud, even when alone—although the enjoyment is even greater in the company of family or friends. When one reads poetry to another, one is not simply reading, but one is sharing the beauty of art.

A poem should be read more than once, just as a painting should be looked at more than once.

Some analytical notes on poetry appear near the end of the technical notes section.

The Pearl

I

In the solar furnace of nuclear fire
Protons and neutrons collide and conspire
To form nuclei new and ever more dense
At temperatures high and pressures immense.

Here and there is a star 'round which its family swings;
Some planets gas giants with beautiful rings.
Most are just cold and quite lonely places,
Cratered and airless with barren rock faces.

Some are too cold and others too hot,
Harsh places like these are no garden spot.
But a precious few worlds in this dark, silent sea
Have been touched by the hand of humanity

And changed, and adjusted, and melted, and warmed
To form livable planets by being terraformed.
The correct mix of bacteria, **lichen**, and plant
Can build up an atmosphere that was formerly scant.

For if water and minerals and sun are around,
Then with proper adjustment, life may abound.
And so to such worlds humanity went,
And washed up upon them like a wave that is spent.

The culture that brought them, that flourished and grew,
Declined and retreated—its life cycle through.
Abandoned and lost on many alien shore
Subcultures continued—the past hidden in lore.

The STC now the trade routes command,
Reaching out to the worlds lost in time's sand.
Restoring trade and communication
Using a free-market system to end deprivation.

Equality's chimera, long since rejected,
Each world keeping what it has protected.
The consequent end, for good or for ill,
In a few cases done by majority will.

Thus, some worlds were rich, full of mirth and delight,
While others lay mired in political **blight**.
The unevenness of wealth and of privation
Is the engine for most of mankind's motivation.

Not merely to live, but wanting to thrive,
Is what keeps the dreams of the dreamers alive:
Hope that the future will be a bit brighter
That problems be solved and burdens made lighter.

Now, the crews of the ships that ply the space lanes
Need courage and wisdom as well as brains.
There, in cultural backwaters lost,
Into these **milieus**, the space crews are tossed.

Yet time and again with decisions confronted
On great and small matters with knowledge blunted
From fatigue and emotion and ignorance blind—
Such is the case for most of mankind.

II

Now, on a world God had blessed with abundant air, land, and water
To a farmer of grain there was born a fair daughter.
Like her mother she was, of blonde hair and good looks,
And like her father, she pored over many deep books.

On this quiet planet, half-covered in grain,
The young woman grew with the wind and the rain.
Though seemingly part of this world's dust,
Hidden within her was a space wanderlust.

Not truly known—not even to her—
'Til the day her betrothed was shown a miserable cur.
The emotional pain of a heart broken and smarting,
Led her to go, from her own world parting.

"I wish you would stay," said her mother, eyes wet,
"But you must decide how your course will be set."
Jana looked at her father, and he gave a small nod.
"If you feel you must go, then go with God.

"Remember the pain of your present condition
When life seems to be a gross imposition
On the hopes that you had and the plans that you made,
Though we really can't know the good if you'd stayed.

"Wherever you go, there's both good and ill—
Rarely much help in showing God's will.
Many decisions that may seem small to you
May be most important from his point of view.

"We'll never know 'til our eternal rest
If a given decision was really the best.
But we can be calm and live without fear
Because we can trust that God's always near."

Jana nodded and promised, though her heart did not feel it.
Against future assaults she had determined to steel it.
In appearance a grown woman of blue eye and blonde curl,
Yet inside remained a young, innocent girl.

"Good-bye, big sis," said her brother, voice low.
She looked up at the young man with his hair of **tow**.
"I wish things had been different," he sighed with a shrug.
"Yes," she whispered, and hid her face in his hug.

Then it was time, the announcement did say,
To board the air transport and get underway.
One last prayer was offered, that God's will would be done,
As they joined hands together—father, mother, daughter, and son.

Jana's moist eyes viewed the ship; her ears heard its whine,
She waved to her family behind the safety line.
She tightened the grip on her guitar's battered case,
Then deliberately back toward the transport she faced.

Resolutely and quickly the walk was completed,
She stowed her things and finally was seated.

The scream of the engines like banshees did wail,
The ship lurched upward, and northward did sail.

From her small window, Jana saw fields far below,
'Neath a few freckling clouds in the gold morning glow.
Just the broad outlines—no details, of course,
But her mind's eye still saw her family, dog, and horse.

Like a mote of fine dust on the wind that is blown,
Part of her felt quite lost and alone.
But part of her still heard her father's strong voice
Reminding her yet that trust was a choice.

And that she was not probability's pawn
Even now as she rode on the wings of the dawn.
But a good plan existed—though not clearly discerned—
And whether she felt it or not, God for her was concerned.

The tools that he uses include the choices we make—
Often to bend us—rarely to break.
He works us and molds us, like a potter's clay jar,
Not willing to leave us just as we are.

As she sat in the transport, surrounded by strangers
She grew more aware of familiarity's dangers.
For most of her young life she had simply obeyed,
'Til the recent events when she'd been betrayed.

Shaken free of all the familiar routine,
She now saw herself as if out of the scene.
While somewhere deep in her analytical brain
She struggled to cope with emotional pain.

Unsure of God's faithfulness, of whom she'd been told,
Now her own faith felt brittle, ancient, and cold.
Her joy was now ashes, her pride now her shame.
From the depths of despair, she called out his name.

And here is the Mystery—what we cannot explain—
The way that God works in our suffering and pain.
We see his hand in Creation, but our vision is dim.
When our night is the darkest, we most often see him.

The calm that ensued came as sweet release.
Strangely, her heart knew a measure of peace.
"It is well," she could hum the ancient refrain,
And it seemed a new person stepped off of the plane.

There was no outward sign—no observer could know
The internal change that God did bestow.
No one really knew, except God and the girl,
How the pain of the heart can form a pearl.

Beneath the Surface

I

A leaf of green is often seen
As common, ordinary, mean.
But each leaf upon close scrutiny
Shows remarkable complexity.

So many parts that synergize
Molecules to synthesize,
Starch to form and air renew
And blossoms of the rainbow's hue.

Each plant from leaf to deep **rhizome**
Helps make a barren world a home,
By meeting the need—and some of the want—
Of the creatures who the surface haunt.

Thanklessly they toil in sun
Benefiting everyone.
They perish unknown, like a morning mist,
Yet without them, life could not exist.

But though we creatures may be unaware
The Creator with everything does share
Awareness—and no small attention,
Sustaining each by his intention.

No creature lives that he not knows it.
No plant survives that he not grows it.
The wind and rain—he knows them well.
(Though sometimes this seems hard to tell.)

And other things, too small to see,
Except with skilled microscopy.
These tiny plants do also toil
In air, in water, and in soil.

Contributing in many ways
To the ecology's complex maze.
No random choice but quite specific
Both **symbiotic** and **parasitic**.

Disparity from place to place
Drove commerce through the depths of space.
The *n*-drive on which all depended
Normal distance all upended.

Some distant worlds were traveled much
While closer ones remained untouched.
Multidimensions—most confusing—
Still not stopping mankind from using.

Traveling the great and wide unknown
Like seeds upon the space winds blown.
Taking root and reproducing
And innovation introducing.

Terraformed worlds thus became **prolific**.
(Humanity thought this was terrific.)
New worlds now fit for habitation
Each awaiting exploration.

Resources few in many places
Of coal and oil there were no traces.
But many held ores of various kinds
So, men soon worked deep in the mines.

II

Thus, on a cold and wintry morn
Thunder boomed on the cold air borne,
As a spaceship made its slow descent
Its flight now done, its crew near spent.

On a bare and windswept plain
The ship at last touched ground again.
A few buildings clustered near at hand:
Outposts in this barren land.

Support vehicles, both trucks and tugs,
Trooped out in lines like wheeled bugs.
In the ship's wind shadow they quickly clustered
To do the tasks for which they had mustered.

Unloading first the great ship's stores
To load back up with precious ores.
Trading the planet's natural wealth
For medicines and food for health.

A saving grace and source of hope—
The radioactive isotope.
Solar cells and fusion reactors
All much in use by space contractors.

The sources varied, clean, and neat,
All stoking mankind's need for heat
To turn the wheels of industry
To make things grow, to sail the space sea.

Like trading ships as in days of old
The ships plied the lanes with bursting hold.
A welcome sight for those feeling drear
On backwater planets with little cheer.

The crew, meanwhile, scanned the ship
Checking systems from tail to tip,
Checking their "bird" so she'd be safe to fly.
(Their care a factor if they'd live or die.)

With auxiliary power on to keep the ship warm
And protect delicate instruments from frost and harm,
The last tug left with driver and crew.
It didn't take much; there were only two.

The captain, a man with eyes narrowed and thin,
His lieutenant a woman—young, lithe, and trim.
Their breath smoked in the cold, frozen air
But being outside the ship made it easier to bear.

The woman glanced up at the cold midday sun.
"Are they still working on this planet, or is it done?"
The captain said nothing, just stared straight ahead.
The driver shot her a glance and then shook his head.

"There's just not enough vapor to trap the sun's rays.
But it's warm enough to do mining, and that is what pays.
With a planet so dry it's an amazing feat
That some lichen can grow, lacking moisture and heat."

Jana whistled a steamy blast from her lips.
"Lichens did *this*?" and she waved gloved fingertips.
Their driver nodded. "Yes, but not with much ease.
"You're seeing the work of over three centuries.

"Now, farther south more heat is found,
But it's here in the north where the ore's in the ground.
If we could move, you know that we would.
A bit of a warm-up would sure feel good."

Jana's smile was small—it was a cautious grin—
She gave a shivering nod in agreement with him.
The captain roused himself and looked around.
"So you spend most of your time, then, underground?"

"Yes," the man nodded, "but we must, you see,
For there's not much on the surface except ice and **scree**.
But underground we have accommodation,
Though not fine enough for commendation.

"There's a pool, a gym, and library,
A cinema, store, and infirmary.
And of course," he added, "there's plenty more—
Labs and units for processing ore."

"A city," Jana said, "but underground, then?"
"Or a prison," the man added, "since the population's all men."
The lieutenant looked to the captain, but he made no sound.
"Are you saying," she asked, "there are *no* women around?"

"It was tried," he said with a small, bitter shrug.
Then followed cold silence—just the whine of the tug.
"What happened?" Jana asked, wanting to know.
She eyed the thermometer, reading twenty below.

"There were ... problems," he said. "At least that's what's surmised."
"Problems with women?" grunted the captain. "I *am* surprised."
The driver regarded him sharply. "I don't think that's funny.
"You got it all easy, flying around with your space honey.

"Our contract is clear," he grumbled. "*No women allowed.*
And some of us got wives, too, for crying out loud.
But there's not enough space for families, they tell,
So we serve out our time on this cold, frozen hell."

"How long do you stay?" Jana asked with concern.
"One to three years," he said, "depends what you'll earn."
"Then it's your choice," the captain put in.
The driver shot a look of irritation at him.

"Look, buddy," he said, "I mean no disrespect,
But you don't seem aware of the attention you direct."
The captain's eyes narrowed, growing ever more thin.
"What do you mean?" he demanded at the driver's weak grin.

"Look, it's a free-market system we all here live by.
When a commodity's rare, then the price is sky high.
Now, womenfolk here," he tossed a gloved hand,
"Can command a good price, since supply's way short of demand."

"Thanks for the review," Jana said, "of basic economics.
You need not explain the resulting ergonomics."
The driver smiled as the tug lowered its whine.
"You catch on quick, lady. I think you'll do fine."

The captain's eyes opened as he looked at her.
How would she respond to this **blatant** offer?
"In a free-market system," she said, "there's mutual consent.
Buyer and seller must *both* be content.

"When either is forced then the market's not free.
Such is the case in a monopoly."
"Well, you're sole supplier," he said. "And by me, that's fine.
You're the one sitting on the potential gold mine."

"A supplier," she replied, "should not be required to sell,
Even if sales would go very well."
The driver arose and gave a small shrug.
"But why turn down a profit?" He stepped off of the tug.

The space crew stepped quickly to the portmaster's door.
The driver led them with no evident rancor.
"It's been nice to meet you—I hope to see you again."
Then he grinned and zoomed off and was gone from their ken.

"So," asked the captain, with once more narrowed eye,
Are you considering sales of your valued supply?"
She frowned and stared into the captain's bland face.
"Sir, these men are one thing, but you know your place."

The officer reddened and looked down at the snow.
"I wasn't asking for me, if you wanted to know."

"Oh?" she asked archly, her gaze penetrating.
"Well," he said slowly, "it's for your professional rating."

She nodded and then they both just let it go,
Stepping into the office and out of the snow.
The portmaster was ready, with his lading complete.
They reviewed the record and asked where to eat.

"The canteen is open most all hours of the day."
(The portmaster's girth proved he knew the way.)
"We run continuous shifts, so everything's in stock,
For breakfast, lunch, or dinner—all 'round the clock."

"Well," said Jana, "if you'd kindly show us the way
We'll have coffee and quickly select an entrée."
The man waved a hand then dug finger in ear.
"No need to show you, since the way is so clear.

"Our complex is laid out in concentric rings
With radii running outward—straight as strings.
There are, at present, four downward degrees,
So three coordinates fix any location with ease.

"This office is level one, ring two, radius four.
The canteen is level two, ring two, but three radii more.
Thus, stay on this ring; drop a level and then three radii up
Will get you your coffee, hot in the cup.

"I'd go with you, but I've some reports that are late,
And also, if you'll excuse me, before you came I just ate."
"Don't worry," said the captain, "we'll be all right.
But we also should know where we'll spend the night."

The portmaster referred to his screen and spoke to them then:
"Level two, ring three, on radius ten."
He looked at the lieutenant; his stare bordered on rude.
In his eyes was a hunger—but it wasn't for food.

They both left the office and a level descended.
At first they said little, conversation suspended.
"Now, Lieutenant," said the captain, "don't get your nose out of joint
But the situation here, I think, makes an important point."

"And what is the point and situation?"
She seemed outwardly calm—as in any conversation.
He cleared his throat. "It's, well, you know, the men.
They're like a coop full of roosters with only one hen.

"Forgive my bluntness, or if I cause some alarm,
But I am deeply concerned that you come to no harm."
"Thank you," she said simply, "for your concern, sir."
(It was not the reaction he'd expected from her.)

"But I think—if I understand male psychology—
That I am far safer than you believe me to be."
"How so?" he asked, doubting the words that she'd said.
"Why, every man here hopes to land you in bed."

"I understand that," she agreed with a smile,
"But I've known that's the case for quite a long while.
It doesn't take long for girl to find
That most men have just one thing in mind.

"When it comes to women—either plain or fair—
The man's mind is, well, you know where.
What keeps women safe from men's dangers then?
The answer is simple—it's other men!"

The captain chuckled, but not very long.
"I sure hope you're right, because if you're wrong
Though I'll do what I can if the worst does come true,
I doubt God himself could even save you."

"I note your concern," she replied, "but consider these facts—
Each one of which could stop the men in their tracks:
One, we're officers under STC command.
Should we be harmed, there'd be strong reprimand.

"Two, you act as a witness, and that all alone
Halts action that the conscience does not condone.
Three, our driver said this was a free-market state.
As supplier, I'm entitled to set my own rate.

"Four, not all of these men are completely debased.
A family man's paternal instincts cannot be completely erased.
Few men with a wife or a loving daughter at home
Will betray their trust, even though their eyes roam.

"And five, despite your lack of faith in his power,
I believe God can use us every hour
In ways that most often come as a surprise.
His will is accomplished—sure as the sunrise."

"I see," he replied. "You've got it all calculated.
Don't forget though, Lieutenant, life's more complicated
Than you might realize in your organized mind.
Such self-confidence may put you in a bind.

"As a space officer you must maintain awareness,
Be respectful and brave and treat all with fairness.
You've shown much skill, but I add as comment,
I am much concerned at your mystical bent."

They reached the galley and ordered their lunch—
Hot soup, a cheese sandwich, and crackers with crunch.
The galley was spacious with an intermittent flow
As the crews for their meals would come and go.

A few of the men stared at the new faces.
Most took a good look then went on to their places.
Conversation was muted, with few excited effusions—
Common in break rooms at such institutions.

They finished their lunch and rose to their feet
When three men also stood up from their nearby seat.
They walked up to the space crew and stood in plain view
"We was wondering, ma'am," one said, "if the rumors was true."

The captain watched closely and tightened his lips
As the miners' eyes moved from her face to her hips.
"Well, boys," she said, her voice loud and clear,
"Some free advice: don't always believe what you hear.

"My profession's space pilot. I don't work on the side.
If you've heard something else, then somebody's lied.
Now that *that's* clear—and I hope that it is—
Are there any more questions, or are we done with our biz?"

The speaker wiped his face with a well-callused hand,
Then glanced at his fellows and shifted his stand.
They looked at each other, and then they looked down.
A faint smile played with the captain's deep frown.

The first man spoke. "Well, there is just one thing.
Does this mean that you ain't gonna sing?"
Jana looked at him sideways, as if caught by surprise.
"You want me to *sing*—you and the guys?"

"Yes," said another, and the third nodded too.
"That's what we heard and wanted to ask you."
"How do you know that I sing?" she then asked.
"Odel was on Tachon," said the man, "when he heard you last."

"That was you, wasn't it?" the miner inquired.
"It's gotta be," said Odel, "or my eyes is tired."
Jana assured them that indeed it was she
Who had sung in the canteen on Tachon Three.

"We'd sure like some music," said Odel, "to brighten this place."
"And no harm in coming," he mumbled, "from such a right pretty face."
"I'll sing for you too," she promised the men,
"But first I must rest. I will sing then."

"Thanks!" said Odel, and his smile went wide.
"I'll spread the word from here to Farside!
Every miner will want to listen, I know.
We'll put it on vid—it will be our own show!"

They arranged time and place so that everyone'd know,
Then she and the captain were ready to go.
They moved out a ring, and up the radial sweep
And shortly thereafter, were both sound asleep.

Jana awoke to the sound of the intercom chime.
It was the captain, who said, "Jana, it's time.
If you're going to put on a show like you said,
It was my understanding that you would *not* be in bed."

She shook the cobwebs of sleep from her eyes.
"You are correct," she replied, and quickly did rise.
"I'll need my guitar if I wish to perform.
And also I want my dress uniform."

"I'll get them," he said, "but it'll take half an hour."
"Meanwhile," she said, "I'll have a hot shower."
"Hmm," he remarked, "this doesn't seem fair.
You in hot water, and I in cold air."

"The change will refresh you." She brushed her blonde hair.
"I'm used to cold water and you with hot air."
"Water," he chuckled, "we take as our predilection,
But the hot air, I believe, is mostly from *your* direction."

He signed off the vid, his grin gone from the screen.
Jana was soon standing, steaming and clean.
She was in a bathrobe when he rang the chime,
Tossed in her things, and was gone in no time.

The captain soon met his lieutenant, now in dress whites,
Her appearance one of the station's most rare of sights.
Gold stripes on the shoulder, gold hair, and eyes like the sky,
As a **seraph** of old, but without wings to fly.

Once more their space boots rang in the halls,
The rhythmic cadence of their footfalls,
The captain, as usual, was silent in thought.
The lieutenant hummed a tune as together they walked.

Finally he said, "I just can't figure you out.
What in the world are you so chipper about?
We're down in the guts of some old mining works,
Soon cheek by jowl with sweaty, dirt-balling jerks.

"Yet, you're smiling away like the Cheshire cat.
I can't help but wonder: 'What's she grinning at?'"
"Yes," she said, "when you look around
There seems not a great deal of good to be found.

"Below, quarters crude and rough remain.
Above, bitter cold, and harsh windswept plain.
The men are sweaty—filthy from toil,
And under their nails this world's soil.

"But just as below this barren earth
The men find ore of most precious worth,
Often, what we may think is no good
Has a wonderful purpose—just not yet understood.

"These men, this place," she waved a small hand,
"Have a value that we but little understand."
The captain smiled his narrow smile.
"Lieutenant, I think that if I wait a while

"I'll soon see you curse your rotten luck
Despite your present appearance of pluck.
Men—all men—are flawed to the core.
But you must have heard all this often, before.

"And even if you succeed a bit,
That still a failure makes of it.
For as you know, even a tiny flaw
Destroys perfection—its nature's law.

"Open your eyes to reality.
Yes, there's some good, but what I see
Are all the little things that seek to destroy
Whatever it is man tries to employ.

"The mightiest chain as you well might think
Is only as strong as its weakest link.
Search for gold in men or in soil
But mostly there's dross for all of your toil."

She nodded. "Yes, of course you are right.
But I choose to see the gold that is bright.
It matters far less how much the dross.
What's more important? To reduce the gold's loss.

"One small deed of kindness carries more weight
Than many great acts of grim, foolish hate.
Far better failure attempting a small charity
Than success and fame at some cruelty."

"Very well," he said, "as you follow your rule,
You are, at least, a happy fool.
And you might be right. But who can say?
We each take the gamble and follow our way."

"Thank you, sir," she said. "I know you meant those words kind,
But I do not think that we are so blind.
We each are given some heavenly light
We know there is wrong. We know there is right.

"We may be in doubt; I'm the first to say,
But of this I am sure: There is a Way.
Our existence, a gift, though filled with strife,
But our Creator still calls us to Life.

"And that is what I think God can see
When he looks at you or he looks at me
Or at any of these men around
In whom his divine spark is found."

At this time they finally reached the place
Where there was many a rough, dirty face.
The smell of sweat was strong in the room,
And in the corners, rocky gloom.

The captain muttered while she was close to him,
“The divine spark, right now, seems mighty dim.”
Then he grinned and nodded and stood back a pace
While Jana went forward and took her place.

The foreman waved to the crowd for a noise reduction
Then he began a brief introduction:
“Boys,” he said, “please give an ear
To this space gal who’s a-sittin’ here.

"I’m told she can really carry a tune
And well, I guess we’ll all find out soon.
For now, I reckon that’s all I will say.
Lieutenant Maines, let’s hear you play.”

Melodious notes sounded from the plucked strings:
The minor sixth, fourth, and fifth followed in the wings.
Her fingers playing both highs and lows
In sliding **glissandos** and rippling arpeggios.

Then her mezzo-soprano voice in a mellow tone
Sang an old ballad that was well-known.
It’s moving words of love and faith
Brought warmth and brightness to this dim and cold place.

The applause was loud and went on long
Dying only when she began her next song.

This a bit of humoresque
A miner's tale she did burlesque.

Of course, this became quite a hoot,
With much clapping, whistling, and stomping of boot.
And so it went on for quite a long time—
The musical rhythm and the rhyme.

She sang of life and death and love,
Of work on earth and heaven above,
Of promises made and promises kept
And more than one man openly wept.

When she sang the last song of her musical show
They did not want to let her go.
But the captain and foreman came to her aid
And at last, her exit finally was made.

The ship left on schedule the following day.
But the story was told for years, they say,
How the rough, rocky walls one night did resound
When the voice of an angel was heard underground.

Opportunity Lost

I

In ancient times the philosophers saw
The hand of God, and they remained in awe
Of what they could not comprehend.
Yet still, they prayed the muse to send—

To bring them light to understand.
Seeing truth as a gift from God's own hand,
For bringing joy and great delight,
To help to make their burdens light.

The eons passed and greater grew
Man's knowledge and skill on how to do
Ever more and clever things.
(But there was still no end to sufferings.)

For Man oft used his clever skill
To hurt and maim and also kill.
Thus, the greater grew technology
The greater grew Man's agony.

At last, Mankind had nuclear fire
With consequences far more dire.
And when they saw what they had wrought
The world had changed—but Man had not.

This crisis passed but left its scars.
Then Mankind learned to touch the stars.
So through the universe they spread.
They lived. They built. They buried their dead.

The crises did not end, of course,
For outward things change not the source—
Which is the heart, the hidden place
Of every child of Adam's race.

But still, beyond, beneath it all
The whisper of the Creator's call
To those who would, his voice heeding,
Space-time no barrier to his leading.

God's whisper often shouted down
By cleric, seer, sage, and crown.
Each claiming to hold the Divine Plan—
Ignoring how God speaks to Man.

But though to God, Man is resistant,
God's love for Man is more persistent.
He finds his own in every place.
Not one is lost, in any case.

He calls and his own hear his voice.
Yet a mystery still—God's will, Man's choice.
Too profound, too deep—none comprehends.
Our pride must cease where knowledge ends.

For only here can faith begin.
Mysteriously one is born again,
And light and life somehow infused.
(Just as mysteriously refused.)

II

So Jana of an evening sat
Admiring a sun, setting red and fat.
A beautiful evening on a chaise
Relaxing in the sun's last rays.

The smell of pine was in the air
Surrounding this high mountain lair.
In a castle, perched on mountainside,
She rested from a long space ride.

This world now had a pleasant mien
With forest, lake, and mountain stream.
For the founders of this world were dead
In conflicts old when blood was shed.

Until at last there were no more—
Such is the cost of total war.
Their cause forgotten in the dust.
Their tools of battle turned to rust.

Glacial chips in her glass did softly clink
As she sipped a fruity drink
And watched in undimmed fascination
The starry evening's constellation.

She sighed and slowly stretched herself
Warm upon her padded shelf.
In vale below, a gray fog bank,
But crystal sky o'er mountain flank.

"Oh!" she sighed. "What a wondrous view!"
A small cough beside. "I agree with you."
She turned in sudden start to see—
Who had arrived so quietly?

"Sir?" she said to the man,
Who moved lightly and with élan.
He strode then to the balustrade,
Sat, and coolly eyed the maid.

He met her look but broke the gaze.
The sun, a ruddy, flaming blaze
At the world's rim and sinking slow.
The stars were shining brightly now.

The woman pulled herself upright,
Cautious in the fading light.
She wrapped her arms around her knees
And asked, "How may I help you, please?"

"Oh, what you are doing pleases me.
I hoped to share your reverie."
She raised a brow—a graceful curve—
This fellow had no lack of nerve.

"Sir, with your cheek none can compete.
You come here on your little cat feet
And invite yourself without consent.
I know neither you nor your intent.

"I warn you, though, far in advance,
I'll tolerate no song and dance.
So speak up, man, clear and plain.
What are you about? Can you explain?"

She was in no mood for verbal footsie,
Nor to be a stranger's tootsie.
She faced him now with gaze unblinking.
He paused in silence, quickly thinking.

"Your pardon, ma'am," he slowly said
And gave a toss of well-groomed head.
"I'm sorry and no insult meant.
My sole intent was compliment.

"And my arrival done so quietly
Was to show respect—not subtlety."
He smiled and bobbed his head again.
"Have I satisfied you, then?"

She sniffed with just a trace of ire.
"Who are you? What's your desire?
Be aware, sir, I am no simple maid,
But an officer of the deep-space trade."

She was now sitting bolt upright.
He leaned back in the dimming light,
Swinging foot from balustrade
While he (she thought) once more delayed.

"My name," he said, "is Renít Mandío.
I, like you, I think you should know
While not a crewman in the strictest sense,
Travel space at my own expense."

Small brows knitted. "Go on," she said.
"Our paths crossed," he quipped, "as by chance we're led."
Once more the little, nervous cough
When he saw she'd not be put off.

"Mr. Mandío, I weary of this charade.
Tell me how your credit's made."
He cleared his throat. "I'm an investor, one could say, of sorts.
I have business dealings in many ports."

"So," Jana said, narrowing eyes of blue,
"Your sneakiness is what you professionally do."
His hand quickly batted at the air.
"Aspersions, ma'am, are neither right nor fair.

"I simply find what's been abused
Or cast aside—no longer used.
The things that others throw away
Still have some uses, anyway."

"Yes," she said. "But are they safe?
Or will they poison some poor waif
Who knows not where and whence its source?
And you will never tell, of course."

"My dear madam!" Renít cried.
"I swear to you, I've *never* lied.
Whenever any asks my source,
I speak the truth as a matter of course."

"Ah!" she shot back. "I'm sure *you* could.
But your clients never would,
Since they are by distress tasked.
These types of questions are seldom asked."

"That may be," Renít admitted.
"But onto me no blame is fitted.
I see a need and then I meet it.
With thankfulness my clients greet it."

"Hmm," she said. "Let all be true.
What then shall I be to you?
A partner in some dubious scheme
To help you skim some tainted cream?"

He rose and said, "Surely you jest.
And I must forcefully protest
Your never-ending accusation
Of my most humble occupation.

"I would ask but little of you—
The smallest act of favor due
To your fellow man who in distress
Simply begs a small kindness."

She shook her head and smiled in spite
Of her doubts that what he said was right.
The man was charming and persistent—
A pleasant rogue, and quite insistent.

"So what small favor do you ask?
Transport a letter, bag, or cask?"
"Uh," he said, "not *quite* that small,
Just a mere three tons of ethanol."

"You are," she said, "the chief of cheaters—
That's about four thousand[1] liters!
And what, then, is your expectation
Of this grainy fermentation?"

"Your ports of call," he said, "I know include
Some worlds that are less imbued
With grain and grape and starchy crop—
Lacking tuber, fruit, or bitter hop.

"I merely seek to bring some cheer
To those who find life very drear.
Surely you would not be so cruel
To let go to waste some excess fuel?"

"Mandío, you're aware, I'm sure,
That fuel may not *be* so pure.
Thus, you'll find me very cold
To carrying this heady load."

"But," he said, "at least I'm told
That this fuel is clean—as pure as gold.
And speaking of this end of grain,
We'd both a good-sized profit gain."

She shook her head. "I'm sure there would a profit be.
But since the choice is up to me
I think I'll pass this profit up
Lest some find poison in the cup."

"Well," at last he sighed. "You cannot say I haven't tried.
Though now in poverty I shall abide.
My only cheer—my own poor stores.
My dreams are shoaled upon life's cruel shores."

"Somehow, Mandío, I do not think
You are the type to helpless sink.
Your wit I have in fact enjoyed.
You could be gainfully employed.

"Why live your life upon the edge
When there are surer ways your bets to hedge?
So many ways that you could gain.
Though, of course, they are mundane.

"Yet, life is made of little things.
They are what real contentment brings.
You may win a long shot, true,
But that seldom is what you should do."

"Madam," he said as he arose,
I will *not* be led about by the nose.
I take the risks, I do admit,
But that's the greater thrill of it.

"What do you know of what should be
From your own vantage of safety?
You live without the slightest care.
No risks, no struggles do you dare."

She rose and to the balcón strode—
She who a space freighter rode—
Who perils daily did confront,
Yet she did not seem to take affront

But only smiled quietly
And gazed upon her astral sea,
Whose depths she'd plumbed a thousand times—
Each trip marked by tiny lines.

"We may choose our options and take our chances
And depend upon life's circumstances
To bring to us what we desire
Until the day when we expire.

"For to each of us many choices given—
Each one a step toward hell or heaven.
And regardless of our state of grace,
We will one day all our Maker face.

"For each word and deed we'll give account,
And all golden treasures will not amount
To any great thing upon *that* day.
Only what was done for love will stay."

"Ah, yes," said he. "You must be her—
The Ice Maiden, preacher, philosopher.
The one who all the answers keeps
And never with a stranger sleeps.

"Why speak of love when you cannot dare
With any man your body share?
Or cast aside a golden horde
For some strange, mystical reward?"

He moved to leave, but then he turned.
It seemed e'er greater his anger burned.
"One day," he said, "in another place
We may again stand, face to face.

"And if the Fates so play their hand
You may be at *my* command."
His finger wagged, time and again.
"Best pray your god will help you then."

He turned without another word.
His footsteps faded, Jana heard.
She shook her head with a small sigh.
Overhead, the silent sky.

The Wind

On a world whose plains
Were covered in grains
In rectilinear patterns arrayed,
A man and a girl
Of blue eye and blonde curl
In the wind on a hill, they both played.

The sky was deep blue
The fields a green hue
And the wind came fresh from the west.
Their laughter did rise
With their kites to the skies
And to them these times were the best.

Deep was the tan
Of the strong farming man

And dark were his beard and his hair.
But his blue eyes, they twinkled
In a face somewhat wrinkled
Contrasting his daughter's so fair.

Their kites soared and flew
In the warm breeze that blew
O'er the green fields about them surrounding,
And the joy welling up
Filled the father's cup
Like a fountain whose flow is abounding.

While the kites soared and danced
At her father the girl glanced
And her fine brow creased in a thought.
"What makes the wind?" she asked,
And once more he was tasked
To give answers to questions she sought.

"Well," he began,
"It's a part of God's plan
To make sure the atmosphere's mixed.
The wind brings the rain
Then dries it again
In a cycle that's forever fixed.

"On mountains so steep
The snow piles deep
When the wind blows bitter and cold.
The peaks keep their grip
Lest the snows away slip,
Their treasures of snow they do hold.

"But the wind it then turns
As the sun's fire burns
And the wind is tempered and warmed.
The snowfall does stop
And then, drop by drop,
Small rivers and streams are now formed.

"The streams then do flow
To the plains down below
And they water the fields and trees.
So, the wind brings us water
To you and me, daughter,
And to all else from flowers to bees."

She shook her head.
"Now, Daddy," she said,
"I still want an answer from you.
Not what the wind carries,
But why the wind tarries

Or blows—and why it wants to."

"My dear, you're persistent
And I'm glad you're insistent.
I'll explain it as best as I can.
But realize, you must
That despite your great trust
I am, after all, just a man."

The kites dipped and rattled
And the two of them settled
On the gentle hill o'er the field.
He pulled out a stem
And she copied him,
Expecting the truth'd be revealed.

"The sun," he waved his hand,
"Warms up the land,
Which warms up the air lying on it.
And like smoke from a fire,
This air rises higher
Pulling in air as a vacuum has drawn it."

She frowned with her eye
On the kites in the sky.
"But the wind doesn't blow up and down.

If the warm air is rising
It seems very surprising
That the wind moves over the ground."

He nodded and smiled.
"That's a good question, my child.
But you see, there's a top to the sky.
The atmosphere's limit
Confines movement within it
So the warmed air rises only so high.

"When the air reaches this top
The rising must stop
And the air mass spreads out and away.
As it cools it will fall
Where below we do crawl,
And it splashes, I guess you could say.

The wind thus is sent
From its place of descent
To the place where the warm air does rise.
Do you now understand
How across sea and land
The wind keeps our kites in the skies?"

She pursed her small lips
And watched the kites' turns and dips.
Then she suddenly narrowed her eyes.
"But the sun's way up there
And shines the same everywhere.
So why doesn't *all* the air rise?"

The man gave a grin
And stroked his bearded chin.
"My dear, you do not cease to amaze!
A light-colored surface is cool
As a general rule,
Though all the land equally feels the sun's rays.

"This difference in heating
Under the sun's beating
Is what drives all the winds blowing free.
So in this huge wind machine
The breeze is made fresh and clean
And is enjoyed by both you and me."

The girl tugged at her string
And she started to sing
And her father wondered and smiled.
His thoughts roamed from birds' wings
To the shape of kite strings

And to the love between father and child.

God's amazing grace,
Though we can't see his face,
Is revealed despite attempted rebuttal,
And his Spirit he sends
Like the movement of winds
Unpredicted, mysterious, and subtle.

The sun was descending
And the day and breeze ending
When the kites finally ended their flight.
Under the sky's darkening dome
Hand in hand they walked home,
A father, guiding his child through the night.

Technical Notes

The following notes will clarify many of the terms and concepts used in the stories. These explanations are instructive but not exhaustive. It is the author's hope that readers are encouraged to further explore the subjects described.

The mathematical solutions presented here are not as concise or compact as experienced mathematicians might prefer, in deference to those who are out of practice in algebra.

The following mathematical operators and conventions are used:		
•	"Equal to" is indicated by the equal sign (=).	2 = 2
•	The approximate sign indicates "approximately equal to" (≈).	2 ≈ 1.999
•	Addition is indicated by the plus sign (+).	2 + 3 = 5
•	Subtraction and negative numbers are indicated by the minus sign (–).	2 – 3 = –1
•	Division is indicated by the division symbol (÷),	2 ÷ 4 = 0.5
	or by the virgule (/).	2 / 3 = 0.5
•	Multiplication is indicated by the dot (•).	2 • 3 = 6

•	Proportionality is indicated by the double colon (::).	if y = 3x, then y :: x
•	Roots are indicated by the radical (√), with the radicand enclosed in parentheses.	Square root: √(4) = 2 Cube root: ^{3}√(8) = 2
•	Scientific notation is of the form a.bc x 10^j	1.45 x 10^2 = 145
•	Roots, trigonometric functions, and subsequent steps are generally rounded to no more than four decimal places.	
•	For clarity, the traditional algebraic practice of simply writing variables next to each other to indicate multiplication is generally avoided to reduce confusion with unit labels: "3 • m" means "three times m," while "3m" means "three meters."	

The following unit labels and variables are the most commonly used:	
m	meters when a unit label; mass as a variable
km	kilometer, or 1000 meters
g	grams when a unit label; gravitational acceleration of Earth at the surface in a general formula, which is equal to 9.8 m/s^2. This means the velocity of an object in free-fall will increase its downward speed by 9.8 meters per second, every second. This is also commonly stated as 9.8 meters per second, per second.
s	seconds as a variable
d	distance as a variable

min	minutes
v	linear velocity as a variable
V	volume as a variable
P	Symbol for momentum or power. The meaning depends upon the context of the formula.
r	radius as a variable
m/s	meters per second
m/s^2	meters per second per second, or meters per second squared
a	linear acceleration as a variable
α	alpha, a Greek letter commonly used to symbolize the rotational acceleration
t	time as a variable
N	Newtons, the metric or SI (from the French, *Système International)* unit of force
F	force as a variable
θ	theta, a Greek letter commonly used as a variable for the measure of an angle
π	pi, a Greek letter used for the ratio of a circle's circumference to diameter, rounded to 3.14.
Δ	delta, a Greek letter generally used as the symbol for "change"

δ	rho, a Greek letter commonly used as a variable for density
λ	lambda, a Greek letter generally used as the symbol for wavelength
e	the number e, rounded to 2.718
ln	natural log; the exponent of e that gives a desired value; $\ln(e^x) = x$

The Derelict

1. Finding the Mass of the Ship and Cargo

The schematics below indicate the side cross-section of a deep-space transport:

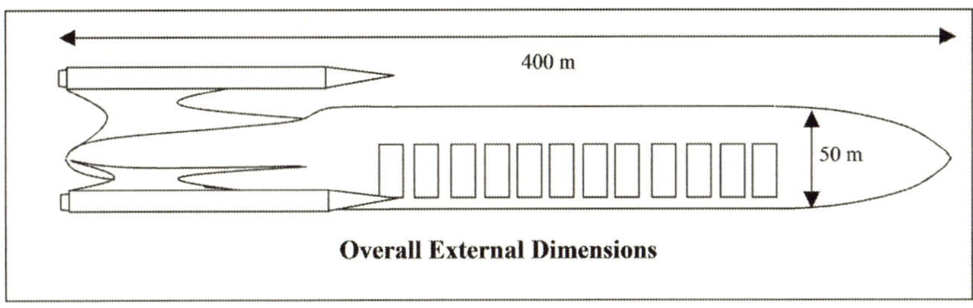

Overall External Dimensions

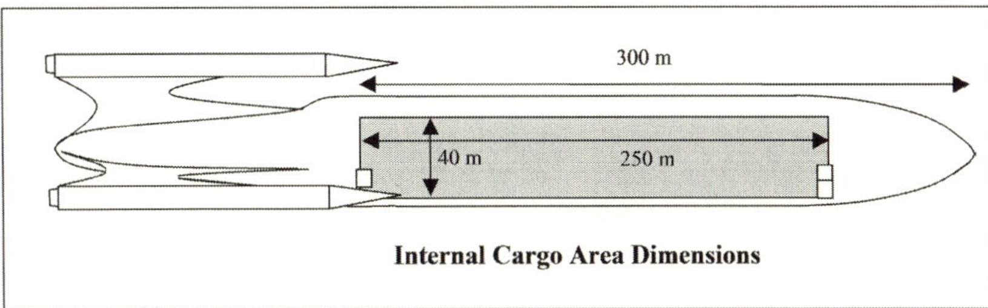

Internal Cargo Area Dimensions

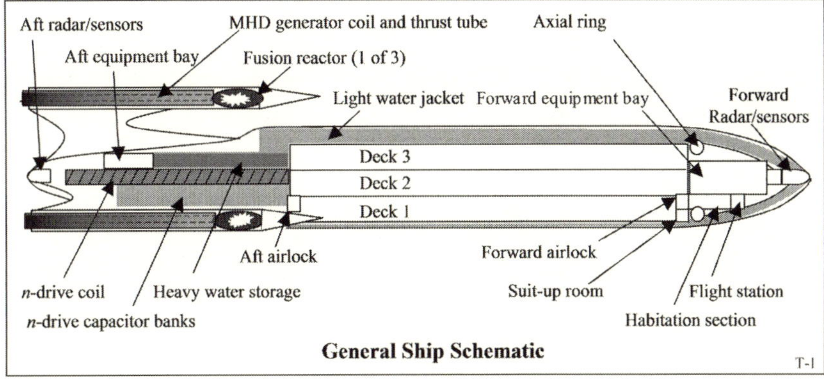

General Ship Schematic

The mass of the ship and cargo is determined in the following manner:

The ship is an approximate cylinder 400m long (L_s) with a diameter (D_s) of 50m.

Given: $L_s = 400m$

And:	$r_s = D_s / 2 = 50m / 2 = 25m$
The volume of a cylinder:	$V = \pi \bullet r^2 \bullet L$
The volume of the ship (V_s) is:	$V_s \approx 3.14 \bullet (25\ m)^2 \bullet 400m$
Simplify:	$V_s \approx 3.14 \bullet 625\ m^2 \bullet 400m$
Simplify:	$V_s \approx 785{,}000m^3$
Density of ti-alum alloy ($\delta_{t\text{-}a}$):	$\delta_{t\text{-}a} = 2800\ kg / m^3$
General formula for density:	$\delta_{t\text{-}a} = \frac{M_s}{V_s}$
Solve for mass:	$M_s = V_s \bullet \delta_{t\text{-}a}$
Mass of a solid cylinder:	$M_s \approx 785{,}000m^3 \bullet 2800\ kg / m^3$
Simplify and express in scientific notation:	$M_s \approx 2.20 \times 10^9\ kg$
Assume 1% of the volume is metal:	$M_s \approx 2.20 \times 10^9\ kg \bullet 0.01$
Simplify:	$M_s \approx 2.20 \times 10^7\ kg$
Convert to tons by dividing by 1000:	$M_s \approx 2.20 \times 10^7\ kg \div 1000$
Simplify:	$M_s \approx 2.20 \times 10^4$ ton
In standard form:	$M_s \approx 22{,}000$ ton

Finding the amount of the reaction mass

The ship's reactors are fueled by *heavy water (D_2O)*—a form of water containing an isotope of hydrogen called *deuterium.* If heavy water is split into oxygen and deuterium through *electrolysis,* the deuterium can be collected and fused into helium in a process called *hydrogen fusion.* Hydrogen fusion is the primary nuclear process that powers the sun and all stars.

A *light water (H_2O) jacket*—surrounds the crew area and most of the cargo area. Light water is ordinary water and serves multiple purposes. The engines can use it as *reaction mass* to accelerate the ship; when stored in a shell or jacket around the ship, it shields the crew from radiation; it can by electrolyzed to provide oxygen for the crew; it serves as a source of drinking water.

The approximate volume of water is a shell with an outer diameter (D_o) of about 50 meters, an inner diameter (D_i) of 40 meters, and a length (L_w) of 300 meters.

The maximum mass of the water (M_w) is found as follows:

Given:	$L_w = 300$ m
And the outer radius (r_o):	$r_o = D_o / 2 = 50\text{m} / 2 = 25$ m
And the inner radius (r_i):	$r_i = D_i / 2 = 40\text{m} / 2 = 20$ m
The net volume of a cylinder shell:	$V_w = \pi \bullet (r_o^2 - r_i^2) \bullet L_w$
Substitute known values:	$V_w \approx 3.14 \bullet [(25\text{ m})^2 - (20\text{ m})^2] \bullet 300$ m
Simplify:	$V_w \approx 3.14 \bullet [625\text{ m}^2 - 400\text{ m}^2] \bullet 300$ m
Simplify:	$V_w \approx 3.14 \bullet [225\text{ m}^2] \bullet 300$ m
Simplify:	$V_w \approx 212{,}000\text{ m}^3$
Density of water (δ_w):	$\delta_w \approx 1000\text{ kg} / \text{m}^3$
Mass = density x volume:	$M_w \approx \delta_w \bullet V_w$
Maximum mass of water:	$M_w \approx 212{,}000\text{ m}^3 \bullet 1000\text{ kg} / \text{m}^3$
Simplify and express in scientific notation:	$M_w \approx 2.12 \times 10^8$ kg
Convert to tons by dividing by 1000:	$M_w \approx 2.12 \times 10^8\text{ kg} \div 1000$
Simplify:	$M_w \approx 2.12 \times 10^5$ ton
In standard form:	$M_w \approx 212{,}000$ ton

The cargo area is roughly a cylinder 40 meters in diameter (D_c) and 250 meters long (L_c). The mass of the cargo (M_c) is found as follows:

Given:	$L_c = 250$ m
The inner / cargo radius (r_c):	$r_c = D_c / 2 = 40\text{m} / 2 = 20$ m
The net cargo volume:	$V_c = \pi \bullet (r_c^2) \bullet L_c$
Substitute known values:	$V_c \approx 3.14 \bullet (20\text{ m})^2 \bullet 250$ m
Simplify:	$V_c \approx 3.14 \bullet 400\text{ m}^2 \bullet 250$ m
Simplify:	$V_c \approx 314{,}000\text{ m}^3$
Density of copper:	$\delta_c = 6000\text{ kg} / \text{m}^3$
Mass = density x volume:	$M_c = \delta_c \bullet V$
Maximum mass of a solid cylinder:	$M_c = 314{,}000\text{ m}^3 \bullet 6000\text{ kg} / \text{m}^3$
Simplify and express in scientific notation:	$M_c \approx 1.88 \times 10^9$ kg
Assume 50% of the volume is cargo:	$M_c \approx 1.88 \times 10^9\text{ kg} \bullet 0.5$
Simplify:	$M_c \approx 9.42 \times 10^8$ kg
Convert to metric tons by dividing by 1000:	$M_c \approx 9.42 \times 10^8\text{ kg} \div 1000$
Simplify:	$M_c \approx 9.42 \times 10^5$ ton
In standard form:	$M_c \approx 942{,}000$ ton

The approximate mass of the cargo is therefore just under one million metric tons.

The total mass of a fully loaded ship (M_t) is the sum of the ship's mass (M_s), the water mass (M_w) and the mass of the cargo (M_c):

$$M_t = M_s + M_w + M_c$$

Substitute known values: $M_t = 2.20 \times 10^4$ ton $+ 2.12 \times 10^5$ ton $+ 9.42 \times 10^5$ ton

Simplify: $M_t \approx 1.18 \times 10^6$ ton

In standard form: $M_t \approx 1{,}180{,}000$ ton

The total mass of the ship including the cargo is therefore slightly over one million tons or one megaton.

2. A *raster pattern* is a method to completely scan a rectangular area. The rectangle is divided into a series of horizontal *scan lines*, where the width of each scan line approximates the width of the search beam. The beam starts in one corner of the box and sweeps across the width. The beam then quickly moves back to the start of the next scan line and once more sweeps across the width of the rectangle. The quick movement of the beam to the start of the next scan is called the *flyback*. This pattern continues until the entire rectangle has been scanned. The beam then goes back to the original starting point and begins the entire raster scan again.

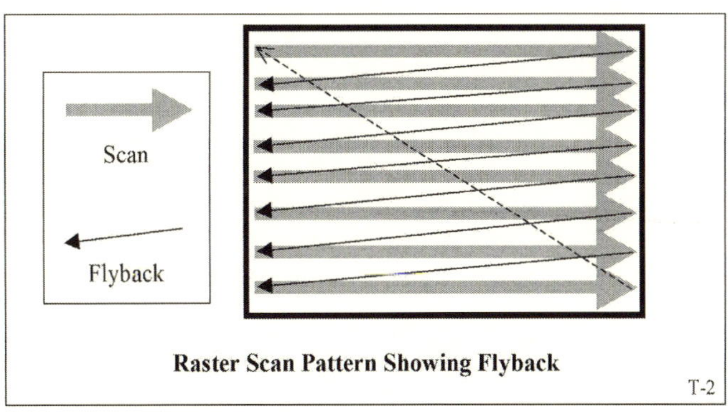

Raster Scan Pattern Showing Flyback

3. The *Doppler shift* is the apparent change in frequency of a wave due to motion of either the source or the receiver.

A stationary wave source will radiate the same frequency in all directions. The concentric circles in the figure below are a two-dimensional approximation of a three-dimensional expanding sphere of wave energy. A sine curve is superimposed over the circles to show the peaks and troughs of the wave pattern.

A moving wave source also radiates the same frequency in all directions, but to stationary observers ahead of and behind it, the frequency will appear to be different. The radiated waves will seem to be lengthened to observers behind the moving wave source and shortened to those ahead of it.

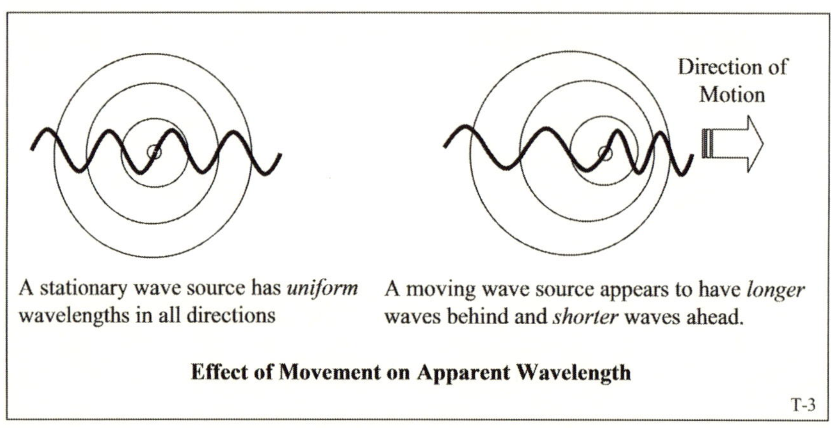

Effect of Movement on Apparent Wavelength

This change in wavelength results in a lower pitch when the sound source moves away from the listener and a higher pitch when the sound source moves toward the listener. In common experience, this is observed as a drop tone of the passing sound of a siren or racecar. In the same manner, light sources are seen as being redder (lower in frequency) to retreating viewers and bluer (higher in frequency) to approaching viewers.

Motion should be considered as *relative motion.* In other words, it doesn't matter if the wave source is moving toward the receiver or if the receiver is moving toward the wave source. The difference is simply the *frame of reference.* In one case, the frame of reference is the source and in the other, the frame of reference is the receiver. But in both reference frames, the source and receiver approach each other at the same rate, so the effect is the same.

Astronomical observations show that the light from all distant galaxies appears red-shifted. This means that these objects are moving *away* from us. The best explanation for this seems to be that the universe is expanding. This implies that if the "clock is run backward" on the universe, it collapses back to an initial point. This is strong evidence that the universe is not eternal, but had a beginning.

4. A Discussion of *n*-Space

The term *space* commonly refers to a 3-dimensional volume measured in terms of length, width, and height. The term *n*-space refers to space with an unspecified number of dimensions.

Space with a single dimension is 1-space. One-dimensional "space" can be visualized as a line. It is important to understand that a true line is not merely a very thin or narrow object, such as a string or even a strand of spider web, but a mathematically thin set of points that have absolutely no thickness. The *only* dimension is length.

In the illustration below, imaginary 1-dimensional "creatures" are shown as darker and thicker portions of the line, but this is only to illustrate them. In the theoretical 1-dimensional universe described, the creatures would have no thickness. The only variation between them is length and color. If sentient creatures inhabited such a linear universe they could never change their relative positions. They could only move freely along the length of the line until they struck another linear creature or object. If that other creature or object couldn't move, there would be no way they could slip past each other.

Linear Creature A	Linear Creature B	Linear Creature C

Imagined creatures in a linear (1-dimensional) universese T-4

This is not to suggest that such creatures actually exist. It is difficult to conceive how any matter could exist or biological processes take place in a truly 1-dimensional universe. We are considering such fanciful sentient beings to clarify the limitations of our own 3-dimensional existence.

By extension, 2-space is the two-dimensional universe of a plane. Creatures of such a place would understand length and width, but not height. The illustration below shows a hexagon, a square, and a triangle occupying an infinite plane. It is drawn from a three-dimensional perspective. We see the plane as if it floats in 3-space. The arrows pointing outward from each side of the plane indicate that the plane continues forever in those directions, and the creatures could move freely about the plane except when they bumped into each other.

We perceive the shapes of the 2-dimensional creatures because we can observe them from above or below the plane. The creatures themselves are locked into the infinitely thin sheet of their 2-dimensional universe and would only perceive each other as "lines," like looking at a playing card edge on.

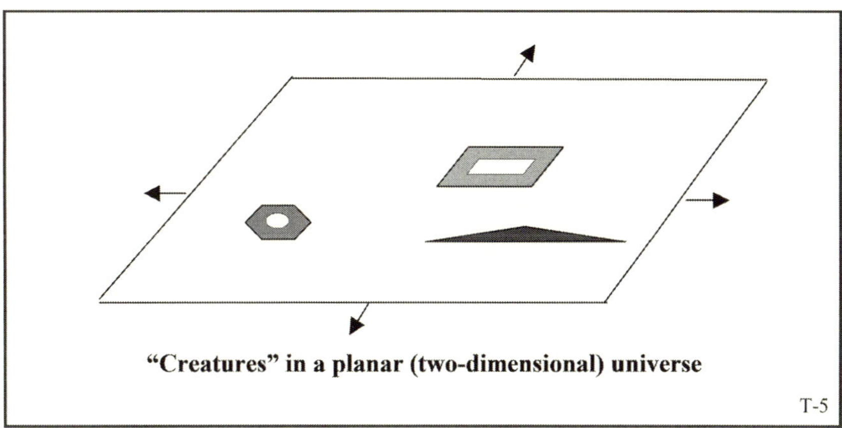

"Creatures" in a planar (two-dimensional) universe

T-5

The 3-dimensional observer has mysterious "powers" compared to the 2-dimensional creature. For example, the 3D perspective shows the square has a hollow center, the hexagon has a circular center, and the triangle is solid. It would be impossible for the 2-dimensional creatures to observe this, and they would find the ability to see "inside" shapes very remarkable.

In the same way, the interior of a closed 3-dimensional box could just as easily be seen from a 4-dimensional perspective—an ability that we would find equally amazing!

The significance and application of *n*-space to space travel is seen when we consider the results of "bending" or "curving" the lower orders of space into a higher dimension.

Curving a 1-space line requires movement into a 2-space plane.

Curving a 2-space plane requires movement into a 3-space volume.

Curving a 3-space volume requires movement into a 4-space hyperspace. It is difficult to imagine 4-space. Because of our perceptive limitations, we will once more utilize the lower order spatial dimensions to explain the higher spatial orders.

Imagine a 1-dimensioinal linear universe as a line with two points, A and B, on this line at some distance from each other. Even though the points are far apart in the perspective of the linear universe, the points can be brought very close together if the line is bent into 2-space. Visually, we could imagine pulling a string into a loop on a table so that two knots are close together. Hence, if a 1-space creature could somehow escape the 1-space universe and enter the 2-space surface of the tabletop, it could simply bypass the intervening 1-dimensional distance between the knots. In other words, a long distance in 1-space could be a short distance in 2-space!

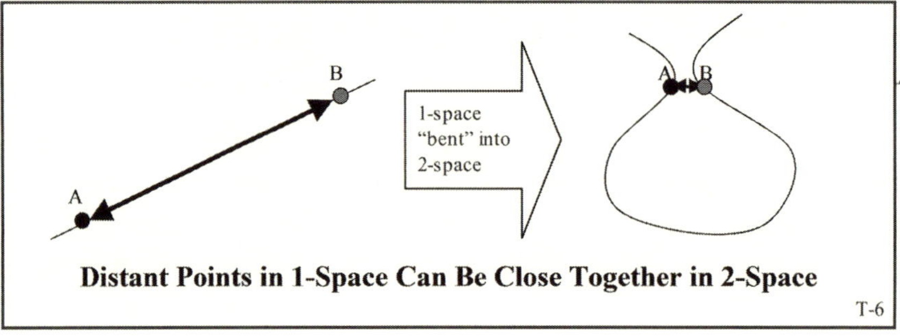

Distant Points in 1-Space Can Be Close Together in 2-Space

In the same manner, a 2-space sheet could be curved into a 3-space volume, making it possible that distant 2-space points are close in 3-space.

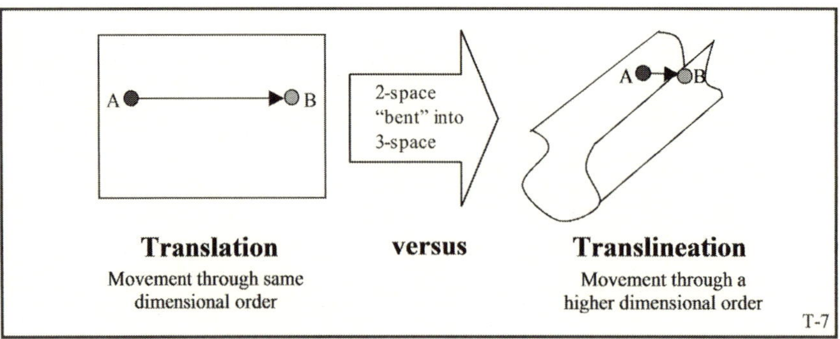

The theory upon which the *n*-drive depends assumes that our 3-space universe is naturally "curved" into a higher order of space. It could be 4, 5, or more dimensions. Since the dimensionality is not specified, it is referred to as *n*-space. Thus, seemingly distant places in our 3-dimensional universe could actually be very close in *n*-space.

This type of movement in multidimensions requires coining a new term. Conventional linear movement in a space is called *translation.* Movement through a higher dimensional space manifold we will call *translineation.*

A Note of Caution

The illustrations shown are simple schematics of complex, hyper-dimensional objects. A great deal of information is lost whenever a higher dimensional object is projected onto a lower order of space. This loss of information is demonstrated when a 3-dimensional object is analyzed by studying its 2-dimensional shadow. The actual properties of 4-space, 5-space, or *n*-space in general can only be assumed.

Three black squares that represent shadows cast by different objects are shown below. Is the object that creates the square shadow a cube, a pyramid, or a sheet of paper? What color is it? Are there any markings on it? No matter how carefully the shadow is studied, such a study cannot answer any of these questions. The shadow, therefore, represents a loss of information compared to the real object.

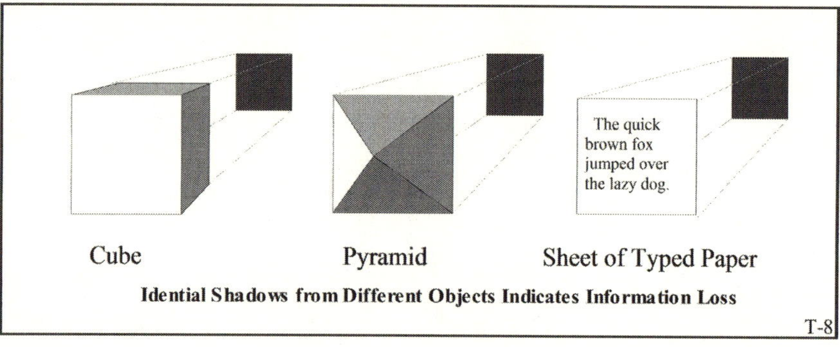

Idential Shadows from Different Objects Indicates Information Loss

Our analysis about the nature of *n*-space must remain tentative. Our comprehension is necessarily limited because we can only analyze a higher-order of space in terms of 3-space. There are likely to be properties of higher dimensional space that cannot be perceived or detected in the lower dimensions, just as the color of an object cannot be determined from its shadow.

What follows are good-natured speculations and an attempt to "think outside the box" while remaining grounded in as much known science as possible.

Time

Space is often called "the space-time continuum" because space-time consists of three spatial dimensions (length, width, depth) plus time. Time is, therefore, frequently referred to as the fourth dimension.

But, consider a 2-dimensional world in which 2-dimensional creatures go about their business. Using the same naming convention, time would be their third dimension. In he same way, 1-dimensional creatures would view time as the second dimension! It is difficult to imagine how time could be measured in a 0-dimensional singularity, or mathematical point, but we can conceive of it existing in time.

It seems appropriate to consider time as the first, or baseline dimension, from which the spatial dimensions follow. Matter can then occupy these temporal and spatial dimensions.

Genesis 1:1 poetically states, "In the beginning, God created the heavens and the earth..." This suggests that the order of the Creation is time, space, and then matter.

Historical Perspective

The concept that there is an aspect to our existence that eludes normal perception is not new. The ancient Greek Philosopher, Plato, (427–347 B.C.), discussed this in The *Republic, Book VII* in the parable of the cave.

Plato compared humanity to prisoners in a cave who are bound so they cannot move or even turn their heads. Behind them is a fire, and between them and the fire move bearers of various objects. The prisoners can only see the imperfect shadows on the wall, but not the fire or the actual objects. He argued that if the prisoners spent their entire lives in such a state, they would regard the shadows as reality—even if one of their members was released, discovered the nature of their situation, and returned and described the real world to them.

The Utility of Folded Space

The actual shape of the *n*-space manifolds could be very complex in design. A complex structure, while difficult to analyze or illustrate, would make a large number of distant and possibly desirable places in the universe accessible to humanity. This concept of using the manifolds of *n*-space for space travel is similar to the way people used natural rivers as relatively easy and efficient avenues for exploration and transportation as they explored and developed the surface of Earth. They didn't create canals for water travel; they used rivers, streams, lakes, and seas that were providentially already in place.

In the same way, the *n*-drive, as proposed, does not warp space. The energy requirements to warp space enough for space travel would be so immense as to be beyond even theoretical possibility.

But, if we assume that space is *already* folded in an organized way, then the only requirement to cross great distances in space is to briefly attain extra dimensionality. In this way, the *n*-drive could exploit the providential natural manifolds of space, just as boats and other watercraft utilize rivers or other bodies of water that are already there.

A simply analogy is driving a needle through a stack of fan-folded computer paper. The paper is unfolded, and a series of holes through each sheet shows that the needle touched each sheet without needing to travel across the full length of even one.

Evidence of *n*-Space

Physicists use atomic colliders to smash atoms. The shower of particles that result is studied in a device called a *bubble chamber.*

The bubble chamber is a tank of liquid helium. When high-speed subatomic particles pass through the helium, they leave tiny trails of vaporized helium. A photograph captures the fleeting images of the bubble tracks. The bubble chamber typically has a magnetic field of known strength and orientation. Charged particles interact with this magnetic field and follow a curved or straight track that depends upon the particle's mass and charge. Heavy particles make wide turns; light particles make tight turns. Positively charged particles turn in one direction while negatively charged particles turn in the opposite. Neutral particles do not turn at all.

The lambda particle seems to appear from nowhere! The lambda particle is believed to be a baryon, or heavy particle, that decays into two mesons, or medium particles called a *kaon* and *pion.* These are just a few of the many subatomic particles.

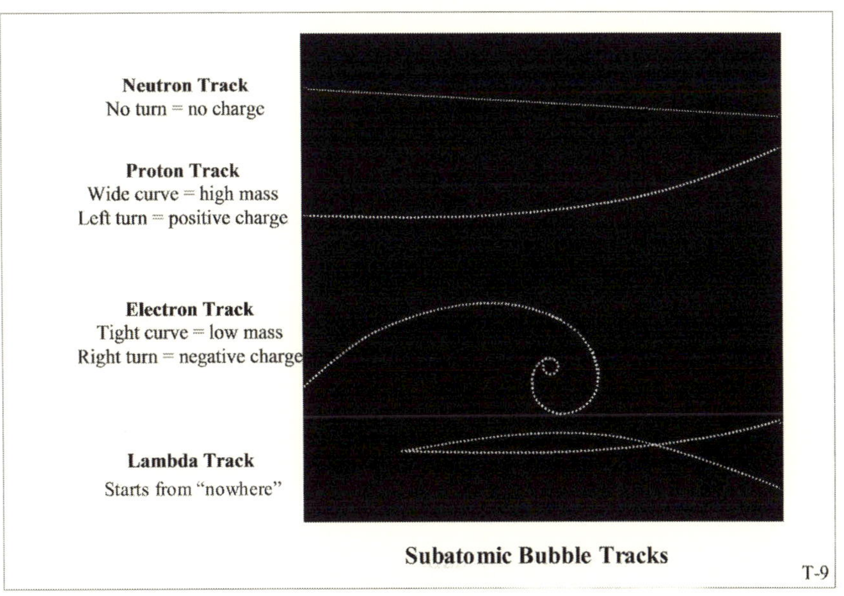

Subatomic Bubble Tracks

T-9

The lambda particle track is not proof of hyperspace, but this effect is what we would expect from a hyper-dimensional particle "dropping" into 3-space from a higher dimension.

String Theory

One model of subatomic particles is that they behave like tiny, vibrating strings. The mode of vibration of a "string" determines the type of particle. The relevant detail of the theory is that it proposes that these strings vibrate in ten or more dimensions. This illustrates why the term *n*-space is used rather than a specific number of dimensions, since the actual number of dimensions of the universe remains undetermined.

Curved Space and Gravity

A rolling ball moves in a straight line on a perfectly flat surface. If it encounters a dip, it changes direction. This seems to be similar to the way gravitational acceleration distorts 3-space. The straight path of a beam of light changes direction if it passes near a large mass with a strong gravitational field. This effect was predicted by Einstein in his general theory of relativity published in 1915 and was observed during a total solar eclipse in 1919.

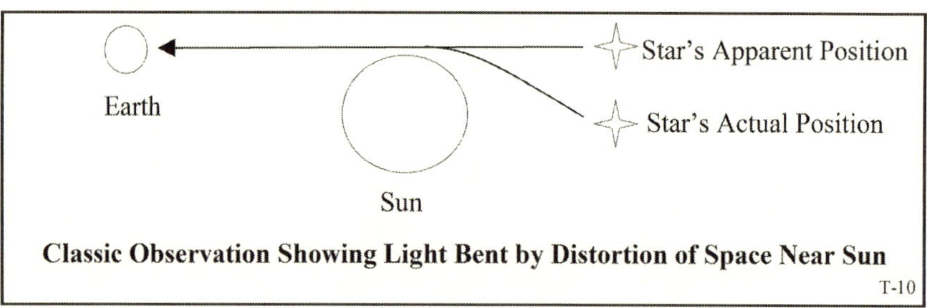

Classic Observation Showing Light Bent by Distortion of Space Near Sun

To help us visualize this concept, we will use a 2-dimensional visual analogy.

Let the 2-dimensional flexible surface of a trampoline represent 3-space. A heavy object, such as a bowling ball, creates a deep depression in the flexible surface. A baseball would create a shallow depression. A small ball would distort the surface very little, but it would tend to roll toward the depressions created by either of the other objects. This is analogous to the way a small object creates very little spatial distortion itself but responds to the spatial distortion, or gravitational field, of a much more massive object, such as a star or planet.

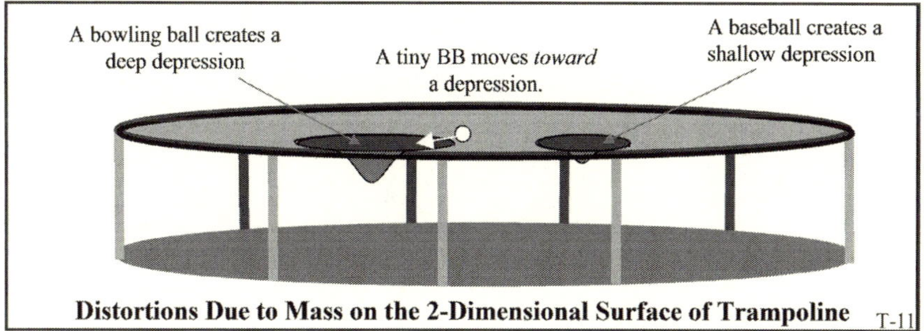

Distortions Due to Mass on the 2-Dimensional Surface of Trampoline

The presence of mass distorts the 2-dimensional surface into the third dimension, which creates a tendency for objects to move toward each other. This is the space-distortion model of gravitational attraction. The logical extension is that since mass distorts the 2-dimensional surface into 3-space, mass must distort 3-space into 4-space.

Suppose our experience with distortions on trampoline surfaces was limited to objects being placed upon them. If a trampoline had a natural sag in it, we would assume the distortion was due to mass. A small BB would create almost no depression of its own, but would roll toward the nearest depression created by a bowling ball or other heavy object. But we would not see any object in a depression formed by such a natural sag, so we could conclude it must be some sort of *invisible mass that is undetectable except for its ability to distort the trampoline's surface.* The mystery could only be resolved with the understanding that the trampoline had a "built-in" distortion that was not caused by an object at all.

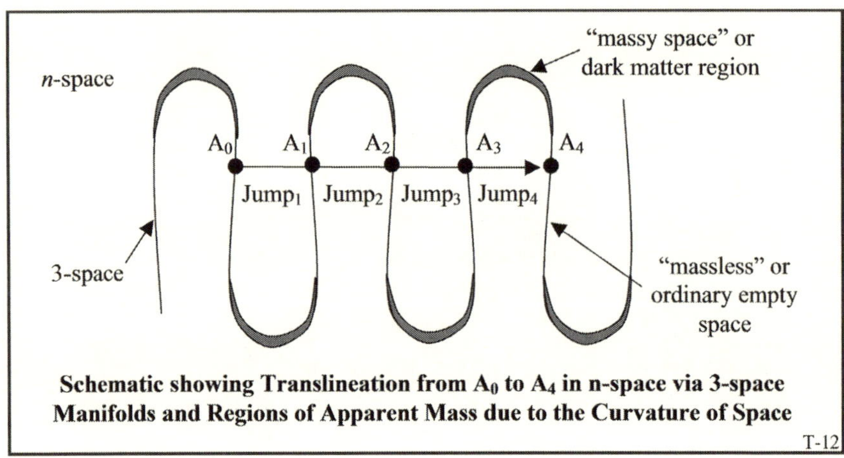

Schematic showing Translineation from A_0 to A_4 in n-space via 3-space Manifolds and Regions of Apparent Mass due to the Curvature of Space

Suppose the 3-dimensional universe is folded as the schematic above suggests. The 1-dimensional line represents 3-space and the 2-dimensional sheet represents 4-, 5-, or more-space, hence it is labeled *n*-space. The strongly curved zones would be volumes of space that experience gravitational distortion. They would be like sags in the surface of the trampoline and would appear as strong gravitational sources, even though no actual mass is present! The curved space itself would have an apparent or *imaginary mass.* Meanwhile the majority of 3-space that is distant from the folds would be gravitationally undisturbed, just as the surface of the trampoline remains relatively flat at a distance away from the bowling ball. These flat areas represent the more familiar region of ordinary, "mass-less" or "empty" space.

As bizarre as this seems, there is evidence that space might really be folded. The clue is referred to as the problem of *missing mass.*

The universe is traditionally understood as an empty void with matter scattered throughout it in the form of gas clouds, dust clouds, stars, and planets. Ordinary matter is seen as the radiant light from stars or in the reflected light from planets, or gas and dust clouds.

Calculations regarding the rate of expansion of the universe indicate that the known amount of matter is insufficient. It seems that about 90 percent of the required mass is missing. *Dark matter* has been proposed to provide this missing mass.

It is further suggested that dark matter does not interact with ordinary matter or energy except for its gravity—exactly the effect predicted as the apparent mass of folded space!

The dark matter theory is conventional in the sense that this invisible material occupies space. It is much like ordinary matter except it is invisible. While dark matter theoretically explains the observed phenomenon, it is without precedent. We know of no invisible matter in practical experience.

But the concept of "apparent" or "imaginary" matter has precedent. There are imaginary forces, such as centrifugal force and the Coriolis force. These forces can be calculated and measured and create real effects—*even though the forces themselves do not exist!* They only appear to exist as a result of the effects of other, real forces. While far from a proof, the existence of imaginary forces are consistent with the idea that imaginary matter could be the result of some other, real phenomenon, such as the folding of space.

Folded Space and the Expanding Universe

[God] stretches out the heavens like a curtain. Psalm 104:2

Astronomical observations indicate that the universe is expanding—just as the Psalmist says. The logical conclusion is that the universe began as some high-energy singularity—commonly called "The Big Bang." This was not simply a cosmic explosion—that is, an outflow of matter into surrounding space for several reasons.

In the first place, the expansion of the universe is not generally considered simply as an outward movement of matter into stationary space, but an expansion of space itself that carries matter with it. Think of the effect like the increasing size of printing or decorations on a balloon that takes place as the balloon is inflated. The printing or decorations "ride along" with the actual balloon expansion.

Additionally, conventional "big bang" cosmology assumes an even distribution of matter throughout the universe. This assumption is made to avoid the problem of the formation of a black hole caused by a concentration of matter near the center of the universe if matter were not evenly distributed.

The assumption, of course, is that all of matter and energy appeared at the same instant. But, suppose an expanding "bubble" of space appeared first. Further assume that energy appeared over a finite period of time. The energy would then both radiate and be stretched outward into and along with the rapidly expanding universe. The expanding energy would then later condense into matter at a great distance from the universal center, and the black hole problem might be avoided.

In any case, the expansion of the universe is *accelerating*—growing larger ever more quickly. Some force seems to be *continuing to pull* the universe apart! What the Psalmist wrote about three thousand years ago, accurately describes what is finally being observed today—that the universe seems to be stretching like the folds of a curtain being pulled apart by some ongoing agency.

A fold in space does not necessarily indicate gravitational attraction. Once more consider the flexible surface of the trampoline. A golf ball will roll toward the dip created by the bowling ball. But a peak or hump would represent "anti-gravity" or gravitational repulsion and the golf ball would roll *away* from it.

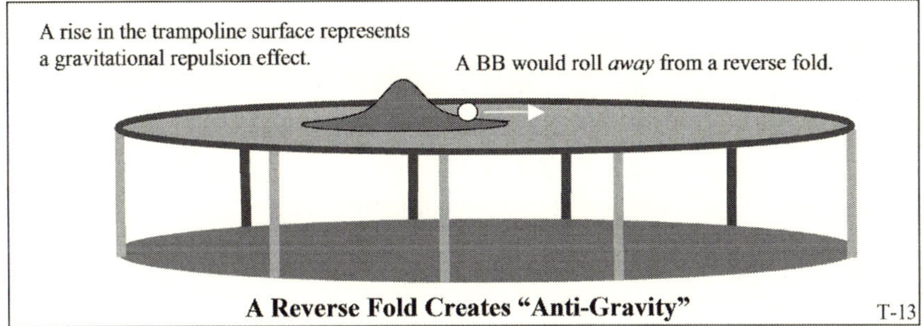

A Reverse Fold Creates "Anti-Gravity"

Below is a more complex model of folded space.

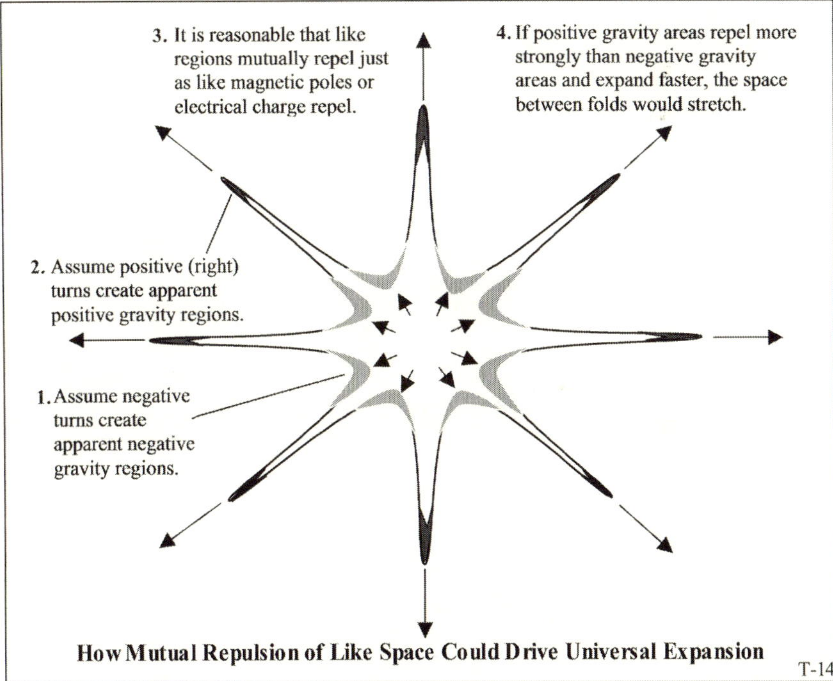

How Mutual Repulsion of Like Space Could Drive Universal Expansion

The "positive" folds in space are like dips in the trampoline and would exhibit positive gravitational attraction. The "negative" folds are like humps that create virtual gravitational repulsion.

The diagram of the folded universe shows the "massy space" regions at the universe's (4-space) outer edges. Because this is a gravitational effect and not an actual mass, the attraction need not be mutual. In other words, the folds would not necessarily tend to collapse toward each other, as would be the case for normal matter. The folds could attract matter, however, just as a dip in the surface of a trampoline attracts a ball that rolls near it. It seems reasonable that the folds might interact with each the way magnetic poles interact: that is, same poles repel and opposite poles attract—yet any pole equally attracts a piece of nonmagnetized iron.

The outward side of the folds could therefore have a tendency to move away from each other, as would the inward folds. If the outward folds moved faster, the overall size of the universe would increase and pull the remainder of space with it. Thus, the curvature of space at the inner and outer 4-space edges would be responsible for the increasing rate of its expansion.

The Contra-Gravity Beam

The *contra-grav beam* is so named as a theoretical device that overcomes the effect of gravity. This does not necessarily imply a true negation of gravity. In a real sense, the force of lift from an aircraft wing or the buoyancy of a hot air balloon are contra-gravity devices.

But if the curvature of space creates gravitational effects, perhaps knowledge of hyper-dimensionality would reveal how to affect gravity on a small enough scale to assist the landing and takeoff of the space transports.

Wave Interference

Since many natural phenomena have a wave nature, it is reasonable to assume that gravity is also wavelike. If this is the case, it might be possible that a contra-gravity device might involve *wave interference.*

A basic wave function has the form: $a = A \bullet \sin(\theta + \varphi)$

Where a = the instantaneous amplitude of the wave

A = the maximum amplitude of the wave

θ = the angular distance in degrees

φ = the phase shift in degrees

For example, below is the graph of the basic wave function for $\theta = 0°$ to $360°$ where $A = 1$ and $\varphi = 0$:

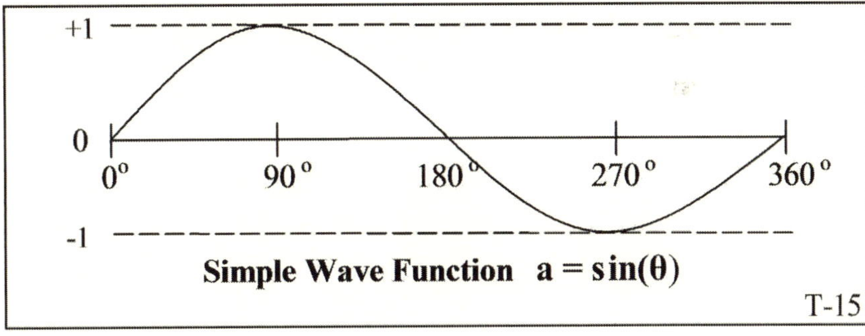

Simple Wave Function a = sin(θ)

Phase Shifting

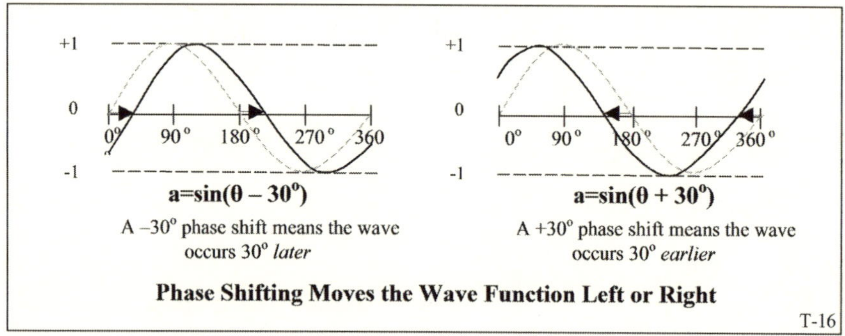

Phase Shifting Moves the Wave Function Left or Right

Frequency

The coefficients of θ adjust the frequency of the function. The larger the coefficient, the faster the function cycles. In the graph of the simple wave function the coefficient of θ is 1, so the function cycles once every 360°. If the coefficient is 2, the function cycles twice as fast.

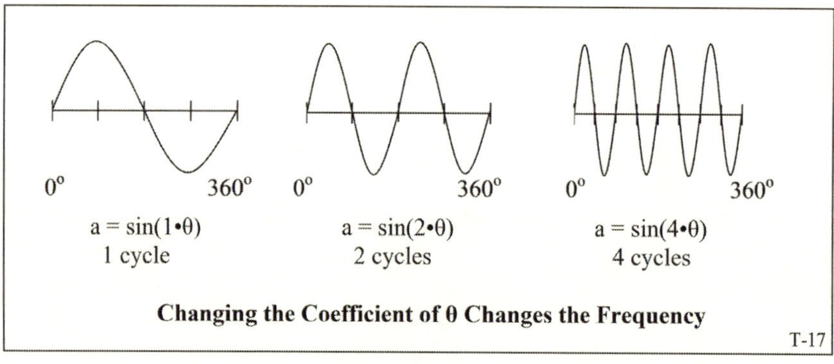

Changing the Coefficient of θ Changes the Frequency

The principle of wave interference is that waves can combine to form a stronger wave of higher amplitude in *constructive* interference, or they combine to cancel each other out in destructive interference. The different cycling rates between two wave functions create the interference pattern shown below. Another term for this wave interference pattern is the *heterodyne,* or *beat frequency.* The beat frequency appears in the graphs as a gray line or envelope of the primary frequencies.

The graph below shows how the addition of two wave functions can alternately combine constructively and destructively:

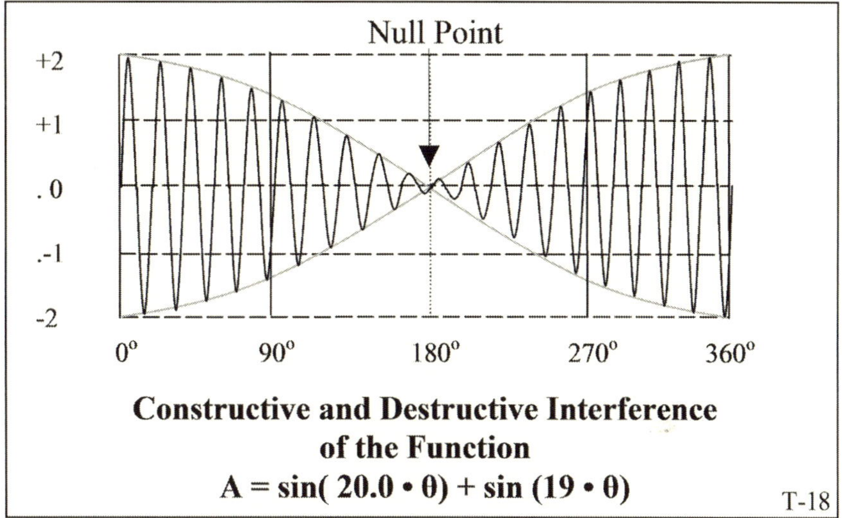

Constructive and Destructive Interference of the Function
A = sin(20.0 • θ) + sin (19 • θ)

Those portions of the function where the peak amplitudes are greater than + 1 or less than –1 are areas of constructive interference. Those portions of the function where the amplitudes are less than + 1 or greater than –1 are areas of destructive interference. Of special interest is 180° where the waves have cancelled each other completely and the peak amplitude is zero! This special point of the function is called a *null point.*

Adjusting the coefficients can move the position of the null point. In the graph below, the coefficient of θ in the second sine function was changed from 19 to 19.2.

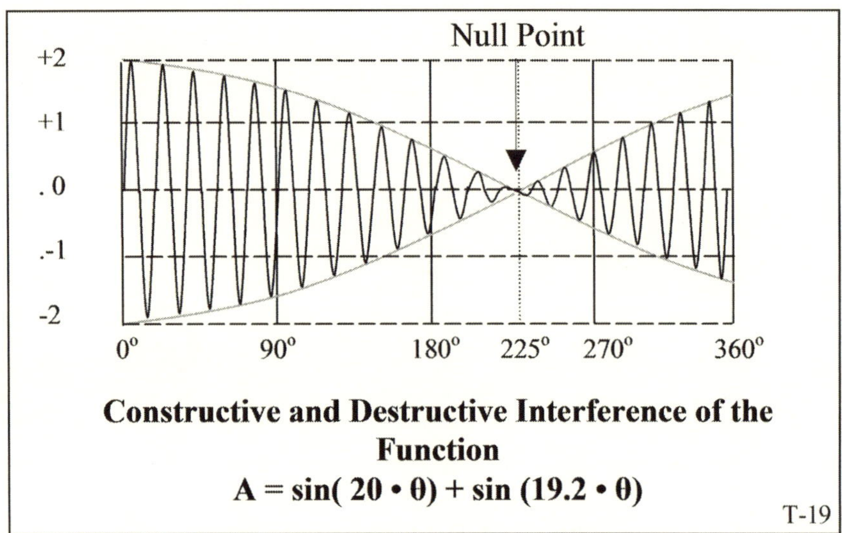

Constructive and Destructive Interference of the Function

$A = \sin(20 \cdot \theta) + \sin(19.2 \cdot \theta)$

T-19

The new null point is at 225°. The null points were found in the following way:

In the first case where the coefficients are 20 and 19:

The difference in coefficients: $20 - 19 = 1$

The heterodyne or beat frequency: $360° / 1 = 360°$

There are two half-cycles in a full cycle.

The null point is: $360° / 2 = 180°$

In the second case where the coefficients are 20 and 19.2:

The difference in coefficients: $20 - 19.2 = 0.8$

The heterodyne or beat frequency is: $360° / 0.8 = 450°$

There are two half cycles in a full cycle.

The null point is: $450° / 2 = 225°$

Linear Distance and Angular Distance

The relationship between linear distance (d) and angular distance (θ) depends upon a wave's velocity (v), frequency (f), and wavelength (λ).

Velocity (v) is the speed of the wave through the medium.

Frequency (f) is the number of complete cycles that take place in one second.

Period (T) is the time for one cycle. The period and frequency are reciprocals. This is written mathematically as $T = 1 / f$ and $f = 1 / T$.

Wavelength (λ) is the physical length of a complete cycle or wave, or, the distance the wave moves in a complete cycle of 360°.

The general equation for distance (d) is: $d = v \bullet t$

Since wavelength is distance and period is time: $\lambda = v \bullet T$

The period is the time for a complete 360° cycle. The distance (d) a wave travels is the fraction of the complete cycle completed.

Mathematically, the distance (d) a wave moves is: $d = \frac{v \bullet T \bullet \theta}{360°}$

For example, suppose $\theta = 180°$ then: $d = \frac{v \bullet T \bullet 180°}{360°}$

Which simplifies to: $d = \frac{v \bullet T}{2}$

But, $\lambda = v \bullet T$, so: $d = \frac{\lambda}{2} = 0.5 \bullet \lambda$

This is exactly what we should expect; 180° is half of a full cycle, so it makes sense that the distance is half a full wavelength. In the second interference example, the null point was determined to be at 225°. This would correspond to 225 / 360 or $0.625 \bullet \lambda$.

This shows that if gravity has a wave nature, it might be possible to create an interference pattern, which would cancel it locally at the null point. The position or distance of the null point could be adjusted by adjusting the interference frequency.

The contra-grav beam would be steered using multiple radiating elements in the same manner that a conventional *phased array radar* beam is steered by selective interference from multiple radiating elements in the radar antenna.

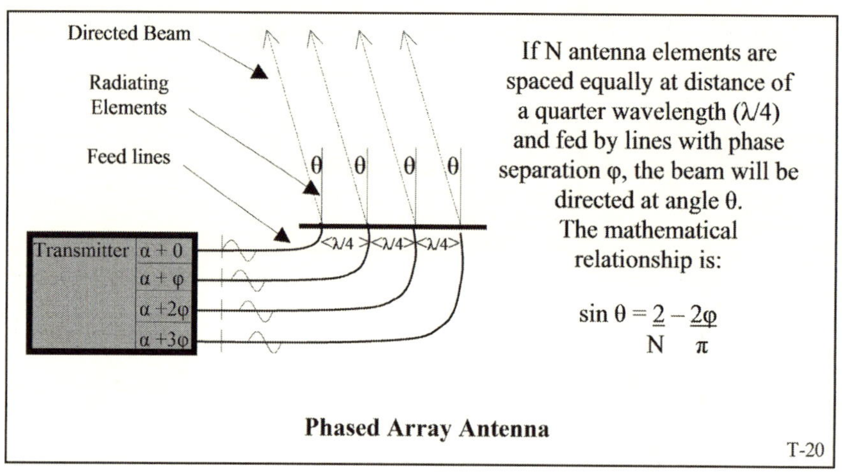

Phased Array Antenna

Radians

The value for the phase shift (φ) in the above formula must be expressed in *radians,* not degrees. Radians are used to measure angles like degrees, but radians are more useful for mathematicians and physicists because there is a natural relationship between the radian value and the circle: an angle of one radian subtends an arc length equal to the radius.

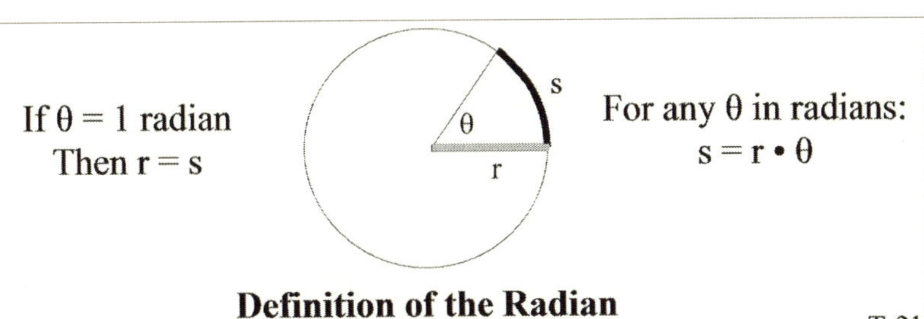

Definition of the Radian

This results in a full circle being 2π radians,

Or: $$2\pi = 360^\circ$$

Or: $$\pi = 180^\circ$$

A phase shift of 30° would be: $$30^\circ \bullet \frac{\pi}{180^\circ} = \frac{\pi}{6} \text{ radians}$$

Using the Phasing Equation

Given: $$\sin\theta = \frac{2}{N} - \frac{2\varphi}{\pi}$$

For N=10 and $\varphi = \pi / 6$ or 30°

Substitute given values: $$\sin\theta = \frac{2}{10} - \frac{2 \bullet \pi}{\pi \bullet 6}$$

Simplify: $$\sin\theta \approx 0.2 - 0.333$$

Or: $$\sin\theta \approx -0.133$$

Solve for θ: $$\arcsin(\sin\theta) \approx \arcsin(-0.133)$$

Simplify: $$\theta \approx -7.6^\circ$$

This means that if a phased array of ten elements is fed a signal where each element's signal leads the previous element's signal by 30° then the beam will be deflected about 8°.

As N increases, the first term (2 / N) becomes smaller. This means that the deflection angle (θ) becomes more sensitive to changes in the phase angle (φ) to some limit.

If N is increased to 100, then the deflection angle becomes –18.2°.

If N is increased to 1000, then the deflection angle becomes –19.3 °.

On the other hand, if N is decreased, the deflection angle becomes less sensitive. The lower limit of N is 2 because you cannot have a phase difference on a single element.

5. The blast shell is the expanding sphere of debris that moves outward from an explosion in space.

An explosion in air or water is accompanied by a shock wave as the energy propagates through the medium. But in a vacuum there is no medium through which a shock wave can propagate. A minimal shock wave will exist only in the immediate area of the explosion. Whatever gas is created in the explosion will quickly dissipate because the volume of an expanding sphere increases with the cube of the radius. This can be shown as follows:

Volume of a sphere of radius r:	$V_1 = 4 / 3 \bullet \pi \bullet r^3$
Volume of a sphere of radius 2r:	$V_2 = 4 / 3 \bullet \pi \bullet (2r)^3$
Expand the cube of 2r:	$V_2 = 4 / 3 \bullet \pi \bullet 8r^3$
The ratio of V2 to V1:	$\dfrac{V_2 = 4 / 3 \bullet \pi \bullet 8r^3}{V_1 = 4 / 3 \bullet \pi \bullet r^3}$
Simplify:	$\dfrac{V_2 = 8}{V_1 = 1}$

Doubling the radius increased the volume by 2^3, or eight times. Tripling the radius would increase the volume by 3^3, or twenty-seven times, and so forth. Therefore, in very short order, the gas would dissipate and the only significant part of the explosion would be the expanding sphere of solid particles.

After the initial blast, the debris will segregate into expanding shells according to speed. The two-dimensional schematic drawing below shows the faster particles as a gray ring and the slower particles as a black ring.

The outer, faster shells will generally contain smaller particles while the inner, slower shells will contain larger particles. A nearby ship would experience a successive series of impacts from small and fast debris at first, to slower and heavier debris with the passage of time.

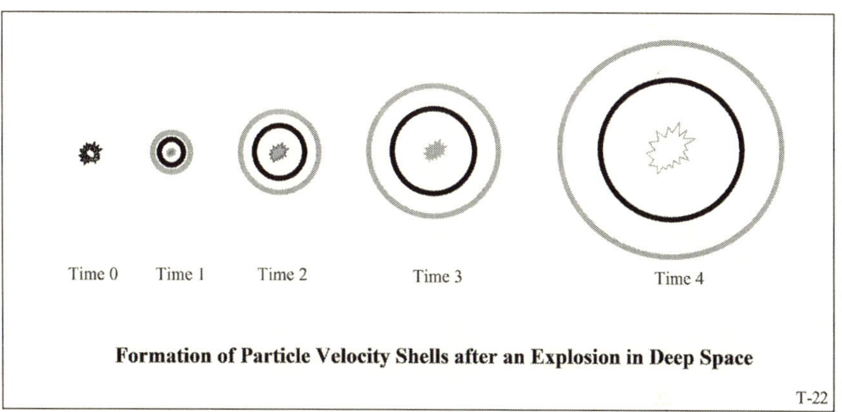

Formation of Particle Velocity Shells after an Explosion in Deep Space

Atmospheric and gravitational effects

Imagine blowing up a box of bricks and feathers in deep space. The explosion releases a given amount of energy, which is imparted to the bricks and feathers by the brief, initial shock wave. By Newton's Second Law of Motion, force equals mass times acceleration, $F=m \bullet a$. Therefore, assuming roughly equal force per cross-section on all the bricks and feathers, the acceleration on a given particle will be proportional to its mass. The smaller the mass, the greater the acceleration. The greater the mass, the smaller the acceleration. The low-mass feathers will fly away from the explosion much faster than the heavier bricks. Because there is no gravity or atmosphere to distort the explosion, the blast shells will quickly separate into a fast-moving shell of feathers and more slowly expanding shells of bricks and brick fragments.

If the same box of bricks and feathers exploded on the surface of the Earth, the feathers would not travel very far before the atmosphere slowed the feathers and they would flutter to the ground. The bricks would fly past them in relatively long arcs.

6. The Irwin-Flyger Scale (IFS) of Technological and Industrial Development:

0	Little or no development
1	Generally nonelectrical technology; no infrastructure or manufacturing
2	Electrical energy available in selected areas; minimal infrastructure or manufacturing
3	Electrical energy available in most areas; moderate infrastructure or manufacturing
4	Electrical energy widely available; well-developed infrastructure or manufacturing
5	Highly advanced technology available in selected areas
6	The most highly advanced technology available planet-wide

As background to the story, Irwin and Flyger were communication specialists who developed a simple set of social, technological, and economic metrics for the STC to categorize planetary systems. Such a system was needed to develop efficient logistical supply and trade routes.

7. Both light and radio waves are forms of electromagnetic radiation that differ in frequency. They both move at the speed of light, which is 300,000,000 meters per second, or 300×10^6 m/s.

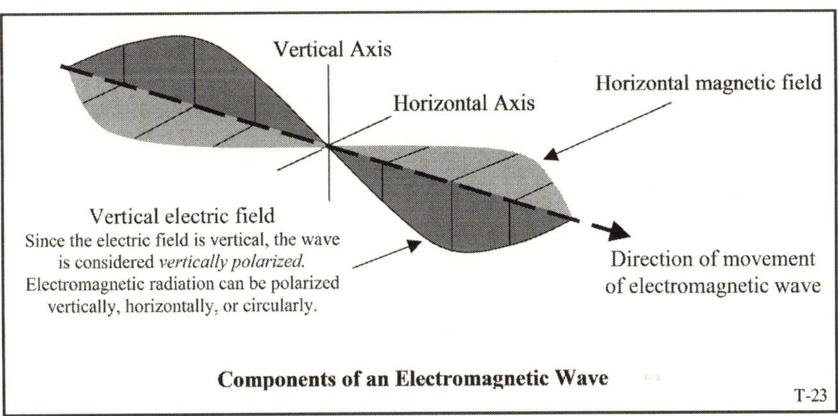

Components of an Electromagnetic Wave

T-23

Radio energy has the characteristics of both a wave and a particle, so physicists refer to a "packet" of electromagnetic energy as a quantum. The plural of quantum is quanta. The shorter its wavelength, the more energy a quantum contains. Blue light, for example, has a shorter wavelength than red light. Blue quanta therefore contain more energy than red quanta. Radio waves are much lower in frequency and thus much longer in wavelength than visible light. The radio quanta therefore have low energy. In general, the shorter the wavelength, the more energetic and "particle-like" the energy will appear. By contrast, the longer the wavelength, the more "wavelike" the energy will seem to be.

Long-wave *red* light

Short-wave *blue* light

The Relationship between Color and Wavelength

T-24

The field of physics used to study atomic structure, subatomic particles, and how quanta interact is called *quantum mechanics.*

8. Binary means, "consisting of two." A binary code has only two symbols—typically a 1 and a 0 in digital computers. Binary codes are used in digital computers because these symbols can be encoded easily by a simple switch with two states: open or closed. An open switch can represent 0, and a closed switch can represent 1. A 1 or 0 is called a *bit* of information, and it takes a separate switch to encode each bit. Switches are grouped to represent letters and numbers. If there are four switches in a group, then the data is handled by a "4-bit" processor. If there are eight switches in a group, then it is an "8-bit" processor. Personal digital computers of the early twenty-first century use 32-bit and 64-bit processors.

Let the variable n represent the number of bits in a group. The number of combinations of 0s and 1s for any group of size n is 2^n. A single bit is a group of 1. A single switch can only represent 0 or 1, so the number of combinations is 2^1, or 2.

A group of 2 have 2^2 ($2^2 = 2 \bullet 2$) = 4 combinations: 00, 01, 10, and 11.

A group of 4 has 2^4 ($2^4 = 2 \bullet 2 \bullet 2 \bullet 2$) = 16 possible combinations: 0000, 0001, 0010, 0011, 0100, 0101, 0110, 0111, 1000, 1001, 1010, 1011, 1100, 1101, 1110, and 1111.

A group of 8 has 2^8, or 256 combinations of 0 and 1.

9. Just as people need a common language to talk to each other, computers require a standard communication rule, or *protocol,* in order to understand each other. The communication protocol is the pattern of information and control bits that computers use to exchange data.

10. *Modulation* is the process by which information is impressed upon a carrier signal. *Amplitude modulation* means the amplitude of the signal

changes according to an informational pattern. *Frequency modulation* means the signal changes frequency according to the information pattern. The drawing below shows the graphical differences of encoding modulating upon identical carrier waves by amplitude modulation and frequency modulation.

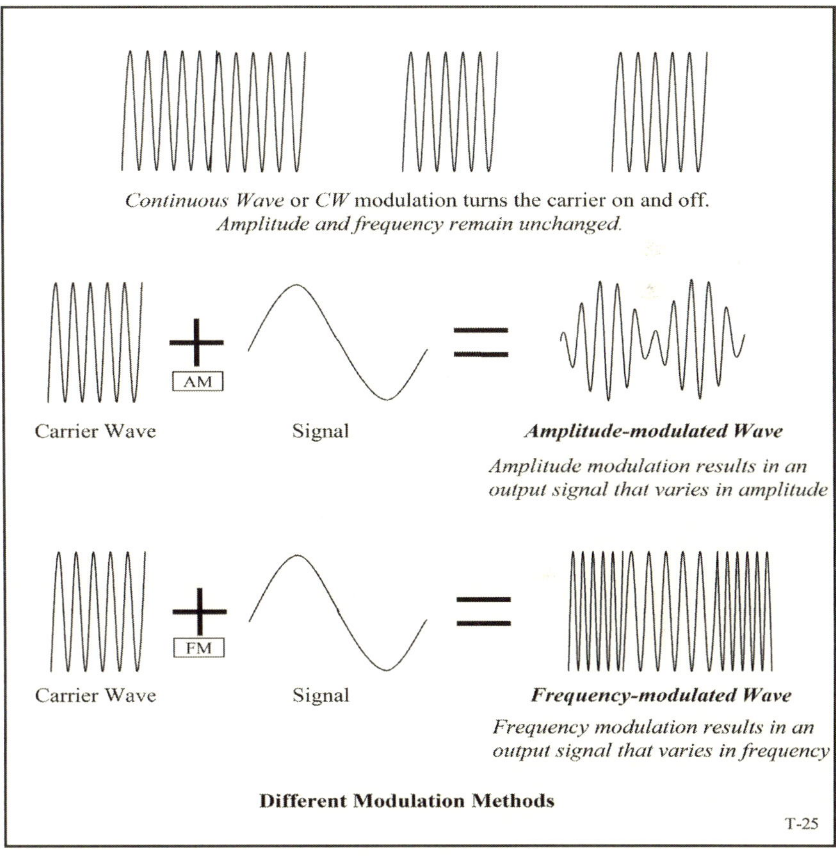

Different Modulation Methods

11. A *spectrum analyzer* is a device that separates a complex signal into component frequencies and displays the frequency domain display. The *fast Fourier transform,* or FFT, is a mathematical method used by the "spec-an" to break down a complex signal into its separate frequencies. The individual frequencies of a complex signal are shown as separate, vertical lines at different places along the horizontal axis, or *domain.* The height of each line indicates the relative strength of that frequency.

Component frequencies are easily differentiated using this type of analysis. If the signal from the derelict had been frequency modulated, the FFT would have shown multiple frequencies.

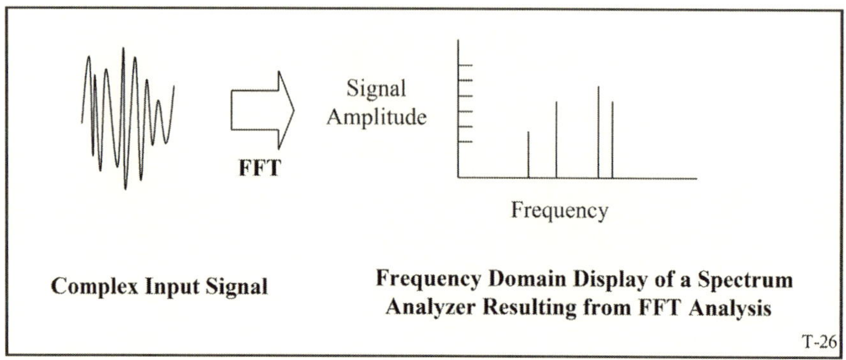

12. In order to increase communication speeds, the International Morse Code used standard abbreviations in addition to the letter and symbol codes. For example, "SOS" (dit-dit-dit, dah-dah-dah, dit-dit-dit) meant, *I need help.* "R" (dit-dah-dit) meant, *I understand,* and "QTH" (dah-dah-dit-dah, dah, dit-dit-dit-dit) meant, *Location.*

13. Particles of *ionizing radiation* are very high-energy quanta. When one of these energy packets strikes an atom, it can energize at least one of the atom's electrons to such a degree that it flies away from the atom. The free electron has a charge of -1. The atom is now short an electron and therefore is left with an electric charge of + 1. The charged atom and the lost electrons are both called *ions.*

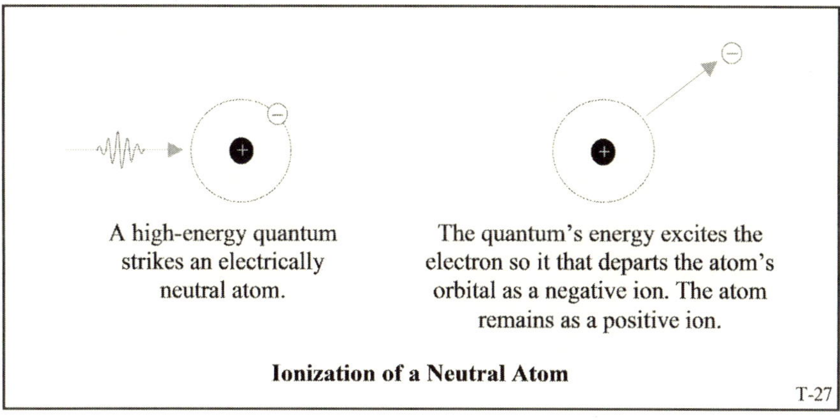

Ionization of a Neutral Atom

T-27

14. Fission

Fission energy is obtained by splitting the nuclei of large atoms, such as uranium-235 or plutonium-239.

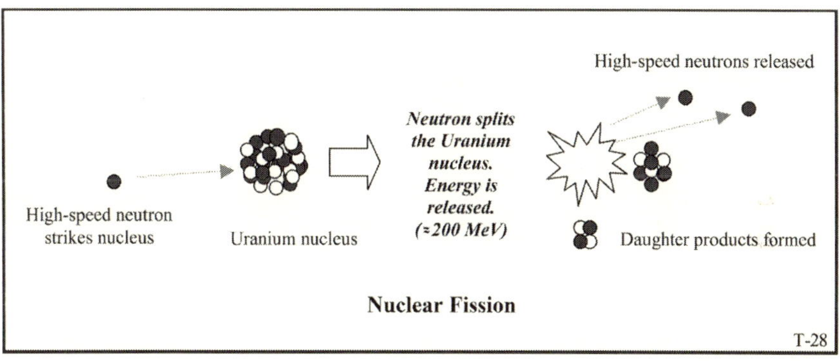

Nuclear Fission

T-28

The number after the name indicates the atom's atomic mass, which is the sum of the number of protons and neutrons in the heavy nucleus. An atom's atomic number is the quantity of protons in the nucleus and identifies the type of atom. The chart below indicates that uranium-235 and uranium-238 both have the same number of protons, but differ in the number of neutrons. They are both isotopes of uranium.

U-235		U-238	
Protons (atomic no.)	92	Protons (atomic no.)	92
+ Neutrons	143	+ Neutrons	146
Atomic mass	235	Atomic mass	238

Uranium Isotope Nuclei Comparison

By comparison, the much smaller helium-4 atom has only two protons, two neutrons, and two electrons.

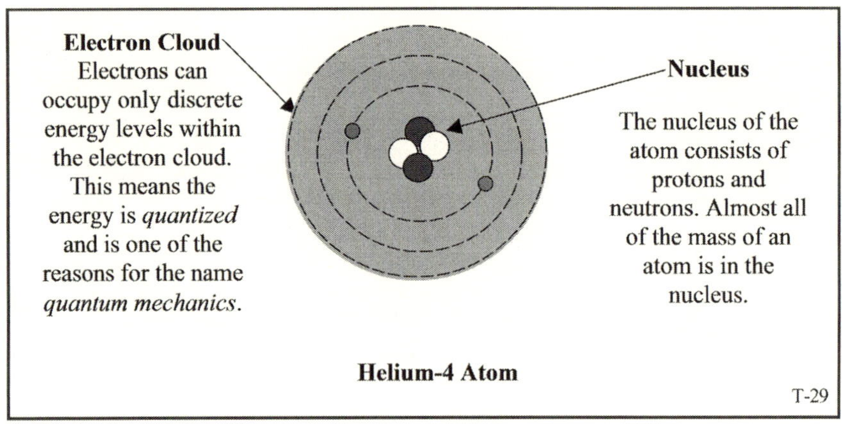

Helium-4 Atom

Fissile nuclei are nuclei that are unstable enough to be split into free neutrons and *daughter products.* The daughter products of fission are also often radioactive. For example, uranium-235 can decay into cesium-137 and strontium-90—both highly radioactive isotopes of their respective atoms. The rate of decay into daughter products can be increased by the presence of sufficient free neutrons, such as in a nuclear reactor, but it will never slow below a minimum rate. Therefore, radioactive fuel cannot be stored indefinitely, because the fissile material will continue to deteriorate or decay over time.

Half of the remaining fissile material decays into daughter products every *half-life period.*

Isotopes of uranium decay slowly. The half-life of U-235 is 4.5 billion years, and the half-life of U-238 is 700 million years.

These half-life periods are not directly observed. They are estimated from the amounts of observed radioactive decay and applied to the following equation: $M = M_0 \bullet e^{-k \bullet t}$

Where:

M is the remaining mass of the radioactive element,

M_0 is the original mass of the radioactive element,

k is an experimentally observed decay constant for the radioactive element,

t is time in units that depend upon the value of k, and

e is the mathematical constant approximately equal to 2.718.

Finding the value of k, the decay constant:

Suppose 10 grams (M_0) of a theoretical radioactive element is observed to decay to 9 grams (M) in 24 hours (t).

Given $M_0 = 10$ grams, $M = 9$ grams, and $t = 24$ hours;

The general decay formula is:	$M = M_0 \bullet e^{-k \bullet t}$
Substituting known values:	$9 = 10 \bullet e^{-k \bullet 24}$
Take the natural log (ln) of both sides:	$\ln(9) = \ln(10 \bullet e^{-k \bullet 24})$
Restate the log of a product as a sum of logs:	$\ln(9) = \ln(10) + \ln(e^{-k \bullet 24})$
Simplify:	$2.197 = 2.303 - (k \bullet 24)$
Subtract 2.303 from both sides:	$-0.106 = -k \bullet 24$
Divide both sides by -24:	$-0.106 \div -24 = -k \bullet 24 \div -24$

Simplify: $0.0044 \approx k$

The constant k is now expressed in terms of hours, so we can determine the half-life in hours by restating the decay formula with half the original material decayed:

If $M_0 = 1.0$, then after one half-life, $M=0.5$

Restating the equation with these values: $0.5 = 1 \bullet e^{-0.0044 \bullet t}$

Simplify: $0.5 = e^{-0.0044 \bullet t}$

Take the natural log of both sides: $\ln(0.5) = \ln(e^{-0.0044 \bullet t})$

Simplify: $-0.693 = -0.0044 \bullet t$

Divide both sides by -0.0044: $-0.693 \div -0.0044 = t$

Solve: $157.5 = t$

The half-life of this theoretical element is therefore 157.5 hours, or about a week. Whatever amount you start with, one week later, half of it will decay into daughter products. The following week, half of the remaining half, or one-fourth of the original amount, will remain, and so on.

We can verify this by doubling the half-life time:	$2 \bullet 157.5 = 314$
Substitute into the decay formula:	$M = M_o \bullet e^{-0.0044 \bullet 314}$
Simplify the exponent:	$M = M_o \bullet e^{-1.3816}$
Solve:	$M \div M_o \approx 0.2512$

The ratio M / M_o is therefore about 0.25, or one-fourth of the original amount after two half-life periods. The ratio does not exactly equal .25 in this case due to rounding off the decay constant.

This type of mathematical function is called an *exponential function* because the input values become part of an exponent. In this case, the input value of time becomes an exponent of e. The chart below shows the characteristic shape of an exponential decay curve. The vertical grid divides the curve into half-life periods. Half of the original element remains after one period, one-fourth after two periods, one-eighth after three periods, and so forth.

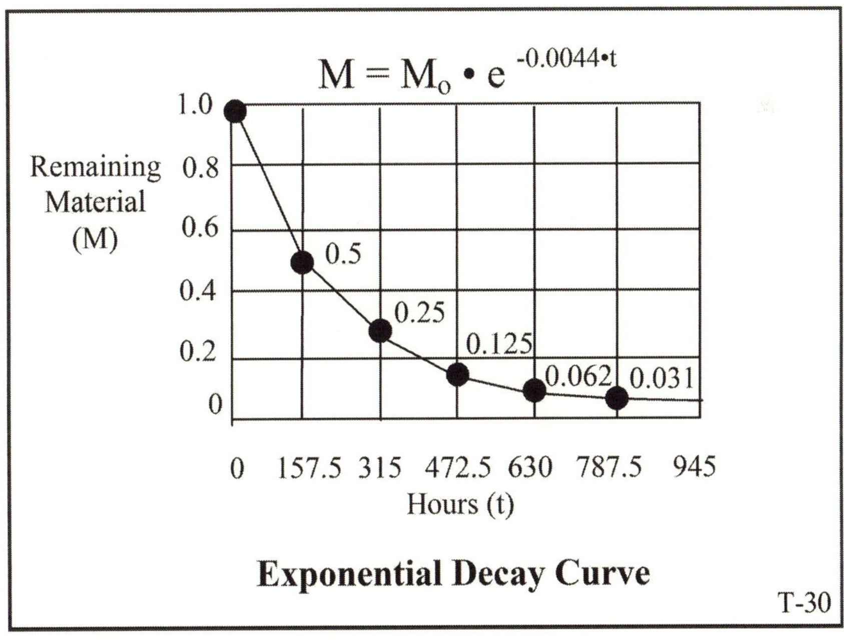

Exponential Decay Curve

T-30

15. Fusion

Fusion is joining, or *fusing*, hydrogen-2, or deuterium nuclei into heavier helium-4 nuclei. The natural stability of the atoms to be fused requires that fusion take place in a high-temperature environment, such as the interior of a star or at the focus of a high-energy laser beam. The deuterium nuclei naturally repel each other, but atoms at high temperature are moving fast enough to overcome this repulsive force. If they collide at sufficient speed, they fuse. The fusion process then releases far more energy than what was required to smash them together, so once the fusion reactor has been started, the energy released can be used to continue fusing more deuterium into helium. The requirement of the initial energy trigger is similar to the use of a small spark or pilot light to ignite a gas jet, which then yields much more energy than the initial spark.

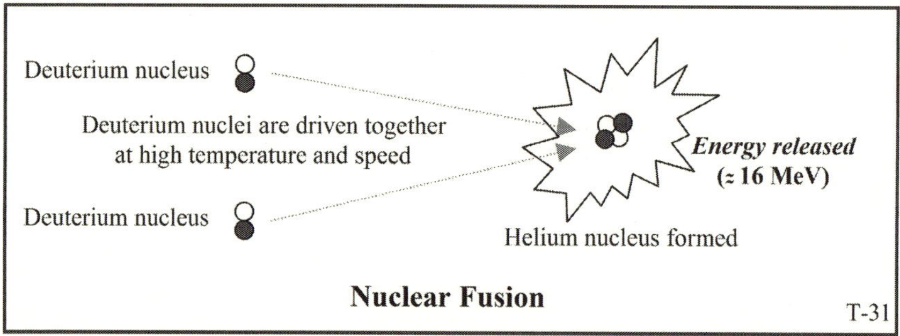

Nuclear Fusion

The energy released for each fusion reaction is less than that of each fission reaction, but because deuterium is such a light atom, less mass is required. A fusion reaction can produce X-rays, but it produces almost no radioactive isotope daughter products. The hydrogen fuel is stable and does not significantly deteriorate over time. The reactor can be throttled up or down and turned on and off very quickly by adjusting the amount of hydrogen fuel admitted into the reactor.

The energy produced per reaction (E_r) is on the order of 16 million electron volts (MeV). We convert MeV to joules (J) in the following way:

Given: $16 \text{ MeV} = 16 \times 10^6 \text{ eV}$

Restating in scientific notation: $16 \text{ Mev} = 1.6 \times 10^7 \text{ eV}$

Given: $1 \text{ eV} = 1.6 \times 10^{-19} \text{ J}$

Convert eV to joules: $E_r = 1.6 \times 10^7 \text{ eV} \bullet \frac{1.6 \times 10^{-19} \text{ J}}{1 \text{ eV}}$

Simplify: $E_r = 2.56 \times 10^{-12} \text{ J}$

Energy and Power

The *joule* (pronounced *jool* or *jowl*) is the SI unit of *energy* or *work* required to move an object against one newton of force a distance of one meter. The dimensions of a joule are therefore the newton meter, or Nm. *Power* is the measure of how quickly this work is accomplished. One joule per second is one *watt* of power. The dimensions of power are the Nm/s or J/s. The same amount of work or energy is needed to reposition an object regardless of how much time it takes. It is logically intuitive, however, that more power will be required to reposition an object quickly and less power to do it slowly.

Mathematically, we can state these relationships as follows:	
Force (F) is the product of mass (m) times acceleration (a):	$F = m \bullet a$
Work or energy (E) is the product of force (F) times distance (d):	$E = F \bullet d$
Power is energy (E) divided by time (t):	$P = E \div t$

These relationships do not manifest themselves so simply in the atmosphere of a planet. In the vacuum of deep space, a powerful rocket engine quickly accelerates a ship to high speed. A weak engine could accelerate the same ship to the same speed, but the engine would have to burn for a much longer time. This is possible because of the complete lack of gravity and air resistance. In the atmosphere and gravitation field of a planet, a weak engine might not be able to overcome the frictional forces to get the ship moving in the first place. No matter how long it burned, the rocket would just sit there, and the engine could accomplish no useful work.

Power of the Engines

The masses of the ships in these stories are very large, so the engines would have to be very powerful to move them quickly.

A typical ship was stated to be about a million metric tons, which is 10^6 tons or 10^9 kg. We can find the amount of power required to accelerate this much mass at 10 m/s^2, or 1 g, in the following way:

General formula for force:	$F = m \bullet a$
Substitute known values:	$F = 10^9 \text{ kg} \bullet 10 \text{ m/s}^2$
Simplify:	$F = 10^{10} \text{ kg m/s}^2$ or 10^{10} N
General acceleration formula:	$d = \frac{1}{2} \bullet a \bullet t^2 + v_0 \bullet t + d_0$
If $v_0 = 0$ and $d_0 = 0$, then:	$d = \frac{1}{2} \bullet a \bullet t^2$
Let $a = 10\text{m/s}^2$ and $t = 1\text{s}$:	$d = \frac{1}{2} \bullet 10\text{m/s}^2 \bullet (1 \text{ s})^2$
Simplify:	$d = 5$ m

So, at an acceleration of 10 m/s^2 the ship moves 5 meters in the first second.

Energy is given as:	$E = F \bullet d$
Substitute known values:	$E = 10^{10}\ N \bullet 5\ m$
Simplify:	$E = 5 \times 10^{10}\ Nm$
Expressed as joules:	$E = 5 \times 10^{10}\ J$
The formula for power is:	$P = E \div t$
Since the time is 1 second:	$P = 5 \times 10^{10}\ J \div 1$ second
Simplify:	$P = 5 \times 10^{10}\ J/s$
A joule per second (J/s) is a watt, so:	$P = 5 \times 10^{10}\ W$
Convert to megawatts (divide by 10^6):	$P = 5 \times 10^{10}\ W \div 10^6$
Simplify:	$P = 5 \times 10^4\ MW$
Or:	$P = 50{,}000\ MW$

Since this is the total power need to be produced by three engines, each engine only needs to produce 50,000 MW ÷ 3, or about 17,000 MW. This can be stated as either 17 thousand megawatts or 17 million kilowatts. Each engine would need to produce about ten times the energy of a large hydroelectric plant, such as Hoover Dam, which can output 1.5 million kilowatts, or about three times the capacity of the Grand Coulee Dam which outputs 6.5 million kilowatts. Fusion reactors would be the simplest and most economical source for this much energy.

Energy per Kilogram of Heavy Water:

Avogadro's constant is the number of atoms in a *mole* of a substance. There are about 6.02×10^{23} atoms per mole.

The mass of a *mole* of a substance is the number of grams equal to the atomic mass units (amu) in the substance. For example, the nucleus of hydrogen is one proton. This is 1 amu, so, 1 gram of hydrogen is one mole of hydrogen and consists of about 6.02×10^{23} atoms. The deuterium nucleus has one proton and one neutron, or 2 amu. It therefore requires two grams of deuterium to obtain a mole of 6.02×10^{23} deuterium atoms. Two deuterium nuclei fuse to form a nucleus of helium, which has two protons and two neutrons. This is 4 amu, so there are four grams of helium per 6.02×10^{23} helium atoms. Each molecule of heavy water (D_2O) consists of two deuterium atoms and one oxygen atom. The atomic mass of the two deuterium atoms in each molecule is 4 amu. The atomic mass of the oxygen is 16 amu. The total mass of the heavy water molecule is therefore 20 amu, so there are 20 grams of heavy water per mole.

The amount of energy produced per mole (E_m) of helium is the number of reactions times the amount of energy released per reaction (E_r):	$E_m = 6.02 \times 10^{23} \bullet E_r$
Restate with known value of E_r (calculated above):	$E_m = 6.02 \times 10^{23} \bullet$ 2.56×10^{-12} J
Simplify:	$E_m = 1.54 \times 10^{12}$ J

This means 1.54×10^{12} joules will be produced for every 20 grams, or mole, of D_2O converted into helium. We can find the energy per kilogram in the following way:

$$\frac{1000\ \text{g}}{1\ \text{kg}} \bullet \frac{1\ \text{mole}}{20\ \text{g}} \bullet \frac{1.54 \times 10^{12}\ \text{J}}{\text{mole}} = \frac{7.7 \times 10^{13}\ \text{J}}{\text{kg}}$$

These numbers are hard to grasp. To try to understand the amount of energy we are considering, let's apply it to a light bulb.

First, convert the energy per kilogram to watt-seconds (Ws) and then to kilowatt-hours (kWh).

Given that a joule is a watt-second: $1\ \text{J} = 1\ \text{Ws}$

Then: $7.7 \times 10^{13}\ \text{J} = 7.7 \times 10^{13}\ \text{Ws}$

Convert to kilowatt-hours (kWh): $7.7 \times 10^{13}\ \text{Ws} \bullet \frac{1\ \text{k}}{1000} \bullet \frac{\text{h}}{3600\text{s}} = 2.14 \times 10^{7}\ \text{kWh}$

An incandescent light bulb rated at 100 watts (W) that burns for one hour uses 100 watt-hours (Wh). If it burns for 10 hours, then it will use 10 • 100 Wh or 1000 Wh, which is 1 kWh.

We found that fusing a kilogram of deuterium can produce 2.14×10^{7} kWh of energy. This is enough energy to power a 100 W light bulb for over 24,000 years!

Divide by 100 W: $\frac{2.14 \times 10^{7}\ \text{kWh}}{100\ \text{W}} = 2.14 \times 10^{5}\ \text{kh}$

Convert kilohours to hours by multiplying by 1000: $2.14 \times 10^{5}\ \text{kh} \bullet 1000 = 2.14 \times 10^{8}\ \text{h}$

Converting to years: $2.14 \times 10^{8}\ \text{h} \bullet \frac{1\ \text{day}}{24\text{h}} \bullet \frac{1\ \text{year}}{365\ \text{day}} = 2.44 \times 10^{4}$

$2.44 \times 10^{4} = 24{,}400$ years

Extracting electrical energy from a fusion reactor

Electrical energy can be extracted from a fusion reactor through a process called *magneto-hydro dynamics,* abbreviated MHD. The fusion reaction creates large amounts of thermal energy and ionized particles. Since thermal energy is actually a form of motion, or kinetic energy, the ionized particles, or ions, will be moving at high speed.

A MHD generator consists of a conducting coil wound around the exhaust tube through which moves the stream of high-speed ions. The stream of electrically charged ions creates a moving magnetic field inside the coil. This moving magnetic field induces an electrical potential in the coil, so electrons begin to flow as in any electrical generator. A moving flow of electrons in a conductor is called *electrical current,* or more simply, *electricity.*

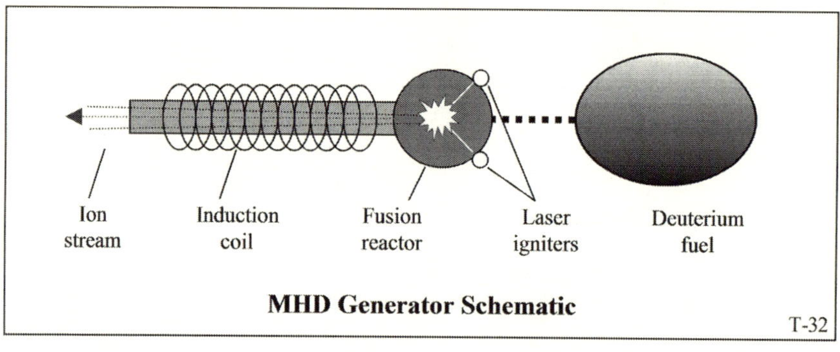

MHD Generator Schematic

The stream of ions can create X-rays. To protect the crew, the MHD generators would be shielded and located in nacelles on the tips of the tail fins to keep them as far as possible from the rest of the ship.

16. The *radio shadow* of the derelict is quite similar to an ordinary light shadow. Radio signals and light rays are both electromagnetic waves although they have different frequencies. Radio waves have a lower frequency, and light waves have a higher frequency. Since the derelict was rotating, it is clear that the visible view of the *Phoenix* would periodically be obstructed as Jana, attached to it, rotated along

with it and disappeared from the view on the *Phoenix*. In the same way, the derelict would obstruct the radio communication signals to create a radio shadow.

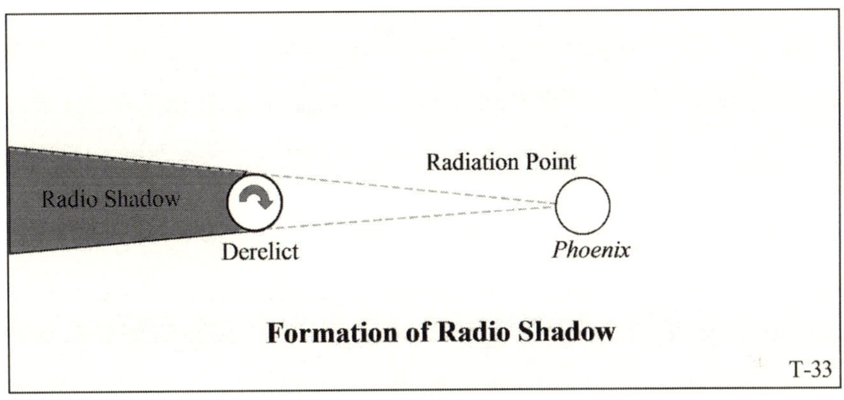

Formation of Radio Shadow

17. An airlock is an efficient way to move between environments of different pressure. The airlock consists of a special opening in the pressure hull of the ship. It has two airtight doors. To use an airlock, the chamber is first brought to the same pressure as the starting environment, which is the pressure from where one is coming. The hatch to that side is opened. The person enters the chamber and seals the hatch. Then the pressure in the airlock is raised or lowered to match the pressure on the other, or, destination side. When the pressure matches the new environment, the hatch facing that side is opened, and the person can leave the chamber at the different pressure.

In the case of space travel, the two most common pressure environments are the vacuum of space and the interior pressure of a ship. The airlock avoids the need to vent the atmosphere from inside the entire ship in order to enter or leave it.

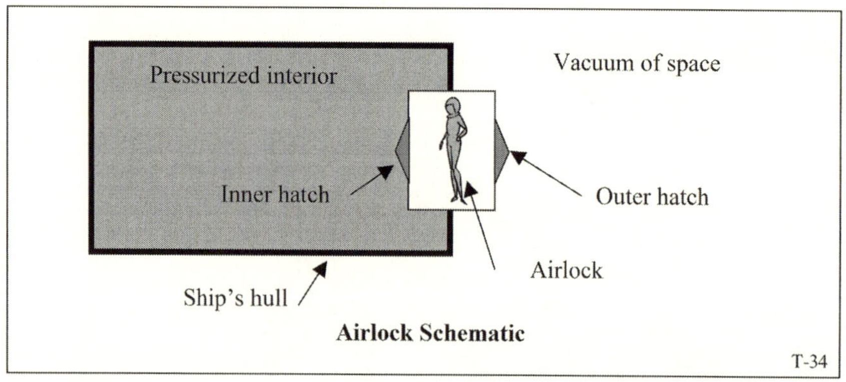

Airlock Schematic

18. The need for artificial gravity became apparent with the dawn of the space age. Early astronauts experienced rapid bone loss *(osteopenia)* and muscle loss *(muscular atrophy)* during extended periods of zero gravity. Subsequent experiments indicated that at least a third of normal gravity ($\approx 3\ m/s^2$) was needed to significantly slow this deterioration.

Artificial gravity is most easily created by angular acceleration or *centrifugal force.* This effect is observed when any object is rotated or moved in a curve. For example, if you turn quickly while driving, you feel your body pushed toward the outside of the turn. This is *centrifugal force.* It is an *imaginary force,* because it results from the tendency of matter in motion to continue moving in a straight line at a uniform rate. This is in accordance with Newton's First Law of Motion, which states that every object in motion will move in a straight line at a uniform speed unless acted upon by another force. In this case, the real force is the *centripetal force.* Centripetal force is the inward pulling force that causes your body and the car to deviate from a straight line. The momentum of the mass of your body makes it seem that there is an outward pulling force—the imaginary centrifugal force.

The feeling of *apparent gravity* or centrifugal force is not identical to gravity. A primary difference results from the *Coriolis effect,* which is named after Gustave Coriolis (1792–1843), who described the apparent twisting force an object seems to experience as it changes its position on the radius of a rotating object or in a rotating frame of reference.

The linear or tangential velocity of a rotating disk varies from zero at the center of rotation to a maximum at the edge of the disk. An object at point r_1, pictured below, will have a given linear velocity, v_1. An object at r_2 will have a greater linear velocity, v_2 because for a given angle (θ), the longer radius sweeps through a greater distance in the same amount of time as the smaller radius sweeps through a shorter distance. The illustration below shows that the change in linear, or straight-line velocity, is proportional to the radius for a solid disk.

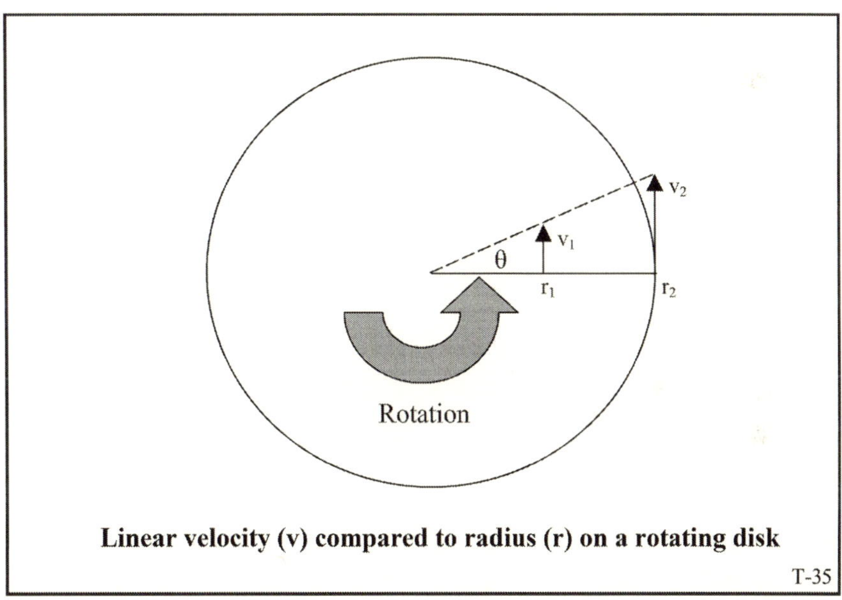

Linear velocity (v) compared to radius (r) on a rotating disk

The ship has an overall diameter of 50 meters. A protective 5-meter water jacket reduces the effective diameter to 40 meters, so the effective radius (r) is 20 meters. If the desired apparent gravity is 0.3 g, we can find the required rotation speed and time in several steps:

Given the desired acceleration is 0.3g:	$\alpha_{roll} = 9.8\ m/s^2 \bullet 0.3$
Solving :	$\alpha_{roll} = 2.94\ m/s^2$
Centrifugal acceleration (α) is:	$\alpha_{roll} = \frac{v_t^2}{r}$
Substitute the desired value of α_{roll}:	$2.94\ m/s^2 = \frac{v_t^2}{20\ m}$
Multiply both sides by 20m:	$20\ m \bullet 2.94\ m/s^2 = v_t^2$
Simplifying:	$58.8\ m^2 / s^2 = v_t^2$
Take the square root of both sides:	$\sqrt{(58.8\ m^2 / s^2)} = v_t$
Solving:	$7.7\ m/s \approx v_t$

The rotational velocity of the illustrated counterclockwise rotating disk is slower at r_1 than at r_2. Therefore, if an object moves outward from r_1 to r_2, momentum will keep its rotational velocity slower relative to the disk at r_2. From the frame of reference of the rotating disk, the difference in velocity will seem to curve the object's path to the right relative to its forward motion. This tendency to curve due to an apparent, imaginary force is the Coriolis effect. Likewise, if an object moves from the edge inward, it will have a greater rotational velocity and will tend to curve right, as well.

The Coriolis effect is responsible for the distinctive pattern of "cloud swirls" around low-pressure systems on a rotating planet.

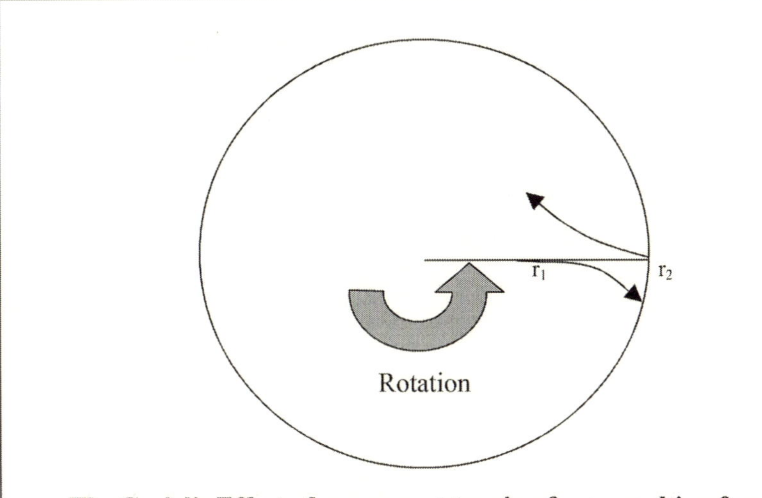

The Coriolis Effect: the apparent turning force resulting from movement inward or outward on the radius

T-36

Finding the Tangential Velocity of the Ship (v_s)

Tangential velocity is the linear or straight-line velocity of a rotating disk perpendicular to the radius. You can think of it as how fast a wheel of radius (r) would move forward over the ground at that rotational speed.

The distance of a rotation is the circumference (C):

$$C = 2 \bullet \pi \bullet r$$

The formula for tangential velocity (v_s) is:

$$v_s = \frac{C}{t}$$

Solve for C by multiplying both sides by t:

$$t \bullet v_s = C$$

Solve for t by dividing both sides by v_s :

$$t = \frac{C}{v_s}$$

Substitute $2 \bullet \pi \bullet r$ for C:

$$t = \frac{2 \bullet \pi \bullet r}{v_s}$$

Replace variables v_s , π, and r with known values: $$t \approx \frac{2 \bullet 3.14 \bullet 20\ m}{7.7\ m/s}$$

Simplify: $$t \approx \frac{126\ m}{7.7\ m/s}$$

Solve: $$t \approx 16.4\ s$$

A ship with a radius of 20 meters must therefore rotate about once every 16 seconds, or about four times per minute, to provide 30 percent normal gravity.

Changing Apparent Gravity by Walking

Walking speed (v_W) is about 1.5 m/s. The tangential velocity of the ship (v_S) was calculated as 7.7 m/s.

Increasing Apparent Gravity

Tangential velocity walking with the spin (v^+_t): $$v^+_t = (v_S) + v_W$$

Substitute known values: $$v^+_t = 7.7\ m/s + 1.5\ m/s$$

Simplify: $$v^+_t = 9.2\ m/s$$

Angular acceleration α + : $$\alpha^+ = \frac{(v^+_t)^2}{r}$$

Substitute known values: $$\alpha^+ = \frac{(9.2\ m/s)^2}{20\ m}$$

Solve: $$\alpha^+ = \frac{84.6\ m^2 / s^2}{20\ m}$$

Simplify and cancel m: $$\alpha^+ = 4.2\ m/s^2$$

Find the ratio of α to g: $$\frac{\alpha^+}{g} = \frac{4.2\ m/s^2}{9.8\ m/s^2}$$

The apparent increased gravity is: $$\alpha^+/g = 0.432 \approx 43\%$$

Decreasing Apparent Gravity

Tangential velocity against the spin (v^-_t):	$v^-_t = (v_s) - v_w$
Substitute known values:	$v^-_t = 7.7\ m/s - 1.5\ m/s$
Simplify:	$v^-_t = 6.2\ m/s$
Angular acceleration α^-:	$\alpha^- = \frac{(v^-_t)^2}{r}$
Substitute known values:	$\alpha^- = \frac{(6.2\ m/s)^2}{20\ m}$
Solve:	$\alpha^- = \frac{38.4\ m^2 / s^2}{20\ m}$
Simplify and cancel m:	$\alpha^- = 1.9\ m/s^2$
Find the ratio of α to g:	$\frac{\alpha^-}{g} = \frac{1.9\ m/s^2}{9.8\ m/s^2}$
The apparent decreased gravity is:	$\alpha^- / g = .196 \approx 20\%$

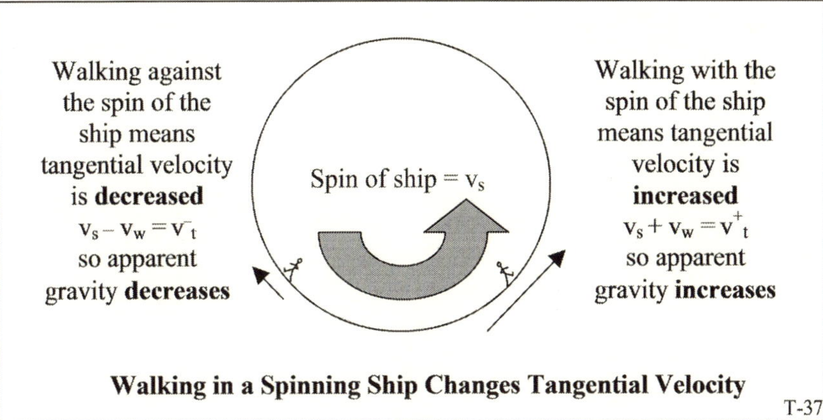

Walking in a Spinning Ship Changes Tangential Velocity

So, one of the "quirks" of apparent gravity is that you would feel heavier if you walked with the spin and lighter if you walked against the spin, but walking forward or aft would not change your weight!

19. *Piezo-electric* substances generate electric potential when they are deformed, and they deform when they are subjected to electrical potential. As of the early twenty-first century, the primary uses for piezo-electric crystals were to generate sparks for cigarette lighters and gas appliances and to act as frequency-control devices in radio circuits. During the mid-twentieth century, piezo-electric crystals were used in the pick-up heads of *phonographs.* These devices sensed tiny variations in the spiral grooves of a spinning phonograph recording, usually a vinyl plastic disk, known at the time as a *record.*

What is proposed here is a space suit that contains a piezo-electric layer of fabric material capable of physically changing shape when charged by an external voltage. The suit could be loose-fitting enough to be easy to put on or take off, but once on, it would electrically adjust to tightly conform to the body within it. This would be an electromechanical means of maintaining pressure within the suit. A simple, elastic material would feel stiff and restrictive, but pressure feedback and logic circuits would relax the piezo-electric material in the joint areas when the astronaut moved. This selective relaxation would make movement easier and more natural.

20. Newton's First Law of Motion states that an object at rest will remain at rest, and an object in motion will move in a straight line at a uniform speed unless acted upon by a force. This is sometimes called *The Law of Momentum* or *The Law of Inertia.*

This is experienced in everyday life when one is pushed back against the seat of a car when it accelerates quickly or feels thrown forward during hard braking. The inertia of your body resists any change in motion.

In the same way, the fluids in the semi-circular canals of the inner ear keep moving after a prolonged period of spinning. If the speed of rotation changes, the inertia of the fluid keeps moving and creates the sensation of dizziness until the fluid matches the new rotation.

21. The *torr* is a measure of pressure exactly equal to 1/760th of a standard atmosphere, or about 1 millimeter of mercury. It is named in honor of Evangelista Torricelli (Tor-rih-**chel**-lee), who discovered the principle of the *barometer,* a device commonly used to measure atmospheric pressure.

22. Two kilometers is 2000 meters. So:

2000 meters ÷ 5 meters / second	= 2000m ÷ 5 m/s	= 400 seconds
400 seconds ÷ 60 seconds/minute	= 400 s ÷ 60 s/min	= 6.7 minutes

In order to accelerate Jana and her equipment, with a mass of 100 kg, to a speed of 5 m/s, the maneuvering pack would have to eject gas at high speed in the opposite direction. This is an application of Newton's Third Law of Motion: *For every action, there is an equal and opposite reaction.*

Momentum (p) is the product of mass (m) and velocity (v): $p = m \bullet v$

Jana's momentum (p_j) is therefore: $p_j = m_j \bullet v_j$

The gas's momentum (p_g) is: $p_g = m_g \bullet v_g$

But, by the Third Law, each momentum is equal and opposite: $p_j = p_g$

Substituting the definition of each momentum: $m_j \bullet v_j = m_g \bullet v_g$

Given that m_j =100 kg, v_j = 5 m/s, and v_g = 1000 m/s

Then substitute these values: $100\ \text{kg} \bullet 5\ \text{m/s} = m_g \bullet 1000\ \text{m/s}$

Simplify by canceling m/s from both sides: $500 \text{ kg m/s} = m_g \bullet 1000 \text{ m/s}$

Divide both sides by 1000: $500 \div 1000 \text{ kg} = m_g$

Solving: $0.5 \text{ kg} = m_g$

A half-kilogram is the approximate mass of two cups of water.

The force of acceleration Jana would experience would depend upon how quickly the maneuvering pack could discharge 0.5 kg of gas. If it could eject 0.1 kg per second, then 0.5 kg would require 5 seconds.

The symbol used to denote change in mathematics is the Greek letter *delta* (Δ), so change in velocity is Δv and change in time is Δt.

Acceleration (a) is : $a = \frac{\Delta v}{\Delta t}$

Substitute given values: $a = \frac{5 \text{ m/s}}{5 \text{ s}}$

$a = 1 \text{ m/s}^2$

Normal Earth gravitational acceleration (1 g) is 9.8 m/s^2, so Jana would experience about 1 / 10 g for 5 seconds. The vacuum of space would provide no frictional resistance, so once the maneuvering pack's acceleration ended she would move in a straight line at a constant speed unless acted upon by another force, in accordance with Newton's First Law of Motion.

The distance (d) required to accelerate from stationary to 5 m/s is found by the following equations:

Given that: $d = \frac{1}{2} \bullet a \bullet t^2 + v_0 \bullet t + d_0$

If $v_0 = 0$ and $d_0 = 0$, then: $d = \frac{1}{2} \bullet a \bullet t^2$

Substitute given values: $d = \frac{1}{2} \bullet (1.0\ m/s^2) \bullet (5\ s)^2$

Simplify: $d = \frac{1}{2} \bullet (1.0\ m/s^2) \bullet (25\ s^2)$

s^2 cancels out: $d = (0.5\ m) \bullet (25)$

$d = 12.5\ m$

Given the same parameters, the stopping distance would also be 12.5 meters.

23. The strength of the centrifugal force must be determined from the information given about the derelict.

The ship was described as three modules connected by external supports that formed an approximate cylinder about 250 meters long and 50 meters in diameter. Since a circle's diameter is twice its radius, the rotational radius of the ship is 25 meters.

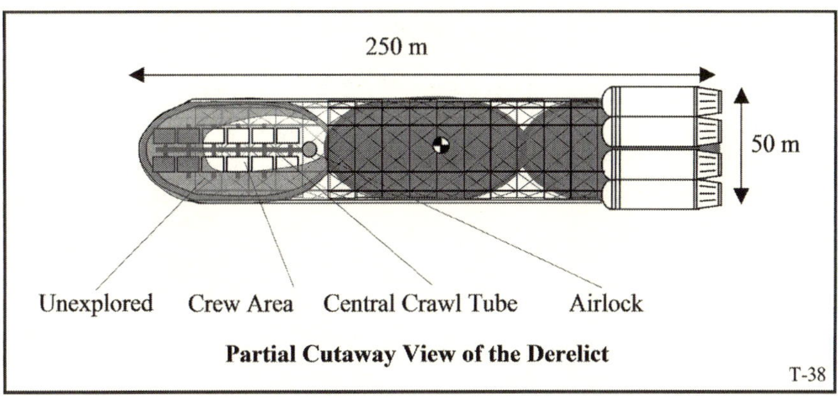

Partial Cutaway View of the Derelict

T-38

The rotation times on each axis of the ship were given as:

pitch—110 seconds

roll—103 seconds

yaw— 400 seconds

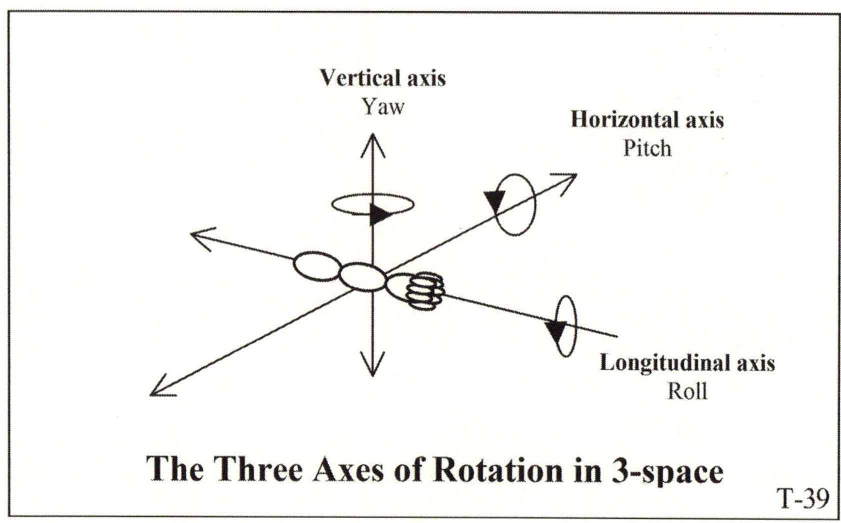

The Three Axes of Rotation in 3-space

Rotational Acceleration on Roll Axis

The roll tangential velocity (v_{roll}) is the rotational distance traveled by a point on the circumference (C_{roll}) of the rotating object divided by the time for each rotation (t).

Written algebraically: $v_{roll} = C_{roll} / t$

The distance traveled in one rotation is the circumference: $C_{roll} = 2 \bullet \pi \bullet r$

Substituting known values: $C_{roll} = 2 \bullet \pi \bullet 25\ m$

Solving: $C_{roll} \approx 2 \bullet 3.14 \bullet 25\ m$

$C_{roll} \approx 157\ m$

Given: $v_{roll} = C_{roll} / t_{roll}$

Substituting: $v_{roll} = \dfrac{157\ m}{103\ s}$

Solving to find the tangential velocity: $v_{roll} \approx 1.52$ m/s

This is about normal walking speed.

Rotational acceleration (α) is tangential velocity (v_t) squared divided by the radius.

Written algebraically: $\alpha = \frac{v_t^2}{r}$

Substituting known values: $\alpha_{roll} = \frac{(1.52 \text{ m/s})^2}{25 \text{ m}}$

Solving: $\alpha_{roll} = \frac{(2.3 \text{ m}^2 / \text{s}^2)}{25 \text{ m}}$

Simplifying: $\alpha_{roll} \approx 0.09 \text{ m/s}^2$

Find acceleration as a ration to g: $\frac{\alpha_{roll}}{g} = \frac{0.09 \text{ m/s}^2}{9.8 \text{ m/s}^2}$

Solve as a ratio to g: $\alpha_{roll} / g = 0.009 \approx 1\%$

This is only about 1 percent of normal gravity (g).

Rotational Acceleration on Pitch Axis

The ship was pitching (turning end over end) once completely every 110 seconds. The ship rotates around its center of mass, so at the center of mass, the only acceleration would be due to the roll. Jana made her approach and attached to the derelict ship at the center of mass because this was the point of least motion. But as Jana moved forward from the center of mass, the pitch and yaw accelerations increased because the radius on these axes increased.

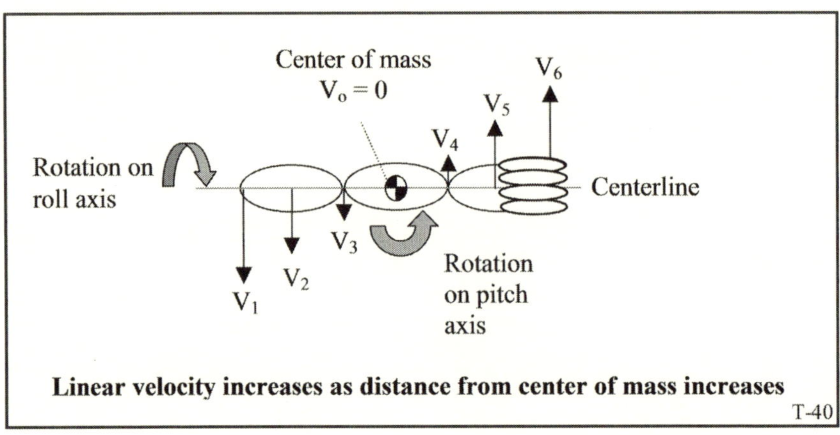

The airlock was stated to be 60 meters forward from the ship's center of mass. The acceleration from pitch rotation is calculated in the same way as roll acceleration:

The rotational distance (C_{pitch}) is:	$C_{pitch} = 2 \bullet \pi \bullet r$
Substitute known values:	$C_{pitch} = 2 \bullet \pi \bullet 60$ meters
Simplify:	$C_{pitch} \approx 377$ meters
Rotational tangential velocity on the pitch axis:	$v_{pitch} = \frac{C_{pitch}}{t}$
Substitute known values:	$v_{pitch} = \frac{377 \text{ meters}}{110 \text{ seconds}}$
Solve:	$v_{pitch} = 3.43$ m/s
Acceleration on the pitch axis:	$\alpha_{pitch} = \frac{v_t^2}{r}$
Substitute known values:	$\alpha_{pitch} = \frac{(3.43 \text{ m/s})^2}{60 \text{ m}}$
Simplify:	$\alpha_{pitch} = \frac{11.76 \text{ m}^2 / \text{s}^2}{60 \text{ m}}$
Solve:	$\alpha_{pitch} = 0.196 \text{ m/s}^2$

Vector Addition of Rotational Accelerations

The roll rotational acceleration vector (α_{roll}) must be added to the pitch rotation acceleration vector (α_{pitch}). This is done through *vector addition.* Vectors are physical quantities that have both a magnitude and a direction and are typically illustrated using arrows. The length of the arrow is proportional to the magnitude, and the direction of the arrow indicates the direction of the vector.

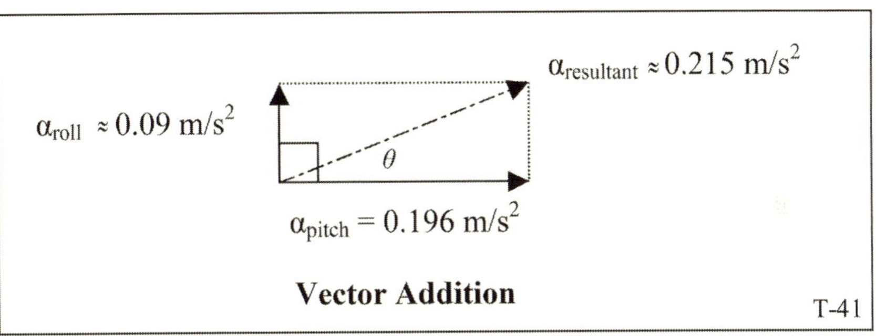

Vector Addition

In this *vector diagram*, arrow α_{roll} represents the roll acceleration and arrow α_{pitch} represents the pitch acceleration. The acceleration vectors are drawn perpendicular to each other (90 degrees apart). The vectors form two sides of a rectangle. When the rectangle is completed, the diagonal of the rectangle represents the *resultant,* or combined acceleration of the two vectors. The angle of the resultant is denoted by the Greek letter theta (θ). In this case, theta is measured from the roll rotational axis.

Pythagorean Theorem of Right Triangles	$c^2 = a^2 + b^2$
Substitute labels:	$\alpha_{resultant}{}^2 = \alpha_{pitch}{}^2 + \alpha_{pitch}{}^2$
Substitute calculated values	$\alpha_{resultant}{}^2 = 0.196^2 + 0.09^2$
Calculate:	$\alpha_{resultant}{}^2 \approx 0.038 + 0.008$

Simplify:	$\alpha_{resultant}^2 \approx 0.046$
Take the square root of both sides	$\alpha_{resultant} \approx 0.215\ m/s^2$
Find in terms of g:	$\alpha_{resultant} \approx \frac{0.215\ m/s^2}{9.8\ m/s^2}$
Solve:	$\alpha_{resultant} \approx 0.022\ g \approx 2\%\ g$
Theta (θ) is found by the definition of the tangent:	$\tan(\theta) = \frac{\text{opposite}}{\text{adjacent}}$
Written symbolically:	$\tan(\theta) = \frac{\alpha_{roll}}{\alpha_{pitch}}$
Substitute known values:	$\tan(\theta) = \frac{0.09}{0.196}$
Solve:	$\tan(\theta) = 0.4592$
Take the arctangent of both sides:	$\arctan(\tan(\theta)) = \arctan(0.4592)$
Yields:	$\theta = 24.7$ degrees

Another vector sum calculation could be made for the acceleration due to rotation around the yaw axis, but since the rotation period is quite long (400 seconds), the yaw acceleration component would be very small and therefore would not significantly change the forces already calculated.

In common English units, the unit of force is the pound. There are 2.2 pounds per kilogram in normal Earth gravity (1 g). The mass of Jana, her suit, and her maneuvering pack was given as 100 kg, which would weigh 220 pounds on Earth. The centrifugal force she would experience holding onto the side of the ship at its center of mass would be 100 kilograms multiplied by 0.09 m/s^2, which is 9 kg m/s^2, or 9 newtons. Developing the conversion factor from newtons to pounds is unnecessary. We can take a "shortcut" by remembering that the acceleration was a fraction (0.009) of normal gravity. The centrifugal force would therefore be simply 220 pounds times 0.009, or about two pounds.

The Difference between Mass and Weight

Confusion often results from the common usage of the kilogram as a unit of weight when it is actually a unit of mass. Weight is a *vector* but mass is a *scalar*. A vector has a magnitude or size and direction. A scalar only has magnitude.

A *force* is a push or pull so it is a *vector* because it has a magnitude and a direction. Weight is a vector because it has a magnitude and direction. Mass has a magnitude, but there is no direction associated with it, so it is not a force. It is only a scalar quantity. Force, as stated above, is the product of mass times acceleration (F=m • a). Common usage causes further confusion when people speak of "the force of gravity." It is more correct to say, "weight." Weight is a force and is the product of gravitational acceleration times the mass of the object.

The SI or metric unit of mass is the kilogram. The SI or metric unit of force is the newton. The English unit of mass is the slug, and the English unit of force is the pound.

System	Scalar Mass Units	Vector Weight Units	Acceleration Units
English	slug	pound	ft/s^2
SI (metric)	gram or kilogram	newton	m/s^2

Comparison of English and Metric Units

Additional confusion results from markings on food and household products that show English units of weight, such as pounds or ounces, next to metric units of mass, such as grams or kilograms. The implication is that they are the same type of unit, but are only equivalent in the relatively uniform gravitational field of Earth. To be consistent, packages should be marked either in units of weight, such as pounds and newtons, or units of mass, such as slugs or kilograms.

24. The ancient Greek philosopher Democritus (Dem-**ah**-kri-tuss) called the smallest possible bit of matter *atomos,* meaning *uncuttable.* The thinking at that time, and for many centuries afterward, was that the atom could not be further divided. It was believed to be the smallest piece of matter possible.

Modern experiments, however, have revealed that atoms are composed of many smaller *subatomic particles. Electrons* occupy various *orbitals* or *shells* around a *nucleus.* The nucleus consists of *protons* and *neutrons.* Further, each of these subatomic particles is made of a variety of even smaller particles, called *quarks.*

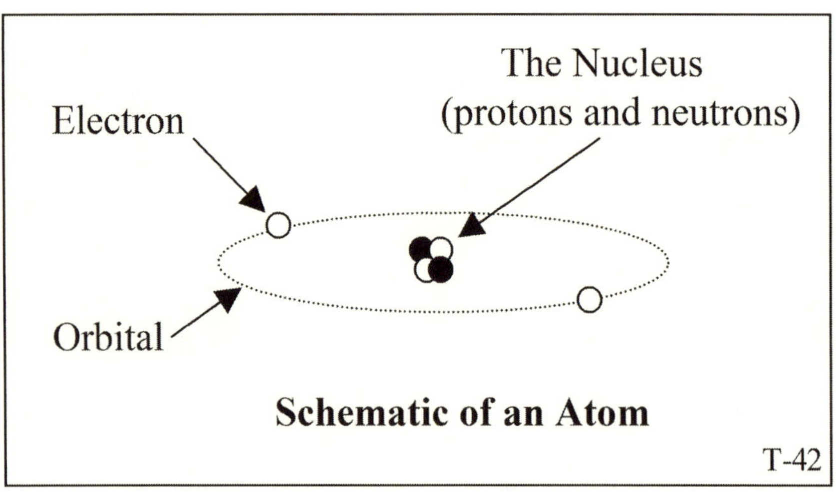

Schematic of an Atom

The drawing above serves only as a schematic to indicate some of an atom's parts. It does not accurately describe the way the atom actually looks. Different models capture one atomic property or another, but a perfect visual model remains elusive.

25. The boiling point of a liquid, such as water, depends upon pressure—or more specifically, the *vapor pressure* above the liquid's surface. If the vapor pressure increases, the boiling point increases. If the vapor pressure is lowered, the boiling point is lowered. If pressure drops to near vacuum, the boiling point of water reduces to the point where the water will boil at room temperature!

This seems counterintuitive, because common experience causes us to expect "boiling" to mean "hot." *Boiling* is the spontaneous formation of gas bubbles within a liquid at a given pressure due to thermal energy sufficient to vaporize the liquid at that pressure. For pure water at one atmosphere of pressure, this occurs at the relatively warm temperature of 100° C. But other liquids have much lower boiling points. Liquid propane boils at -42.7° C, liquid carbon dioxide boils at -79.5° C, and liquid oxygen boils at -118.8° C.

Because higher pressure increases the boiling point, propane, for example, is stored in a pressurized tank. The high pressure in the tank raises the propane's boiling point above room temperature, so the propane in the tank used for a patio grill remains liquid even on a warm summer afternoon.

Conversely, lower pressure reduces boiling points. Living things contain fluids. If a live body is exposed to a hard vacuum, any fluid in the body, such as blood, begins to boil.

In order for water to undergo the change of state from liquid to gas, however, 1000 calories per gram of water, the *energy of vaporization,* is needed to change the liquid water to water vapor. This change of state does not cause a change of temperature, so this energy is "hidden" and is called *latent heat.* Initially, liquid water exposed to a vacuum will boil by absorbing the thermal energy already present in the water. If no additional energy is added, the remaining liquid becomes colder as energy is lost to the vapor at it absorbs its latent heat. At some point, the remaining liquid water will lose enough energy to freeze. The surprising result is that *under a hard vacuum, liquid water will boil until it freezes!* Once the water is frozen, it will no longer boil. It will slowly vaporize directly into the gas form of water from the solid form in a process called *sublimation.*

In the story, Jana's suit was rinsed with pure water that was then boiled off in the vacuum of the airlock. The ice crystals that formed on her suit were then sublimated into vapor by supplying them with energy from infrared heat lamps.

Latent heat is important in the transfer of energy by water vapor. When water condenses—changes its state from a vapor to a liquid—the latent heat is released and warms the surrounding air. The warmed air rises and this release of energy is evident in the "boiling" appearance of towering cumulus and thunderhead storm clouds. The thermal mechanism of latent heat causes the formation of thunderstorms and hurricanes.

Let us return to our patio grill example. You can also observe the absorption of latent heat by the propane evaporating inside of the tank by feeling that the tank is cooler than the surrounding air. If the day is warm and humid, the tank may "sweat" as moisture condenses on it. In this case, the water vapor in the air is giving up its latent heat and transferring it to the propane in the tank. The propane absorbs this heat and vaporizes. The vaporized gas then flows through the pressure regulator and then through a pipe to the flame unit in the grill, where it burns.

In very cold climates, outside air temperatures can fall so low that insufficient energy is transferred to the liquid propane from the surrounding air, and the liquid propane in the tank cannot vaporize. Propane devices do not work well if the storage tank is too cold.

The Prophecy

1. *Orographic lifting* occurs whenever the wind forces air upward over rising terrain. As the air moves upward, the pressure decreases, and the air expands. Whenever air expands, it cools. Cooler air holds less moisture than warmer air, so if the air is lifted far enough, the air becomes saturated, and the water in it condenses into clouds and perhaps rain. The windward slopes of mountain ranges tend to receive the most rain of any region on any planet. The downwind slopes experience the opposite effect: the air descends, warms, and absorbs moisture. The downwind slopes of mountain ranges are therefore usually dry, desert regions.

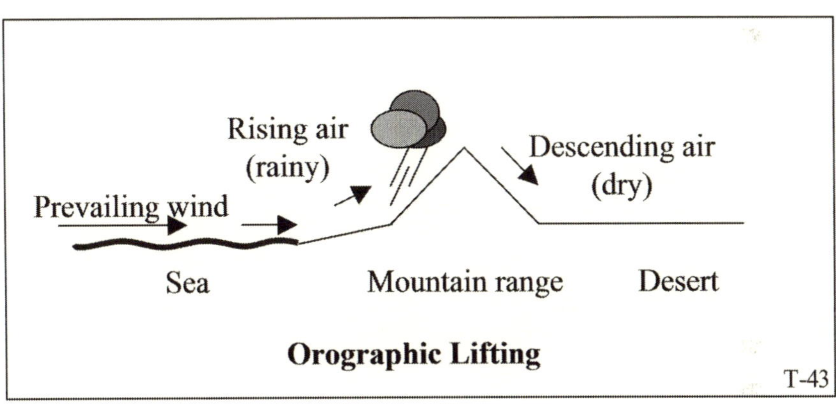

Orographic Lifting

2. A rainbow is the result of light *refraction* and *reflection,* as Jana explained in the story. The following diagram illustrates the respective light paths of a red ray (light line) and a blue ray (dark line) into and out of a raindrop. The idealized raindrop in the diagram is shown as perfectly round. In reality, raindrops are distorted. The average shape of millions of quivering raindrops, however, is spherical.

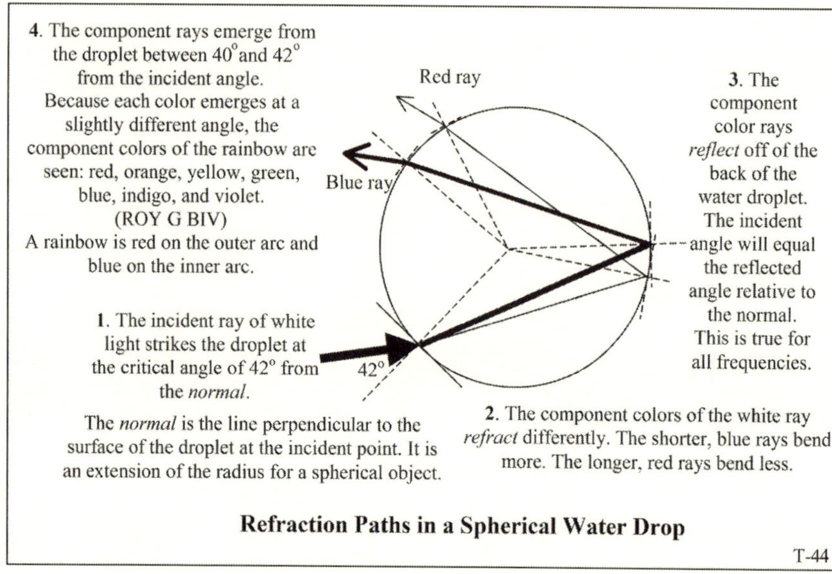

Refraction Paths in a Spherical Water Drop

3. The chromatic scale is a progression of twelve sequential notes.

There are eight primary notes in the even-tempered Western musical scale: A, B, C, D, E, F, and G. Most of the named notes are one musical step or tone apart. The exceptions are a half step between B and C and a half step between E and F. Half-steps are called *semitones.*

The half steps between the rest of the notes are called *sharps* or *flats.* A half step above A is A-sharp. This is the same musical tone as a half step below B, which is called B-flat. The entire even-tempered twelve-tone chromatic scale is shown below. The musical distance between any two adjacent positions shown on the circle is a semitone or half-step interval. For example, the musical distance from A to C is three semitones. The second chart indicates that a musical distance of 3 semitones is a *minor third.*

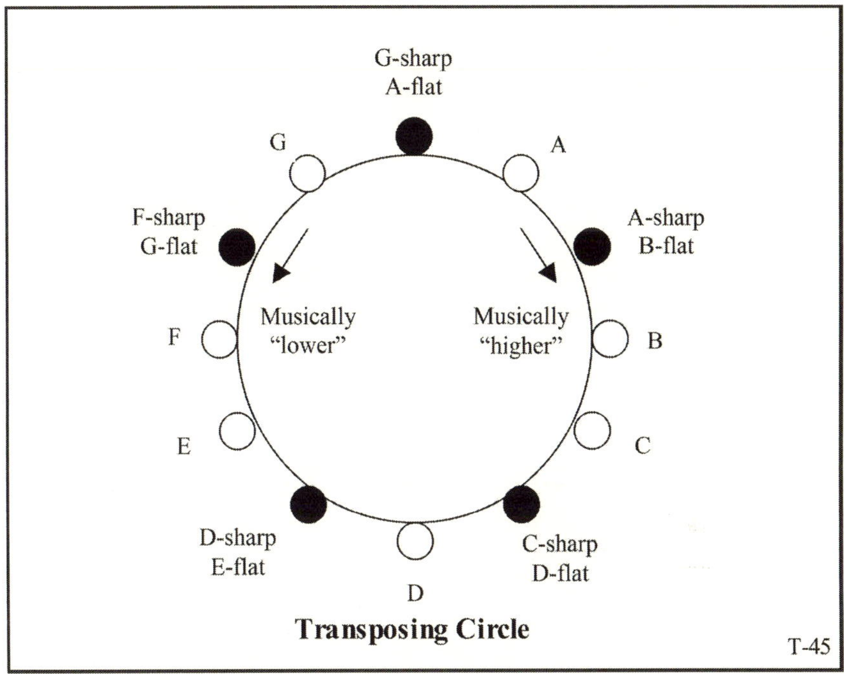

Transposing Circle

Musicians have named the musical intervals. The following chart indicates the musical distance, interval name, and an example interval:

Semitone Distance	**Named Interval**	**Example**
0	unison	G–G
1	minor second	G–G#
2	major second	G–A
3	minor third	G–A#
4	major third	G–B
5	perfect fourth	G–C
6	tritone	G–C#
7	perfect fifth	G–D
8	minor sixth	G–D#
9	major sixth	G–E
10	minor seventh	G–F
11	major seventh	G–F#
12	octave	G–G

A *chord* is three or more notes played at the same time. Many of the basic chords are composed of notes that are either a major or minor third apart The three notes are called a *triad.*

A *major chord* starts with a root note and adds the note a major third above the root and one a minor third above that. For instance, the notes of the G major chord are G, B, and D.

A *minor chord* starts with the root note and adds the note a minor third above the root and then another a major third above that. The notes of the G minor chord are G, B-flat, and D.

D	D
} 4 semitones (major third)	} 3 semitones (minor third)
B-flat	B
} 3 semitones (minor third)	} 4 semitones (major third)
G	G
Minor Triad	*Major Triad*

Musical Structure of Triads

The chord sequence of the first song in the story, "Even If," is G, Am, C, and D. This is a common chord sequence of a root, minor second, fourth, and fifth pattern in the key of G.

The key of a song is the scale, or set of notes that are used in the song and which are based upon a *home note.* The home note is also called the *tonic.* Most music ends on the home note to provide the listener with a sense of musical rest or completion.

The chart below illustrates the same chord relationships in different keys.

Key	Root	Minor 2nd	Fourth	Fifth	Minor 6th
G	G	Am	C	D	Em
D	D	Em	G	A	Bm
C	C	Dm	F	G	Am

The musical basis of much Western music is a root chord, a fifth, and a fourth. The root chord is called the *tonic,* the fifth is called the *dominant,* and the fourth is the *subdominant.*

Chord construction is part of the study of music called *musical theory.*

4. *Sound cancellation* uses the property of wave addition to eliminate an unwanted noise. A sound-canceling device senses a wave and generates a mirror image of it. A sound wave's mirror image is 180 degrees out of phase; that is, the sound is identical except that the peaks and troughs are reversed. Sound is a wave phenomenon, which means that the sum of the original sound and its opposite will cancel to silence.

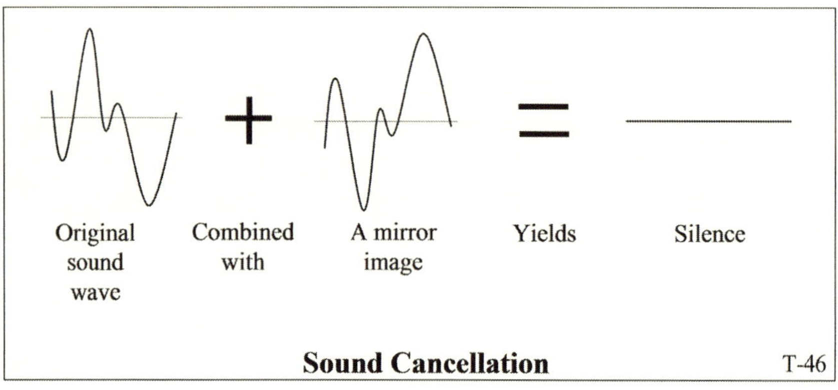

Sound Cancellation

In the twenty-first century, this effect was used commercially to make background-noise-canceling headphones and microphones.

5. One megawatt (1 MW) output of an engine is about 1340 hp. This was found in the following way:

Given: $1 \text{ hp} = 746 \text{ watt}$

And: $1 \text{ MW} = 10^6 \text{ watt}$

Therefore: $$10^6 \text{ watt} \bullet \frac{1 \text{ hp}}{746 \text{ watt}} = 1340.48 \text{ hp}$$

A typical output of two megawatts would therefore be equivalent to about 2680 horsepower. This is similar to the output of two twenty-first century JT15D engines, commonly used on small business jet aircraft, which can each produce about 1700 horsepower.

6. A *subsonic sedator* or *psychotrope* is a theoretical device that uses low-level sound to relax its hearers and reduce their inhibitions. It is based on the following observed phenomena:

Absolute silence, such as found in an *anechoic chamber,* a sound-absorbing room without echoes, is mentally disquieting. Any sound generated, such as speaking or hand clapping feels as if it is being sucked away. These chambers are appropriately called "sound-dead rooms."

On the other hand, most people find low-frequency, rhythmic sounds, such as ocean waves, very relaxing. Waves are a type of natural *white noise.* White noise is a mixture of many frequencies and sounds like a hiss that can have a lower or higher overall tone, depending upon the average of all the generated frequencies. "Sleep machines" are devices that generate rhythmic patterns of white noise to mimic the relaxing sound of waves.

Tension and relaxation are mental states. The presence of white noise or absolute silence can alter a person's mental state. What is speculated in the story is that a particular frequency, combination of frequencies, or modulation of frequencies could be used to provide a subliminal influence, inducing a sedative or hypnotic effect.

The Prophet would be less affected by such sounds because he was aware of them ; the power of subliminal phenomena is generally greatest when they remain below the threshold of consciousness. Realization of manipulation increases the victim's resistance to it. Also, as was hinted in the story, the Prophet had a sound-canceling device concealed in his brooch.

7. Religious philosophy is generally divided into two broad categories: *theism* and *atheism.*

Theism assumes a supernatural being brought the natural or physical universe into existence.

Atheism assumes that nothing exists beyond the physical universe. The physical universe consists of all that is, all that was, and all that ever will be—including any theoretical hyper-dimensional, impersonal, creative process that brought everything else into existence.

Neither philosophy is monolithic; there are many variations within each group.

Two broad groups within theism are *polytheism* and *monotheism.* Polytheists believe that there are multiple divine beings with varying personalities and degrees of authority or interest in the affairs of humanity. Monotheists contend that there is but a single, supreme, divine being with a singular personality and purpose.

Monotheism is further divided into at least two main categories: *active monotheism* and *passive monotheism.* Active monotheists believe God is personally interested and involved to varying degrees in the lives of each person. God has a purpose for each individual and can directly influence the physical universe to bring about his ultimate goals. *Judaism, Islam,* and most forms of *Christianity* are examples of active monotheistic religions.

Passive monotheists believe that God created the universe and its natural laws, but she / he / it has little or no further involvement. Some forms of *deism* are passive monotheistic.

Another theistic variation is *pantheism,* which holds that the creator and creation are one and the same. An impersonal creative force exists in a diffuse way in all things.

The distinguishing feature of atheism is the assumption of the nonexistence of any ultimate creator with a distinct personality or purpose. Atheists hold that everything must be explained only in terms of matter, space, time, and energy. There can be no appeals to any supernatural interference to explain why things happen. Simply put, the divine doesn't exist, therefore, divine intervention cannot exist.

Miracles must be, as Mr. Herzog and the Prophet contend, either natural processes for which an adequate explanation has yet to be found, or the results of chance and coincidence.

It is worth noting that both theism and atheism are faith systems. They differ in the basic axioms believed, but ultimately, the adherent of either system can only present the evidence that convinces them that their belief is valid. Each conclusion is therefore considered self-evident, not demonstrable, because each system interprets the same evidence through ***a priori*** assumptions.

The following parable illustrates this concept:

Two explorers are deep in a trackless jungle and come upon what appears to be a cultivated garden. Trees and bushes are planted in perfectly straight lines. Various flowerbeds are set up in neat squares with a circular pond located at the center of the garden.

"I wonder who planted this garden?" asks the first explorer.

"No one," answers the second. "The jungle is uninhabited, and it is too far for anyone to travel back and forth from civilization to maintain it. This area appears to be under cultivation, but due to its isolation, it can be nothing but a remarkable example of coincidences."

The first explorer insists that there must be a gardener, so they take turns standing watch. But no gardener is seen, even though they wait and watch for several days.

"Maybe he comes at night when we can't see him," suggests the first explorer.

They set up an electrified fence, and post guard dogs. But no shrieks ever indicate someone has touched the wire, and the guard dogs never bark or give any sign that a stranger is roaming the grounds.

"Perhaps the gardener is invisible, insensitive to electric shocks, silent, and odorless," the first explorer suggests.

"Wait a minute!" the second explorer exclaims. "What is the difference between your invisible, silent, odorless gardener and a gardener that is simply imaginary?"

"The difference," the first explorer replies, "is the garden. I am trying to explain its design. You are trying to explain it away."

The first explorer, representing the theist, points to the order and structure of the garden. Such order and design is never observed to appear without a designer, so he concludes that the gardener, though unobserved, must exist.

The second explorer, representing the atheist, admits that the garden appears designed, but since the gardener has never been directly observed, he concludes the gardener must not exist.

Neither conclusion can be demonstrated; either position requires faith.

But there at least two pragmatic or practical differences between the conclusions. The first is illustrated by the inconsistency of the atheist position when it is applied to a real-world situation: SETI—the Search for Extra Terrestrial Intelligence.

SETI uses radio telescopes to examine signals from space, trying to find a signal containing information that could not have been naturally produced. This is a telling admission that the conclusion of the first explorer, the theist, is valid: Certain patterns require an intelligence to create them.

What kind of signal would this be? It could be as simple as a series of pulses indicating the first few values of pi: 3-1-4-1-5-9; or e: 2-7-1-8-2-8; or the Fibonacci series: 1-1-2-3-5-8.

If radio waves carrying this information were detected, their discovery would be considered as almost certain evidence that an intelligent civilization existed on a distant planet.

It is inconsistent for an atheist to search for information in a simple digital radio sequence to prove the existence of intelligence capable of creating a designed signal—and yet maintain that the complex creatures that created the signal themselves came into existence by chance and undirected natural processes!

A second pragmatic difference is that theism does not ignore the evidence of human experience. A sample of observations is listed as a mnemonic acronym: QUESTION. Each letter of the acronym represents a key word in a series of questions about observations of the natural world: Question, Universal, Existence, Sin, Teleology, Induction, Order, No natural explanation.

Question

What is the source of the Question about the existence of God? There are only three possible origins for such a concept: an individual's random thought, a culturally transmitted idea, or a genuine awareness of the Creator.

Universal

Why is the question Universal? The vast majority of cultures in all times and places acknowledge a Creator. This seems to rule out the concept as a random thought by an individual.

Though there are great religious differences among cultures, ranging from monotheism to polytheism, a truly atheistic culture is almost unknown. If the concept of God is a mere cultural construct, then it would seem that atheism should be more common. This seems to eliminate the theory that the concept of a Creator is just a culturally implanted idea.

The observed evidence, therefore, indicates that each person has an innate awareness of a Creator that is independent from mere cultural transmission.

Recent history is replete with outspoken atheists. Clubs, societies, and even entire governmental systems have been established with the intent to eliminate the knowledge of a Creator. Despite brutal and violent methods, including imprisonment of millions of individuals and the deaths of hundreds of millions more, all such efforts have had only slight and temporary measures of success. To paraphrase Queen Gertrude in *Hamlet,* Act 3, scene 2, "The atheist doth protest too much, methinks."

Existence

Why does the universe Exist? There are only four possibilities:

1. The universe is an illusion and doesn't actually exist. This explanation is a non-explanation. If scientific observation is to have any value, then it must be determined to be false because it contradicts the testimony of all of our senses. It also begs the question of self-awareness. The source of the ability of any mind to have the capacity to perceive an illusionary universe remains unanswered.

2. The universe is eternal and has always existed. This idea was popular in scientific circles during the nineteenth century. Astronomical observations by Edwin Hubble in the twentieth century conclusively demonstrated that the universe is expanding and, therefore, must have had a beginning.

3. The universe created itself. This possibility is self-contradictory. A thing that doesn't exist cannot be a cause for itself. It is sometimes speculated that our universe is a fluctuation in an eternal, quantum field in which universes, such as our own, pop in and out of existence at random. This is pure speculation, lacking any observational support whatsoever.

4. The universe was created by something from outside the universe. This is the most reasonable explanation.

Sin

Why do all cultures have a sense of Sin, good, right, and wrong? Every culture maintains that some things should not be done even if you can escape detection and punishment. This is difficult to explain in terms of simple genetic programming through natural selection. Selfless individuals benefit others by placing their own survival at risk. If a sense of right and wrong are dependent upon genetics, as the atheist contends, then the genetic contribution of the selfless individuals must diminish until it becomes extinct. A few examples show how this is the case.

Consider a tribal member in a hunter / gatherer society who selflessly shares or even gives up food to save others in the tribe. This might allow the tribe, consisting of a mixture of selfless and selfish individuals, to survive, but each such altruistic act will reduce the selfless individual's survival chances. He will be hungrier and weaker than he could have been if he had kept all the food for himself. The selfish members of the tribe will keep what they find and eat better, thus increasing their chances of survival. Over time, the population of individuals with the supposed genetic tendency for selflessness must therefore decrease, and the proportion of selfish individuals must increase.

Consider a man who runs into a burning house to save another man's child. Suppose the child is rescued, but the rescuer is badly burned and dies. If the man had no children, then his potential contribution of altruism to the gene pool ends. If he has children, his death reduces their chances of survival. If he was the only altruistic member of that society, his children would be left to starve.

In any case, without the concept of a transcendent moral authority, nothing is really "wrong." Lying, cheating, stealing, rape, and murder are only undesirable if the perpetrator gets caught. Genetic or cultural programming might explain the fear of retribution from angry victims, but it cannot explain the sense of "ought" that prevents individuals from acting selfishly even when they could avoid detection. Nor can genetic programming explain the admiration and honor all cultures generally give to such selfless behavior.

The seemingly inborn sense of right and wrong or good and evil has been called natural moral law. The most reasonable explanation for the existence of natural moral law seems to require the existence of a moral lawgiver.

Teleology

Why does almost everything in the universe appear to be Teleological, that is, to have been designed for a specific end purpose or function? There is no question that the universe appears designed. Living and non-living systems interact in complex and interdependent ways that strongly indicate purpose and design rather than careless or haphazard arrangements. A universe that is the result of random chance would seemingly contain an abundance of failed experiments. What is actually observed, however, is a universe that functions with the efficiency of a precision-tuned machine.

But beyond the apparent design and purpose of the universe is the human need for an ultimate purpose. Without this sense of purpose, man sinks into despair. The atheist Camus wrote of the "absurdity" of hanging onto life, even though there is no meaning in it. Another atheist philosopher, Sartre, called man "a useless passion," and described existence as a "horror and mystery."

It seems that something beyond mere physical survival or self-gratification is vital for the mental health of most individuals and societies. This is consistent with a Creator bringing sentient beings into existence with a specific purpose in mind.

Induction

How does Induction demonstrate a Creator? Induction is the logical formulation of general principles from specific examples. We observe that a watch is made by a watchmaker, and an automobile is made by an automaker. By inductive logic, therefore, a universe is made by a universe maker.

Order and Information

Where does Order and information come from? There is only one known place, and that is a mind.

The universe contains a high degree of order and information. While some order does result from purely natural forces, such as the formation of crystals, informational order never appears without intelligence.

Despite atheistic claims that the complex information contained in the biologic code could have appeared by chance or through some yet-to-be-discovered natural-ordering process, such spontaneous appearance of information has never been observed. The most reasonable explanation is that the source of information found in the universe is from the intelligence and mind of its Creator.

No Natural Explanation

There is no natural explanation—supported by experimental evidence—that accounts for the existence and arrangement of the known universe. The concept of an external Creator of the universe is the most reasonable, rational, and empirically supported theory of the origin of the universe available.

Summary

The theist makes the single, reasonable appeal that a personal Creator exists outside the universe. Theism provides satisfying answers to three important philosophical questions:

Where did I come from?	I was created by God.
Why am I here?	My purpose is to learn and fulfill the Creator's plan for me.
What happens after death?	There is an eternal existence beyond the grave.

Atheists make multiple appeals to unknown processes and improbable events. They have no satisfying answers to the same three questions.

Where did I come from?	I am an accident—the chance result of a mindless process.
Why am I here?	There is no reason for me to exist.

What happens after death? I become worm food.

Agnosticism is often loosely understood to be a state of philosophic uncertainty. The agnostic simply isn't confident enough in the evidence to declare faith in either the existence or nonexistence of God. The strictest definition of agnosticism as a philosophical system, however, is not that the holder is personally uncertain, but that certainty about the existence or nonexistence of God can never be known. This position is internally inconsistent. It claims certain knowledge about what it claims must remain uncertain!

8. "When the debate is lost, slander becomes the tool of the loser," is a statement generally attributed to the ancient Greek philosopher, Socrates, c. 400 BC. What is known of Socrates is found in the writings of his students, Plato and Xenophon.

The Two Hundred Million that Almost Got Away

1. The classification of living things is called taxonomy. A common scheme that biologists use has the following structure:

Kingdom – Phylum – Class – Order – Family – Genus - Species

A helpful mnemonic, or aid to memorize this sequence, is the following sentence:

"Kids Play Chess On Fine Golden Sand."

Examples:

Kingdom	Animalia	Animalia	Animalia
Phylum	Chordata	Chordata	Chordata
Class	Mammalia	Mammalia	Actinopterygii
Order	Carnivora	Carnivora	Perciformes
Family	Felidae	Felidae	Cichlidae
Genus	*Panthera*	*Panthera*	*Tilapiini*
Species	*tigris (tiger)*	*leo (lion)*	*thysi*

Typically, a species name consists of two names, according to *binomial nomenclature.* The tiger, for example, is identified as *Panthera tigris,* or more simply, *P. tigris.* There are many species of tilapia. *T. thysi* is cited as only one example.

2. The speed of a wave (v_w) on a liquid surface is proportional to the square root of the gravitational acceleration (g).

We can write this as: $v_w :: \sqrt{g}$

The gravitational constant of Oceanus ($g_{Oceanus}$) was given as 0.85 g. Therefore, the speed of ocean waves would be proportional to the square root of the ratio of gravitational accelerations.

Write the proportion: $v_w / v :: \sqrt{(g_{Oceanus} / g)}$

Substitute known values: $v_w / v :: \sqrt{0.85g / g)}$

Simplify by canceling g: $v_w / v :: \sqrt{0.85}$

Solve the root: $v_w / v \approx 0.92 = 92\%$

The ocean waves under 85 percent normal gravity would therefore travel only about 92 percent as fast as they would travel under one g.

The ocean-going ship that was briefly mentioned, however, would sink as deep on one planet as on any other, even under reduced gravity. A ship experiences buoyancy due to the weight of the water displaced. Under reduced gravity, the weight of the ship would be less, of course, but so would the weight of the displaced water. Both weights would *decrease* by the same proportion. The same effect holds true under increased gravity. In such a case, the weight of the ship and the weight of the water would *increase* by the same proportion. A ship will sink to the same depth regardless of the strength of gravity in any gravity field greater than zero. At zero gravity, the concept of buoyancy is meaningless, since the ship and the water would have no weight.

At some level of increased gravity, however, the weight of the displaced water will exceed the crush strength of the hull. At that point, the hull will collapse, and the boat will rapidly sink to the bottom!

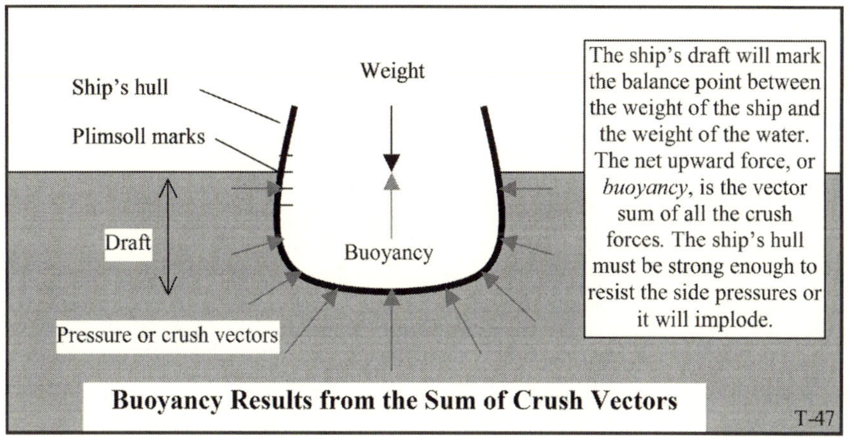

Buoyancy Results from the Sum of Crush Vectors

A ship's depth, or *draft,* will change as the ship is loaded. The ship will ride lower as it is loaded more heavily and ride higher when empty. Because of this, ships often have a depth gauge painted on the side near the waterline. These indicators are called *Plimsoll markings* and effectively function as a giant scale to measure the ship's weight.

3. A ship that rises on a contra-grav beam must gain potential energy. If it accelerates forward it also gains kinetic energy.

Without the transfer of kinetic energy to the ship in the direction of the planet's spin, it would drift backward and appear to have a *retrograde* motion. This would result from an increase in radius without an increase in tangential velocity. The diagram below illustrates why this would happen.

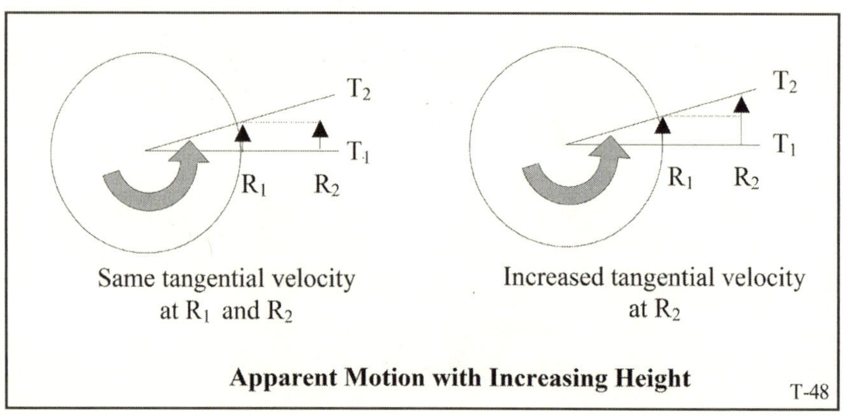

Apparent Motion with Increasing Height

The drawing on the left shows the tangential velocity arrows at R_1 and R_2 of the same length. The spaceship at R_2 falls behind the vertical line over the launch point at T_2.

The drawing on the right shows that in order to remain over the launch point as the altitude increases to R_2, the tangential velocity must also increase.

4. Human travel in deep space requires a variety of protective layers to reduce the exposure to ionizing radiation particles. There are four main types of ionizing radiation: alpha, beta, gamma, and neutron.

A particle of alpha (α) radiation consists of a helium nucleus, two protons, and two neutrons. It is a very slow and heavy object on the atomic scale and is easily stopped by a sheet of paper.

Beta (β) radiation is fast-moving electrons. A thin sheet of metal, such as aluminum foil, will stop this form of radiation.

Gamma (γ) radiation is made of very high-energy photons called X-rays. Only a layer of dense matter, such as lead, can stop these rays. The more dense the matter or the thicker the layer, the greater the level of protection.

Neutron radiation is a stream of high-speed neutrons. Neutrons have no electrical charge, so they are unaffected by the electrical fields of the negatively charged electron cloud or the positively charged nucleus that make up the atoms of matter. As a result, they penetrate most materials quite well. A high-speed neutron can easily penetrate many inches of lead.

Protection from neutron radiation is accomplished by *neutron scattering.* Neutrons are scattered by collisions with light hydrogen atoms. Hydrogen is abundant in water and wax, so a water jacket would be one way to protect a space crew from neutron radiation.

Atoms are *ionized* when they gain or lose electrons. Ions have different chemical characteristics from nonionized atoms. When ionizing radiation penetrates a living cell, the formation of ions creates chemical interference and contaminates the normal metabolism of the cell. This chemical interference disrupts or kills the cell and is called *radiation sickness.*

In addition, high-speed particles damage DNA, the complex genetic information code. This reduces or destroys the cell's ability to reproduce by sterilizing the cell or introducing genetic abnormalities.

5. *Escape velocity* is the minimum required speed moving away from a gravitational source that ensures that the moving object will not fall back. In the case of Earth, the escape velocity is about 11,200 meters per second (abbreviated as 11,200 m/s). This can be derived several ways. A noncalculus method is as follows:

Potential energy (P) for any object of mass (m) at distance (r) at gravitation (g) is:	$P = m \bullet g \bullet r$
Kinetic energy (K) for any object of mass m moving at velocity v is:	$K = ½ \bullet m \bullet v^2$

Assume an object is at distance r with zero velocity. Kinetic energy is therefore zero and potential energy is at a relative maximum. As the object begins to fall, it gains velocity and loses altitude as its potential energy converts to kinetic energy. Assuming no losses due to friction, the instant the object reaches the surface, altitude and potential energy are both zero. At the same instant, velocity and kinetic energy are at a maximum, and all the potential energy has been changed to kinetic energy.

This means that: $K_{max} = P_{max}$

For free-fall objects, generally stated as: $K = P$

Substituting: $\frac{1}{2} \bullet m \bullet v^2 = m \bullet g \bullet r$

m cancels out: $\frac{1}{2} \bullet v^2 = g \bullet r$

Multiply both sides by 2: $v^2 = 2 \bullet g \bullet r$

Extract square root from both sides: $v = \sqrt{(2 \bullet g \bullet r)}$

This establishes the relationship between free-fall velocity, the local gravitational acceleration, and the distance from the gravity source. Therefore, the equation for the escape velocity can be stated as: $v_{escape} = \sqrt{(2 \bullet g \bullet r)}$

Note that since the value of g decreases as r increases, escape velocity is not a fixed value. It will be smaller the farther the initial starting point is from the center of gravity.

In the case of Earth, the value of g is $9.8\ m/s^2$ at the surface, which is about 6,400,000 meters from the Earth's center.

Substituting: $v_{escape} = \sqrt{(2 \cdot 9.8\ m/s^2 \cdot 6{,}400{,}000\ m)}$

Simplifying: $v_{escape} = \sqrt{(125{,}440{,}000\ m^2/s^2)}$

Solve: $v_{escape} = 11{,}200\ m/s$

The gravitational acceleration of Oceanus was given as 85 percent g. The radius of the planet was not specified. But since mass is proportional to volume, and if we assume a similar density to Earth, finding the radius of a sphere with 85 percent the Earth's volume will provide an estimate of the radius of a planet with 85 percent g.

Formula for volume of a sphere: $V = 4 / 3 \cdot \pi \cdot r^3$

The ratio of volumes for 85% is: $0.85 = \frac{V_{Oceanus}}{V_{Earth}}$

Substitute: $0.85 = \frac{4 / 3 \cdot \pi \cdot r_{Oceanus}^3}{4 / 3 \cdot \pi \cdot r_{Earth}^3}$

Simplify: $0.85 = \frac{r_{Oceanus}^3}{r_{Earth}^3}$

Solve for $r_{Oceanus}$ cubed: $r_{Earth}^3 \cdot 0.85 = r_{Oceanus}^3$

Take the cube root of both sides: $\sqrt[3]{(r_{Earth}^3 \cdot 0.85)} = \sqrt[3]{r_{Oceanus}}$

Restate: $r_{Earth} \cdot \sqrt[3]{(0.85)} = r_{Oceanus}$

Substitute radius of Earth (6400 km = 6,400,000m = 6.4×10^6 m):

$$6.4 \times 10^6 \text{ m} \bullet \sqrt[3]{(0.85)} = r_{Oceanus}$$

Solve: $$6.4 \times 10^6 \text{ m} \bullet 0.947 = r_{Oceanus}$$

$$6.06 \times 10^6 \text{m} = r_{Oceanus}$$

Divide by 1000 to convert to km: $$\frac{6.061 \times 10^6 \text{m}}{1000 \text{ m / Km}} = r_{Oceanus}$$

Solve: $$6061 \text{ km} \approx r_{Oceanus}$$

The estimated radius of the planet is therefore just over 6000 km.

Escape Velocity of Oceanus at the Surface

The value of $g_{Oceanus}$ at the surface is: $$g_{Oceanus} = 0.85 \bullet g_{earth}$$

Substitute: $$g_{Oceanus} = 0.85 \bullet 9.8 \text{ m/s}^2$$

Solve: $$g_{Oceanus} = 8.3 \text{ m/s}^2$$

Given: $$v_{escape} = \sqrt{(2 \bullet g \bullet r)}$$

Substituting: $$v_{escape} = \sqrt{(2 \bullet 8.3 \text{ m/s}^2 \bullet 6.061 \times 10^6 \text{m})}$$

Simplifying: $$v_{escape} = \sqrt{(1.006 \times 108 \text{ m}^2/\text{s}^2)}$$

Yielding the result: $$v_{escape} = 10{,}030 \text{ m/s}$$

The escape velocity of Oceanus at the surface is therefore 10,030 m/s.

Gravitational Acceleration

The most general formula for gravitational acceleration is:

$$g = \frac{G \bullet m}{r^2}$$

Where:

m is the mass of the gravitational source, such as a planet;

r is the distance or radius from the center of mass; and

G is an experimentally derived gravitational constant, approximately equal to $6.674 \times 10^{-11}\ m^3 / (Kg \cdot s^2)$. The value of this constant in terms of how the universe operates on the grand scale is extremely sensitive and significant to at least twenty decimal places. This degree of precision is a clue that the universe operates as a finely tuned and delicately balanced machine.

Gravitational Inverse Square Law Relationship

The gravitational acceleration can be calculated directly from the above equations, but since the value of g_o is known at a given radius r_o, then an *inverse square law relationship* can be used to calculate the value of g at another radius r.

Given the initial gravitational acceleration:

$$g_o = \frac{G \cdot m}{r_o^2}$$

If g is the acceleration at some radius r, then:

$$g = \frac{G \cdot m}{r^2}$$

Set up these values as a proportion:

$$\frac{g}{g_o} = \frac{G \cdot m / r^2}{G \cdot m / r_o^2}$$

G and m cancel out:

$$\frac{g}{g_o} = \frac{(1 / r^2)}{(1 / r_o^2)}$$

Which simplifies to:

$$\frac{g}{g_o} = \frac{r_o^2}{r^2}$$

Solve for g:

$$g = g_o \cdot (r_o^2 / r^2)$$

Simplify:

$$g = g_o \cdot (r_o / r)^2$$

Time to Reach Escape Velocity

The ship's engines accelerated the ship at 10 m/s^2. The time required to reach this velocity at the given acceleration is found as follows:

Given: $a \bullet t = v_{escape}$

Solve for t by dividing both sides by a: $t = \frac{v_{escape}}{a}$

Substitute known values: $t = \frac{10{,}030 \text{ m/s}}{10 \text{ m/s}^2}$

Solve: $t = 1003 \text{ s}$

Solving for minutes by dividing seconds by 60: $t = \frac{1003 \text{ s}}{60 \text{ s/min}} \approx 16.72 \text{ min.}$

Escape velocity is thus obtained in less than twenty minutes.

6. The distance (d) covered in 1003 seconds of acceleration at 10 m/s^2 is found by:

Given that: $d = ½ \bullet a \bullet t^2 + v_0 \bullet t + d_0$

If $v_0 = 0$, $d_0 = 0$, and $t = 1003$ s, then: $d = ½ \bullet a \bullet t^2$

Substituting given values: $d = (½ \bullet 10 \text{ m/s}^2) \bullet (1003 \text{ s})^2$

Simplifying: $d = 5 \text{ m/s}^2 \bullet 1.006 \times 10^6 \text{ s}^2$

s^2 cancels out: $d = 5\text{m} \bullet 1.006 \times 10^6$

$d = 5.030 \times 10^6 \text{ m}$

Divide by 1000 to convert to km: $d = \frac{5.030 \times 10^6 \text{ m}}{1000 \text{ m / Km}}$

Simplify: $d \approx 5030$ km

The ship will therefore reach escape velocity at about 5000 kilometers.

Accelerating for an additional thirty minutes

Find seconds in 30 minutes: $30 \text{ min} \bullet \frac{60 \text{ sec}}{1 \text{ min}} = 1800$ seconds

Given that: $a = 10 \text{ m/s}^2$

$v_0 = 10{,}030$ m/s

$t = 1800$ seconds

Accelerated distance (d'): $d' = ½ \bullet a \bullet t^2 + v_0 \bullet t$

Substitute: $d' = ½ \bullet 10 \text{ m/s}^2 \bullet (1800 \text{ s})^2 + 10{,}030 \text{ m/s} \bullet 1800 \text{ s}$

Simplify: $d' = 1.62 \times 10^7 \text{ m} + 1.805 \times 10^7 \text{ m}$

Simplify: $d' = 3.425 \times 10^7$ m

Convert to kilometers: $d' = \frac{3.425 \times 10^7 \text{ m}}{1000 \text{ m / km}}$

$d' = 34{,}250$ km

Total accelerated distance (D) is: $D = d + d'$

Substitute values: $D = 5030 \text{ km} + 34{,}250$ km

Simplify:	$D = 39{,}280\ km$

The gravity at this distance:	$g = g_o \bullet (r_o / r)^2$
Substitute:	$g = (8.3\ m/s^2) \bullet (6{,}061\ km / 39{,}280\ km)^2$
Simplify:	$g = (8.3\ m/s^2) \bullet (0.154)^2$
Simplify:	$g = 8.3\ m/s^2 \bullet 0.0237$
Simplify:	$g \approx 0.197\ m/s^2$

The total acceleration time is:	$t = 1003\ s + 1800\ s$
Simplify:	$t = 2803\ s$
Convert to minutes:	$t = \frac{2803\ s}{60\ s/min}$
	$t = 46.7$ minutes.

The final velocity is:	$v = a \bullet t$
Substitute known values:	$v = 10\ m/s^2 \bullet 2803\ s$
Solve:	$v = 28{,}030\ m/s$

The engines are shutdown at this velocity and the ship then coasts on momentum.

Energy and Fuel Requirements

The amount of energy required to accelerate to this speed is approximately the following:

The formula for kinetic energy (KE) is:	$KE = ½ \bullet m \bullet v^2$
The mass of the ship (m) is approximately	$M_t = 1.17 \text{ x } 10^9$ kg
The velocity (v) is:	v = 28,030 m/s
Substitute known values:	$KE = ½ \bullet 1.17 \text{ x } 10^9 \text{ kg} \bullet (28{,}030 \text{ m/s})^2$
Simplify:	$KE \approx 4.6 \text{ x } 10^{17}$ kg m/s^2
Restating in Joules:	$KE \approx 4.6 \text{ x } 10^{17}$ J
Energy per kilogram D_2O:	$7.7 \text{ x } 10^{13}$ J/kg
Heavy water (deuterium) to fuse (m_d) is:	$m_d = \dfrac{KE}{7.7 \text{ x } 10^{13} \text{ J/kg}}$
Substitute known value of KE:	$m_d = \dfrac{4.6 \text{ x } 10^{17} \text{ J}}{7.7 \text{ x } 10^{13} \text{ J/kg}}$
Simplify:	$m_d = 5.97 \text{ x } 10^3$ kg = 5970 kg
Convert to pounds:	$m_d = 5970 \text{ kg} \bullet 2.2 \text{ lb/kg} = 13{,}130$ lb

Ordinary water is 8.3 pound/gallon.

The atomic mass of water (H_2O) is:	1 + 1 + 16 = 18.
The atomic mass of heavy water (D_2O) is:	2 + 2 + 16 = 20.

Therefore heavy water is 20 / 18 or 1.11 times as heavy as ordinary (light) water.

A gallon of heavy water is therefore:	8.3 lb / gal • 1.11 = 9.22 lb / gal
Convert (m_d) to gallons:	13,130 lb • gal / 9.22 lb = 1424 gallons

This amount of heavy water would be difficult and expensive to find on Earth. Analysis of the atmosphere of Venus indicates that heavy water is about one hundred times more abundant than on Earth. Venus might provide sufficient quantities of heavy water for initial deep space exploration. Other planets might then be discovered that could provide even more heavy water—possibly oceans of it—much like the providential reserves of coal provided the energy for the Industrial Revolution.

Reaction Mass

The amount of light water, or, ordinary water, needed to be ejected at 10^6 m/s (v_w) is found using the principle of conservation of momentum: The momentum of the ship (P_s) must equal the momentum of the water reaction mass (P_w).

Given:	$P = m \bullet v$
And:	$P_s = P_w$
Then:	$m_s \bullet v_s = m_w \bullet v_w$
Solve for m_r by dividing both sides by v_w	$\frac{m_s \bullet v_s}{v_w} = \frac{m_w \bullet v_w}{v_w}$
Simplify:	$\frac{m_s \bullet v_s}{v_w} = m_w$

Or: $m_w = \frac{m_s \bullet v_s}{v_w}$

Substitute known values: $m_w = \frac{1.18 \times 10^9 \text{ kg} \bullet 28{,}030 \text{ m/s}}{10^6 \text{ m/s}}$

Simplify: $m_w = 3.28 \times 10^7 \text{ kg}$

The maximum amount of water carried: $M_w \approx 2.1 \times 10^8 \text{ kg}$

The number of burns possible is: $\text{burns} = M_w / m_w$

Substitute known values: $\text{burns} = \frac{2.1 \times 10^8 \text{ kg}}{3.28 \times 10^7 \text{ kg}} = 6.3$

The ship would therefore have more than enough reaction mass for three starts and three stops from planets with surface gravitational accelerations of about 1 g.

Water Pump Requirements

The rate of injected water: $\Delta m / \Delta t = m_w / \Delta t$

Where

$\Delta m = m_w = \text{change in mass}$

$\Delta m = 3.28 \times 10^7 \text{ kg}$

$\Delta t = \text{change in time} = 1800\text{s}$

Substitute known values: $m_w / \Delta t = 3.28 \times 10^7 \text{ kg} / 1800 \text{ s}$

Simplify: $m_w / \Delta t = 1.82 \times 10^4 \text{ kg/s} = 18{,}200 \text{ kg/s}$

This amount is divided between three engines: $\frac{m_w / \Delta t}{3} = \frac{18{,}200 \text{ kg/s}}{3} = 6074 \text{ kg/s}$

By definition, one liter of water is one kilogram. Therefore, 6074 kg/s is equal to 6074 L/s.

Convert to gallons per second:	$6074\ L/s \bullet 1.057\ qt \bullet \frac{gal}{4\ qt} = 1605\ gal/s$
Convert to gallons per minute (gpm):	$1605\ gal/s \bullet 60\ s/min = 96{,}300\ gal/min$

Each engine would therefore have to eject almost 100,000 gallons of water per minute to accelerate the ship at 1 g when fully loaded. This requirement would decrease as the water load decreased.

Engine Thrust

Thrust is a measure of the force, or push, of the engines. The combined thrusts (T) of the three engines are found in the following manner:

General equation for thrust:	$T = v_e \bullet \frac{\Delta m}{\Delta t}$	
Where:	T = thrust	
	v_e = exhaust velocity	(10^6 m/s)
	m_w = change in mass	(3.28×10^7 kg)
	Δt = change in time	(1800 s)
Substitute known values:	$T = \frac{10^6\ m/s \bullet 3.28 \times 10^7\ kg}{1800s}$	
Simplify:	$T = 1.82 \times 10^{10}\ kg\ m/s^2 =$	1.82×10^{10} N

For comparison purposes, the space shuttle's solid rocket booster (SRB) produces about 14 MN (1.4×10^7 N)—about a thousandth the thrust of the proposed space transport engines.

Specific Impulse

A measure of rocket engine efficiency is *specific impulse.*

General equation for specific impulse:	$I_{sp} = v_e / g$
Substitute known values:	$I_{sp} = \dfrac{10^6 \text{ m/s}}{9.8 \text{ m/s}^2}$
Simplify:	$I_{sp} = 1.02 \times 10^5 \text{ s} = 102{,}000 \text{ s}$

This indicates an engine well beyond the efficiency of any we can produce today.

For comparison purposes, the specific impulses of the space shuttle's SRB and main engine are about 250 seconds and 460 seconds, respectively.

7. If the ship's engines were shut down at a distance of 39,280 km (3.928×10^7 m) at a velocity of 28,030 m/s heading away from the planet, it would begin to slow with an initial retarding acceleration of 0.197 m/s^2. Deceleration in the equations below is shown as $-.197\text{m/s}^2$.

The coast time was given as eight hours. Convert this to seconds:

Given: $t = 8 \text{ h}$

$t = 8 \text{ h} \cdot 60 \text{ min/h} \cdot 60 \text{ s/min}$

$t = 8 \cdot 60 \cdot 60 \text{ s}$

$t = 28{,}800 \text{ s}$

Approximate Coast Distance

Given: $d = \frac{1}{2} \bullet a \bullet t^2 + v_0 \bullet t + d_0$

Substituting: $d \approx \frac{1}{2} \bullet -.197\text{m/s}^2 \bullet (28{,}800\text{ s})^2 + 28{,}030\text{ m/s} \bullet 28{,}800\text{ s} + 3.928\text{x}10^7\text{ m}$

Simplifying: $d = -8.17 \text{ x } 10^7\text{ m} + 8.073 \text{ x } 10^8\text{ m} + 3.928 \text{ x } 10^7\text{m}$

$d = 7.649 \text{ x } 10^8\text{m} = 7.649 \text{ x } 10^5\text{ km}$ or 764,900 km

This formula will work for short times, but it is inadequate for longer times because the rate of deceleration will decrease as the ship moves away from the planet. Because this formula assumes a constant deceleration, it will underestimate the coasting distance in the given time.

Dividing the coasting time of eight hours (28,800 seconds) into two sections of 14,400 seconds each will provide a better estimate.

We find the coasting distance in the first time period:

$d_1 = \frac{1}{2} \bullet -0.197\text{ m/s}^2 \bullet (14{,}400\text{ s})^2 + 28{,}030\text{ m/s} \bullet 14{,}400\text{ s} + 3.928 \text{ x } 10^7\text{ m}$

$d_1 = -2.042 \text{ x } 10^7\text{ m} + 4.036 \text{ x } 10^8\text{ m} + 3.928 \text{ x } 10^7\text{ m}$

$d_1 = 4.225 \text{ x } 10^8\text{ m} \approx 422{,}500\text{ km}$

The velocity (v_2) at this point is:

$v_2 = a \bullet t + v_2$

$v_2 = -0.197\text{ m/s}^2 \bullet (14{,}400\text{ s}) + 28{,}030\text{ m/s}$

$v_2 = -2837\text{ m/s} + 28{,}030\text{ m/s}$

$v_2 \approx 25{,}190\text{ m/s}$

The gravitational acceleration at 422,500 km is:

$g_2 = g_o \bullet (r_o / r)^2$

$g_2 = (8.3 \text{ m/s}^2) \bullet (6{,}061 \text{ km} / 422{,}500 \text{ km})^2$

$g_2 \approx 0.0017 \text{ m/s}^2$

Apply these values in the distance formula for the second portion:

$d_2 = ½ \bullet -0.0017 \text{ m/s}^2 \bullet (14{,}400 \text{ s})^2 + 25{,}190 \text{ m/s} \bullet 14{,}400 \text{ s} + 4.225 \times 10^8 \text{ m}$

$d_2 = -1.763 \times 10^5 \text{ m} + 3.627 \times 10^8 \text{ m} + 4.225 \times 10^8 \text{ m}$

$d_2 \approx 7.834 \times 10^8 \text{ m}$

$d_2 = 7.834 \times 10^5 \text{ km or } 783{,}400 \text{ km}$

As the number of steps increases, the total coast distance will increase to a limiting value. This can be approximated without calculus using the following BASIC computer program. In order to run it, you need a PC with BASIC programming language installed.

There are various versions of BASIC available to download on several internet websites as an executable (.exe) file. The following program was written in GW-BASIC, but should run on most other versions.

GWBASIC and the short BASIC program shown below can be downloaded from www.janamaines.com.

You do not need to know how to program, but some programming knowledge is helpful. Type in the code exactly as shown below. Each line of code is identified by a line number. Press the ENTER key after every command line is typed. A code line can run off the right side of the screen and continue onto the following visual line, but as long as a new line number has not been entered, the program sees it as a single line of code.

Type RUN to begin the program. If you make a mistake, do not worry. The BASIC language will display a error message and give you the opportunity to correct the line.

A few BASIC conventions:

Zero appears with a slash	Ø
The letter "oh" has no slash	O
Multiply is the "splat"	*
A power is the carat	^

A few BASIC commands that are helpful to know:

Press the ENTER key to initiate any command.

CLS	Clear Screen
RUN	Begin the program
LIST	Display all the lines in the program
LIST XXX	Display line XXX. Example: LIST 100
LIST XXX-YYY	Display lines XXX to YYY. Example: LIST 100-150
SYSTEM	Exits BASIC
Control-Break	Press both keys together to stop the program
SAVE "filename"	Uploads program to the current drive
LOAD "filename"	Downloads program from the current drive
FILES	Displays all programs on the current drive

Your mouse or other pointing device will not work in the BASIC window. Use the arrow keys to move the cursor to the desired location on the screen. If a line is changed or edited, you must press ENTER to register the change.

REM	Remark. The information is for a person studying the code. The computer ignores anything after a REM statement, so you need

not type lines 100 through 140, or the REM statement in line 180, or any other line.

```
1ØØ REM ** This program calculates the final velocity of a falling space ship
11Ø REM ** integrated between specified altitudes in a varying gravitational
12Ø REM ** field. Initial velocity is also specified.
13Ø REM ** Calculations are for vertical movement only. 'Angled shots' are not
14Ø REM ** considered. User selects time or distance limits.
18Ø CLS        :REM clears screen
19Ø ON ERROR GOTO 18Ø        :REM traps errors
2ØØ T$="* Velocity Integration Simulator *" :REM title string
21Ø PRINT TAB(4Ø-LEN(T$) / 2);T$:PRINT        :REM centers title on screen
22Ø INPUT "Planet Radius    (Km)    ";RØ
23Ø RØ=RØ*1ØØØ   :REM converts RØ to meters
24Ø INPUT "Planet g(m/s^2)          ";GØ
25Ø PRINT:INPUT "T= time limit  D = Distance limit  (t / D)  ";I$
26Ø IF I$="t" OR I$="T" THEN I$="T"
27Ø IF I$<>"T" THEN I$=""
28Ø INPUT "Starting altitude (Km)   ";R1
29Ø IF I$<>"T" THEN INPUT "Ending altitude  (Km) ",R2 : RE=R2
3ØØ INPUT "Ship Velocity ( + up -dwn) (m/s)        ";V
```

```
31Ø IF I$="t" OR I$="T" THEN INPUT "Time limit  (seconds) ";TL

32Ø S=SGN(V):IF S=Ø THEN S=-1

33Ø TI=.1 + .1*R1^.2            :REM sizes time increment

34Ø T=TI       :REM sets first time increment

35Ø PRINT

36Ø R1=Rl*lØØØ     :REM changes R1 to meters

37Ø R2=R2*1ØØØ    :REM changes R2 to meters

38Ø R1=R1 + RØ: R2=R2 + RØ: R=R1          :REM changes altitude to distance.

39Ø G=-GØ*(RØ / R)^2        :REM finds g at distance R

4ØØ V=V + G*TI       :REM increments velocity

41Ø R=R + V*TI         :REM increments distance

42Ø IF SGN(V)<>S THEN S=SGN(V):PRINT "The ship slowed to Ø m/s at an  altitude of "(R-RØ) / lØØØ "Km after "T " seconds.":PRINT

43Ø     REM ** tests for direction reversal and prints information if true

44Ø IF R1>=R2 AND R<=R2 THEN 52Ø

45Ø      REM ** if end altitude was less than start altitude, tests if current  distance (R) is now less than end altitude and ends routine if true

46Ø IF Rl<=R2 AND R>=R2 THEN 52Ø

47Ø     REM ** if end altitude was greater than start altitude, tests if current distance (R) is now greater than end altitude and ends routine if true
```

48Ø IF R <= RØ AND V<=Ø THEN PRINT "Ship did not reach"RE"Kilometers. It fell short and struck the surface after ":GOTO 54Ø

49Ø REM ** tests if current altitude (R) is less than radius of planet (RØ) and ends routine if true

5ØØ IF I$=""THEN T=T + TI:GOTO 39Ø :REM increments timer

51Ø IF T<TL THEN T=T + TI:GOTO 39Ø :REM tests if time limit reached

52Ø PRINT "The ship was at an altitude of "INT(R / 1000)" Kilometers after: ":PRINT

53Ø R=R / 1ØØØ:R=INT (1ØØ*R) / 1ØØ:R=R-RØ:IF R<Ø THEN R=Ø

54Ø PRINT INT(1Ø*T) / 1Ø,"seconds or" :REM rounds time (T) to .1 second

55Ø PRINT INT(1Ø*T / 6Ø) / 1Ø,"minutes or" :REM rounds time (T) to .1 minute

56Ø PRINT INT(1ØØ*T / 36ØØ) / 1ØØ, "hours" :REM rounds time (T) to .Ø1 hour

57Ø PRINT:PRINT "The final speed of the ship was "INT(1Ø*V) / 1Ø "m/s "

58Ø PRINT:INPUT "Another calculation with this planet (Y / n) ";Z$

59Ø IF Z$ ="n" OR Z$="N" THEN 61Ø :REM stops program if response = n or N

6ØØ V=Ø:T=Ø:R1=Ø:R2=Ø:GOTO 25Ø :REM resets variables

61Ø CLS

62Ø INPUT "Do you want to exit BASIC (Y / n) ";Z$

63Ø IF Z$<>"n" OR Z$<>"N" THEN SYSTEM

```
640 END
```

Below is an example of what your BASIC window should display with the given inputs. If your screen looks different, the output values are different, or you get an error message when you RUN the program, then LIST the program and examine your code for an error.

```
              * Velocity Integration Simulator *

Planet Radius         (Km)                              ? 6061
Planet g              (m/s^2)                           ? 8.3

T = time limit        D = Distance limit   (t / D)      ? T
Starting altitude     (Km)                              ? 39280
Starting velocity     (m/s)                             ? 28030
Time limit            (seconds)                         ? 28800

The ship was at an altitude of 846834 Kilometers after:

28800.8               seconds or
480                   minutes or
8                     hours

The final speed of the ship was 27802.2 m/s

Another calculation with this planet (Y / n)?
```

We found above that a one-step calculation of the coasting time of 28,800 seconds resulted in an approximate distance of 764,900 km.

Dividing this into two steps resulted in an approximation of 783,400 km.

The BASIC program divides the coasting time into thousands of increments that approaches a limiting value near 846,834 km.

The programs computational steps are:

Divide the coasting time into approximately one-second increments;

Calculate the gravitational acceleration at that distance;

Calculate the change in velocity for that time interval at that acceleration;

Add the change in velocity to the current velocity;

Calculate the change in distance for that time interval at that velocity, and;

Add the change in distance to the current distance.

The program repeats these steps until:

The specified time is reached, or;

The specified distance is reached, or;

The ship reaches the surface of the planet.

The direction flag is the variable S in line 320. Positive velocities are "up," or away from the planet. Negative velocities are "down," or toward the planet. The positive or negative sign of the velocity initially entered in line 300 will set variable S. The only way this direction will change in a free-falling object is if it is initially thrown "upward" and then loses enough energy to start falling back toward the planet. The change of direction is detected in line 420. The first increment that shows a change in direction will flag the program to display the distance and time at that point.

The digitally integrated result is 846,834 km. The integrated distance is greater than the simpler, manual approximations because it more accurately reflects the decrease in the strength of gravity the ship experiences as it moves away from the planet.

The same is true when a ship approaches a planet on a free-fall trajectory. The closer it approaches, the faster it picks up speed. Integral calculus, or discreet numerical modeling such as is used here are needed to compensate for the changes in the strength of the gravitational field.

The program above is very simple in that it computes only a linear, "up / down" velocity. In reality, a ship could have other velocity components. These components are critical once the ship reaches the planet, as their values will determine whether or not an orbit is possible. But, for the purposes of this story, determining the approximate changes in approach and departure velocities was sufficient.

8. The Peltier effect is an electrical phenomenon that causes junction pairs of dissimilar metals to change temperature as a result of electrical current flow. A junction is the physical meeting point of the two conductors. When two wires of different metals are connected into a loop, a junction pair will always form. Depending on the direction of the current and the nature of the metals, one junction will heat, and the other junction will cool.

The following diagram illustrates an iron/copper junction pair and the resulting thermoelectric effects:

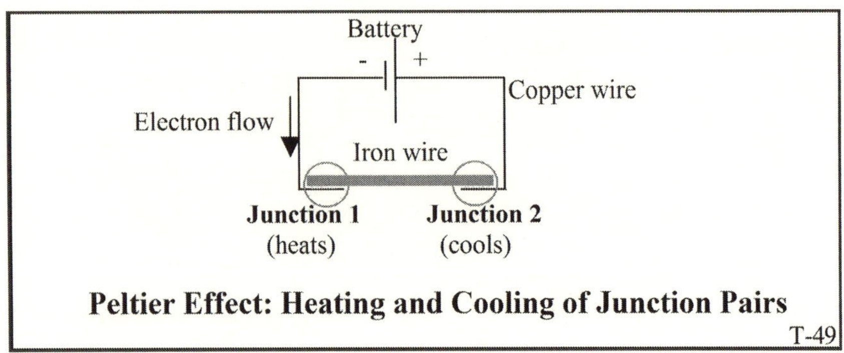

Peltier Effect: Heating and Cooling of Junction Pairs

T-49

9. Absolute zero –273.15° centigrade or Celsius, is the temperature at which molecular motion ceases. The Celsius scale divides the freezing temperature of pure water and the boiling point of pure water at one atmosphere of pressure into one hundred degrees. The Kelvin scale uses the same temperature change per degree, but begins the scale at absolute zero rather than at the freezing temperature of pure water.

Hence the freezing point of water (0° C):	0° C + 273.15° = 273.15° K
A comfortable room temperature (20° C):	20° C + 273.15° = 293.15° K
The boiling point of water at one atmosphere (100° C):	100° C + 273.15° = 373.15° K

The kinetic theory of heat describes heat, or thermal energy, as the motion of molecules. Energy of motion is called kinetic energy. The molecules in a substance with thermal energy are moving. The higher the temperature, the greater the average molecule movement, and, therefore, the more kinetic energy.

At *low* temperature, molecules simply vibrate in position and hold a *solid* shape.

At *medium* temperature, molecules vibrate enough to slip and slide over each other as a *liquid*.

At *high* temperature, molecules vibrate so vigorously that they fly about the container as a *gas*.

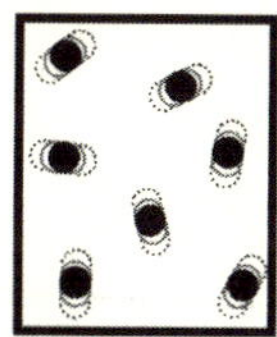

Temperature and the Kinetic Energy of Molecules

T-50

10. A blackbody is a theoretical object with a surface that reflects none of the light that strikes it. Such a surface does not exist, but a practical equivalent is a light-absorbing chamber that effectively traps any light that enters it.

The blackbody chamber is of experimental value in the laboratory because it exhibits the characteristics of a true blackbody.

All light rays that enter the cavity are completely absorbed. The opening into the cavity thus appears as a true blackbody to an outside observer. It appears as a "virtual object" that reflects no light at all.

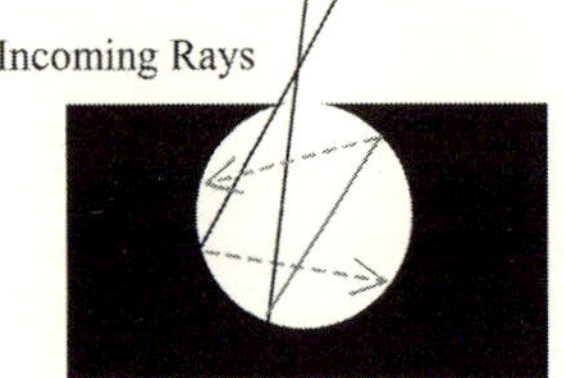

Cavity with interior walls of low reflectivity absorb the light rays in one or two reflections

Side View of the Interior Structure of a Blackbody Cavity

T-51

The open hatches of the Aegis would not function as perfect blackbodies because of the cosmic background radiation. This is the echo of the intense, high temperature that accompanied the creation of the universe. As the universe has expanded, this energy has been stretched and cooled to the microwave regions, and indicates an average temperature of the universe of about 2.725° K.

Planck's Curves

The patterns of radiation from a heated object are called Planck's curves. Max Planck (1858–1947) is credited with finding the mathematical solution to the problem of blackbody radiation.

Any object above absolute zero radiates energy in a band of wavelengths. A hotter object will primarily radiate shorter wavelengths and a cooler object will radiate longer wavelengths.

This can be observed when a metal bar is heated. At lower temperatures, the bar glows a dull red. As the bar's temperature rises, the wavelengths become shorter and the color becomes bright red, orange or yellow. If heated to a very high temperature, the radiated energy would be at very short wavelengths and the color would become blue.

The chart below shows how the frequency bands change with temperature. Three representative temperature curves are shown to illustrate the spectrum of each temperature in relation to the band of visible wavelengths.

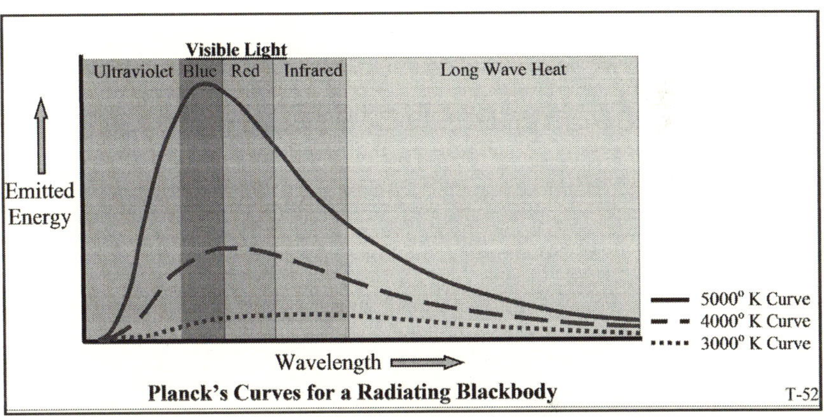

Planck's Curves for a Radiating Blackbody

The chart illustrates how the color of a star indicates its temperature. A red star is cooler than a blue star and therefore generally emits longer wave, or red and infrared energy. Careful measurement of the exact spectrum enables astronomers to determine the temperature of the sun and other stars even at very great distances.

The ship's engines are said to emit sapphire, or blue light. This indicates they are operating at a very high temperature.

11. The distance to Blueworld can be calculated using the speed of light (c). The speed of light is 300,000,000 m/s or 300 x 10^6 m/s. Since the distance from the Aegis to Blueworld was given as three light-

seconds, we can find the distance by using the fundamental equation for velocity.

Given	$d = v \bullet t$
Substitute the symbol c for velocity:	$d = c \bullet t$
Given	$t = 3$ s and $c = 300 \times 10^6$ m/s:
Substitute these values:	$d = 300 \times 10^6 \text{ m/s} \bullet 3 \text{ s}$
Simplify:	$d = 900{,}000{,}000$ m
Divide by 1000 to convert to km:	$d = \dfrac{900{,}000{,}000 \text{ m}}{1000 \text{ m/km}}$
Simplify:	$d = 900{,}000$ km

The actual distance was therefore 900,000 km, or just under a million kilometers. In the story, the slang term for a million kilometers was a megaclick.

12. The descent to Blueworld from a million kilometers out is analyzed in the following manner:

Assume Blueworld has a radius of 6,000 km and a gravitational constant of 10 m/s^2.

Then:	$r_o = 6{,}000$ km
And:	$g_o = 10 \text{ m/s}^2$.
Given the value of g at range r:	$g = g_o \bullet (r_o / r)^2$

The values for g at various distances are shown in the following table and graph:

Distance (Megaclick)	Distance (km)	g (m/s^2)
0 (Surface)	6,000	10
.1	100,000	0.0360
.2	200,000	0.0090
.3	300,000	0.0040
.4	400,000	0.0023
.5	500,000	0.0014
.6	600,000	0.0010
.7	700,000	0.0007
.8	800,000	0.0056
.9	900,000	0.0044
1	1,000,000	0.00036

Table of Blueworld's Gravity vs. Distance

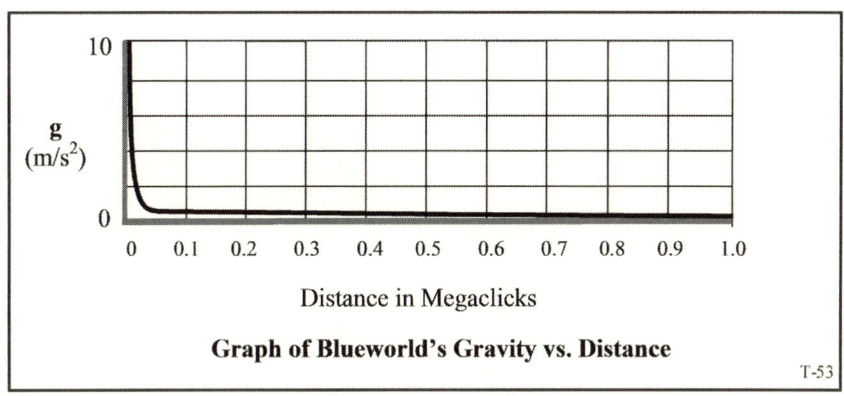

Graph of Blueworld's Gravity vs. Distance

As shown by the chart, a linear approximation of velocity beyond 100,000 km is reasonable since gravitational acceleration at those ranges is uniformly small.

Since the initial speed of the ship toward the planet was given as 23,000 m/s, we can assume the ship will be traveling at about that rate most of the time. It will gain relatively little speed until it is within 30,000 km or so, based on the graph above.

The maximum time possible, therefore, to travel 900,000 km is found using the simple velocity equation once more:

Given: $t = \frac{d}{v}$

Convert m/s to km/s by dividing by 1000: $v = \frac{23{,}000 \text{ m/s}}{1000 \text{ m / km}}$

$v = 23 \text{ km/s}$

Substitute: $t = \frac{900{,}000 \text{ km}}{23 \text{ km/s}}$

Solve: $t \approx 39{,}130$ seconds

Find minutes by dividing by 60: $t \approx 652$ minutes

Find hours by dividing minutes by 60: $t \approx 10.9$ hours

The BASIC program's integrated value for falling the entire distance is 650 minutes, or 10.8 hours. The integrated time and the simple approximation are close because the gravitational acceleration is very small for most of the distance.

If you have entered the program and verified its correct output, you can use it to calculate the final velocity after falling from 900,000 km to 100,000 km. The speed increases from 23,000 m/s to 23,123 m/s—very little change in velocity after 9.6 hours of falling. This confirms what we suspected earlier: since g is small, the velocity remains relatively unchanged.

The program also calculates a time of 4.83 hours to travel from 900,000 km to 500,000 km.

The ship needs to lose this speed before it reaches the planet or it will burn up due to friction with the atmosphere. This is what happens to a "falling star" or meteor. Unlike a meteor, which is an inert piece of space debris, the ship can use its engines and slow down, or decelerate.

The amount of time required for the engine burn can be estimated as follows:

Assume the engines provide 1 g of negative acceleration. The minimum time needed to lose the velocity of 23,123 m/s is:

Given: $$a = \frac{\Delta v}{\Delta t}$$

Then: $$\Delta t = \frac{\Delta v}{a}$$

Substitute: $$\Delta t = \frac{23{,}123 \text{ m/s}}{10 \text{ m/s}^2}$$

Solve: $$\Delta t = 2312 \text{ s}$$

Convert to minutes: $$\Delta t = \frac{2312 \text{ s}}{60 \text{ s/min}}$$

Simplify: $$\Delta t \approx 38 \text{ minutes}$$

We can now use the time of 2312 seconds to find the approximate stopping distance by using general formula for distance covered during acceleration:

Given:	$d = \frac{1}{2} \bullet a \bullet t^2 + v_0 \bullet t + d_0$
Where:	$a = 10.0 \text{ m/s}^2$
	$t = 2312$ seconds
	$v_0 = -23{,}123 \text{ m/s}$
	$d_0 = 0$
Therefore:	$d = \frac{1}{2} \bullet a \bullet t^2 + v_0 \bullet t + 0$
Substituting:	$d = \frac{1}{2} \bullet (10\text{m/s}^2) \bullet (2{,}312 \text{ s})^2 - 23{,}123 \text{ m/s} \bullet 2{,}312 \text{ sec}$
Simplify:	$d = 2.67 \text{ x } 10^7 \text{ m} - 5.35 \text{ x } 10^7\text{m}$
	$d = -2.68 \text{ x } 10^7 \text{ m}$
	$d = -2.68 \text{ x } 10^4 \text{ km}$
	$d = -26{,}800 \text{ km}$

The negative distance indicates travel in the opposite direction of the acceleration.

In summary, the ship will fall toward the planet in an approximately linear fashion for about ten hours at a rate of about 23,000 m/s. At a distance of about 30,000 km, it will need to fire its engines to slow down. An engine burn at negative 1 g for about forty minutes will cancel most of the speed. During that time it will travel about 27,000 km and be at an altitude of about 3,000 km.

Further calculations cannot use the altitude of 3,000 km directly in the formula for gravitational acceleration because the ship is now so close to the planet that its radius is a significant part of the distance to the gravitational center. We must add the planet's radius to the altitude to find the distance to the theoretical gravitational center:

$r = r_o + \text{altitude}$

Substitute: $r = 6{,}000 \text{ km} + 3{,}000 \text{ km}$

$r = 9{,}000 \text{ km}$

Given: $g = g_o \bullet (r_o / r)^2$

Substitute: $g = 10 \text{ m/s}^2 \bullet (6{,}000 / 9{,}000)^2$

Simplify: $g \approx 4.4 \text{ m/s}^2$

If g at the surface is 10 m/s², then the average acceleration is: $g_{ave} = (g + g_o) \div 2$

Substitute: $g_{ave} = (4.4 + 10) \div 2$

Solve: $g_{ave} = 7.2 \text{ m/s}^2$

If the ship were to free-fall from 3000 km with an initial velocity of zero, then the approximate time to reach the surface would be:

Given: $d = ½ \bullet a \bullet t^2 + v_0 \bullet t + d_0$

Where $g_{ave} = 7.2 \text{ m/s}^2$

$v_0 = 0$

$d = 3{,}000 \text{ km} = 3{,}000{,}000 \text{ m}$

$d_0 = 0$

Therefore: $d = ½ \bullet g_{ave} \bullet t^2 + v_0 \bullet 0 + 0$

Simplify: $d = ½ \bullet g_{ave} \bullet t^2 + 0 + 0$

Or: $d = \frac{1}{2} \bullet g_{ave} \bullet t^2$

Solve for t: $(2 \bullet d) \div g_{ave} = t^2$

$\sqrt{(2 \bullet d \div g_{ave})} = t$

Or: $t = \sqrt{(2 \bullet d \div g_{ave})}$

Substitute: $t = \sqrt{(2 \bullet 3{,}000{,}000 \text{ m} \div 7.2 \text{ m/s}^2)}$

Simplify: $t \approx 913$ seconds

Or: $t \approx 15$ minutes

The BASIC integration program provides a more precise value of 18.8 minutes.

Of course, the ship will not really free-fall to the surface. It will continue to fire its engines to slow down, and eventually encounter the contra-grav beam that also reverses the influence of gravity during the critical last stages of its arrival. Such a device will greatly reduce the demand on the engines to provide a slowing force as the ship nears the surface.

The point of these calculations is to provide an approximate idea of the times involved. They illustrate the long period of near-uniform motion toward the planet until the critical point where the gravitational field and velocities begin to rapidly change.

13. Johnson noise, or Johnson-Nyquist noise is the white noise, or hiss, that results from the motion of individual electrons within an electronic circuit. The amount of noise self-generated in any circuit is dependent upon its temperature. All other things being equal, a cooled circuit will exhibit less internal noise and a lower noise factor

than when it is warmer. Extremely sensitive amplifier circuits require cooling with liquid nitrogen or other cryogenic means to reduce their noise factors.

Opportunity Lost

1. Density (δ) is the amount of mass (m) per unit volume (V). Stated mathematically:

$$\delta = \frac{m}{V}$$

The density of ethanol, or ethyl alcohol, is:

$$\delta = .78 \text{ kg / liter.}$$

Given the general formula for density:

$$\delta = \frac{m}{V}$$

If m = 3 tons or 3000 kg, then:

$$.78 \text{ kg / liter} = \frac{3000 \text{ kg}}{V}$$

Solving for V:

$$V = \frac{3000 \text{ kg}}{.78 \text{ kg/liter}}$$

Solving:

$$V = 3846 \text{ liters}$$

Notes on Poetry

The poems in this book are examples of dramatic poetry or dramatic verse. Dramatic poems tell stories in which the characters are the actors in the poem.

Poetry differs from prose by having a meter or rhythm. There are several methods or schemes to analyze the meter of poetry: syllabic, stress, and foot-verse.

Syllabic meter counts the total number of syllables per line and establishes a poetic rhythm based on that pattern. For example, haiku always has five syllables in the first line, seven syllables in the second line, and five syllables in the third line:

A strange, ancient ship	(five syllables)
With its crew long forgotten,	(seven syllables)
Is now found at last.	(five syllables)

The following excerpt shows a syllabic meter of alternating lines of eleven and ten syllables:

In the solar furnace of nuclear fire	(eleven)
Protons and neutrons collide and conspire	(ten)
To form nuclei new and ever more dense	(eleven)
At temperatures high and pressures immense	(ten)

Stress meter establishes a rhythm that depends on the number stressed syllables in each line rather than the total number of syllables. The following passage has four stressed syllables per line:

In ANcient TIMES the philOSophers SAW
The HAND of GOD, and they reMAINED in AWE
Of WHAT they COULD not COMpreHEND
Yet STILL, they PRAYED the MUSE to SEND.

Foot verse meter distinguishes the patterns of stressed and unstressed syllables per line. The smallest repeating pattern is called a foot. Each pattern of stressed and unstressed syllables, or foot, has a name. Analyzing poetry into feet in this manner is called scanning or scansion.

Here are some common examples of poetic feet:

Foot Name	Example	Spoken as	Scansion	Oral Scan
iamb	retire	re-TIRE	-/	duh-DUH
trochee	crayon	CRAY-on	/-	DUH-duh
dactyl	indolent	IN-do-lent	/- -	DUH-duh-duh
anapest	interfere	in-ter-FERE	- -/	duh-duh-DUH

Example 1:

In the solar furnace of nuclear fire
- - / - / - - / - - /

Protons and neutrons collide and conspire
/ - - / - - / - - /

To form nuclei new and ever more dense
- - / - - / - / - - /

At temperatures high and pressures immense.
- / - - / - / - - /

The above sample does not scan perfectly anapestic. That is, not every foot has the - - / pattern. However, the anapest is the predominant pattern, with generally four anapestic feet per line. Since tetra is Greek for four, the passage is said to be written in anapestic tetrameter.

Example 2:

In ancient times the philosophers saw

- / - / - - / - - /

The hand of God, and they remained in awe

- / - / - - - / - /

Of what they could not comprehend.

- / - / - / - /

Yet still, they prayed the muse to send

- / - / - / - /

The first two lines scan half iambic and half anapestic. The last two lines scan perfectly iambic. Again, since there are four feet per line, this example is predominantly iambic tetrameter.

Songs

Everyday Miracles
RCM Schmidt
Ev ry day as we make our way through this maze of life, with its twists and turn ings we per
i...... ence man y gifts of God, some things that we know and some things to be learn
ing! Ev - ry day mir a cles! Look be-yond the com mon ness that just can't quite dis guise it! Ev ry day mir a cles!
They're real ly all a round if we just would rec og nize it! Oh! We look for signs and
won.... ders, and great things to in spire. And I guess it's on ly nat' ral that we - do.
But God is in the lit le things, not just the storm and fire The
still, small qui et Voice that dail y calls to me and you. Ev' ry day, as we

38
Em C Dsus4 D G
make our way through this maze of life, with its twists and turn ings, we ex per i ence. ma ny
42
Em C Am Dsus4 D Em
gifts from God. some things that we know and some things to be learn ing Ev'
46
D C Dsus4 D Em D
ry day mir a cles! Look be yond the com mon ness that just can't quite dis guise it! Ev' ry day mir a cles!
51
C Am Dsus4 D G Em
They're real ly all a round if we just would rec og nize it! The heav'ns de clare the
56
C Dsus4 D G
glory of Go - - - - d

Glossary

aft – nautical term for rear or rearward

ambient – all around, surrounding

anomaly – an exception or peculiarity

a priori – reasoning from theory rather than observation

antithesis – direct opposite, reverse

arpeggio – playing the notes in a chord in rapid succession instead of together

basso profundo – a low, deep voice, or someone with such a voice

billet – job, professional position

blatent – offensive, obtrusive

blight – destructive disease or influence

bulkhead – nautical term for wall

cadre – staff, personnel, officers

cerebral – having to do with the brain

cerebral cortex – the portion of the brain that processes thought, speech, and memory

chromatic – in music, a scale of twelve distinct notes, each separated by a half-step

chronometer – a precise timepiece, precision clock

cranial – having to do with the skull

cryogenic – having to do with very low temperatures

cryonic – preservation of bodies in extreme cold

deck – nautical term for floor

disparity – difference, inequality

eclectic – made up from selections from various sources

effluvia – odor, discharge

ennui – boredom

entrepreneur – a person who organizes a business for profit, a capitalist

epinephrine – also adrenaline; a hormone secreted by the adrenal gland during periods of stress

Flying Dutchmen – in sea lore, a ghost ship generally believed to be a bad omen

glissando – sliding from one musical note to another

head – nautical term for restroom or toilet

hectare – a unit of area equal to ten thousand square meters; a square one hundred meters on each side equivalent to 2.471 acres

hiatus – period of inactivity, pause

hypersonic – a speed at least five times the speed of sound or faster

intravenous – within the vein, injecting directly into the vein

kilohectares – one thousand hectares

ladder – nautical term for a steep stairway

lading – shipment, cargo

lick – a musical improvisation based on a melody

light-year – the distance light travels in one year, about 9.6 trillion kilometers lobotomy – a surgical procedure that severs nerve connections in the frontal lobes of the brain

logistical – having to do with planning, moving, and supplying a planned activity

megaclick – slang term for one million kilometers

mess– shortened nautical term for mess hall; the place where meals are taken

mezzo-soprano – a medium or midrange female voice

milieus – surroundings

millisecond – The prefix milli means "one thousandth." A millisecond is a thousandth of a second. A pulse of 300 milliseconds would be 300 / 1000ths of a second long, or about a third of a second.

nexus – connection, tie point, link

nominal – a very small, insignificant amount

overhead – nautical term for ceiling

ozone – a form of oxygen (O_3) with a strong, pungent odor, formed during electric arcing

parasitic – feeding from a host

pathogens – disease-causing microbes, such as bacteria or viruses

pentatonic – in music, a five-tone scale

pitch – to change angle up or down on the horizontal axis

planetesimal – a very small astronomical body or object

port – shortened nautical term for portside, the left-hand side of the vessel when facing forward

prolific – producing much

refract – to bend a wave, such as light or sound, from a straight course

rhizome – an underground and root-like stem of a plant

roll – to rotate around the longitudinal or lengthwise axis

saline – salty, saltwater

seraph – an angel

scree – loose rock or gravel

sortie – a single mission; an excursion, expedition

spurious – not genuine or authentic

stanchions – supports, locking frames

starboard – nautical term for the right-hand side of the vessel when facing forward

sublimated/sublimate – to change directly from a solid state to a gaseous state

symbiotic – the association of two unlike organisms for their mutual benefit

temperate zone – the middle latitudes of a planet, between the tropics and the polar regions

tenet – a doctrine or creed followed by a group or organization

terraform – to transform a planet with suitable raw materials and conditions into a more earthlike state by seeding it with bacteria, algae, and lichen to release oxygen and water

ti-alum – a laminate of aluminum and titanium

tow – white flax straw (archaic), as in towhead, meaning "having white or pale blonde hair"

unorthodox – uncommon, irregular, unusual

vindictive – unforgiving, spiteful

virulent – very poisonous or deadly

white noise – the sound of an entire range of audible frequencies

wry – twisted, turned to one side, or grimly humorous

yaw – to turn left or right on the vertical axis

yeoman's work – efficient and faithful service

zenith – the highest point

zephyr – a breeze or gentle wind